Praise for
Heidi Wessman Kneale

All romance stories need a little magic, and Heidi Kneale has told us a romantic story brilliantly.... [MARRY ME] deserves to be on the top of your TBR pile.

—Kayden Claremont,
author "Timeless Passion"

"I enjoyed [AS GOOD AS GOLD], well written and with well-rounded characters."

—Long and Short Reviews

"...Kneale succeeds in reversing reader expectations in more ways than one."

—Chris Butler, The Fix:
Short Fiction Review

"Heidi Kneale has so much imagination. She's one of the best I've seen."

—Anne Wingate, author
Deb Ralston series

"...the world introduced [in AS GOOD AS GOLD] was intriguing and there seem to be more possibilities to be explored, always a sign of a strong tale."

—Margaret Fisk, author
Uncommon Lords & Ladies series

Dedication

For their Ladyships,
Lady Sarah and Lady Amy.
Go forth and be mighty.

Bride of the Dark

by
Heidi Wessman Kneale

Of The Dark—Book 2

Enjoy.

Bride of the Dark

Book 2 of "Of The Dark" series.

Other titles in the **Of The Dark** series:

- God of the Dark (Book 1)
- House of the Dark (Book 3)

Cover Design: HW Kneale and SR Kneale

ISBN: 978-0-6484228-2-2

IngramSpark version 1.0—18 Oct 2018

Printed on planet Earth by human beings.

This book is also available in a digital edition for those who adore carrying hundreds of books on their smartphones.

License Statement

Table of Contents

⟡

Our Story So Far...

Adrastea, a journeyman healer, never gave much thought to the gossamer strands that connected everything to Creation. She naturally assumed if she could see them, so could everyone else.

Then she learned she could touch them, to send vibrations through them in a new way. While this new gift had its uses, it also had its consequences. By doing so, she unwittingly announced her presence to the universe, and to a god.

Mor-Lath, God of the Dark, comes to Adrastea and proposes marriage. While his proclamation sounds more commandment than courtship, he does offer her a choice. He will not abduct her nor force her to her vows but wishes to win her hand voluntarily.

However, he leaves her with a betrothal gift, a black line embedded in her skin. At first it seems little more than the Dark One marking his own, but Adrastea quickly learns that it is a connection that works both ways. Through the line, she is able to gain insight into this god and his bemusing courtship of her.

Not that Adrastea has any intention of agreeing to this marriage. After all, she is a follower of the Light, and intends to remain that way. Raised on chilling tales of this chthonic being, marriage to Mor-Lath was the last thing she desired.

Not that Mor-Lath had any intention of giving up on his suit. He woos her, not with flattery and flowers, but by showing her that she has talent in the Deeper Power—a talent normally reserved for priests. Not that Adrastea has any desire to become a priestess. If anything, the village of Sacred Spring would more likely burn her as a witch, should they learn the true identity of her suitor.

Those few who do know her secret—namely, her family—vow to do their best to aid her. The village priestess, especially, does her best to guard and guide Adrastea. She would do anything to save Adrastea's soul, even if it means killing her by slitting her throat with a sacred shard of glass.

Surprised that the priestess would go so far in the name of faith, he kills her and heals Adrastea, rending the priestess' last desperate act moot.

This death reminds Adrastea just who her suitor is—the Dark God. No way would she ever marry him now. In her anger, she flees to the sacred spring, thinking that he cannot reach her there.

The death of the village priestess cannot be hidden. The people of Sacred Spring knows evil walks among them and they begin to question many things.

News of impending invasion comes to them from a nearby town. The foreign army that invaded the great city of Feown was now set on conquering further inland. Refugees flee to the village, giving the villagers something to think about other than their own troubles. A temporary village is erected for the refugees.

Torn between protecting Sacred Spring and protecting his niece, the Mayor sends Adrastea to help the villagers as their healer. He hopes, by keeping her out of the village he may avoid having to deal with the situation sooner rather than later, at least, until he can sort out this new influx of desperate people.

Mor-Lath does not hide his courtship from the villagers or the refugees. As far as most people believe, he is merely from another village, or maybe from the city of Feown, who came and took an interest in their journeyman healer. He appears helpful enough as the villagers prepare a place for the refugees to live. Many find him likeable and suspect nothing.

A new priestess arrives at the request of the Mayor. Now, more than ever, he knows Sacred Spring needs all the ecclesiastical help they can get. But the new priestess is not impressed by Adrastea. It is not long before she discovers Adrastea's secret, and condemns her as a Dark Priestess.

Meanwhile a few others are learning that Mor-Lath may be more than he seems.

The foreign army moves quickly, sending scouts to follow the refugees. While the villagers do their best to stop the scouts from reporting back, one does escape, carrying news of the village, and of a marked maiden...

The army, having conquered the nearby town, come in force to Sacred Spring, determined to convert or kill all those who do not worship the One True God. There, a foreign priestess recognizes Adrastea as the one her master was looking for.

Sacred Spring refuses to surrender, and they prepare to withstand attack, even though they know they will not survive.

Mor-Lath offers Adrastea a choice. If she marries him, not only will he save her village, but protect it for three generations.

Adrastea weighs her options. If she refuses, she will watch her village be destroyed. Mor-Lath will not allow her to die, but will continue to follow her, no matter where she goes, until she gives in.

To save everyone she knows and loves, she agrees to marry the God of the Dark.

Chapter 1

She'd done it. Adrastea had married Mor-Lath, God of the Dark. A strange haziness overcame her as soon as the vows had left her lips. The world wavered up and down.

Married. Wait...

Had this really happened?

This was not how she had envisioned her wedding—certainly not in the middle of war. Adrastea looked out from the hill above the village of Sacred Spring to the army that surrounded it. Tall machines, their poles high in the air and dangling with ropes, stood sentinel over so many soldiers. The crops were gone, trampled to dust.

Plumes of smoke rose from the village below. Cries of young fear echoed up from the smithy. As she looked at the incredulous faces of Uncle Natan and Ari, her heart ached. She'd done it to save them. She'd done it to save everyone. Her face stung. She put a hand to her cheek, but the pain did not last long. Had she imagined it?

Did she imagine this whole thing?

She shook her head in a vain attempt to knock the haziness out of it.

Mor-Lath's arm slid about her waist. He drew her close to his chest. "Mine," he murmured in her ear. A wave of triumph washed over her—his, she presumed.

Adrastea shuddered. What had she done? Her throat ached from smoke and tears.

Mor-Lath called upon the Deeper Power, letting it fill him. The lines on Adrastea's face—there were two now—sang in harmony with the Power he held. He reached... somewhere distant... and grasped onto something.

Shift.

Adrastea's heart felt like had been tugged from the inside out, the rest of her following through. Her head spun as she lost orientation. The image of Sacred Spring wavered and blurred as if disappearing. If it were not for Mor-Lath's arm about her waist, she would have fallen.

Her feet connected to something solid, not the grass she stood upon moments before. The scent of different air filled her nostrils, also smoke but of a different kind.

They were no longer at Sacred Spring.

When Creation resolved itself, she looked down onto a vast city. How high up were they? Her head swam with vertigo and she clung to the strong arm around her waist.

In the distance, a mighty silver river snaked its way by the city. A smoky pall covered the sky, muting out the sun.

Outside the city walls wall a multitude of small white patches, like tiles, filled the empty spaces between the fallen buildings and across fields. Adrastea squinted for a better view, for she did not recognize them at first through the blurriness.

Tents. Thousands of tents pitched before the wall, scattered about like confetti. And the miniscule moving figures? Horses, possibly. Or people. So many!

"Welcome back to Feown," Mor-Lath murmured, his baritone voice touched with excitement. It nagged at her, as if she was supposed to feel it too.

Well, she didn't.

He buried his nose in her hair and inhaled. All she smelled was smoke.

"Where are we?" Her head had recovered from the sudden change of height.

"It's called the Maiden's Tower. Interesting story, but we don't have time. It's the highest point in Feown." He breathed warm air into her ear. "I believe part of our bargain, my Bride, was the salvation of your little village?"

Sacred Spring. Her heart thumped. Was it all right?

"Feown, too. You belong to it by right of blood. You are very much the daughter of this once-august city. You can save it as well."

Feown? Hers? Except for the last time Mor-Lath had brought her here she had never been to Feown. The city was too far away, at least two weeks' travel. Ari had been there before as a journeyman.

But for a country girl like herself? The furthest she had ever been was to Crossroads.

Now she was the Bride of the Dark. She looked beyond the walls of

Feown, to the vast pallor of smoky and speckled camps of the army. Surely this was not the same army that threatened Sacred Spring? "What do I do?"

Mor-Lath pressed his cheek to hers, sending the new line on her cheek singing. "Every life in Creation is connected to it by a thread of Power. In turn, each person is connected to others by more threads.

"Below us, in the depths of the palace is a man by the name of General Miniver. He is in charge of the force invading Feown, and ultimately, those who are currently battering your village. Right now, he is doing terrible things to the Duchess of Feown—things that would make your innocent heart cringe."

Oh? The memory of a memory, a blond man, his heart full of ill intent, drawing bloody lines on her skin with a knifepoint before— What could possibly be worse than what Mor-Lath had shown her?

"Focus on him. Concentrate on the Lines that connect him to his war council, his captains and lieutenants, his sergeants and so forth."

Adrastea closed her eyes. She drew on the Deeper Power. With him behind her, it came to her easily. "How do I find the General?"

"Think of his name. It is by our names we are connected."

General Miniver. As she focused on the name, the bright sparks of people's lives within the palace opened to her. Everything else faded but those little spots of humanity. They flew past her awareness like fuzzy little mayflies as she sought the spark called General Miniver.

Every spark was an individual, with its own personality of being, its own mix of emotions and thoughts. She wanted to stop and explore. She wanted to reach out and stroke them, for each one sang its own note. Together, their song called to her.

Mor-Lath warned, "Stop that. We're running out of time."

She found General Miniver. His spark burned fierce and red as he tortured a woman. Her spark flickered and fluttered, an angry simmer of water droplets on a hot grill that refused to evaporate. Immediately Adrastea's heart went out to the woman, to comfort her.

"Don't waste time!" Mor-Lath snapped. "You'll end her suffering soon enough. Focus on the General."

She felt the Dark God's personal strength flow into her as his arms tightened about her waist. "Focus on the General, then follow the Lines that connect to him. Soldiers will feel different from everyone else. Their song sings of battle."

Adrastea saw what he meant. She had never noticed before but each

Line that connected the General to the Duchess to the soldiers to the others in the palace, to the palace itself and to her, each Line had its own song.

The Line between the general and the woman had its own feel. It was different from the Line between him and the other men. The general fought the woman. The antagonism between them was strong. Between him and the men—subservience, obedience, and something else.

Mor-Lath murmured his approval. "Now, follow that Line and all the others like unto it until you have reached every last one. Be warned; there are many."

Her consciousness skipped along the Lines, locating bright sparks of life like beads on a string. She kept a hold of the strings as more were added. "How many?"

"There are half a million."

"Half a million?!" She nearly dropped the Lines. Adrastea had no idea there were that many people in the world, much less that number of soldiers. But if this army was that huge, imagine how many people there were in the world beyond that.

His arms tightened once more. He gave her a little shake. "Don't lose focus. Every second you let your mind wander is another second that army has to assault your Sacred Spring."

She increased her efforts. Soon, her mind raced over the sparks until they became a blaze of light. Every spark was found. Was it a moment or was it a year?

"There," Mor-Lath said. "That's the whole army."

How did he know? Adrastea refocused her mind. Have to save Sacred Spring. "Now what?"

"Imagine yourself grasping the Lines of Power that connect you to everyone you've touched. When you are ready, pull on those Lines. Imagine lifting each life up and through you. It's important that you imagine every single Line going through your heart. They must go through you, or it won't work. Are you ready?"

She trembled. Her hands tightened on his arms. Her heart thumped hard. She felt his heart beating in parallel with hers. Why couldn't it slow down?

Are you ready?

She nodded.

"Good. Let's begin." He pulled on the Deeper Power.

He called to Creation. It answered him, flowing through her, to him and back. His hands slid, one moving down around her belly while the other reaching upwards across her bodice to her collarbone until he enveloped her whole body with his. As the Power enveloped them, they blended together, no longer her and him but them. He poured all the Deeper Power he held into her, giving it to her freely.

She gasped as it overwhelmed her in its warmth and sweetness. This was very different from the times he'd tempted her with Power before. Before, was a mere sip of water. This was a torrent that threatened to pull her down. "Don't let it overpower you," he urged. "Stay focused." There was a hint of desperation in his voice. She brought herself back. "Ready? Can you see them all?

The Lines. She redirected her attention there. A half-million lives pulsed, their multitudinous symphonies sang to her through the Deeper Power. So many but she could count each one.

"Now pull."

Adrastea pulled. She imagined every single one of those half million lives being lifted up and away from where they were. An unimaginable amount of Deeper Power came away from them. It flowed down the Lines until it contacted her. But instead of flowing through her, the Power poured into her. So much! Who knew there was so much Power?

Did she scream? How would she hold it all?

Somewhere she thought she heard a voice of protest but then Mor-Lath's voice was in her head. "Do not let yourself be distracted by anything. Keep pulling until you are finished."

She felt the Power of a half-million lives pour into her until all was contained in her. Oh, how it burned! Once inside, it shrieked and twisted as if not sure where to go. She wanted to cry out in pain, in passion, in surprise but too much was happening. Voices chattered in confusion, adding to the chaos.

She felt the Power in every speck of dust that was her. The intensity increased, if that was even possible. The specks of dust began to melt, to move.

Adrastea began to change.

Her spine straightened ever so slightly. Her limbs lengthened. Her eyes focused and she felt her skin move like the vibrations of a hummer toy. Her teeth slid to their proper places and her voice changed a few notes deeper. Her waist narrowed, and her hips rounded. Something within her tuned up until the song she had gathered to her vibrated in perfect harmonies. Oh, the beauty of the song.

It felt too much. Her knees buckled. The very world felt as if it would tear apart. She grasped at Mor-Lath to keep from falling.

Panic rippled through Mor-Lath, washing over Adrastea. Vast power surged back through her, along those lines she had pulled, pushing through to that world that trembled under the effort. He pushed and coaxed and pleaded with... what?

Soon the rumbling eased, and Mor-Lath relaxed, relieved.

Together they tumbled to the stones, panting, weak from effort. Even the God of the Dark was drained from their efforts. He lay next to her, hand thrown across her chest, his head cradled on her arm.

A chuckle came from inside him, erupting as a laugh of triumph. "Well done," he congratulated her. He turned her face to his and kissed her.

With her new-found clarity, she realized what had happened. She scrambled for the stone parapet. Her eyes, no longer blurry, gazed out across Feown, the same stone buildings, the same pillars of black smoke, the same speckles of tents, everything in the sharpest of focus.

And then...

Mortal eyes could not have seen what she now witnessed. Hundreds, thousands, and eventually half a million souls wandered the earth in great astonishment, torn from their bodies. They were not only in Feown but beyond, to the plains and finally to the mountains. They were across the great river to the east and far away, all the way to a distant kingdom and... and... How strange. She felt as if there was supposed to be someone else, in the distance, to express shock at the sudden mass-murder of so many people. But there was no one. Was he gone too?

They were all dead. Every single one of them.

"What have I done?" Adrastea moaned.

The whole of the army, from a commander-in-chief so many hundreds of leagues away, to General Miniver down below, to the lowliest potboy, had died.

Her vision turned grey with the horror of it all. She'd killed. Not once, or a dozen times but... Her head spun. She had to lie back down.

Mor-Lath caught her. Together they sat against the parapet wall. He smoothed back her curly brown hair and folded her hands neatly on her waist. "There was no other way," he murmured. "Oh, no. Thanks to the noble sacrifice of so many, you are now immortal."

She sat up and scooted backwards away from him. Her hand touched a dark stain on the stones beneath her. It sang out to her: a child had died here, not too long ago. She pushed herself to her feet and fled to the parapet to look again. He had to be mistaken. He had to be! How could she kill half a million people and not realize it?

"What have you done to me? What have you done?!" She turned to him, her eyes blazing, fists balled. The Deeper Power came easily to her now. She gathered it up, ready to open the ground beneath his feet and have the earth swallow him whole.

He moved to her swiftly and caught her hands. "Let us wait a moment."

"No!"

He enveloped her two hands in one of his and laid a finger on her lips. "Wait. Listen." He looked about as if expecting something.

She drew in a breath. Listen for what?

"Do you see any angels come for vengeance? No. Do you see the Light Themselves come to chastise you? No. Because They know this was meant to be."

"But a million people. Dead!"

"Half a million but it was enough." He tilted her chin up. "There is one more thing we must do. I'm sorry, but this will hurt."

Adrastea pulled from his grasp. "No. No more."

"Silly creature. This is just between you and me."

A warm glow suffused her face as she thought she caught his meaning. "What? Here?" She gestured to the stones, open to the elements. "Outside?" Her body still buzzed from the echoes of the Deeper Power, but the sickness of her heart pushed away any thought of pleasure. Surely, he didn't mean to consummate their marriage now?

After a moment of bemusement, Mor-Lath failed to conceal his smile. "Just give me your hands." He took them and placed them on either side of his face. "Now demand the comprehension of language from me. It must be a demand."

She hesitated.

"Come on. Demand it from me."

"Why?"

"It is the quickest way, believe me."

She nodded. She drew on the Deeper Power but not as much as before. "I demand the..."

"Comprehension."

She swallowed. "Com-pre-hension of language."

He closed his eyes. She felt his pain as something flowed from him to her. It was as if her head filled with warm water. To her surprise and relief, it didn't hurt her. She allowed herself a moment of schadenfreude.

When it was finished Adrastea released his head and stepped back. Mor-Lath pressed his fingertips to his forehead as if to dispel the rest of the pain. "*Comprene-toah?*" he asked.

She nodded her head. It was the strangest thing. She heard a different language, but it resolved itself in her mind and made sense. Do you understand me? he had asked.

"*Owi,*" she replied in the affirmative. "*Ge comprene.* Will I know every language?"

"Just the ones I know. So yes. Every language." His fingers were still pressed to his temples, the vestiges of pain still in his eyes. "Let us go home, Bride of the Dark."

⁂

Natan and Ari watched the exploding munitions pelt Sacred Spring. Cannonballs rained down, sending explosions of dirt flying upwards. In the village, the nearer homes were crushed as the munitions found their mark. Jak Carpenter's home lost half his workshop. Mira's house was completely demolished.

"Damn it," Natan cried as tears of rage ran down his face. "I should have known he would lie to us!"

Ari wept and clung to Natan. Together they watched the army load the cannons and the catapults, gauge them and fire them, their aim improving every time. One good aim had taken out the forge side of the smithy. Ari could hear the screams of terror from within. "Natan, the children. We have to get them out." She fled towards the smithy, heedless of Natan calling her to stop.

Then the cannon fire ceased.

"Ari, wait," called Natan. He pursued her.

Ari stumbled around a crater and slowed. It would not do anyone any good if she sprained an ankle.

Panting hard, she leaned against one of the few remaining trees and looked out towards the army.

Quietude spread across the village; no more cannon fire. Every single soldier had fallen to the ground, unmoving. They did not get up.

Natan caught up with her. Together they clung to the tree, watching and waiting.

Children and women streamed from the back door of the smithy and fled up the hill. Every child shrieked in terror as they clambered past torn trees and gaping holes in the earth, panic fueling their little legs.

Still, the soldiers did not rise.

"Is it a trick?" Ari wondered.

Natan didn't answer.

Ely came down, his spindly legs wobbly from terror. "Natan, what's happening?"

The mayor shook his head. "I don't know."

Ari clung to the tree. "You don't think..."

"What?" Natan uttered. "That he did this?"

"I'm having a closer look." Ely ran off. He sprinted the length of the village until he went out past the walls to the fields.

Natan and Ari followed at a slower pace. A few of the Crossroaders came as well, curiosity overcoming their caution.

Had Mor-Lath kept his promise? What did he do?

It was not long before Ely returned. "Natan? It's all right. It's over." He gasped and wheezed as he clambered his way back up the hill. "Natan, they're dead, every one to a man. It's over."

Natan's hand stole into Ari's. She turned into his arms. Long after the sun's edge touched the mountains, they clung together and grieved.

Quiet. Saraym, the Duchess of Feown, let it wrap about her in the darkness. Only her ragged breaths and the beating of her broken heart made any sound. Here, in this prison of a cellar, quiet was the first luxury she'd had.

She lay on the cool stone floor, the weight of dead men on her outstretched arms. She was certain they were dead, every last one of them. Death had a quietude about it, a stillness that life could not imitate.

Death was beauty. Death was release. It was a gift utterly wasted on the monsters surrounding her.

There were her two jailers, holding her down. Another had stood in a corner with the lamp. It, too, had fallen to the ground but didn't break. It provided a wan light, gently illuminating this cellar room.

And there was General Miniver, collapsed at her spread feet. She knocked his head out of the way and brought her legs together. Never again, would they part for any man.

Her husband was dead. Her children were dead, their young heads bashed against the marble columns of the throne room. Attendants, household staff and more, all dead—humiliated, violated, murdered. For all she knew, the rest of Feown was dead, all by the Cithran Army.

Why wasn't she dead? Why had the Light spared her? Or did she live in spite of Her? Not that she would call the others' deaths a blessing.

The Cithrans had their One True God. What was his opinion, assuming he existed?

Saraym sat up. Pain. Lots of pain. Yes, definitely alive. Alas. Her back ached from the cold of the cellar. Her arms burned where the soldiers had gripped her. Many, many days ago, General Miniver had plucked out her right eye, because it had offended him. A broken toe throbbed, and she refused to think of the state of her loins. Her skin was mottled, though whether by dirt or bruises, she could not tell in the wan light.

What was left of her clothing hung on her in rags, barely enough to cover her nakedness.

She nudged the soldiers with her foot. Nothing. General Miniver, the same. He was a slim man. His coat could not reach about her fleshy shoulders. She considered the uniform of one of the bulkier soldiers to clad her body. All high-ranking officers sported sashes over their coats. The lesser had badges sewn on sleeves. The higher the rank, the more decorations a uniform had, until they covered it so much, one could barely tell what color the uniform had once been.

Greys and blues and greens marked soldiers belonging to different divisions. Not that one could distinguish the color here in the darkness.

As she took a uniform off an unprotesting soldier's corpse, she studied it closer. No. She would not wear it. She would never wear it. It was the clothing of the enemy.

She lifted the sash of General Miniver, white satin, as favored by the highest ranks. This, on the other hand, was a trophy. Feowan tradition favored the claiming of a token from a fallen general, usually a sword or other weapon of war. General Miniver carried no steel.

As she tied the sash about her waist, her gaze fell upon the unbuttoned trousers of the general. He had been preparing to violate her yet again when his unfortunate death struck him.

Wait. He did have a weapon of war, one he'd wielded against her many times.

She nudged the flap open with her toe. His phallus lay there, frozen half-erect in death.

One of the lesser soldiers had a knife on his person. With this, she removed General Miniver's favorite weapon, also those of the other soldiers.

The General's boot made an ideal container for her trophies.

Saraym, Duchess of Feown, lifted the lantern, to guide her out of the cellar and up to the palace.

Her palace. Her people, her duchy.

She had survived.

How did she get to be so unlucky?

*S*hift.

The stone of the tower faded from Adrastea's view. Mor-Lath had moved them again. With her new eyes, she saw how Mor-Lath did it. It was a simple matter of moving oneself along the Lines to where one wanted to be. She would attempt it when she had the chance... assuming she was ever left alone again. A glance at Mor-Lath's possessive expression suggested she would never be alone again, whether she liked it or not.

Where were they?

A pleasantly warm air caressed her skin, warmer and drier here than in Feown. Before her rose the columns and fine lines of a giant temple. It stood white and sparkling in the morning sunlight, higher than any building she knew, including the Maiden's Tower. Eight columns supported the front. Adrastea looked up even further. Her breath escaped her. This temple had been carved into the side of a mountain.

The Deeper Power sang in her bones, residuals of her earlier abominations. It didn't care that she'd done such a horrible thing. It hummed along in her blood. The earth itself also hummed along, its song echoing the relief of escaping a close call.

Mor-Lath released her. Her legs gave way. He caught her and lifted her up. "Best you stand for now. Look strong."

Stand? She didn't want to stand. She wanted to collapse and have a good cry.

"Ah-ah," he cautioned. "Not now. You can have your little morality crisis later, in private." His eyes glanced towards the temple.

The front of the temple had stone steps leading down to the courtyard. A young woman, only just touched by the flush of puberty, swept those steps with a broom. She had long, glossy-black hair. A bandolier wrapped around her young breasts, leaving her belly bare. Across her hips hung a gauzy divided skirt of a gentle blue fabric that was gathered around her ankles. She moved with a grace Adrastea never had as a child.

The young woman sweeping the steps caught sight of them. In delight, she dropped her broom and came running. "Holiness!" she shouted before she launched herself at Mor-Lath, wrapping arms around his neck and legs about his waist.

Her voice had an accent. She had spoken in another language. Would Adrastea ever get used to that? What language was that? She sorted through her new memories. Tredan, the language of the nomads. The girl looked Tredan with those almond eyes and broad cheekbones.

Adrastea's head spun for a moment. Had he really taken her as far as the Western Tribes? They lived on the other side of the mountains. A few caravans came through Sacred Spring, once every few years.

Mor-Lath laughed and caught the girl. He swung her around as a doting father would his favorite daughter.

Holiness? Adrastea thought. Holy was the last word she would have used to describe Mor-Lath. For one brief moment, the irony tickled her fancy.

And who was this slip of a girl, little more than a child, who made herself so free with the Dark God? Adrastea cursed her naivety. Of course, there would be others. It felt as if her whole insides fell to the bottom of her stomach. So much for being unique. Mira had been right.

This girl did not have any fear when faced with the God of the Dark.

"Now, now," he chided her, his tone gentle. "Where's your propriety?"

The girl realized her faux pas and released him. Blushing, she knelt in obeisance, her excitement barely contained.

With a nod of his head, Mor-Lath gave the girl permission to rise. She flung herself at him again in an adoring hug. He returned her hug then gently disengaged himself.

"Go fetch the others, Garie. No doubt they are as eager as you for my return."

She genuflected, then fled into the temple, occasionally looking over her shoulder.

Mor-Lath had a fond smile on his face. "That is Berengaria, the youngest of my priestesses. Do not let her age fool you. She will be a most formidable woman as soon as she learns to control her passions."

Adrastea didn't want to meet any of the other priestesses. All she wanted to do was open up the earth and let it swallow her whole, to bury her in its cold, dark depths, never show her face to the light of day again. Her conscience ached. What had she gotten herself into?

Mira had warned that bad things would happen if she accepted the hand of the Dark God in marriage. Now half a million lay dead. The Light would never forgive her this.

Oh, Light! Sooner or later They would come for her. Her heart pounded hard. She put a hand to her forehead. She would have to pay for what she did. What would They do to her?

Mor-Lath grabbed her hand and led her towards the temple. "Come, my dear bride. Meet my priestesses."

About a dozen came running, from young Berengaria to older women. They all wore the same flowy clothing of jeweled hues. They had the same dark glossy hair, the same graceful limbs, the same large, dewy almond eyes. They were like a rabble of gaudy butterflies.

Unlike Berengaria, the other priestesses' eyes were not full of the eager innocence of youth but something harder, some with wisdom and experience, others cunning and calculating. Each one of them noted her but made no further acknowledgement.

First, they greeted Mor-Lath fervently, bending their knees to him before throwing themselves at him with joyous hugs as if he'd been gone far too long. They all called him Holiness. Every time they did, it didn't sit right with Adrastea.

She stood back. Let them have their little reunion. They were happier to see him than she was.

Mor-Lath pried himself loose from their embraces. He held up his hand to prevent any more puppyish attention and gestured to Adrastea.

"May I present to you Adrastea, my Bride," he said simply.

The news of this rippled through the priestesses, a susurrus of astonishment. Their mood closed. They backed away. The curiosity in their eyes changed to a guarded wariness. It was as if a dark cloud had moved between them and the sun.

"You told us you sought a bride," one of the older priestesses said. "We did not expect you to get one so soon."

"The end of time draws near," he explained. "You know it was foretold."

The elder priestess, perhaps a little older than Ari, didn't reply. While her poise was one of control, her eyes betrayed her worry. The other priestesses gathered behind her, still whispering to each other.

Adrastea suspected trouble ahead. This must be Mor-Lath's high priestess, who had control of the temple when he was gone. Women did not take kindly to being usurped by a newcomer, especially one who looked lesser in age and experience. What else did Mor-Lath share with her?

A little niggle pulled at her stomach. Mor-Lath must have sensed her uneasiness, for he drew Adrastea forward. To his priestess he said, "Do not be fooled by her appearance; she is powerful. And don't annoy her for she's had a bad day. My bride is immortal as I am. She has a capacity for the Deeper Power beyond all but me." He shot Adrastea a smile as if they shared a secret. If there was a secret, he hadn't told her yet.

"Here," he said to Adrastea as he tossed her a stone. Where did he get a stone? "Show them a trick or two."

Adrastea caught it. She looked at the stone, a smooth, grey river stone slightly larger than her palm. What sort of game he was playing now? Dissolving rocks was one of the first things he'd taught her. Still, was she no more than a performing dog?

The priestesses in front of her watched in expectation but there was doubt in their eyes. She saw she would have to earn their respect, or they would make her life miserable. She'd just escaped a destiny of ostracism and didn't need to enter a life of cattish nastiness.

They waited for her demonstration.

She drew on the Deeper Power. How easy it came to her now. She commanded the rock to dissolve. It crumbled in her hand and the dust flowed away like water.

Then the young priestess Berengaria clapped as if she had watched a feastday trick. "Do something else," she begged before she got an elbow in the ribs from one of the others.

The other priestesses disapproved of Berengaria's outburst, did they? They watched Adrastea closely, to see what else she could do. Their gazes made her shoulders itch. No doubt every one of those priestesses could touch the Deeper Power and dissolve rocks for fun.

Forming rocks was harder. Adrastea knelt. As she did, she noticed her skirts were dowdy and ugly compared to the graceful gauze the priestesses wore. They were also spattered with mud. No wonder they didn't think much of her.

No time for weakness. If they wanted a demonstration she'd give them one.

She laid her hand down in the pile of dust that was once a rock. Then, closing her eyes, she began to draw on the Deeper Power from Creation itself. As she called to it and it answered, it flowed into her easier than ever before.

The ground rumbled in response to her. Worry rippled through the priestesses as they murmured to each other in alarm.

"What is she doing?" one of the younger priestesses whimpered, her voice rising higher with her growing panic. Adrastea glanced up but did not stop pulling in Power.

The earth began to shake.

The priestesses clung to one another. "Holiness?" they implored.

But Adrastea was nowhere near her full capacity. Past experience said she needed as much as she could hold to reform the rock.

Mor-Lath calmly lifted Adrastea up. "No need to frighten the children," he said to her. "They understand how powerful you are. I hope you do," he murmured to her, low so the shaken priestesses couldn't hear. He stroked the new mark on her cheek, a mirror of the first he gave her in the beginning. It sang under his touch. A little thrill rippled through to the end of her limbs, one that woke up her skin.

In all the calamity and grief of the past few days, Adrastea had forgotten how he'd tempted her with the sensual arts through the Deeper Power. Those memories came flushing back.

Only this time, with the benefit of matrimony, she had no compunction acting upon them. She had spent so much time trying not to think about it, that now she felt guilty admitting the rights of marriage were now available to her.

With the God of the Dark.

He drew in a deep breath as if inhaling her essence. His hand lingered before he snatched it away.

"What have you done to me?" she asked, her voice as low. Sure, the Deeper Power came so much easier to her now. But what was she going to do with it?

He let his lips brush her hair ever so slightly and did not answer her question. A frission of excitement rippled through the lines on her face.

His priestesses gazed upon Adrastea in awe tinged with fear so strong it rippled along the line. The eldest priestess refused to be cowed.

However, wariness overshadowed her eyes.

When he turned to them, they all bowed their heads as one. "You serve her now as you serve me," he told them. His hand stroked her skin. "Do not invoke her wrath, for she has killed half a million men today and would not think twice about making it half a million and one."

His priestesses dropped to their knees, hands and eyes to the ground, all but the eldest. Only she remained standing and did not wait for permission before asking a question. "An earthquake shook the ground today. I presume that was you, then?"

Adrastea's stomach wrenched. Did he have to bring that up when the pain of it was still so raw? She turned her head away so nobody would see her cry.

He took her turned face into his hands. With his thumbs, he sponged away her fresh tears. Then softly, just to her, "It was necessary, and it was your destiny. Accept that and show no weakness, especially to them. If you must cry, do it in the privacy of your own room."

A tendril of lust snaked itself through her belly. Was that him, or was that her? Why now? Couldn't she simply feel one emotion at a time? There were too many for her to deal with all at once.

"Desideria," said Mor-Lath.

"Yes, Your Holiness?" It was the eldest, who had questioned Adrastea's status earlier.

"As my high priestess, it is your job to make sure that my bride's wishes are fulfilled. You can delegate, or you can serve her yourself, I leave that up to you. No doubt currying her favor will serve you well."

"As you wish," Desideria replied, her voice too neutral for true acceptance.

Desideria's attitude sent a shudder up Adrastea's spine.

Chapter 2

Mor-Lath congratulated himself. He'd convinced Adrastea to marry him of her own free will. It was simply a case of negotiating the right bride price, and it had only taken a month. How easy was that?

He put his arm about Adrastea's waist and guided her into the temple. Her touch was electric. Even her proximity sent thrills up his spine. With her suffused with the Deeper Power, her pull was even stronger.

He fought it. He could not give in. He measured his steps, resisting the siren call of his bride.

His bride. How that sent a ripple of excitement through his body.

He pushed his impulses away. Business first.

The priestesses followed. Yes, they were pleased to see him return—they always were—but today, things were different. He felt their curiosity and caution. Too many startling things had happened today. They did not speak openly as they followed him in. He sensed their meaningful glances behind his back. A new variable had been added to their lives and they were not yet sure what to make of her.

Desideria, his current high priestess, had worry and concern foremost in her mind. While he was not completely privy to all her thoughts, he felt them tumbling about. The earthquake had worried her. If only she knew how close he'd come to destroying the whole world for the sake of Adrastea. Even that consequence had surprised him. At least the elements obeyed his command to reform themselves and utter disaster had been averted.

The revelation of his bride had pushed the worry of the earthquake out of her head as if it had never happened.

He should have warned Desideria. He should have told her

everything. As they climbed the temple steps, he felt her behind him, head bowed, hands clasped before her, lost in her calculations. She did not study Adrastea as the others did but let herself be overtaken by her own thoughts.

Sure, he'd mentioned that he'd been considering taking a bride, but it had been as an idle remark here and there. As soon as he had found Adrastea by the manifestation of her power, he should have come straight to Desideria to speak of it. That was thoughtless of him.

Desideria knew him better than any other mortal, than any of his priests or priestesses. Yet he'd neglected to mention Adrastea to her. Had he been so focused on winning his new bride that he forgot to include anyone else whose lives might be impacted?

He would make it up to her later. At least Desideria was wise enough to do as he bade. He'd answer her questions at a better time. He would have to reassure her that Adrastea was not taking her place as high priestess.

He felt Adrastea's grief, a bubbling welter of tar that kept threatening to engulf her. She fought hard to keep that at bay, but the flavor of her emotion spilled about her so strongly he wondered if even the weakest of his priestesses could sense it.

Also, there was a self-consciousness about her, the awkwardness of a maiden. He'd played with her sensuality in an attempt to win her over. She fought it now as she fought it then. Perhaps it was unfair to have jerked her away from her provincial life so quickly.

No matter. She was immortal now. She would adjust to her new life. Besides, it would not do for the Bride of the Dark to live in some dinky little clapboard country cottage.

She belonged here. She belonged with him. Oh, he wanted to run his hand through her dark hair. He wanted to drink of her essence and taste her skin.

As they passed between the granite pillars, she looked up at them in awe. He reached out and stroked a pillar as they passed. He felt rather proud of this temple. He'd done a fine job of it.

Once inside, the priestesses divided up. Desideria turned down a corridor to carry out his instructions. A few selected younger priestesses followed her. The rest remained with him, their curiosity stronger than their sense of propriety.

Adrastea studied the high-ceilinged stone corridors and the wooden doorways they passed. At least it was better than her staring at nothing but the floor.

"This temple was carved by hand several thousand years ago," he told her, but she wasn't listening. Her arms were folded tightly about her waist and her gaze darted about, not so much from curiosity but more as if trying to remember the route they took. Remembering her way so she could escape? As if something as simple as a stone temple could keep her penned in.

Not that the layout of the temple was labyrinthine in any way.

One might expect his temple to be dark and mysterious inside but that was not so. Self-glowing glass balls of light lit the interior, driving away any gloom. He was rather proud of those too. There were no furtive shadows here. He liked it bright and cheery.

She studied the lights. A funk of depression washed over her and flowed into him, as if her capacity for shock and grief had been filled. Was he going to feel it every time she got upset?

"Your thoughts have changed," he said, watching her closely. "I hope they are not bad ones."

Her eyes narrowed at him in an answer, but she did not speak.

"You will wish to rest after such a busy day." He stopped at a particularly ornate double door. A few of the priestesses whispered to one another. For as long as any of them knew, these doors had never been opened. They'd never seen the inside. Mor-Lath had forbidden it.

He gave a small flicker of his fingers to the priestesses. Almost as one, they sank to the floor in genuflection, awaiting his further command. They would get their chance to assuage their curiosities.

He swung open the doors. Taking Adrastea by the hand, he led her in, leaving the priestesses out in the hallway. As one, they craned their necks to see what lay beyond.

The door closed, shutting out the priestesses, much to their disappointment. No matter. They'd get their chance later.

Mor-Lath and Adrastea were alone. Adrastea let out a small sound of awe. She drifted in to this humongous chamber illuminated by the same lights as the rest of the temple, coming to rest as the spectacle overwhelmed her. That satisfied him. He'd prepared this chamber especially for her. It had been waiting for her well before she'd been born.

Oh, sweet solitude. He could do anything he wished in here. But not everything he wanted.

He drew a breath and took a hold of himself. Some things were not worth the risk, no matter how tempting.

She tempted him so.

Thick warm carpets covered the polished granite floor. Along the wall stood the kind of furniture a woman would enjoy—a dressing table, several mirrors, from small hand mirrors to a full-length framed looking glass, soft-cushioned chairs of delicate design with matching tables. He'd carved a closet in one side of the room, a giant chamber full of ornate clothing selected especially for her. No doubt she would wish to discard her dowdy country homespuns in favor of exotic silks and cottons, once she convinced her country self it was all right.

On the other side of the room a curtained doorway led to a bathing chamber, hosting a large tub set into the floor. He'd engineered the piping to ensure it was always filled with warm water. A quick check showed his previous actions had not disrupted the system of pipes nor the clever heat transfer system he'd created.

Adrastea looked like she could use a good bath. The battle this morning left her quite filthy, as did her sojourns in the woods around Sacred Spring.

In the middle of the room he'd placed an ornate bed with a canopy and curtains. The mattress was not straw but the finest of eiderdown. Only the best for his bride.

Adrastea looked about, her eyes briefly touching on its furnishings before she turned her gaze to the bed. Her heart thumped harder. He watched her pulse quickening in her neck and waves of apprehension warred with the grief and also with passion.

No, he would not ravish her, no matter how much he wanted to. An image of washing the dirt of her creamy skin tricked its way into his head. He pushed it away.

"This," he said, more to distract himself rather than reassure her, "is your room. You are a lady now, despite your upbringing but not despite your birth. It would seem odd if you did not have a room of your own."

"Ah," was all she said. Her heart continued to race. Now she looked about, anywhere but at the bed. That amused him, for she could not stop the idea of sensuality rising within her. Did she know he knew?

Mor-Lath's own thoughts strayed to the bed. What delights awaited them there? Before he could stop himself, he'd reached up and stroked her curly hair. Oh, immortality had improved her. All those little mortal flaws were gone. She was a beautiful, elegant woman, with curves in all the right places. Her new height had raised her hemline a few inches, betraying her ankles. Even the flush of embarrassment on her cheeks set his own blood aflame.

Yes, she had been thinking of the bed and what it would mean for a new bride.

Oh, that.

He drew a breath to steady himself. No matter how enticing she was, he could not risk it. No matter how tempting.

He stepped back and laid a hand on her shoulder. She jumped. No. Even if he was so inclined, she was not ready for consummation. Conflict tore at her heart.

And if he had his logical way, that would be never. Shame, really. Her passions were as strong as his own.

"Fear not, my bride. I have no desire to bed you today." Well, not quite true. He desired her greatly. At the moment, there was nothing he wanted more than to run his hands through her hair, his lips over her skin and certain parts of him through certain parts of her. She ignited a fire in his soul. He so wanted to give in to its heat. He'd always preferred dark-haired women.

Only fear kept him in check. Fear of a prophecy.

"You would be terribly offended by my attentions at this time. I have no wish to invoke your wrath." When she'd pulled the Deeper Power that had connected the souls of a half-million people through her, he'd realized just how powerful she could be. She was created to be that powerful, but he'd forgotten. He would have to woo her and break her of the bad habits Mira Priestess had taught her.

They had work to do together. It wouldn't do to have her go squeamish on him at a critical time.

Until then, he wished he could sink himself into the deliciousness of her. He ran his hand from her shoulder to her back. Before he could go farther, he pulled away to keep his passion from taking over his common sense. "Rest and reconcile yourself to your new life."

He plucked at her homespun skirt. "You have new clothes, suitable to your station but keep your old things if you so wish." He had personally chosen the most beautiful gowns from several cultures around the world, things that would suit her color and figure. He would dress her in the finest.

And how he itched to take them off again. He brought his thoughts away from the brink.

"Desideria has already made her selection of priestesses to serve you personally." Indeed, he could sense his high priestess out in the hallway. She'd given her orders. Now she stood waiting his pleasure.

"I'd say treat them kindly but knowing what I know of them, you are better off causing them to fear you. Indeed, I may say they already do." As well they should. He feared her. Should she ever discover her true capabilities before he had completely won her over, she could do some serious damage to him.

The danger made his blood sing. He loved powerful women, not to subdue them but to share their power. It made their passion stronger. That was the greatest turn-on of all.

He couldn't help it. Mor-Lath reached out and drew her to him. His body still echoed the faint song of her translation to immortality. He stopped himself before his lips met hers. A moment more and he would give in.

Best to flee now before he did something he would surely regret. Without even a kiss on the tip of her perfect nose, he abandoned his bride while he still could, leaving her very much alone. His legs refused to obey him, so he willed himself directly into the corridor. He needed a chaperone.

In the hallway, the priestesses startled at his appearance. Only Desideria remained unmoved, kneeling on the floor. Radelisa, Garsinde and Berengaria knelt beside her, awaiting orders. Yes, she chose well.

"Beyond this door," he told them, "Stands the most powerful woman in the world."

Berengaria peeked up, concern in her eyes. He laid a gentle hand on her head. "Don't worry. I'm sure she'll like you, Garie." Everyone liked Berengaria.

Berengaria's wan smile did not convince him.

"You are chosen to serve her. Scrub her down, dress her up, make her feel more comfortable. After all, she's had a long day."

To Desideria he said, "Cater to her every whim. Do not invoke her anger. Even I fear her from time to time."

That sent a ripple of surprise through them. What could be so bad that it caused a god to tremble?

To the others: "Dellie, Sindie, Garie, behave yourselves.

"I have something rather important to take care of." And he felt he'd explode if he didn't take care of it soon. "I shall give you further instructions upon my return."

And he left them before he could embarrass himself.

Mor-Lath stood on top of his mountain and looked across the world. The wind blew through his hair and the evening rays of the sun cast long shadows over his valley. A vast city, the capital of the wanderlusty Tredan peoples, filled it from mountain to mountain. There were hundreds of thousands of people there, most of them town-bound denizens of the once-nomadic Tredan tribes. Many still roamed the world in caravans or ships, engaging in trade of goods and ideas. The sense of so many people sounded like the cheer of a great crowd, or the roar of ocean waves. He loved it.

But today it was not strong enough to drown out the annoying buzz of his lust.

Oh, his new bride stirred his soul, by both her strength and her potential. The thought that he was that much closer to his final goal also buzzed in his ears, making him feel giddy and igniting his passions. He'd nearly made a very dangerous mistake.

He could not sate himself with Adrastea, no matter how strongly he felt the pull. The power that set his blood on fire had the potential to destroy him.

He could not scratch the itch on his own. Unsatisfying. He needed a partner, one he'd never had before. A substitute. Whomever he chose, she had to be just right. Someone he didn't care about.

Sex was one of his greatest pleasures in life, more so in his godhood. His personal preference: a willing woman who held no fear in her heart. With no fear, she'd open herself to pleasure. With willingness, she'd need no convincing, though seduction held its own merits. With his talents, he could pay attention to what woke the passion within her. He'd feed on that and give back to her his lusts and thrusts. Then, when she arrived at the zenith, he'd share her pleasure, as well as his own. The sensation was overwhelming.

He loved it! Fear and terror were all right, in their way, when one wished to awe and inspire. There was a certain pleasure to be gained from a clever turn of wit and playing with words. But when it came to sheer pleasure, nothing beat a good orgasm.

He pushed aside thoughts of Adrastea. How powerful, how intense would she be, with her newly-wakened abilities in the Deeper Power? His loins stirred at the thought.

There were a few women about the world he'd had in the past when his desires got the better of him. Most of them had no idea of his true identity. A few—select priestesses—knew. Of all the women he'd had, they were the most passionate, the most giving, possibly because they knew exactly who he was. The others were fine in their own way. He derived a certain pleasure in their not knowing they were making love to a god.

But overall, the priestesses were the most fun. Other than their willingness, the consequences of their night of passion made for interesting politics in their rank.

Being "Favored of Mor-Lath" held a certain status. The shaking of their world amused him sometimes.

Today, he didn't want someone he'd had before. Today, he wanted a casual fling, no strings attached, and certainly no emotional connections.

He sorted through the living souls pledged to him. Were there any currently ripe for the picking?

He found one named Desmone, a rather shallow soul who spent much of her personal prayers in begging for his favor.

Desmone served in a temple southeast in Avelia, a small nation not too far from Feown. She was willing and desperate for attention from him. He didn't care why at the moment.

Perhaps now he should hear her pleas. She was an ambitious woman who craved more power. No doubt his favor would serve her purposes.

She was pretty enough, with dark hair and a slim figure, though not as well-developed as he usually preferred. Also, she was not a virgin, so he would not have to take the time to seduce and ease her.

And the best thing, he had no particular emotional attachment to her, so she'd make a nice substitute.

She was perfect.

The sun had long set in Avelia. Most priests and priestesses had finished their evening devotions. Avelians were not as faithful as Tredans. Once they finished their lip service to him, out they went into the city for whatever purposes they saw fit.

The temple was nearly abandoned and would remain so until morning. Only Desmone remained at the altar, pouring out her desperate prayers.

She was a dramatic person and he felt urgent. He appeared on the other side of the altar where she prayed. A small ripple through the stone floor, a faint rumble of thunder. She'd love it.

Her name floated on his baritone voice. "Desmone."

Desmone opened her dark eyes and looked up. He saw surprise, then the fire of smug ambition in her eyes. She rose to her feet. Although she had never seen him before, she knew him. He felt her mind tumbling.

She'd do admirably.

"You wish my favor?" he asked her.

"Yes," she panted.

He strolled around the altar. "You would serve me?"

"Forever." The pulse in her neck quickened.

He held out his hand. "Will you come to me willingly?"

"Yes."

Good enough. He pulled her to him and ravished her mouth with a fierce urgency he'd barely kept under control. The power of his lust surprised even him. He surrendered to it. The fear was there as well, as it always was but he fought that back.

Desmone gasped for air and couldn't. Only when he threw her on the altar could she breathe. He took her, hard. He fed her the taste of his ache for release until it overwhelmed her. She cried out in passion and pain, so strong was her arrival. So strong but so quick.

He felt his release a moment later. He let his body spend into hers.

It left her lightheaded. She fought the waves that threatened to pull her under into unconsciousness. Mor-Lath distanced himself from her emotions. No good getting caught up with this one. She was merely a tool.

He felt physical relief, and a little cold. While she lay prone on the altar, he laid his hand on her belly and seared the cradle of life within. No prophecies fulfilled today. Then he lowered her robe and left her there to sink under the dark surface of sleep. The other priestesses would find her in the morning, they who had nothing better to do than gossip and scheme.

Before he left, Adrastea fully believed Mor-Lath would pull her to that bed and... Her cheeks flushed with the thoughts of consummation. That was what had to happen next. She didn't know how those who followed the Dark got married. In the tradition of the Light, they shared their hearts, they shared their intentions, they shared their bodies. A flicker of lust licked at her insides.

She and Mor-Lath had shared their intentions before Carles Priest.

They'd spoken the words. The moment on the wall above Feown, when they'd joined together in the Deeper Power to make Adrastea immortal. Could that have been considered sharing their hearts? Or had her willingness to sacrifice herself for the sake of the village been the sharing of her heart? If so, it was a one-sided deal. She would have to ponder on that further, if her heart ever came unburdened with the horror of what they had done.

He desired her. He wanted her. So great was his need for her to marry him, that he stopped at nothing to secure her. It was not love. It was need, an overwhelming need for her. He wanted her. He got her. Was that his sharing of the heart?

That left the sharing of bodies, the consummation.

But that hadn't happened. What was he waiting for? She'd married him, willingly. Another frission of desire rolled within. What other obstacle lay in their path?

He disappeared, leaving her in the hands of his priestesses.

For a moment, she stood alone in the room—her room. A strong wave of lust rolled over her. Where had that come from? With this new body, everything came easier. The Deeper Power responded to her unlike before. Why not passion? Another wave of desire rolled through her. She fought it.

Or should she? Ever since the first day he'd appeared, she'd felt an attraction to him, one she had resisted, one she had been encouraged to fight.

There were a few times she almost gave in.

So here she was, married, with absolutely no reason, logical or moral, to need to fight her attraction. If she wanted, she could give in and assuage that ever-present desire for her—dare she say it?—husband.

The doors opened. High Priestess Desideria entered the room, smooth and graceful. Three other priestesses followed her, one of whom was Berengaria. The three knelt but Desideria remained standing.

"Mistress," Desideria began. "We have the honor to serve you." She gestured to the women behind her. "May I present Radelisa, Garsinde and Berengaria. They shall serve you personally. If they fail to please, I beg you to send them to me for punishment." Desideria did not wish for her to discipline them. Was she afraid that 'the Mistress' would go too far and cause irreparable damage to one of them? Not that Adrastea would ever be so cruel.

The priestess feared Mor-Lath's wrath, should anything happen to them. Her concern flowed along the Lines of Deeper Power strong enough for Adrastea to feel it. They hummed with tension.

Was she more sensitive to the Lines now? Nothing but neutral respect showed on the High Priestess' face, yet behind that face tumbled a thousand thoughts.

Desideria fell silent. The others remained kneeling on the floor, not saying anything. They waited for something.

"Is that all?" Adrastea asked, keeping her voice level. What was she waiting for?

"Unless you wish more, Mistress."

Adrastea shook her head. Desideria waited to be dismissed. "You may go," Adrastea told her.

Desideria touched her forehead with two fingers, then held her palm face-up as if offering something. She departed the room, closing the door behind her. The other three remained.

Now what?

Adrastea looked about this opulent prison in which Mor-Lath—*her husband*—had placed her. He gave her a prison mistress and three jailers. Couldn't they have just left her alone? She had some grieving to do. Yes. Focus on the grieving. Lust could wait.

She'd killed a half-million people. She would never have done what he had told her, if she knew that would be the result. All Adrastea wanted to do was curl up in a corner under a heavy blanket and cry until the darkest pit swallowed her.

Garsinde appeared to be the eldest, though she couldn't be too much older than Adrastea. "We wait to attend you, Mistress."

"Attend me?" What would that entail?

The three rose and looked about the room. Had they never seen it before? Berengaria dashed to the curtain on the other side of the room and pulled it aside. She let out a small squeal of delight when she saw a bathing room, this one bright with blue light. "Oh, it's beautiful."

The other two came to her side. "Has this been here the entire time?" Radelisa asked.

What? Had Mor-Lath created this just for her? Did he wave his hands five minutes previous and here it was? Adrastea followed.

Beyond the curtain lay another large room, also gently lit by those strange glowing balls. This room had a single purpose—bathing. The pool in the middle of the room was larger than some ponds back home. A cabinet on one side held bottles and boxes. Stacks of soft fluffy terrycloth lay on shelves. Even a few mirrors hung on the walls.

Their curiosities satisfied, Radelisa and Garsinde approached her and began to unlace her bodice. This surprised Adrastea. She pushed their hands away and backed off a few steps. They fell instantly to their knees. Berengaria, investigating the bottles, also fell to her knees.

"Forgive us," Radelisa begged. "We do not know your desires."

Adrastea retightened her bodice strings. "At least tell me your intentions before you carry them out."

"Forgive us."

Adrastea sighed. "Please don't do that. I—" She was about to say, *I'm new to this* but Mor-Lath had given her the impression that she was not to show weakness.

Why? What would these priestesses do?

"Just... What do you want?" she asked them.

The three rose once more but did not touch her. "His Holiness suggested that you could use a good bath," explained Garsinde. "And then, lunch. I fear it will not be as sumptuous as you are used to, for we were not expecting His Holiness back so soon, especially not with..." With what? A bride? "...with you, Mistress."

Berengaria quipped, "And it's more like afternoon tea, since lunch was several hours ago." Garsinde shushed her. Berengaria dropped her head.

Adrastea's stomach heard the word 'lunch' and put in a hearty request. She had not eaten since yesterday afternoon, when she grabbed a simple meal between all the chaos of battle. "Food sounds good. Keep it simple." Her heart did not want to eat but her body demanded it.

Berengaria asked, "Do you wish to bathe before eating? The pool looks ever so nice."

Adrastea nodded. A sudden desire to be clean of all her guilt filled her. How long would she have to scrub before a half-million deaths were erased from her soul?

Where was the sacred spring when she needed it most?

Her fingers tore at her bodice strings, unlacing them faster than ever. She dropped it to the floor where Garsinde fetched it. She pulled out her blouse and lifted it up over her head and laid that too in Garsinde's waiting hands. Her skirt, still filthy from battle, fell to the floor. She stepped out of it. Her shift was soon to follow.

Berengaria held a white robe of a soft, fluffy material in which to wrap her Mistress. Adrastea accepted it.

"Your skin is so bronze," Berengaria breathed. "It's pretty."

It was not often Adrastea had been called pretty in her life. The compliment caught her by surprise. "It is?"

"I wish I had perfect skin like you."

Perfect? Adrastea looked at her, puzzled. Berengaria's skin was a lovely almond color that suited her long, black hair. She must have frowned, for the priestess immediately fell to her knees. "I'm sorry. I did not mean to offend."

The priestesses' immediate apologies for whenever they thought they had offended her were rather frequent. What did Mor-Lath do to them when they did offend?

"You didn't. I wasn't expecting—" She paused. How much should she share with these priestesses? She barely knew them. And, belonging to Mor-Lath, how much could she trust them?

Who could she turn to now? Who was her ally? Who was her protector?

Adrastea felt alone.

By the wall stood a wide mirror, large enough to reflect everyone in the room.

Adrastea could tell the difference between Radelisa and Garsinde. Radelisa had a wider face and was just a little bit taller. Otherwise, they looked very much alike, with their straight dark hair and their large eyes. Were they, were all the priestesses, related?

But it was the figure between them that confused her for a moment. Who was that beautiful woman?

She blushed. It was herself.

Forgetting the priestesses, she skirted the pool of water and approached the mirror. If this was immortality, she'd changed.

The unruliness of her hair had smoothed into a lovely curliness. Her face had aged. She looked more adult now, with her puppy fat gone and her cheekbones more prominent. The lines Mor-Lath had drawn made her face paralleled her contours. She had a matching pair now. While her eyes were not as large as the priestesses', she preferred hers, simply because they were the most familiar thing about her. The brown had more depth of color. There were even a few flecks of gold in them that weren't there before.

She opened her robe to inspect her naked form. Her face and hands were quite filthy, making the skin of her arms and belly quite smooth by comparison. Her waist was smaller, her hips bigger. Her hands roamed up to her chest. Alas, her breasts were still the same small size. Pity.

Radelisa's voice broke her reverie. "Do you wish to bathe now, Mistress?"

Adrastea turned to her, embarrassed. She looked to the deep pool of water. She thought of the sacred spring, its pool of cold water bubbling up from deep within the earth. The spring was supposed to wash away evil, to cleanse one of sins. To drink the water was to lift one's heart and bring one closer to the Light.

Oh, how Adrastea wanted to be clean!

Berengaria took her robe. Adrastea descended steps at the edge of the pool and sank into the beautifully warm water. She let out a sigh that shuddered like a sob.

Garsinde brought out bottles of potions and set them down on the side. "May I wash your hair, Mistress?" Adrastea heard a touch of longing in the request.

She looked up at Garsinde and shook her head. She didn't want to be handled right now.

Adrastea ducked her head under the water. There, she could cry as much as she wanted.

Down here, under the surface, was a different world. The water enveloped her. It shut out everything else. Here, it was just Adrastea and the water. She imagined she was enveloped in the warmth of the Light, that the past day had been but a nightmare. Maybe she was tucked in her mother's bed, or better yet, ensconced in her corner of Ari's loft. Tomorrow she would swear off whatever it was she had sampled from Ari's cellar or her private garden...

Then she felt something so strong it startled her. Immediately she rose from the water and pressed her hands to her cheeks. Whatever it was she felt, it came through those infernal lines with which Mor-lath had marked her.

"Mistress?" asked a surprised Garsinde.

"Shh," Adrastea hissed, focusing on the sudden emotions she'd felt under her skin.

Passion. And lust. But not hers. His? She had been getting undercurrents of desire from him all morning, but he kept his distance.

She felt a touch of frustration and after a moment, there was a faint undercurrent of fear. So, it wasn't just passion.

Adrastea settled back against the side of the pool. Her eyes wanted to cry. She let them. Water streamed from her hair down her face.

It felt like she was eavesdropping on some sort of conversation where she couldn't hear the words.

"Mistress? Shall I leave?"

Was she experiencing the residual emotions from those she had killed?

No, that wasn't right. It should have been fear, surprise, sorrow. Lust is the last thing one would expect the dying to feel.

The lust sated itself after a minute or so but the fear, no longer masked, remained. People feared death. Then the fear was cut off and everything faded.

Out of the corner of her eye, she saw Radelisa and Berengaria kneeling and whispering together. When they saw her, they stopped.

"Sorry," Adrastea apologized. "My mind was elsewhere."

Out of habit, Radelisa and Berengaria touched their hands to the floor. "No need to apologize, Mistress," Radelisa said.

"We're used to the ways of gods," added Berengaria. "Well," she amended. "A god."

Adrastea sat up. Mor-Lath told her she was immortal. He never said anything about her being a god. She certainly didn't feel like one.

Garsinde had scooted away from her. Adrastea held out her hand for the bottle Garsinde clutched. "I'll wash my own hair for now. I have some thinking I need to do."

"As you wish," she replied, her relief quite obvious. The others also nodded and departed.

Adrastea studied her body. Is this what Mira fought? Did she fear what Adrastea would become? Did she even know?

She sank into the water until it lapped about her mouth and filled her ears. Away from the soft sounds of the priestesses, Adrastea was alone with her thoughts. How much did Mira know? Did she realize that Mor-Lath intended to make Adrastea immortal? Or did Mira simply fear he would turn Adrastea into a Dark priestess, taking her away from the Light?

She glanced at the attending priestesses who moved in and out of the bath chamber on their business. They didn't seem so sinister. Still, she wished they would go away so she could cry in peace. She dunked herself under the water several times and ran her fingers through her hair.

Desideria entered the bathing room but she did not kneel. "I have brought you a humble repast. Please accept it."

"Thank you." Adrastea rose, and warm water ran off her body in rivulets. Berengaria brought the white robe to wrap her in while Garsinde bundled a towel of the same fabric around her hair. She needed food.

Desideria inclined her head and departed.

The priestesses dried off Adrastea and led her back into the bedroom. Radelisa helped her into a shift of a fabric Adrastea couldn't identify. A beautiful green dress lay on the bed. When Radelisa lifted it up to pull it over Adrastea's head, it felt like the best-quality cotton. A pang of sadness flowed through her as she remembered her mother. What she wouldn't have given to know fabric of this quality.

The dress was overly long, pooling on the floor at her feet. It had long, flowing sleeves whose tails reached nearly as far. The neck was far too low for Adrastea's sense of modesty. The dress hung loose like a blouse but when Radelisa wound a golden cord around Adrastea's waist, it cinched in to fit her figure. Adrastea felt disconcerted there was no other form of undergarment. Is this what all Tredan women wore?

"His Holiness has brought you fine clothing of the latest fashions from all over. I hope you are pleased."

Adrastea ran her hands over the smooth fabric. "It's nice." But it wasn't her. Homespuns were what she was used to.

The priestesses exhaled in relief.

Berengaria seated her at a table where a fine meal was spread. She had no idea what was placed before her, except for the bread and the soup. Even that had elements of unfamiliarity.

She sampled a meat dish. It was dark like beef with mushrooms. This was lunch? Adrastea didn't care. It was delicious. She devoured the food, for she'd not eaten properly in three days. Also, there was a plate of unfamiliar salads. She ate that too. Then a bowl of soup with soft, crusty bread. The cup did not contain wine, as Adrastea first thought but a juice that had a creamy texture to it. This she gulped down. Oh, she was hungry.

Before she finished her meal, Desideria entered once more. She dismissed the other three priestesses with a look. "When you are finished, Mistress, His Holiness commands that you be brought to the library."

"A library?" Adrastea was not that fond of reading.

"His Holiness wishes you not take too long over your lunch."

Adrastea sensed a feeling of urgency from Desideria. She sighed. "Very well." But food first. If Mor-Lath didn't like it, that was his problem.

Saraym emerged from her prison. In the corridors of the palace, dead Cithrans lay scattered like so many fallen rag dolls among the flotsam of war. Blood and horror spotted the floor. Discarded shoes, scraps of food, the ragged remains of Feowan clothing lay here and there.

She slipped her feet into a pair of abandoned shoes and wrapped a torn pelisse about her shoulders. Being too long for her short stature, it dragged along the floor. General Miniver's sash she kept about her waist. His boot with its gory contents stayed tucked under her arm.

Only her footsteps echoed through the marbled hallways of the palace. No other living human soul roamed here.

The rats were present, of course. Let them have their feast. May they not get indigestion.

She came across a few more familiar officers. She claimed their sashes and their staffs. The sashes she tied about her waist, their genitals she added to the boot.

She gave up dismemberment when the boot reached capacity. But sashes she collected until her waist fluttered like a beribboned young lass on May Day.

It was thus the braver Feowan souls found her, stalking the courtyards of the palace.

She limped along, a frightful sight—missing eye, gore-filled boot in one hand, blood-stained knife in the other.

At first, her subjects ran away. She let them.

As she gathered a few more sashes—they were fewer to find, the further one got from the palace—one unlucky young man approached her.

Before he could draw near enough for a conversation, she slashed at him with a knife. "All men are forbidden within the palace!"

She gave chase, hobbling the best she could on a broken toe. The young man easily outdistanced her.

She returned to her collecting, silent, angry, and cold.

The young man was not there for curiosity. Panting and heaving, he made his way back outside the gate. There, a carriage with the Jeratigue family crest waited for him.

"I found her," he reported to the woman within. "But she has forbidden all men within the palace."

"Well then," replied Lady Jeratigue, opening the door to her carriage. "It is a good thing I am a woman."

After Saraym had made the rounds of the palace, she returned to the main courtyard near the stables.

Unlike before, the courtyard teemed with people—her people. From where did they come? In groups of three or four, they dragged away the Cithran bodies. Quite a few of the crowd were children, given to sweeping and picking up random objects.

Saraym stopped cold. "Who the hell are you?" she shouted at the nearest group. They had grabbed the legs of a rather large Cithran soldier and were trying to drag him across the yard.

At the sound of her voice, they dropped the body and gave sketched curtseys. "Your Grace." Yes, she'd startled them all right.

She looked over the busy crowd. They were all women, as far as she could tell. Good.

Only one was not working. Saraym squinted with her remaining eye. Tall, slim, well-dressed, doing nothing. A noblewoman. Whoever she was, she'd survived the Cithran Purge. Not only had the Cithrans sought to kill every priest in the city but had wiped out a fair bit of the upper class.

So, how'd this one escape?

Ignoring the first group, she staggered her way to the noblewoman.

As she drew near, she recognized Lady Jeratigue, a rather ambitious lady whose opinions often rubbed Saraym the wrong way. Still, she was no simpering miss. No one who looked at Lady Jeratigue could mistake her backbone of steel.

Saraym dispensed with pleasantries. They, along with everything else of great social value, had perished in the siege. "What are you doing?"

Lady Jeratigue, dressed in a morning gown of spotted blue, folded her arms. "Overseeing the cleaning of the palace."

"Ah. Been promoted to head maid, I see."

Lady Jeratigue frowned over her aristocratic nose. Yes, that insult had struck home. She looked Saraym up and down. "Forgive me for saying this but you need a bath."

Saraym brandished her knife. "Not until I know that Feown is safe."

"It's safe. Every Cithran is dead."

Saraym took this in. "Every one?"

"Yes, Your Grace."

"How did they die?"

Lady Jeratigue confessed, "I don't know."

Saraym's eyes narrowed. "I thought all high-ranking nobles were killed. How did you survive? Or does one of your grandfathers have some dirty laundry?"

Lady Jeratigue drew herself upright. "My genealogy is impeccable, even if my health is not. I had a terrible cold that day and had stayed home. When the soldiers came knocking, I hid."

Saraym snorted at this. "Who else survived?"

Lady Jeratigue shook her head. "I don't know."

"Find out." She looked out over everyone's effort. "Keep up the good work. You'll have this palace sparkling in no time. Meanwhile, seek out any survivors and set them to the task of removing every single Cithran body from the city. None is to remain within my walls, what's left of them." Honestly, she had no idea of the state of her city. The Cithrans made quick work of their invasion of Feown, making it all the way to the throne room on that first day. Saraym shuddered and pushed away that memory. After the horrors of the throne room, she'd been dragged down to the cellars. She had been there until this morning.

"Don't forget the bodies in the cellars under the palace. If you don't get them out soon, they'll stink up the place."

She dumped out her boot of trophies. "While you're at it, get rid of these. I recommend sticking them on spikes outside the city walls."

Only now did Lady Jeratigue's will falter. She paled as she stared at the gory pile of dismembered phalluses. "Is that... are those..." Her gorge rose. She doubled over and lost whatever breakfast she'd had earlier.

Saraym studied her blood-caked palm. Her hand shook as she scrutinized it. Perhaps Lady Jeratigue was right. Maybe a bath, or at least a bit of a wash, was overdue.

"One last thing," she said to Lady Jeratigue. "No one is to disturb me." She twirled the knife in her hand. "I'm sure you understand."

Lady Jeratigue, still overcome by the pile of dismemberment at her feet, covered her mouth with her hand and nodded.

Chapter 3

That evening, disquiet rumbled through Nyabern, the capital of the mighty Cithran empire. A man rode his solitary horse through the empty Military Quarter. Stark stone barracks stood row after row, echoing the ring of his horse's shoes on pavement. Flags denoting each company fluttered in the breeze. Other than the flag, the only other movement was the scurrying of rats about the perimeter.

No living soul remained in the Military Quarter. Only the man and his horse. He was the secretary of the Speaking Minister of the High Council, or so he let everyone believe, and he'd come to see what had happened.

There was no one in the Military Quarter to note his passing. At midday, every soldier there had died. They'd perished where they stood—in the streets, in the mess hall, on patrol. Suddenly and inexplicably died. Even the earth itself threatened to perish, so strong had been the sudden wave of mortality.

The bodies still lay there, for no one wished to approach the scene of so much death. But the secretary had to investigate. His horse stepped over limbs, dancing nervously.

The secretary dismounted. With a touch of Power, he quieted his reluctant horse. So many dead but only soldiers.

Not all who lived in the Military quarter were of the army. Those who did not die, had fled. These people, fueled by confusion and panic, bore their horrible tale to the rest of Nyabern.

Did the soldiers die of plague? Did they perish from some new weapon? After all, those who dabbled in science came up with some rather peculiar things. Surely, they weren't all executed? What happened? Who would die next?

The secretary pushed a lank of blond hair back behind a handsome ear as he studied a dead body. No apparent trauma, no sign of disease. He laid a hand on its chest. No movement.

He closed his eyes and reached out to the universe. "Come to me," he commanded the Lines of Deeper Power. They rose from the dead soldier and wrapped themselves about the secretary.

There was no one about to see him work his magic. Such knowledge was considered sorcerous, and therefore illegal. He liked it like that.

The secretary let the Lines wrap about him. He listened to them. "Who killed this man?" The question carried along the Lines that connected the soldier to his platoon and sergeant, who answered to lieutenant, and so up the line to General Miniver and the War Minister. Someone who bore the Deeper Power greater than any other the secretary knew, had not only killed this soldier but every other soldier in the entire Army. His gut clenched in horror. The whole army. Dead. How could anyone in the world do something so mighty? He couldn't.

He wanted to.

A niggle rose in the back of his head, accompanied with fear.

"Who are you?" he inquired of the Lines. Who was so strong?

They returned the impression of a woman most powerful. Behind her stood a man, of whom the secretary knew. Mor-Lath.

So. The God of the Dark had found the Bride. A fresh wave of terror mixed with elation filled the secretary. His knees buckled. He was running out of time. She'd been found.

He located his nervous horse and hastened back to the Rotunda.

The Bride had been found by the last person he wanted to find her. All his work, all his study, and someone else had beaten him to her.

It was not until he'd reached the Rotunda, where the High Council met, he realized he'd forgotten to sever the Lines of the Deeper Power.

The secretary did not like being tied down. One by one, he cut the Lines to the dead body, feeling them snap back into his soul with tiny little pings.

Interesting. Their severance did not sting. Why not? Had the mass death something to do with that? He reached out to the body once more with the Power, then severed his ties. Again, the lines pinged back, without their usual painful snaps. That was an implication he'd have to investigate further.

Free and unencumbered, the secretary sought the Speaking

Minister. The High Council would have to be called. With the army completely destroyed, the whole of Cithra was vulnerable. It was not so much the neighboring nations he feared but the Bride herself, and the one who claimed her.

Desideria brought Adrastea to the tall double doors of the library. "His Holiness awaits you inside." She opened one of them.

Adrastea stepped in and drew in a breath of amazement. It was as if the whole mountain had been carved into one giant cave. Rows upon rows of tall wooden shelves filled this room so large she couldn't see to the far end. She never imagined that there could be so many books. The shelves went on forever.

A reading table about the length and breadth of her new bed stood between the door and the books. A few wooden chairs, more for practicality rather than comfort, surrounded it.

Mor-Lath stood in front of the shelves, reading to himself from a large book. When she came in, he glanced at her then went back to his reading.

Adrastea peered down the aisles. "Have you read every single one of these?"

He looked up, his countenance pensive. "I believe I have. Thousands of years are a long time." He closed the book but did not replace it on the shelf. "I wish we had enough time for you to read them all as well."

"Oh, I'm not much of a reader." Ari had taught her, as had Natan but she had found it difficult to concentrate on the words for long. It took too much time to suss them out.

He handed her the book, a brown leather tome with a wooden spine. "You may find your tastes have changed."

Adrastea opened it. As her eyes scanned the page, her head picked up the information. It was as if the words jumped straight into her brain, as if they wanted to be there. She didn't have to wrestle with them like before.

The book was about Feown, the Duchy to which Sacred Spring belonged. She turned the page and read more. All that information wanted to be inside her head as fast as her eyes could scan it. This was the city she saved. Would she remember everything so easily?

If only she could forget those half-million dead. The memories of every single one of those lives pulled at her heart with the Lines of Creation that bound them all together—those same Lines with which she'd ended their lives. Would she ever get used to that?

Mor-Lath put his hand on the page she was reading. "As fascinating as the history of Feown is, I would prefer you save that for later. Come with me."

Adrastea picked up the hem of her gown. Unless she lifted the voluminous fabric, she stumbled over it. She tucked the book under one arm and threw the train of the gown over it, clutching all to her chest. She followed Mor-Lath through the stacks until he came to a stop.

He selected a smaller book off a shelf. "Read this one first, especially page sixty-seven."

After some awkward shuffling on her part, Adrastea handed the larger tome to Mor-Lath and let her hem fall to the floor. She opened the small book.

Page 67: *The Dark One shall have his bride as he has desired, and he shall mark her as his own, so that the whole of the world, should they gaze upon her, know who she is. She shall be his equal, his half and thus complete him as he wishes. For this purpose, has she been designed, that she may fulfill the measure of her creation.*

As she read it again and again, a frown creased her face. Her heart raced. A cold pit opened in her stomach. She shook her head. "No. You're lying to me again."

He turned the pages to the title: *The Aviseriad: His Prophecies of the Light.* "These are Light prophecies—a translation but the idea is the same. They, the Light, have foretold your existence and your destiny. In fact, They helped me design your soul."

Her jaw dropped. "Design?"

He gave her an amused smile. "Did you think souls just 'happened'? Well, most of the time they do, and they turn out well enough. But once in a while, the gods take an active role in creating a certain type of soul for their purposes. The Light create Their mashiahs, and I created... well, you."

The bottom dropped out of her world. Her chest tightened before going numb. "But I thought I was a daughter of the Light..." She rested her fingertips on her lips. She wanted to cry again. She wanted to throw up.

"You are. Make no mistake about that; I had some input into you, but They did most of the work. Indeed, I think they put a little too much of the Light in you." He sounded annoyed.

A sob escaped her. "So... this whole..." She waved her hands. "Your," she didn't want to use the word 'courtship', "your pursuit of me, the war, my agreeing to marry you, it was all a lie? I thought I had a choice." She sobbed again. She couldn't breathe.

"You did," Mor-Lath confessed. "And had you continued to resist me, not only would you serve to forever frustrate me but could have gone on to live a rather plebeian existence in your little village. Imagine a glorious future of listening to dull sermons by your Light priestesses for the rest of your short mortal life. I'm sure the Light would have been more than happy to see that happen," he finished wryly.

Adrastea broke out into noisy tears. She clutched the book to her chest as if it could fill the empty place that opened under her ribs. She wanted to collapse in upon herself until nothing was left. All that time she'd been trying to be good... had it all been a sham?

He let her cry for a moment while he selected another book. "All those with destinies have choices despite those destinies. For destiny is not so much that one particular mortal is locked into their potential but rather destiny is the choice of mighty consequences that is given them. Should they choose one path or another, those paths lead to great things."

Adrastea fell against a bookshelf and slid to the floor. Drops of tears left wet patches across the fabric of the dress as it lay across her knees. The enormity of her choice struck her. Stay as a mortal and lose all those she ever loved. Save those she loved and lose more lives. Some choice. Either way featured far too much death. "So, what would have happened if I'd always said no?"

He crouched down in front of her. "Imagine your fame as the only mortal able to thwart the Dark God."

She curled up into an even tighter ball. Shame pricked her insides. She could have said no. Always no.

He rose. "Perhaps this has been too much for you today. And to think, this morning all you wanted to do was sleep in. Who thought so much could have happened in one day?"

She cried harder. Her frustration mounted in her as well as her grief. As it fed the emptiness inside her, she called upon the Deeper Power to come and comfort her.

Mor-Lath relieved her of the book, took her hands and helped her to stand. He scooped her up and carried her to her bedroom. There he laid her on the bed, still fully clothed. He held her in his arms while she cried out her sorrow.

She didn't care that it was Mor-Lath, author of her misery, who held her. Oh, she felt so lonely.

"You'll feel your pain now; it will be but a moment and will soon pass. Tomorrow you shall feel better."

Adrastea doubted that. She pushed him away. He did not resist.

He placed the books on the foot of her bed. "There is something for you to read on the morrow. I do hope you enjoy them, for the knowledge will come in handy. When you are done, we shall go to Feown, where you can meet those whose lives and whose country you have saved."

She didn't answer him but rolled away. It wasn't much of a salve for her soul, his promise. She surrendered to the dullness that the emptiness had born.

He laid his hand on her forehead. "*Sleep*," he murmured. "You need it."

The Deeper Power washed over her and pulled her down into oblivion. Like a blessed relief from pain, she closed her eyes and embraced the inky depths.

By the next morning, the whole of Nyabern rang with the news. The Military Quarter was no more.

The secretary had informed Thofferson the Speaking Minister and suggested an emergency council. Notes went out, hand-delivered, to call in the High Council. The urgency and the nature of the note sent every Minister flying towards the Rotunda of the High Council. Not a single one delayed his departure, abandoning meals, illicit beds, gaming tables and other such pleasures of the rich and powerful.

Every man of them but one.

"The War Minister is dead," Thofferson informed them upon arrival, one by one. Behind him the secretary, dressed in livery and nigh invisible in the background, kept track of everyone as they arrive. He held a ledger. As he brushed his lanky blond hair out of his handsome eyes, he made notes and marks.

At first, most Ministers were annoyed that they were called to a meeting of utmost importance to be told this news. Most of them knew it anyway. The gossip had made its rounds. On a personal level, most of the ministers did not like each other. They were rivals for political power, for social influence and more. Sure, they cared that another died, for that left a vacancy over which to be argued.

In the Rotunda, a good three dozen seats surrounded the polished marble floor, each one equal in status and power. These belonged to the Ministers. Behind them were back benches and desks and more for the staff and lesser politicians who supported the ministers.

Soon, every seat was filled. The murmur of curious and irate ministers buzzed through the domed Rotunda, questions and gossip passing.

Thofferson, who held the right of assembly and generally kept order, rose. The buzz settled but did not stop. Speculation hissed back and forth. Rumor had it that it wasn't just the War Minister who'd died.

"As you may have heard," the Speaking Minister said, "Lord Emerey, our War Minister, has died of unknown causes."

The buzz of the back benchers rose.

"What you may not know is that not only has the Military Quarter been emptied but the entire Army has perished as well." Thofferson swallowed. He adjusted the chain of office about his neck. "Every last soldier."

The whole High Council paused. Silence settled for a few moments, then the buzz of low conversation burst forth like angry wasps, reverberating through the high dome of the Rotunda. Many of them had heard these rumors as well. They had not expected it to be confirmed so soon.

Thofferson pounded and pounded his gavel until the noise settled down.

One Minister rose. "But how could such a thing happen?" The others added their voices.

The secretary consulted with Thofferson, their heads bowed towards each other for a moment. The Minister cleared his throat. "A new threat has manifested itself. It seems we have offended the Bride."

A rumble of discontent rolled through the Ministers. "What?" called a Minister. "Isn't she a figment of Feowan imagination, a non-existent god?"

The secretary murmured in Thofferson's ear. He nodded before answering his fellow Minister. "Is she a god? No. There is only One True, and only he." The secretary prompted the minister again. "She is merely a foreign sorceress, albeit a powerful one."

The Ministers murmured again. To defeat the evilness of sorcery was why the Cithrans went to war in the first place. The Faith Minister, a rotund man dressed in the opulent robes of religion, stood and requested acknowledgement from the Speaking Minister. Thofferson granted the Faith Minister permission to speak

Here was a man who took especial delight in pomp and circumstance. From the precision of his fingernails to the grand sweep of his arms, he spared no effort in the hallmarks of his exalted calling. The secretary allowed him his self-righteous drama. The masses enjoyed a spectacle. Helped keep them in line.

"Our research hinted of a powerful being; foreign religions are never clear. Some of their history speaks of a Bride to come, who cleaves to darkness itself. Such a metaphor speaks of the evil that would rise in the West. Now we have seen it come to pass."

Murmurs of assent rolled through the Ministers. However, a few voices rose in dissention. "We've had no proof of a sorceress commanding the Feowans!" said one. "Did the War Minister know of this Bride?"

Behind the empty chair of the late War Minister, his remaining backbenchers and staff—civilians all—murmured amongst themselves.

One unlucky chap received an instant promotion, being pushed forward to speak for the War cabinet. "Um," he hesitated before turning back to the men behind him. One man, dressed in the livery of a secretary, leaned forward, his blond hair sweeping over his elegant face. He whispered to the de-facto War Minister, prompting him, before slipping away.

"Uh, it seems that the War Ministry did have knowledge of such a sorceress." More promptings. "It seems rumors from the West had narrowed her location to the mountains."

"Well," Thofferson demanded. "Did they find her?"

The de-facto Minister swallowed several times. "I... I think it is more that she found us."

The blond secretary leaned over to the Faith Minister and prompted him. "It is clear that we must return to the West, seek out this evil sorceress and kill her!"

Shouts of agreement rang out through the Rotunda. The Faith Minister stood proud with his declaration. He ignored the buzzing little secretary who tugged at his robed and tried to whisper in his ear. Eventually, the secretary gave up.

The Speaking Minister pounded his gavel for silence.

A rumble shook the Rotunda, shaking the floor.

"NO."

A mighty voice rang out, echoing against the copper domed ceiling. As one, every man in the Rotunda fell to his knees, some prostrating themselves on the floor in hopes it would swallow them. Some whimpered, others cried as quietly as they could.

When the One True god spoke, everyone listened.

The Speaking Minister looked around for the Faith Minister. The fat old man had buried his face in his hands. Thofferson swallowed and genuflected. "Mighty be the voice of One True, he who he be." He bowed his head to the floor. "Forgive my ignorance. Have you not sent us out to destroy the blasphemy of the Western faiths? Would you not have us seek out the Bride? She has destroyed our army to the last man. Why would you spare her life?"

"FIND. HER." One True's voice shook the whole Rotunda. "BRING. HER. TO. ME." The rumbling stopped.

Thofferson swallowed the dust in his mouth. "How shall we—" A ping of pain struck Thofferson's heart. Everyone else around him also put their hands to their chests.

One True had spoken. Now he had departed from them.

A quiet chaos bubbled up from the assembled crowd. Many junior ministers, who'd never heard the voice of their god before, had fainted or fled. Those who'd had the experience before sat most subdued. The Ministers murmured between themselves. If One True wished for the Bride to be brought to him, how would they accomplish that without an army?

One group sat with their heads close together, consulting deeply. Thofferson noticed them. He banged his gavel for attention. "Intelligence Ministry," he called out. "Have you any insight to add to this?"

The Intelligence Minister rose. "Indeed we have, Speaker. It seems the Bride is offended by an army." He looked over to the decimated War Ministry and the Faith Minister. "Perhaps we have been too heavy-handed. As we now have our own homeland safety to look to, perhaps we should attempt to recover the Bride by more subtle means."

Thofferson nodded. "Do you have a plan?"

The Intelligence Minister bowed. "Allow us a few more days to finalize details."

Thofferson nodded. He leaned back to his secretary. "You. What's your name? Make a note to remind me to follow up with the Intelligence Minister in a few days' time."

The secretary's blond hair fell over his face as he made his notes. "Of course, Minister." The secretary was most interested to see what the Intelligence Minister had in mind. Perhaps declaring war was killing a fly with a mallet. However, it had exposed the Bride. Things were looking up.

In the morning, Adrastea came to consciousness when a hand smoothed the hair from her face. Immediately, she sensed the whole of her surroundings, including the warm male body lying next to her on the bed. Mor-Lath's presence didn't alarm her. In fact, this was the best she'd felt since...

Oh.

Her memories seeped back into her heart as sleep retreated from her head. Her heart settled heavy into her chest.

Mor-Lath smoothed a curl behind her ear. Through the Lines, she felt his interest, albeit tightly reigned. He reposed safely above the covers and fully dressed. Adrastea pushed away a tendril of disappointment.

She looked about the bed and into the chamber. The soft light in the room came from glowing balls along the edge of the walls. Curious. Those were worth investigating later.

She felt a surge of Power from Mor-Lath, gentle and local.

Two priestesses entered the room as summoned, bearing a breakfast tray. They sat it on the table and then knelt to await further orders. Their clothing, those same billowy trousers with full blouses, appealed to Adrastea's fashion sense. At least they weren't showing so much skin.

Mor-Lath propped himself up on an elbow. "You know, I've been thinking about what that True Faith priestess said to you."

"What?" For a moment, Adrastea had no idea who he was talking about. "When?"

"Yesterday morning, when the horses bolted, leaving them in a rather embarrassing mess. She said something I did not expect her to say."

Adrastea remembered the parley that had come to Sacred Spring, five soldiers and a priestess. The priestess claimed to serve the True Faith. Adrastea had assumed she had meant the Light, but she had a feeling the priestess—Mydala was her name—served the Dark and didn't even know it.

So, what had she said? Adrastea couldn't remember. All she knew is that the horses had bolted. Why? Something about how they all shied at once. What spooked them?

Mor-Lath. He did it to ruin a chance of peace, even an occupied peace, and incited them to war.

"She said, 'My Master's been looking for you.'"

Adrastea didn't care what Mydala said. "Mor-Lath," she said in a low, dangerous voice. "You spooked those horses, didn't you?"

"Kindly don't change the subject."

"Oh, no," she said, unwilling to be swayed. "We are going to talk about this right now. You spooked those horses so they'd think we'd—" the anger rose within her and rage lit her eyes. "—we'd... You did everything you could to provoke that battle."

Mor-Lath sat up. "I don't think that's important right now."

"I think it's damn important." She felt the Deeper Power flow into her. She sat up and swung her legs over the side of the bed. She had slept in the green gown from yesterday. Its rumpled skirts tangled about her legs as she rose.

The two kneeling priestesses scooted away until they reached the far wall. They kept their eyes on the floor and their mouths shut.

Mor-Lath drew on the Deeper Power himself. "And if I did? They needed provoking, so I could see their true colors."

"People died because of it."

"You say that as if it was my fault."

"It was."

He regarded her for a moment. "We can sort out blame later. Now, stop scaring my priestesses. You'll give them nightmares."

He went to the cowering women by the wall and helped them up. "You do well to fear my bride but don't get carried away. You'll quite like her once you get to know her." He gave them reassuring hugs. "Choose for her a grey gown. Today we go to Feown."

Mor-Lath sat on the bed, after commanding the bedclothes to straighten themselves. The priestesses, now chatting to each other, hurried off to the dressing room. Adrastea stood in the middle of her chambers and scowled at the Dark God.

"Now," he continued, "as I was saying before our little sidetrack, I have put some thought into what Mydala said before she ran back to her little commander. 'My Master has been looking for you.' But who is her master?"

Adrastea snorted. "So, you don't know everything."

He glanced at her. "I never claimed to." Then he returned to his thoughts. "I didn't think much of it at the time, for my mind was on other things but when she said, "Master," she didn't have a name."

Adrastea folded her arms and rolled her eyes. "And that would be significant because...?"

"I can locate anyone if I know their name." He rose off the bed and paced while he pondered. "But it was the way she said it. Something does not sit right with me. I aim to discover why."

The two priestesses returned. Adrastea wished she could remember their names.

The elder one spoke, "We thought this would be suitable." She held up a grey dress of exquisite cut and the foundation garments to go with it.

"I'll trust your judgement," he said. He kept his eyes on Adrastea.

Pleased, they laid the clothing on the bed in preparation for dressing their Mistress.

Mor-Lath reached out a finger as if to stroke her cheek. "Perhaps I was rash to mark you thus, but it was a good idea at the time. For the most part, I stand by that decision." He regarded his handiwork. "Cosmetically speaking, I think it enhances your look."

Adrastea scowled at him. "And to think I never gave you anything for our wedding."

He grinned rakishly at her. "Oh, you've given me plenty." His hand lingered on a tendril of her hair. His finger trembled before he turned away from her.

Adrastea caught the repressed smiles of the two priestesses as if they were in in on some intimate joke. The younger—Berengaria, that was her name—stooped for the hem of Adrastea's gown. "Must get you dressed."

Adrastea sighed and waved her on. Chances were if she tried to remove the full-skirted gown, she'd get lost in the fabric, never to emerge again.

The priestesses helped her into a light shift then into a heavily-boned corset. She protested loudly at this when they strung her in too tight.

"Forgive us, Mistress," the murmured, though they did not stop their ministrations. "Fashion will make its demands."

As Adrastea figured out how to breathe with the top half of her lungs only, the priestesses girded her with several layers of petticoats. "This is what they wear in Feown?" Adrastea tried to think back to the ladies' catalogues that came every so often in the mail. Were their illustrations this ridiculous?

"I have a mind," said Mor-Lath, resuming a seat on the other side of the bed so as to not disturb the laid-out clothing, "to seek out Mydala's soul. I dare say Death has been so busy that she has not yet had a chance to get to this one yet. I would like to see what she has to say."

Whether he meant Mydala or Death, Adrastea never found out. As one priestess buttoned her dress up the back, another brought out a hat with a long, light veil. "Please allow me to dress your hair," the priestess said.

Adrastea stared at her.

"I think Efanda would find it easier to minister to you if you sat at the vanity," Mor-Lath hinted.

Efanda. Did she meet her yesterday? Adrastea followed Efanda to a chair that sat before the large mirror. After arranging the voluminous folds of her dress, Adrastea sat as comfortably as she could. If she had thought a bodice restrictive before, it was nothing compared to a corset. She had no choice but to sit stiff-upright. If she slumped in the least, the boning poked her under her arm.

Adrastea let the priestess ply the brush and pins. "You're Efanda," she said to the first. "And you're Berengaria, right?" she asked the other.

Berengaria squirmed in delight. "Yes, mistress."

Mor-Lath leaned against the wall and observed the toilet. "Someone other than myself is extremely interested in you. I want to know who. Meanwhile, we are going to visit the Duchess of Feown. She, poor creature, has suffered a far worse loss than you. We must offer our condolences and our aid."

The Duchess. Of the few things Adrastea knew of her, the Duchess of Feown walked in the Light. "She won't accept it."

"She is steeped in bitterness and grief, all set simmering by the steady burn of revenge. She will listen to us and accept our proposal."

Adrastea endured some fierce backcombing of her hair. "And what," she said when she had respite, "were 'we' going to propose?"

"That now is the best time for revenge. She shall gather together what little of her army remains, train more as necessary. Then we shall descend upon Cithra and crush them."

Adrastea pushed Efanda's hand away from her face. "We're going to do what?"

"Wage war," he replied, a faint smile playing his lips.

"We just stopped a war." Adrastea leapt to her feet. She wanted to slap the smugness off his face. "You want to start another one?"

"We stopped a war that was not in our favor. We're going to start one that is."

Adrastea frowned at him. "All war is in your favor."

"Perhaps," he admitted. "However, there are other advantages to war other than my collection of souls."

He slipped his arms about her waist. That familiar thrill sent shivers over her skin. Why did he have to tempt her so? Especially when she was upset at him.

She snorted her disapproval. He laughed at her disapproval. He gave her a quick peck on the cheek. "I distract you too much. Dress your hair, admire your beauty, then we shall leave. Until then, I wish you to think about something: what you want more than anything else?" He departed but not before leaving a lingering touch on her shoulder that sent waves of warmth into her.

"I want to be rid of you," she muttered but not loud enough for the priestesses to understand. She wanted to mean it with all her heart but for some reason, the words failed to ring true. His touch echoed under her skin.

No, what she really wanted was to undo yesterday—the deaths, the marriage, the everything. Maybe it would have been better that she'd been struck by a cannonball and killed.

After they had put up her hair and pinned the hat to her head, the priestesses draped the veil over her face and across her shoulders, creating a soft feminine look. They gazed at Adrastea in the mirror, smiles of satisfaction on their face.

She tried not to think about her newfound beauty; it had cost her far too much.

Berengaria laughed and clapped her hands. "Oh Mistress, you look perfect. You look like you could be twenty-five."

That old, huh? What would they say if she told them she was but two and twenty?

"Better," Efanda gushed. "I'd swear you were no older than twenty."

The priestess' comments astonished Adrastea, who had been brooding over what Mor-Lath meant by his last statement. "Twenty-five," she mused, studying herself in the mirror.

"R eady?" Mor-Lath asked her. While the priestesses had been helping her dress, he'd change into what Adrastea supposed was the height of fashion in Feown: tight-fitting pants to the ankle, high-buttoned waistcoat over a generously-cut shirt, biased cut jacket and a large overcoat. He held a tall hat of satin in one hand and a black cane in another.

Adrastea stopped pacing. "I don't know why I'm doing this." While the full skirts of her current dress were a vast improvement over the too-long train of the green gown, she still had difficulty walking in it. At least it covered her bosom enough for the sake of modesty.

"Because you are the Bride of the Dark. You need to know the world. Your country ways will not serve you in your new role."

"But by starting a war?"

"First lesson: you cannot prevent every bad thing from happening. But you can control how they happen."

"And what is my new role?"

Mor-Lath sighed and studied her as if trying to read her mind. "Do you feel like a god?"

"No," she replied peevishly.

That answer disappointed him. "Ask me tomorrow, then."

But Adrastea wouldn't accept that. "That's not an answer."

"If you want an answer, I could give you one. But I'm sure you wouldn't want it unless it was the right one."

She opened her mouth again, but he shushed her. "Let us discuss this later. You always choose the most inconvenient moments for an argument." He pulled her to him with an arm about her waist. His cane pressed a gully into the fullness of her skirt. "How about you take us to Feown this time?"

Her? "I can't. I don't know how."

He gave a dramatic sigh and plunked the hat on his head. "You've seen me do it often enough. I thought you'd have picked it up by now."

Adrastea didn't like being insulted. "So, pretend I'm an idiot and explain it to me."

"I was thinking more of 'born yesterday'." By his reckoning of time, this must seem true. She felt young and clumsy. "Remember the Maiden's Tower?"

"I'm not likely to forget." She shuddered from her memories.

"Imagine where it is, then command Creation to align you with it."

"That's it?"

He nodded. "That's it. We have Creation at our command. Or rather, Creation wants to do what we ask it. However, a word of caution: whatever you choose to do, think about how Creation will choose to obey you. Think of the consequences, for whatever you change in Creation, there will be another reaction equal and very often opposite to what you have commanded. Most of the time its best to let Creation do what Creation does best."

Adrastea turned her face away from him. "Hasn't stopped you from meddling in people's lives."

He wrapped his other arm around her waist. "Ah," he purred into her ear. "That's a different set of rules. People are the Creation-Changers. Theirs is to transform the world. And they have been doing so for as long as I can remember. You wouldn't believe how much they've changed the world in the past two hundred years. No doubt their ability to change the world will accelerate even faster in the future. Imagine how it will be in a hundred years' time. Or even fifty. No doubt something marvelous. Can't you wait to see it?"

"Mor-Lath, I'm still trying to get used to you."

"Ah, yes. I forget. I've had years and years to think about you. You've only had what? Not quite two months?"

"When I dreamt of getting married, this is not what I had in mind."

He loosened his grip on her waist. "How about this? We go comfort Her Grace and give her what she needs to rebuild again. Then we shall return, and you can spend the next little whenever getting used to your new life. Spend your days with the priestesses. Go out to the town with them if you like or peruse the library. Go home and walk around your village, if you so wish."

Adrastea perked up. "I could do that?"

"There's not much you can't do, Darklet."

"And what do you plan on doing?"

He released her waist and took her hands. "The end of an Era draws near. I have things I must do before that happens. I need you to help me. I didn't marry you simply because you are pretty."

What does one say when the God of the Dark offers a half-compliment?

"Now," he ordered, "take us to the palace at Feown."

Adrastea closed her eyes. The Power filled her, and she imagined the tower from yesterday. She pulled on the Lines. The whole world shifted around her.

The temperature dropped, making her shudder. A breeze stirred her veil. When she opened her eyes, she saw they stood on the Maiden's Tower.

They had arrived in Feown.

"I did it," she exclaimed. "Oh, Light, I did it." She dashed to the parapet to look down on the city below.

"Mm hmm," was all Mor-Lath said.

They entered the palace. Locked doors opened to his silent command. A few servants and other survivors of the siege paused in wary silence to watch them go by.

The hallways and corridors were made of stone. The walls bore large pale squares where tapestries and pictures once hung. The palace at Feown seemed like a woman who'd been stripped of her fine clothes and forgotten to be given rags.

Mor-Lath had given Adrastea only one line of instructions. "You may say whatever you wish; clearly I cannot stop you there. But please think a moment before you speak. Your words have a stronger impact than you realize."

They came to a wooden door, its finely carved and painted surface marred by planks of wood nailed over what looked like axe marks. Had someone failed to chop through the door, or did they succeed? The rough and hasty repairs did not do its once-splendor justice. He did not open it. "We will arrive with a more dramatic appearance. It will make an impact." He laid a hand on the door and listened. "Ask the door to show you what lies on the other side."

Adrastea laid a hand on the door and made a silent request with the Deeper Power. She found the Power obeyed her more readily now that she was immortal.

The door yielded its secrets, showing her all that lay beyond, images imprinted directly into her head. It also showed her whose hands had touched it earlier and the things it had overheard. Yes, an axe did splinter the door, enough for it to be forced open. According to the door, quite a few things had happened recently, few of them pleasant. She tucked this information away in case it might be useful later.

The door showed a chamber beyond. Paneled walls still bore shreds of silk, testifying to the delicate beauty that once resided there. A few pieces of mismatched yet comfortable furniture sat in the room, with several quilts and rugs draped over them. A deeply-silled window looked out across Feown. This room faced sunward and the light shone in the open casement to pool on the floor. Adrastea thought it odd that no dust motes swirled in the sun beam. A breeze blew in and the black-clad figure sitting by the window shuddered.

Saraym Blanqiva, Duchess of Feown, the door said. The door had much more to tell her concerning Her Grace's sorrow. It also told her what wasn't there: three children. Their absence was most conspicuous.

Adrastea snatched her hand away. "I don't know if I can do this."

"You would leave this woman to suffer in frustration? Believe me, the best cure for the blues is action."

"I think she suffers far more than the simple blues."

"Then it will require far more than simple action."

"Ah," he sighed. "Did you hear that?"

Adrastea listened. The door whispered to her of a faint wistfulness in the words, "Help me..."

Mor-Lath straightened his sleeve. "Let us go pay our respects."

Chapter 4

Jonathan Pennexter, Priest of the Light, was a coward. A coward has no qualms about running away or hiding. Because of this, he had survived.

When the Cithrans breached the walls of Feown, they invaded the temples and killed every priest they found. Light, Dark, other, it didn't matter.

His great-niece Hannah had stood up for her faith. He remembered her, tall and proud, like a Pennexter should be. She shouted her unwavering faith at the oncoming invaders, claiming she would never depart the Light until her death.

Look what it got her.

Jonathan's sister Dassie, Lady Pen, was brave. As the current head of the Pennexter family, she saved her grief for her granddaughter until later. Nobody knew where Stobol Pennexter was. He'd been gone for years, lost in the Cithran Empire in the service of Her Grace. For all they knew, he was well and truly dead.

Lady Pen also knew that if she didn't hide her brother Jonathan, he would die as well. Then the whole family would suffer.

As long as one of each generation of Pennexters had been dedicated to the Light, the family would prosper—this blessing had been given to them so long ago, they could not remember it not being so.

Was their rise through the merchant class and eventual elevation to the nobility due to their obedience? Not a single member of the clan was willing to risk that it was not.

Hannah was dead. Josephus had been missing for years. Only he was left.

Lady Pen had stuffed her brother into in the secret rooms of Pennexter House. Every merchant family had their warehouses near the docks of the river. They also had secret rooms and passages in their private residences, as well as catacombs beneath. Here they stashed their most precious commodities—in this case, Jonathan.

Lady Pen insisted that Jonathan hide away when the first reports of priest-killing reached their ears. "It is not so much that I love you, dear brother," her normal curmudgeonly attitude brittle with stress, "but that I save you to save the whole family."

Then she shut him up inside the walls with enough food and water to last several months, should needs demand.

Jonathan sighed as the light of day disappeared. At least he would live for now. But it was a cowardly way to survive.

Three weeks later light filled Jonathan's tiny, windowless cell. Two bright angels appeared at the foot of his bed, gazing fondly upon him. "Wake, son of the Light."

Jonathan startled, his blanket sliding off his tiny cot. He retreated until his back hit the cold stone wall of his cell.

He believed in angels. He had only witnessed them from time to time as brief flickers of light from the corner of his eye, quick enough and faint enough that one with lesser faith would dismiss them as an optical illusion.

These angels did not flit away but regarded him with soft eyes and gently folded hands. "We bring you a message from the Light."

Jonathan swallowed. "Me?"

"You will go to Saraym, Duchess of Feown and give her instruction."

Jonathan's throat was too dry to swallow. Why him? Why didn't they appear to her directly?

"The nature of the world changes," the angels told him. "The end draws nigh. Those who were once enemies shall unite as allies."

To his growing horror, they laid out the Light's plan for Saraym.

If it had been anyone else but angels who told him these things, he would have sworn they were of the Dark.

"You are proposing the destruction of our way of life." Jonathan's stomach sank. "How can I ask her to do this?"

"The Light commands. Put your trust in the Light. All will be well." One angel tilted her head. "Do you doubt?"

"No," he replied hastily. "I will obey." His gut sank. His heart hammered in his chest and his head felt faint. Why had the Light chosen him?

Was he truly the last priest in Feown? That thought sent a shudder down his spine. Everyone... gone?

"What if she doesn't believe me?"

"She will."

Jonathan swallowed again. "What if Feown doesn't listen to her?"

"They will."

Jonathan blinked. "Awfully sure of yourselves."

"Fire burns in her soul." Then so he would understand, they showed him every single painful thing that had befallen Saraym. She had been torn from her bed. She was forced to watch the torture and death of her family. Before her eyes, the Cithran soldiers had swung her children by their legs, to bash their heads against the wall. Her husband, the Duke Consort, had suffered various physical humiliations in front of his wife until they released him through death.

Saraym wasn't as lucky. No death for her. She had been imprisoned and subjected to tortures that made Jonathan flinch. He tried to turn away but closing his eyes could not erase the vision from them. He witnessed every single moment of her suffering. His body shuddered in grief and sympathy. How could one woman withstand all that and live?

Still, she lived. Still, she remained unbroken. She lived to see the death of her captors, When had that happened, Jonathan wondered?

The Light had allowed her to be dragged through the nadir of human experience so that when she was called upon to do that which the Light saw fit for her, she would not balk nor flinch but act with swiftness and surety.

"Jonathan Pennexter." When the angels spoke his name, he heard a warning in their voice. "Your House has been blessed by the Light. Continue to serve the Light and your family shall prosper. If you fail in this task, woe shall befall you all.

"Do not tarry long."

The angels departed, plunging his cell into darkness. And with that darkness came the doubt—heavy, enveloping, and cold. Their departure left him feeling quite deserted. How could they show up without warning, give him this overwhelming task and then leave him on his own? While he did not overly enjoy the company of people, once the angels left, he wished there was someone there to share his burden.

Jonathan curled up under the covers and tried to chase away the horrors they left in his mind.

He passed a most unpleasant night in the company of his own dreadful thoughts.

⌘

Saraym, Duchess of Feown, locked herself away in a salon, alone and isolated in her grief. None dared approach her in her solitude, for she kept that terrible knife.

The day passed and the night. Then day came again. Saraym couldn't sleep.

The salon featured a large recessed casement overlooking the remains of her vast city. If she opened the window, the scent of the smoke floated in on the gentle autumnal breeze. Funeral pyres burned here and there, taking good Feowan souls to the Light. As for the Cithrans, they suffered the insult of being dumped into graves like refuse.

Her head spun, and her vision played tricks on her. But she did not dare close her eyes.

Every time she did, the images of her children's heads smashing against marble pillars haunted her. She could not push the vision of her husband the Duke Consort away, as the Cithrans humiliated and violated him over and over. She'd been forced to watch.

For two days she dared not sleep. She could not close her eyes.

How could Saraym mourn her lost husband and children without thinking about how they died? Her heart wanted to be dulled and numbed, to be cut off from the pain—and what it stood for—which still wracked her body. It made it uncomfortable to sit, to stand, to do anything. Most of all she wanted to take the pain give it back to those who caused it.

But they were dead. How? Why?

As she sat in the window, she struggled against her memories, trying to will them away. With great concentration she could clear her mind. But the moment she let her focus slip, they would push past her barriers and invade her mind again. The longer she didn't sleep, the harder it became.

"I am sorry," she murmured in one final prayer. "I have been calling out to You from the beginning."

For her, there was no mercy. There was no death. There was nothing. "Oh, my beautiful children. I cannot forgive." And those was her last words to the Light.

Her heart turned to darker thoughts. Her missing eye throbbed but the good eye could see clearly now.

"Help me," she murmured to who? She did not know. She never meant it as a prayer.

A strong wind blew in through the open casement, rippling her skirts and billowing the curtains about the room. Saraym leaned out and swung the windows closed. She tied the curtains back.

She was not alone.

"Saraym, widowed Duchess of Feown, we hear your prayer."

Saraym leapt to her injured feet, ignoring the pain. She gripped the knife she had hidden in the folds of her black skirt. "Who are you?"

An unfamiliar man and woman stood in the middle of her salon, dressed in the height of fashion. Where had they come from? Her door was still locked.

"No man may enter here." Her hand gripped the knife tighter, keeping it well-hidden.

He removed his hat. "Ah but I am no mere man. I am a god. Your god."

"No, you're not." These were not the Light. "I have no god." She looked to the lady in grey. She was taller than Saraym—not that that was difficult—and of finer figure as well. She had twin lines on her face, one on each cheek, almost like a tattoo. Was she foreign? Her grey clothes were Feowan in design, accentuating her narrow waist. Saraym had always bemoaned the girth of her waist, back in a time when fashion had been one of her biggest concerns. Her copper skin and curly hair looked Feowan, almost familiar.

"Put your knife away," he said. "We mean you no harm. If we did, we wouldn't have stopped for pleasantries."

"No." How did he know she was armed? She held her knife steady, bringing it out from hiding.

He shrugged. "Suit yourself. You can't harm us anyhow."

The man held out his hand, palm up. The knife wriggled free from Saraym's grasp and flew, hilt first, to his hand. He casually tucked the knife into an inner pocket of his coat. "Is that any way to greet your god?"

Saraym took a step back. "You're not the Light."

"We never claimed to be."

Her heart thumped in her chest. Saraym rarely spent any time alone since she inherited the Duchy from her father. She had always had someone around to support her, to back her up, to even protect her, if necessary.

Here, she had no one. "Who are you?"

"I am Mor-Lath, God of the Dark."

Saraym stumbled back until her legs hit the sill. Her legs gave out and her rear sat down hard on the window seat. Pain shot up through her injured back. Was he truly the Dark God or simply a pretender? He seemed mortal enough, in manner and dress. But she had to admit there was something about him that made her nervous.

Maybe whatever it was made the lady in grey nervous as well. She'd been fidgeting the whole time. Saraym regarded her. "And who are you?"

Mor-Lath, if that's what he wanted to be called, said, "Permit me to introduce my bride, Adrastea."

"Adrastea?" That was a rather Feowan name. So, not foreign after all. "Wait. You said, 'bride'?"

That's what General Miniver had called Saraym. "Bride of Feown," as he referred to her. Not that his Feowan was very good. He'd made several vocabularial mistakes.

At least, she knew her doctrine. "The Dark has a bride?"

The man who called himself Mor-Lath inclined his head. "Why is everyone surprised that I am married? Ask your priests if you doubt me. They shall confirm prophecy fulfilled."

Were there any priests left in Feown? Those who did not have the good sense to flee or hide were surely dead. She folded her arms. "There are none left."

"While I'm sure you regret the loss of those attached to your household. You will rebuild. There will be priests aplenty for you to choose from. I'll even let you have some of mine."

"No, thank you." She put a less-injured arm on the seat to adjust her position. Oh, she hurt. No position hurt less than another. Many hurt worse.

Adrastea's fingers flew to her lips. "You're really in pain."

Saraym glared at her with her remaining eye and said nothing. Her head ached as well as everything else.

The grey lady came forward. "Let me heal you." Did she have a country accent?

Saraym drew back. "And what would that cost me?"

Adrastea hesitated. "Cost? Nothing." Definitely a country accent.

She looked away. "No, thank you."

Mor-Lath (that name was as good as any other) rolled his eyes. "Charge her two beers like any other country doctor and fix her up. We have business to discuss. I'm sure it'd be easier if she's not hurting. Though I doubt her beer would be as good as Ari's."

Country doctor, eh? Saraym looked at Adrastea. She could believe she was a country lass. She didn't sit right in that dress. "Herbs and snakeskin, I suppose." What good could a country doctor do against injuries like these?

"Not quite," Adrastea replied. She reached for her. "Give me your hand."

So, spit in her hand three times and draw a circle? Even better.

Adrastea's hand waited for hers. "Come on."

Saraym, too tired to protest, flopped her less-injured hand into Country Adrastea's. Let her see what this 'bride' could do.

As Adrastea concentrated, feather-light touches of the woman's presence search through Saraym's body like slender fingers. This woman had to be a priestess of the Dark. Only the Dark used the Deeper Power to their own ends. If she was a Dark priestess, then was Mor-Lath who he said he was? Was he really the God of the Dark?

Saraym didn't sense any malice or evil in the tendrils of the other woman. She sensed a regret, a sorrow and a bitterness within her. Did this connection work both ways? It must, for the flavors of these emotions were not her own. For a brief moment, Saraym did not feel so alone.

Then the healing began.

It surprised her. Something warm and gentle, like bathwater, flowed through her veins. As soon as that warmth hit her back, the strains disappeared. She didn't expect her pain to be released so quickly. Her body knit together. Her shoulders unknotted. Within her belly and loins, the burning went away. Her toe mended.

Alas, the eye remained missing, even if the socket healed completely.

Relief flooded her shattered nerves but also a sliver of fear. The Dark never gave things away.

She never asked for this healing, welcome though it was. She could refuse to pay whatever price they demanded of her.

Her body whole once more, Saraym slumped to her knees. "I walk in the Light." She refused to show gratitude, no matter how it made her look in their eyes.

"Walk there if you wish," Mor-Lath said. "Pray to the Light, if that is your desire. But take comfort in the fact that we shall be there for you, to aid you in the difficult times ahead." He considered her words for a moment. "I could tell you that the Light has given you to me, but I believe you would require some proof. Is not your salvation from the hands of your enemy enough?"

The Cithrans were dead, to the man. "I have no proof their deaths were caused by your hand."

He toyed with the brim of his hat. "They weren't," he told her matter-of-factly. "You may direct your gratitude to my bride. It was by her hand that they were reft of their lives."

Adrastea startled. "Don't you pin the blame on me," she retorted.

Her reaction didn't bother him. He slipped a fond arm about her waist. "Oh, come now. Don't be so modest. Your altruism is so vast that humility is almost an insult."

Adrastea folded her arms and snorted her disapproval. Of all the things this man had told her, Saraym could at least believe they were married.

Mor-Lath turned his attention to Saraym. "We are here to aid you. I know what desire lies deepest in your heart."

Saraym stiffened. While revenge burned deep within her, it was not a charitable thought. "No. I will not believe my salvation was by your hand. You're trying to deceive me."

"Believe what you want. You cannot hide forever, Your Grace. Sooner or later your people will look to you to save them.

"The Cithran army on your doorstep may be gone but you have no guarantee that another one won't follow. Or maybe one of your other rivals will learn of your weakness and exploit that? The Avelians to the south, perhaps. They may not seem like much of a threat when you are at full strength, but your weakened state may tempt them.

"You need to restore your army and your government, else your lands will dissolve into chaos and anarchy. Do it alone if you wish. I tell you now, I know for sure that you alone lack the strength to see it through."

She put fingertips to her forehead, even though her headache was gone. Weariness was her biggest complaint now. "I'm too tired to discuss anything regarding the future of Feown. Please, leave."

Mor-Lath placed his hat on his head. He slipped an arm about his wife once more. "Sleep well this eve, for tomorrow will be busy. Time refuses to stop for mourning."

Then, before her very eyes, they disappeared into nothingness, leaving aught but a faint swirl of air in their wake.

Being already on her knees, Saraym offered up a silent prayer to the Light. "Are you even there?"

A warm breeze blew across her face.

Chapter 5

Chamque, devotee of the god Mor-Lath and high priestess of this humble Avelian temple, startled awake at the sharp knock on her cell door. It took her a moment to gather her fuzzy wits about her. She'd fallen asleep in her chair. She rescued her fallen book from the floor, rubbed the sleep from her old eyes and said, "Come." She stretched her aching old bones and scratched her silvered head.

Awena, a young priestess on the cusp of puberty, slipped in. "Guess what I found," she whispered, although they were alone. Awena was prone to gossip, though not maliciously. Chamque groaned. She was woken for some tidbit of news that she most likely didn't care about?

Awena wore the soft brown kirtle that all Avelian priestesses wore. This she twisted between her still-chubby fingers. "I found Desmone on the altar."

Desmone. Much older than Awena and a lot more ambitious. While she was not terribly impressed with Desmone—who sought more for her own glory than that of their god—Chamque did not mind sharing her duties. Let the younger priestesses offer the morning praises, she reasoned to herself. Truth was, her old bones complained of the coolness in the mornings as the days shortened. Soon it would be Autumn and the rainy season.

Awena danced as if she had to go relieve herself. "She was naked!"

At this, Chamque groaned. What now? All she wanted was to go back to her book, or rather, sleep.

But Awena's next words, "It's the Sign," woke her faster than a bucket of cold water ever could.

She leapt to her feet and ignored her old body's protest. "What?"

"I saw it. A hand print on her belly. I'm sure of it."

Chamque's thoughts tumbled. She had seen the Sign before, once, when she was a little younger than Awena. A priestess from her first temple had been visited by His Holiness. Her Sign had been verified. Chamque remembered the upheaval that brought.

She did not look forward to the disturbance this would bring her temple now. There had been enough worry in the city, with the news of Feown's siege upriver. News as well as bodies had floated downriver to the kingdom of Avelia, which shared a highly-contested border with the Feown Duchy to the north. However, with the invasion of Feown by Cithra from the east and the threat that smaller Avelia could be next, hostilities had been temporarily suspended. Feowan border patrols had been recalled. Avelian border patrols were busy keeping an eye on the situation while they surreptitiously moved the border markers northward.

The high priestess set aside her book and rose. "Where is she now?"

Desmone woke as the cold of the altar stones seeped into her bare back. Where was she? She sat up.

On the floor lay her clothing. Ah, yes. Her skin burned with the memory of His Holiness' touch. She closed her eyes and bit her lip, tasting the faint saltiness of their love. Oh, how her loins ached for him. No boy, no man had ever ignited her fires thus.

Her hand slid down her belly to stroke over her pubis and slip a finger even further. He had been exquisite. He'd been everything she imagined.

She wanted more.

She wanted him.

It had been powerful but too quick. The world dimmed with the thought that no one else would ever satisfy her like he had.

Would he visit her again? Her heart ached with desire.

As a child, she and the other apprentice priestesses would share dark stories late at night about the forbidden things. Somewhere there had been journals kept by priestesses who'd received, as they called them, 'special blessings'. Someone had read them. Tales were told.

As she had blossomed into womanhood, Desmone had dreamed of such little secrets.

She wrapped her arms about her bare legs. Once chosen by the god, did he come visit you a second time?

She hoped so. Desmone wanted to feel that good again.

In the coolness of the temple, she shivered. Her brown kirtle and robe had been discarded thoughtlessly on the floor. She pulled on the robe and belted it. The kirtle she draped over her arm. Lifting it to her nose, she inhaled. Did his scent linger on it?

Before she could leave the chapel, Chamque and Awena entered. Desmone had never seen the old priestess move so fast. Awena dogged her heels, dancing like the eager puppy she was. What a snitch.

She didn't need to guess; they already knew.

"Desmone," Chamque commanded. "Let me see."

Desmone knew exactly what Chamque was looking for—the Sign. They said His Holiness' seed was so powerful it would burn out the womb of a mortal woman. The seeping of blood was the first triptych of the Sign. Had she bled? She hadn't bothered to check the altar.

Second, a mark would appear on the belly of the woman touched by his Holy Passion, remaining for as long as a week, then gradually fading. Desmone looked down. There, between her belly button and pubis was a distinct mark of a hand. Chamque reached out as if to touch it but her fingers stopped just short of Desmone's skin. Desmone pulled back. If she was favored of the god, surely that put her above frigid old Chamque.

Third, she would never bleed as a woman again. Desmone wouldn't miss that one bit, not if it meant she could have the passion His Holiness had shared with her. A small groan rose within her. How long would she have to wait?

"It's the Sign," Awena breathed.

Well, well, thought Desmone. She was not the only one who had listened to surreptitious stories told after dark in the dormitories of younger priestesses.

"We've got to get you out of here," Chamque urged. She pulled off her cloak and wrapped it around Desmone.

Desmone balked. "Why?" she looked around. There was no one else. Shame. Wouldn't all the other priestesses be jealous when they learned.

Chamque did not answer her but pushed her along.

"Show some respect," Desmone snapped at her.

As the other priestess hurried her out of the chapel Desmone allowed herself a small smile. He had visited her. The rest of the Sign would surely show, and her place would be assured.

Then Chamque thrust her into a cell and locked the door.

Chamque hurried back to the chapel before anyone else had arrived. She stood before the stone altar and traced a finger over the dried blood left there.

Now, was this a true Sign, as Awena believed? Or was this more of Desmone's political manipulation? Chamque would not put such silly games past Desmone in an effort to gain prestige and power. All she ever thought of was herself. Oh, that stupid girl.

"Fetch me a lamp, Awena. My eyes aren't what they once were." She wanted to investigate the stain further. A woman often bled after her first sexual encounter, especially if the man had not been gentle. However, Desmone was no maiden. Chamque was wise to the girl's silliness. She knew the younger priestess slipped out of the temple and into strange beds. Did her victims know she was a priestess? Or was that what drew them to her?

Chamque closed her eyes. Would His Holiness forgive her for not removing such a creature from the temple and from the face of the earth? She should have done it long ago.

Ah, now there was a sticky spot. What if His Holiness had visited her? What if he favored her in this most intimate way?

No. He couldn't have. Surely, he would have known her for the faithless creature she was. Why would he choose her above all the others? Desmone was shallow, unspiritual.

This had to be a trick on Desmone's part. It wasn't going to wash with Chamque.

Awena returned with a lamp. Chamque set it on the altar and studied the blood closely. How did one tell that this was blood from a Sign and not Desmone's scheming? Chamque ran a finger over the dried blood. Would it be sacrilege to remove it?

Even so, she should clean it up as quickly as possible. Awena she could swear to secrecy. Desmone she could control for as long as necessary—no more than a month. But blood? Blood always told. Should anyone else see this, word would get out. After that, her temple would be turned into a shrine.

Chamque would remain high priestess but Desmone would be exalted. All the honor and favor would be hers, not Chamque's, and the gifts and invitations and the influence—

She drew a sharp breath. It shouldn't be like this. Had they forgotten their honor to the God of Wealth and ended up worshipping the wealth instead?

Awena bounced on her toes, awaiting Chamque's pronouncement.

Chamque never liked Desmone. She was too ambitious. "The mark might be false."

"But what if it isn't?" Awena replied.

"But what if it is?" Inwardly, she hoped this was true. Desmone was putting on a sham to gain power. Indeed, she will have succeeded for a few days until the deception could be uncovered; it would be enough to cause problems. Chamque didn't need this sort of drama at the moment. "There have been many who have tried to fake the Sign. Good never comes of it."

Awena's face twisted in disappointment. "It could be real."

"There hasn't been a true Sign in the past forty years. If it is real, then so be it. Though I do question the reasoning behind the choice of Desmone."

Awena drew in a breath through her nose but didn't voice her thoughts. If this was a true Sign, what she'd just said could have been considered blasphemy.

Chamque had to mollify Awena. "As this is Desmone we speak of, I am certain she is faking it."

But the doubt still lingered in her own heart.

esmone gasped as her hands and knees scraped on the floor of the cell. "You'll regret this," she growled at Chamque, who had just thrown her in. Then the old witch slammed the door. She heard the distinctive *snick* of the key in the lock. "Let me out!" she cried.

No answer. Desmone pounded on the door and rattled the lock. "You bitch! You'll see."

Still no answer. No doubt Chamque would have told all the others to leave her alone.

This cell had been some priestess' bedroom. Danah's, perhaps? Not much here. Desmone sniffed. Stupid little bed and only a chest. That was it. A quick rifle through the chest yielded clothing, a few books and not much else. Boring.

Maybe there was another way out? But the walls were solid. Like most walls within the temple, these were stone. The only window was small and up high. Despite the approach of autumn, the shutters hadn't been brought out yet. There was some light in through the grille, though it was too high for her to see anything but sky. It rarely snowed in winter but many of the nights did suffer from chill. The shutters did little to keep out the cold.

Desmone shivered. Was Chamque going to leave her here? How unfair.

She was one of the Chosen. She should be given better rooms, with fireplaces. Or maybe a stove. There were the little potbellied stoves with a flat top for a kettle, and the large stoves, all black and iron and with a large tank on the side for heating water. Or maybe she'd get one of those new donut stoves she'd seen in the marketplace. Its primary purpose was heating a room, nothing else. A donut stove was considered pure luxury.

She deserved it. After all, hadn't the god favored her above all others?

Another change she would see in her life—long hot baths. If she managed to find the coin, she sometimes slipped off to one of the city's bath houses and indulged in the luxurious steamy delights. Sometimes other delights could be found there for the right price. Sometimes her youth and beauty were all the price required.

A key scraping in the door lock shook her from her pleasant memories. She sat up on the bed.

Old Chamque, the high priestess, entered the room, as well as two other senior priestesses, their hair dark against their long-sleeved robes. Awena was nowhere to be seen.

They stood by the door while Chamque sat down on the bed. Desmone scooted away. She did not want to be within reach of the old hag. Chamque's bony frame was clad not in the day-to-day kirtle they customarily wore but in her full ceremonial robes. Horrid old bat. Did she think she could capitalize on Desmone's glory?

Chamque might have been the one in power but that was about to change.

"So, you think you bear the Sign," Chamque began without preamble.

Instead of dreaming about baths, Desmone realized she should have been crafting replies to potential questions. Of course, Chamque would wish to question her. Desmone hadn't been expecting His Holiness' favor and had been quite surprised when he turned up. She was not suitably prepared.

"I never said any such thing," Desmone replied. It was always best to play it safe with Chamque.

"Yet you were found sprawled like a wanton, dripping your blood onto the sacred altar." She rose to her feet and moved to the door. "Either you bear the Sign, or you don't. Only time will tell. Until then, I shall make sure everything that could cause counterfeit to be removed from the room."

Desmone looked around. There was only the bed and the trunk. Then it sank in; Chamque planned on locking her in there until the Sign proved itself.

Chamque motioned to the two priestesses, who lifted the trunk and carried it out of the room.

"So, I am to stay in here for a whole month?" Desmone asked, afraid for confirmation. She hadn't thought ahead as to what would happen after the blessing.

The two priestesses pulled the dressings off the bed.

"Wait," Desmone cried. "What are you doing?"

"Not your blankets," Chamque explained.

Desmone felt foolish. No doubt the previous owner, whoever she was, would be given Desmone's cell.

"You can't do this."

Chamque gave her a cold smile. "Oh, but I must. How else will we know for sure that this sign is genuine? A month of fasting and prayer will do you good."

Then the priestesses carried the bed out as well. "Where will I sleep?" she protested.

"On the floor, I imagine, unless you have mastered levitation. If so, then you are welcome to sleep on the ceiling."

When the bed had been removed, Desmone found herself in a very empty room.

The priestesses returned one more time and reached for Desmone's clothing.

Were they going to strip her of even her clothing? Oh, no they wouldn't! She slapped one of them, Calaire, across the face.

Chamque chose well. Calaire, an ugly, fat thing, shook off the blow and slapped her back.

As Desmone lay on the floor, her tears more rage than pain, the priestesses removed her clothing. "Those are my robes!" She shook herself free from the priestesses, the air uncomfortably cool against her bare backside.

Chamque, in her place by the door, didn't move. "You won't need them." She tossed Desmone a single blanket of undyed wool. "I don't want anything that could be construed as a counterfeit device. I'd remove the walls themselves if I could, but one must draw the line somewhere."

"So, I won't be getting any more clothing or blankets?"

"None."

"But I'll freeze. Nights are getting colder." Desmone wrapped the inadequate blanket about her. It wasn't long enough. There was a bit of dried blood on her leg, remains of the second mark. She'd been taken so quickly, she hadn't had time to tidy herself. She wanted to scrub it off but not in front of Chamque.

"You won't freeze if you keep moving."

"How can I keep moving if I'm asleep?"

The wrinkled skin around Chamque's mouth moved as she smiled with tight lips. "You won't be sleeping tonight."

"Torture?" gasped Desmone. "You wouldn't dare."

"Oh, no torture at all. It's simply the way things are. We can't have anything in the room that could possibly be used to fake the third mark, assuming you're being less than honest with us."

Desmone's mouth gaped. How did one fake a cessation of one's cycles? It wasn't as if one could cross her legs and hold in her monthly blood.

"And should you be true, we would not wish to clothe you, so that we may better observe the failure of the third mark. Due to this inconvenience—"

"Inconvenience indeed," Desmone snorted in interruption.

Chamque ignored her bad manners. "...inconvenience, you may find it to your advantage to reverse your habits." Chamque moved through the doorway. "Many other priestesses would be quite envious of you right now. You are excused from duties and chores for as long as I see fit. You are given an opportunity to laze around and do whatever you want." She looked around the bare cell. "Well, within reason. I recommend some meditation and prayer if you're bored. If you're sensible, you may want to sleep during the day. The afternoons are still quite warm. I would dearly love to sleep them away and commune with the stillness of night. No doubt you will find much to do should you put your mind to it."

Desmone had been cornered. It wasn't like she'd planned any deceptions. She had received the favor of Mor-Lath. She bore two of the three marks of the Sign, the handprint and her Last Blood. The third sign—a cessation of monthly blood for the rest of her life—should manifest itself soon. Her cycle was due in a fortnight. Then they would all see. "What about food?"

"Your needs will be provided for. There will be someone to see that you eat enough. Then the remains will be taken away, so none will doubt."

Desmone wrapped her arms around herself, for the cell was still chilly from last night's coolness. "Thank you." She tried not to let too much sarcasm creep into her voice.

Chamque made mock sounds of pity. "Do not think we're abandoning you. I shall station two priestesses outside your room to keep you company. They'll watch you and your little handprint there." She gestured to Desmone's bare belly. "They'll also keep watch for the last mark, should it fail to manifest."

"You'll see," Desmone replied in a low voice. "Just you wait." She didn't care whether Chamque heard her or not. Within the month, she would fail to bleed. They all would see.

Mor-Lath put his arm about Adrastea. She felt him pull on the Deeper Power. Time to leave Feown.

Adrastea had expected to return to the temple after Feown. As the world shimmered and changed around them, the appearance of Ari's back garden startled her. Mor-Lath had brought them to Sacred Spring.

She was home.

Beyond the distant wall the cannons and Cithran war machines remained abandoned in the fields. They creaked occasionally as the afternoon breeze touched them. The breeze also brought a stench that reminded Adrastea of the Poulters' abattoir a few days after a slaughter. The bodies of the dead had not yet been cremated. Yet Adrastea smelt smoke when the breeze shifted.

"What are we doing here?" She knelt to bury her face in the fragrant lavender bushes. Would the stink ever go away?

He removed his hat. "Selfish reasons. Mydala's soul will be here. I warrant Tanat has not gotten this far yet in her collection." He inhaled deeply of death's scent. Adrastea wrinkled her nose. How could he stand it?

Before Adrastea could ask who Tanat was, Mor-Lath gave her further instructions. "While I'm off sorting souls, why don't you pop in and see if Ari's got more of that excellent beer? You might want to secure the recipe, for we cannot depend on Ari's good nature forever."

A rustle came from behind the rosemary bushes. Ari rose up. Her hands, filthy from working, were wrapped around great swathes of pruned rosemary twigs. "Damn it, Mor-Lath! I thought you were gone for good."

Adrastea jumped. It had not occurred to her that Ari would be in the garden. When Ari saw who she was, the anger smoothed into surprise. The rosemary she'd gathered dropped from her hands. "Adrastea?"

Adrastea gave her a sheepish smile.

"Oh, my dear girl, it is you! I didn't recognize you." Ari ran forward and caught her journeyman in a big hug. It had only been two days, yet Ari was crying like it had been a year. "You're all right."

Adrastea let Ari hug and cry at her. Adrastea wanted to cry but the tears wouldn't come. It didn't matter. To be hugged by someone who genuinely loved her was the greatest feeling in the world. She let its warmth wrap around her.

Mor-Lath backed off silently and went to roam the fields beyond.

Eventually Ari released her and held her at arm's length. "Oh, you look so different. What happened to you? I mean, it's you but it's not."

Adrastea plucked at the folds of the fine dress she wore. "I'm told it's the latest fashion in Feown."

Ari shook her head. "No. I meant your face."

Adrastea's hand stole to her second line. "Oh."

"You look older."

Ah, that. "That's immortality."

A wrinkle of envy crossed Ari's forehead for a moment. Adrastea felt Ari's emotions as they flitted through her heart. Another gift of the immortality? If so, no wonder Mor-Lath had been able to manipulate hers so easily. Did he know what she was thinking as well? Even if he only sensed feelings, it was almost as good as reading one's thoughts.

"Believe me, Ari. This is one gift whose price is too high." Adrastea looked back over the fields beyond the wall.

Ari's eyes followed. "Why? What did he do to you?"

"Me? Nothing. However, he sacrificed the lives of a half-million people to give me this gift."

Ari's horror spilled over to Adrastea. "He didn't," she whispered.

Adrastea's bleak expression said all. Another breeze blew the funk of death to their noses.

Ari looked out over the fields. "He could have cleaned up after himself if he was going to kill that many people," Ari's harsh words couldn't hide her sorrow from Adrastea, who felt even guiltier about the deaths. "I don't know what Susan's going to do about the harvest. Those soldiers have all but ruined it."

Would the villagers help Susan and Sergan Farmer move them before too much of the crop was ruined, assuming it hadn't been completely trampled in the first place? "Is there no one to help?"

A mask came over Ari's face. "The rest of the villagers have their own problems to worry about." She pointed to the billow of smoke rising beyond the roof of the stillroom. "Sergan's there, along with far too many of our people."

Adrastea didn't need to see the village green to know the largest funeral pyre ever still burned there, two days later. How many of her friends and neighbors had gone to the Light?

Could she have saved them, had she said yes to Mor-Lath earlier? Her stomach clenched. Was there never a better way?

Adrastea looked to the field. Empty patches in the wheat fields betrayed where the fallen bodies lay.

Perhaps she could do something about the wheat. Adrastea closed her eyes and stretched forth her hand. She sent out a silent request to Creation to allow her to find all the wheat standing in the field. When she had located every last stalk, she called them forth from the earth. They came up, roots and all, to be suspended over the torn earth. Then she commanded the earth to open further and the dead to fall in. She commanded it to close, efficiently burying over hundreds of bodies. Only then did she place the wheat back into the ground. How simple.

When she opened her eyes, Ari had stepped back until she leaned against the rosemary. Her mouth opened but no words issued forth.

Adrastea felt a blush rise to her cheeks. "I'm sorry. I should have warned you." Her corset felt restrictive and she couldn't breathe. She struggled for breath and then drew in a great lungful, as much as the corset would let her.

"And what price did you pay to be able to do something like that?" Ari asked.

Adrastea folded her hands tightly. "I— there wasn't a price."

"There wasn't a price yet," Ari corrected. "There is always a price, whether you pay before or you pay after."

Adrastea hadn't thought of that.

Suddenly Mor-Lath appeared beside her, startling her. He was covered in dirt and his fine clothes were quite rumpled. "You could have warned me first." He knocked dirt off his clothes.

Ari snorted. "I see it didn't kill you."

He took off his coat and shook it out. "Nah."

Adrastea's pride stung. "I was only cleaning up your mess." She wrapped her arms around herself and turned away from him.

"Don't you blame this on me," he said, brushing dirt from his front. "You're the one who killed them."

"You what?" Ari reached out to Adrastea but afraid to touch. "No." She retracted her hand. "You couldn't have done that."

Dispersing the last of the dust from his raiment, Mor-Lath set himself to rights. "Oh, she did. It was quite amazing. Who knew she had such potential for destruction?"

What was it about Mor-Lath that brought such rage to her chest? She let out a single shriek and knocked Mor-Lath's face sideways with a well-placed punch.

He exhaled hard, though whether from astonishment or pain, she didn't know. What she did know is that she surprised him. He did not see that coming.

When he turned back to her, his eyes burned with displeasure. "That was uncalled for."

But Adrastea was not done with her anger, nor was she going to shrink away. "It was perfectly called for! You use me to accomplish your ends but whenever I act on my own—no matter what I've done—you disapprove like I was some child."

"You are a child."

"According to you, I'm old enough to be married. By society's reckoning, that makes me a woman, not a child."

He seized her by the arms, his grip painful. She refused to let him see how much it hurt.

He held her face close to his. "You do not want to know what makes a woman by my society's reckoning but if you are curious, I'm sure I can find someone who would be more than eager to oblige you. He might not leave too many bruises when he is finished."

Hot tears filled her eyes and spilled down her face. She couldn't strike him again; he would see it coming. His superior experience with the Deeper Power ruled that sort of attack out as well. But her heart burned with the desire to hurt him, to break his smug pride, to shake him and make him see her as more than some tool or asset.

And then she remembered the one advantage she did have. While he still gripped her upper arms, her hands were free. She clenched the front of his waistcoat in her fists and pulled him towards her as she leaned backwards. At the same time, she thought of the one place he couldn't go. Adrastea called on Creation and it obliged.

They translocated to the sacred spring, appearing at its edge. Adrastea could sense its coolness behind her descending back.

For the second time in as many minutes, Mor-Lath had been surprised again. In the three moments it took for them to fall to the water, the first he wasted with astonishment. The second, he gathered his thoughts. The third, he disappeared, leaving Adrastea to splash down into the frigid alpine water alone, her fists still grasping his empty waistcoat.

As she clambered out of the cold spring water, she lifted her head to the heavens and shrieked out her frustrations. "Damn you, Mor-Lath!"

Chapter 6

Her dress, heavy with water, made it difficult to pull herself from the spring. Even standing was hard as the weight of the dress hampered her. She unpinned the waterlogged hat and its veils to let it fall on the bank. Perhaps she could use her new-found skills and command the water to leave her dress.

Before she could do it, a bright light shone down upon her, causing her to shade her visage. When her eyes adjusted, she saw two angels standing before her. "Adrastea, Bride of the Dark, you are summoned."

At first, Adrastea did not know what they meant. Then cold realization dawned upon her; the Light wished to speak with her. Her stomach knotted in fear. She backed away, stumbling over the rocks as she returned to the Spring. Her feet sank into mud. "I— I can't see the Light." The faces of the half-million she'd killed flitted through her head so fast she couldn't tell individuals, but she had seen them all, not as numbers but as people. She would probably see them for the rest of her life whenever she closed her eyes. Despair and shame warred with the fear. She sank to her knees amid the flowing water and buried her face in her hands.

"The Light commands it," the angels told her. Together they reached out and laid a hand each on her shoulders.

Adrastea jumped to her feet when their hands touched her. Angels and mortals couldn't touch.

But she was immortal now—changed.

Before her, the world shimmered, the stones and moss beneath her were replaced by smooth polished marble. A warm glow suffused the air about her. Two beings of a brightness that exceeded the noonday sun stood before her.

One was a woman of tall, statuesque beauty, full of bosom and of hip. She wore long flowing robes of white that flattered her figure. Her hair, like her clothing, was white and fell in gentle waves.

The other was a white-bearded man, dressed in similar robes of a more masculine cut. Instead of being strong and bulky, he was tall and lithe. He looked like he spent more time running through fields rather than ploughing them.

The woman argued with a dark man whose stark contrast seemed out of place in this ethereal peace. It took a moment to recognize Mor-Lath. Until now, she thought he was the most powerful being in Creation.

His superiors stood before her.

Adrastea didn't belong either, her hair in rattails and her dress wet and dowdy.

The woman held up her hand to Mor-Lath and pointed to Adrastea. "Your bride has arrived."

All three turned to Adrastea. The man and woman smiled welcomingly at her. Mor-Lath scowled.

Adrastea knew, in her heart, who the two were.

They were the Light.

The knot of fear grew into a stone, which weighed down her heart. Guilt consumed her strength. She sank to her knees. "Oh, Light." She'd be punished now for her role in the unexpected deaths of so many. "I'm so sorry." She bowed her head and awaited her fate. Unlike her husband, They would be merciful. Was it too much to hope for quick and painless? But no. She deserved whatever They chose to mete out. She would accept it fully.

Mor-Lath hauled her up by her arm. "Get up. We don't kneel before Them."

Adrastea added anger to her cocktail of despair. How dare he humiliate her before Them? She struck out, raking his cheek with her nails. He hissed in pain and drew back his hand.

"Stop," They commanded. A force stronger than both Mor-Lath and Adrastea drove the fighting pair apart. Anger contorted Mor-Lath's features. Adrastea's nails had left red welts across his cheek. They faded as they healed before her eyes. How unfair.

"You deceived me," he spat at the Light. He jabbed a finger in Adrastea's direction. "She is not what We agreed on."

"She is exactly what We agreed upon," the female Light replied, Her voice shaking Adrastea. "She is the perfect woman for what you need. We have been true to Our word and have helped you create the best bride. We have not deceived you but rather have given you everything you have asked for. There could be none better for you than Adrastea."

These words angered him further. "She is stubborn, willful and aggravating!"

The female Light folded Her arms. "She is strong, self-confident and sure. Anything less and you would accuse Us of cheating you."

Mor-Lath rounded on the Light. "You are still deceiving me." He gestured to himself. "I am the same as I have always been. Nothing has changed."

"That is your fault, not Ours."

Adrastea felt cheated by the Light as well. Was there no other purpose in her life but to serve Mor-Lath? What about what she wanted?

Her heart clenched in her throat. Her head bowed, and the tears flowed once again from her eyes. What about her? Didn't she have any say in this at all?

Gentle fatherly arms wrapped around her and sent a soft warmth into her heart. "Oh, My dear daughter, do not fret."

She turned into the comforting embrace and sobbed as hard as she could.

He held her while she expressed her full agony. He eased her pain with a gentle touch. His kindness slipped into her soul and undid the knot of fear and despair. He untied it as a parent would a child's knotted shoe lace. As soon as the ends of sorrow were free, they evaporated into nothingness.

In the end, there remained nothing but calm and reason. She looked up into one of the kindliest faces she had ever seen. She could not have said what color His eyes were, for they seemed to be all colors at once.

"Feel better?" He asked.

She nodded. She truly felt better.

"The weight of so many wrong deaths weighed heavily on your soul." He kissed her on the forehead. "I forgive you every whit."

The burden of a half-million lifted from her. For the first time since that fateful day at the creek when she first met Mor-Lath, Adrastea felt free.

His warm, chocolatey voice rolled over her senses. "I know, had you full knowledge of what you were about to do, you would have said no. He tricked you. For that reason alone, you are absolved. Walk clean in the Light."

His blessing settled on her, soft and still.

"I am Phyl," He introduced Himself. "She over there is My wife Lucea. We are the God of the Light. 'I am the Light and I am the Love, to brighten your life and gladden your heart,'" He quoted. Adrastea recognized it. Mira sometimes used that phrase when she spoke of something pleasant, like a good meal or a lovely day.

"I never knew there were two of You."

Phyl started to say something, then smiled. "I thought he would have told you. Let me guess. In his pride, he only tells you what you need to know, if that, and only after you need it."

Adrastea made a moue of disappointment. "I don't think he tells me even that much."

He looked at her dress, still damp from her dunking in the Spring. He didn't lift a finger. The water obeyed Him and evaporated.

Phyl led her away from where Lucea and Mor-Lath were arguing. Rather, Mor-Lath was doing the arguing and Lucea was listening. She sat on some marble steps, Her hands wrapped loosely around Her knees while he ranted and raved and paced before Her. Then She'd say something which seemed to enrage him more. Adrastea did not know what They were arguing about—though she would like to, for Mor-Lath was losing. She raised a hand to her face in hopes of eavesdropping through the lines.

"No," said Phyl, His arm around her in a fatherly manner. "You don't want to know what they argue about. It is about you. I'm afraid it's best you not know everything they are saying."

That didn't assuage her curiosity, though.

"I will tell you something of which They speak. I shall also answer the question you were going to ask before I distracted you."

This surprised her. "Was I going to ask a question?"

Phyl shrugged. "No, there are not two Gods of the Light. Rather, Lucea and I *are* the God of the Light. Gods are not a single being but are comprised of two halves, male and female."

It all made sense, why Mor-Lath wanted her. "He is not a god after all?"

"Well," conceded Phyl. "He is a demi-god, a half-god. He is the holder of the Mantle of the Dark which qualifies him as enough of a god, rather than a mere immortal. To become a full god, he needs the other half—you."

Adrastea's head felt like it wanted to expand out and beyond. "I'm not a god too, am I?"

"Not yet. That will come when he is ready."

The hope in her heart died upon hearing this. "It all depends on him?"

"I'm afraid so. This is what Lucea and Mor-Lath are arguing about. She's telling him what he needs to do. He's refusing to do it."

"If he knows what he has to do in order to become a god, why is he so reluctant?"

"Pride. And a few other things." They were too far away for Adrastea to hear what Lucea and Mor-Lath were saying. But she knew what he was feeling.

Mor-Lath was unhappy. And afraid. Adrastea could feel his fear, a knot of many ropes centered around his heart. "I think I can sense the feelings of others," she said to Phyl. "I can't read their minds, though."

"You won't know their thoughts, but you will know their emotions. But with Mor-Lath, it will go deeper." Phyl chuckled and looked back to the others. "Oh, I can see trouble ahead."

"Why? What do you mean?"

Phyl wrapped his arm about Adrastea's shoulders. They walked back to where Mor-Lath had grudgingly accepted defeat. "It is harder to read the feelings of another immortal, because they are on the same level of existence. However, Mor-Lath made one little mistake. He gave you a gift— a pair, actually."

He meant the lines on her face. Her hand stole up. She traced the right line, the first one, with her finger. She felt Mor-Lath's frustration through them.

Phyl explained: "He left behind something of him when he drew those, something embedded in your skin. This created a connection between you, mainly in your favor.

"He makes a great many mistakes, he does. They will be his downfall, whether for the moment, or for the rest of his life. As soon as he learns how not to make mistakes, he will achieve his greatest desire."

Adrastea folded her arms. "To be a full god."

Phyl pondered for a moment. Adrastea couldn't hear the others, but she wondered if He could.

Then He said, "Let me tell you a story. Mor-Lath became the God of the Dark relatively late. He was not the first, though he may very well be the last."

"Who was the first?"

But Phyl shook his head. "I have so much to tell you and not enough time. Let Mor-Lath tell you that story when he is ready.

"So Mor-Lath became the God of the Dark. He realized his limitation and sought Us to question why he was only a demi-god. We told him: he needed a wife to become complete."

"He's got a wife—me. Right?" Doubt niggled at her conviction, causing it to wobble.

Phyl corrected her. "No, he's got a bride. You are not yet his wife. Being a wife means sharing everything from a bed to your hopes, secrets and fears. Mor-Lath, being a man of pride, may have difficulty letting down his walls. He is not used to admitting his fears to himself, much less anyone. It is a difficult thing."

"But You've managed it," Adrastea stated. "How did You do it?"

Phyl thought about that one. "You know, I can't rightly remember. It was such a long time ago. I simply focus on the here and now. Lucea and I do everything within Our power to please the other person—not that I'm recommending that path for you; Mor-Lath is not ready. For now, he needs someone strong to stand up to him.

"You, too, suffer from pride. Whenever you feel its sting, let it go. Do not use it to fuel your anger. Both you and Mor-Lath need to learn that you are not out to defeat one another. You are allies. You should be lovers." He and Lucea had made eye contact for a brief moment.

Phyl's love for His wife saturated Adrastea. Her heart yearned for it. "I wish I had that kind of love." Her gaze returned to Mor-Lath, still sulking. "But I don't think I'll get it."

Phyl stroked her hair. "Do you love him?"

Adrastea searched her heart. That she wanted love was clear. Her need ached inside her. Ever since she was a child, she grew up wanting what every village girl wanted—a skill, a home, a good husband, a family.

She looked at a sullen Mor-Lath, still discussing things with Lucea. Something inside her stirred but she could not call it love.

"No," she replied. "I don't think I do. And I don't dare risk it; the pain would be too great."

"Oh. That's too bad. How about Respect?"

Adrastea didn't expect that. Reluctantly, she had a respect for Mor-Lath, though whether for the man or the mantle, she wasn't sure.

"You could easily be friends and allies," suggested Phyl. "That would be the best place to start."

Adrastea rubbed her arms. She had a sudden chill. "I don't know…" She looked to Phyl. "I am the weak one in this. Whatever I do isn't going to change him."

"I disagree." He put His arm around her again. They returned to the other pair. "Lucea advises him to treat you as an ally at the very least. Maybe even offer friendship. Anything beyond that he's going to have to learn for himself. We could tell him every single scrap of knowledge he'd need for success. Either he wouldn't believe Us, or he wouldn't be ready."

"Am I? Ready, that is?"

Phyl laughed. "You were born ready."

Their conversation over, Lucea turned from Mor-Lath, who brooded silently to himself. She came to Adrastea with open arms. "I trust you enjoyed your walk, Daughter?"

Adrastea nodded. She then felt an overwhelming urge to hug this comfortable woman. Having no reason to resist, she gave in to her impulse. She received a warm embrace in return. "Come back any time," Lucea said. "You are always welcome here, Daughter of the Light."

Adrastea did not want to let go but she had to. Lucea stepped back. "Do not regret the life you have chosen, for you are now in a place where you can do much good. Tell Me. Did you enjoy being a healer?"

Had she? Adrastea thought back to her time with Ari. While there were moments when Adrastea wished she could have shirked her work, overall, she did enjoy it. Ari's stillroom was home to her, from her brews and beers to her lotions and potions. "Yes, I did. I was a journeywoman until…" her eyes flicked towards Mor-Lath.

Lucea nodded. "So why not continue your work? Here you are, having journeyed to a new place. Why not explore new herbs and new medicines? Surely your husband would not begrudge you a stillroom of your own." That sounded like a commandment.

Lucea lifted Her hand to Mor-Lath. "Be at peace, God of the Dark. You are your greatest enemy when you give in to pride and anger."

Phyl moved to Lucea's side and put an arm about Her waist. Together They spoke. "We give you a commandment." The way They said it told Adrastea that she was included. "Cease to provoke one another. Forgive one another. Cease to be angry with one another. For if you fail in this, you shall surely fail in your greatest desire."

This did not sit well with Mor-Lath. "You would deliberately cause me to fail? You who are pledged to do no harm?"

"We would not cause you to fail. You yourself would cause you to fail. There is a reason you are not a god. For that reason alone, would you fail at the end. We do not need to do much more than what We have already done. The rest is up to you, Mor-Lath. Though We know you. You have faults. These faults could be your undoing."

"That is not true," Mor-Lath stated. Adrastea's jaw dropped at his audacity. Even after all the Light said to them—even giving them the clues they needed to achieve godhood—he would turn and call Them liars to Their faces?

Mor-Lath pointed a finger at them. "You have plagued me with mashiahs, even to the prevention of my advancement. I don't care what you say. You have set me up to fail."

"We have set stumbling stones in your path. Should you not be diligent and watch where you walk, you may fall. But as you proved last week, you are more than capable of seeing and removing these stumbling stones."

Lucea raised a finger to point at Adrastea. "She is the key to your greatest desire. However, you are the lock."

The glow of light around Them grew in intensity until even Mor-Lath had to shade his eyes. They departed, leaving Adrastea and Mor-Lath alone.

Adrastea looked to Mor-Lath and held her head high. "I received forgiveness for my greatest sin. What did you receive?"

"Useless words and meaningless riddles."

Mor-Lath had refused to speak further. He disappeared, leaving Adrastea alone in the domain of the Light, to find her own way home.

Where to go? She felt too embarrassed to return to Sacred Spring. Eventually, Adrastea gave in and returned to the temple.

Adrastea's feet touched the cobblestones of the courtyard. The warm breeze of the afternoon wafted through her curly hair. When she looked around, she was alone.

There was no Berengaria to greet her on the doorstep. She entered the temple alone, skirts swishing. The first chamber was the main chapel. As Adrastea approached, she heard voices chanting in worship.

The large double doors were open, so she peeked in. The chapel was a high chamber, carved out of rock and lit by the same glowing orbs that lit the rest of the temple. There were no benches, nor chairs nor any other piece of furniture, save a large altar towards the other end, on a raised dais. Before this, all the priestesses knelt. Led by Desideria, they chanted their litany of praises for Mor-Lath, their musical voices echoing throughout the chamber. They wore black robes that covered them completely except for their raised arms and their bare heads. Their hair hung loose down their backs.

Adrastea took a tentative step through the doorway and quietly cursed her skirts as they rustled.

One of the priestesses on the end of the back row turned and looked for a moment. It was Berengaria. She gasped and opened her mouth to say something, but Adrastea held a finger up to her lips and waved Berengaria to silence. She did not feel like drawing the attention of the others to her. Berengaria turned back.

Adrastea listened to the litany. It was more of a poetic canticle extolling the traits of their god and the power he gives to mankind that they may rise above the weak, et cetera, et cetera. This was the last thing she wanted to listen to right now.

Her clothes were too much. But how would she change without help?

Wait. She was an immortal with command over the Deeper Power. She could very well undress herself.

She retreated to her chambers where she willed the tiny buttons on the back of her dress to undo themselves. They obeyed, and she let the dress, worse for wear after its unexpected dousing in the Spring, slide off her figure to the floor. The laces of her corset obliged as well. She dropped the steel-bound monstrosity with great relief. A pox on Feowan fashion.

Clad only in her shift, she gathered the clothing up and left it lying on the bed for the priestesses to care for. She approached the wardrobe and looked inside.

Did she say wardrobe? This was no mere wardrobe, but a giant chamber filled with all manner of clothing. Sumptuous gowns of Feowan design, long swathes of fabric that had not yet been tailored or was that deliberate, to be tied and draped somehow? She stroked her hand over billowy, diaphanous garments that reminded her of the clothing of the priestesses, court robes, puffy shirts...

While she ought to be grateful to her new husband for his generous provision of a wardrobe, he didn't honestly think she'd be comfortable in these frocks. Why couldn't there be something simple? She dug through the assortment to seek out anything even remotely serviceable.

She was still in the wardrobe snarling at the inappropriate clothing when Desideria and Berengaria, still dressed in their black robes, entered. They knelt to the floor and murmured, "Mistress."

Adrastea threw the latest bit of froth to the floor and stalked out of the wardrobe. "Find me something appropriate to wear."

Berengaria looked to Desideria, whose eyes remained on the floor. "What do you mean by 'appropriate', Mistress?" the high priestess asked.

"Something I can work in."

Berengaria lifted her eyes. "Work? You work?"

Desideria's fingers whipped out in a sharp tap to Berengaria's thigh. The younger priestess dropped her gaze and blushed.

Adrastea flung a hand back to the open wardrobe. "Nothing in there is suitable. I have work to do. I do not want to be hampered in full skirts."

Her odd request did not flummox Desideria. "What sort of work did you have in mind? I will find something suitable. I'm sure His Holiness has provided."

She rose to her feet, but her eyes did not meet Adrastea's as she moved past her to the wardrobe.

Adrastea put a hand to her forehead. "I do not need his permission to do what I have always done."

The high priestess paused and inclined her head. Her back remained towards Adrastea. "I was under the impression that he approved of your actions, whatever they are to be."

Adrastea smelled something suspicious. "When did you speak with him?"

"It was not in the manner of speaking." Her hand stole to her side.

Adrastea walked around to face Desideria. "Then how was it?" Her eyes fell to Desideria's waist. There, under the hand, tucked into the waistband of her robe, was a small scrap of paper. "He left you a note?"

Desideria looked up. There was no meekness in her eyes but rather a careful guardedness. "Yes."

Adrastea folded her arms. "And what did it say?"

"In regards to you, that you had much work to do. We were to aid you in any way you saw fit." After a moment's hesitation, she added, "Mistress."

"Is that all?"

"That you were to be given what was required to complete your tasks."

"Did he say what that was?"

"No."

"Anything else?"

"Yes. He said that he had many important things to do and that he was not to be disturbed."

Adrastea snorted her disbelief. More likely he was sulking after his dressing-down. Still, she would not disparage him in front of his own priestesses. That would have been contravening the Light's commandment. Though she was the Bride of the Dark, she still felt subject to the Light.

"I'm sure he'll be back next week," Berengaria blurted out, then squeaked and scooted away from Desideria, possibly fearing punishment. Apprehensive, that was Berengaria.

Adrastea addressed her question to Desideria. "How long do you expect him to be gone?"

"Truthfully? I don't know." To Berengaria, she said, "Not that it matters to you, child." She emphasized 'child'. Berengaria turned her face downward. The label of 'child' irked the young priestess, though nothing showed externally. The chastisement was like a tugging on the heartstrings of Berengaria's soul, a thrumming through the Lines. Berengaria could be a useful ally, if only she could win her over.

Desideria spoke the truth. The high priestess seemed concerned about something, possibly something within the letter. Her fingers itched to snatch it out of the black belt at Desideria's waist. She could not afford to ruin her reputation with Mor-Lath's priestesses.

Adrastea regarded them for a long pause. Instead of fidgeting at the discomfort of silence, they patiently waited. Berengaria shifted, not from awkwardness but from curiosity. Did the younger priestess know the contents of the letter?

"Now, what aren't you telling me, Desideria?" Adrastea asked.

"Nothing," she replied. Then, without prompting or even an inflective pause, she rose, pulled the letter from her belt and handed it over.

Adrastea opened it. For a missive from a god to his high priestess, it seemed rather informal. She recognized the script as the same that illuminated her copy of the Book of Mor-Lath. For a moment, she wondered where it was, before remembering she had packed it with the rest of her scant belongings in preparation to leave Sacred Spring. She made a note to retrieve her belongings, including some sensible items of clothing, later.

Desideria,

There are some pressing matters I must attend to. My bride, likewise, has some tasks ahead of her. Give her what she needs to complete them. Aid her as she sees fit. Above all, keep her busy, for when she is idle, she will create trouble for you. I know not when I shall return.

He did not sign it. He didn't need to. Adrastea handed back the note without comment. Where was he?

Adrastea laid her hands to her cheeks and closed her eyes. *Mor-Lath, where are you?*

Go away. I do not want to talk to you right now.

A wall came up between them. He had to concentrate to keep it up and shut her out. Her first thought was of surprise. She hadn't meant to communicate with him like that—hadn't even known it was possible. Did he? He did not seem surprised at her communication.

Regardless, his refusal irked her.

"Shall I find you suitable raiment?" Desideria asked.

"What?" Adrastea came out of her reverie.

"I don't think there's anything common—" started Berengaria but one look from Desideria silenced her.

Desideria picked up the discarded clothing Adrastea had thrown on the floor in frustration. "What sort of work?"

"I—" she started and then changed her mind. "Do you have a stillroom?"

The high priestess swept a too-long gown into her arms and carried it into the wardrobe. "We do, such as it is."

"Then I wish for something suitable for working in the stillroom."

Both priestesses looked at each other as if this was the oddest request they have ever heard. Berengaria rose to her feet, undid her belt to her formal robe and sloughed the fabric from her shoulders. Underneath she wore the same sort of short bodice she had before, and the same full, divided skirt gathered at the ankles. Her shoulders and her belly were bare. The gauzy fabric of the skirt barely hid her legs. "Will this do, Mistress?"

Desideria let out a small gasp of surprise. "Berengaria!"

But the younger priestess did not cover herself back up. She gave a subtle yet defiant look to Desideria.

Adrastea's gasp was a bit more pronounced. "I couldn't wear something like that."

Berengaria covered herself again. "I know it is common, but it is suitable for working."

"But your belly is bare."

"And you are standing around in your underwear."

"Berengaria!" Desideria's shocked voice rang out. "You will not speak to her like that again."

Berengaria threw her hands over her mouth. Tears streamed down her face. She sank to her knees and gave herself over to sobs. "Forgive me, Mistress," she whimpered. "I did not mean to be so forward."

Adrastea could not have been more shocked than if Desideria had slapped the younger priestess.

"You didn't have to do that," she told Desideria.

"His Holiness would not have permitted such impertinence."

"I am not His Holiness."

"But you are the one he chose to marry," Desideria said, with a flavor of disapproval. Whatever the high priestess thought, Adrastea was sure of one thing: her heart did not wholly rejoice in the marriage. Whether jealous, or fearful of change... or perhaps even envious, Desideria did not approve.

"Yes. We all wonder at his choice." As soon as she said it, Adrastea knew she shouldn't have. Desideria was thinking. Oh, what she would give to know what went through the priestess' head.

"Tell me everything," Adrastea ordered. Now that she was lawfully wedded—acknowledged by the Light Themselves—she did not want to be cuckolded, even if her husband was the personification of all things Dark. She opened herself further to the Deeper Power and drew it in like a thirsty horse draws water.

Berengaria squeaked and scuttled away to the far side of the room. Desideria stood her ground but worry cracked her resolve. Adrastea felt it. Desideria had enough talent to sense what Adrastea was capable of. What Desideria didn't know was what Adrastea would do. Adrastea herself didn't know but that didn't matter. The fact that she could inspire fear in the other woman was enough.

It was more than enough. It was thrilling, addictive. No wonder Mor-

Lath enjoyed it so much. But it was not her desire for the Deeper Power that drove her need to call upon it but her fear that she was only an object, a trophy, a final key for Mor-Lath's personal gain, and there being little reward for herself. No wonder she was so angry.

Adrastea grasped Desideria by her holy robes. "You will tell me everything between you and Mor-Lath," she demanded. "You can give it to me of your own free will, or I shall take it from you."

Desideria maintained her mask of calm but Adrastea felt the conflict within. Fear also worried away at her foundation of strength. The high priestess warred between choices. To what they were, Adrastea was not privy.

Adrastea felt the release within the other woman as she made her choice. A calm came over Desideria. "Would it be such a terrible thing to give my life in sacrifice to guard the secrets of my god?"

Adrastea frowned at the quandary. If she pushed hard enough, she might be able to learn what the other woman knew but at what cost to Desideria? Here was a woman willing to die for something she believed in. She stood there, her body rigid as she fought off fear. After all, she was ready to die here and now.

Adrastea wasn't ready to kill again. Not ever.

But she couldn't back down. "I don't want his secrets. I want yours." She had taken Mor-Lath out of the equation. It was between her and Desideria now.

To her surprise, Desideria relaxed. Her knot of tension and fear loosened. "What? Is that all?"

Adrastea released her grip on Desideria's robe. She smoothed out the wrinkles she'd created. "Sorry," she muttered without realizing she said it. "I... I didn't mean it. I'm sorry."

What had she become? How stupid she felt, having let her anger and jealousy get the best of her. "I should never have done that."

"I believe you. I am not your rival, if that is what you are thinking."

Adrastea felt even more embarrassed. "Still, I should not have taken my anger out on you. You've done nothing."

Desideria smoothed her skirts and folded her hands. "May we start over?"

"Please."

"What do you want to know?" Desideria asked.

"Everything."

Desideria took a breath. "Please be more specific. I've been a priestess a long time."

But Adrastea didn't know any delicate way to put it. It would not do to scream out, how often has he taken you to his bed? Even worse, if Adrastea did not maintain some kind of control, her jealousy could cause her to spill her own secrets—the fact he had not taken her to his bed yet. Until Desideria had made that remark about marriage and choice, Adrastea didn't realize how important consummation was to her.

That wasn't completely true. It had been in the back of her mind since that first day, shoved there by the horror of having been tricked into murdering all those people. When Berengaria had greeted Mor-Lath at his return, it hadn't seemed all that innocent. But Berengaria was still a girl, and would be for at least another four, maybe five years. The others had been as enthusiastic, if not quite as physically demonstrative.

And then after he had shown her to her (not their) bedroom, she feared it would happen then but in the back of her mind, she wanted it.

Ever since she'd first met him, she'd wanted it. His continual tempting of her with the Deeper Power only reinforced the idea.

Had they been so truly busy the past few days that he could not have made some time for her?

And now they'd had that terrible argument. It certainly wasn't going to happen any time soon, unless he was feeling particularly mean. But then it wouldn't be called consummation.

"I have known many jealous wives," Desideria said. "I know what is foremost in your mind."

Adrastea broke off her musing and her eyes flashed dangerously. "Just how many wives has he had?"

"What?" Desideria stepped back. "You are the first, as far as I know." She proceeded with caution, pausing to choose her words carefully. There was a certain resignation in her voice. Then Adrastea realized that Mor-Lath had warned his high priestess about his wife in the letter. He knew her better than she thought and that irked her.

Silently, she begged Desideria's forgiveness again and released her anger. It wasn't the priestess' fault they were in this situation.

Desideria continued. "I only meant that I know of many mortal men who think nothing of straying from their marriage bed. You question the fidelity of your husband." She observed Adrastea for a moment as if gauging how she received this.

"And your role?" Adrastea asked, trying to be gentle.

Desideria pondered this for a moment, possibly trying to avoid another temper eruption from Adrastea. When Adrastea's meaning sank in, she fluttered her hands before her as she inspired in surprise. "Oh, no, no! Mistress, not that. We none of us have ever shared— Oh, no. Nothing like that." That had flustered her. "Did you think that he and I— No. His Holiness makes a special point of not engaging in that sort of, well, engagement. Not with me, not with any of us here at the temple. That rule is unbreakable."

She spoke the truth.

"I will confess each one of us has let our young hearts be broken by it..." She drew in breath as if to continue but seemed to think better of it. "In my wisdom, I see it is all for the best. I am sorry if you did not know."

Adrastea folded her arms. "He hasn't told me anything." Adrastea legs wobbled. She flopped onto the bed. Desideria sat down on the bed beside her. Berengaria remained against the far wall.

"Ah," Desideria sighed. "I wonder if that task has fallen to me?"

Adrastea raised her head. "Why? What is everything?"

"I don't know," the high priestess confessed. "I thought you knew, as it is what you wanted to know."

Adrastea sat up. "Assume I know nothing. I want you to tell me everything, even if you think I may already know it. I want to know about the priestesses, I want to know about your religion, your culture, your food. Everything. Pretend I grew up in some country village on the other side of the mountains and know nothing. Unless you know for sure I know it, assume I don't."

Desideria blinked. "All that, right now?"

Adrastea waved her hands. "Oh, no, not right now. Just... whenever. Talk to me all the time. Just because I'm, well, whatever it is I am, don't assume that you aren't allowed to speak in my presence. I want you to speak to me all the time.

"I think my biggest problems come when I don't get told what I need to know. He's the biggest culprit. I think he forgets I don't know everything."

A moment of silence fell between them. Desideria rose. "Perhaps we should find something suitable for whatever it is you need to do. And the stillroom is yours, Mistress."

While Desideria dug through the closet, she shared her story. "I first came into His Holiness' service when I was eight. I was the bastard daughter of a scullion and the most powerful Shiah in our tribe. I did not know it at the time but His Holiness himself came for me. I am not sure what he paid my mother, but she was more than happy to let me go. She knew that as a priestess, I would have a better life than as a servant.

"He came for me because of my ability to read the lines of Deeper Power."

And thus, did Desideria proceed to educate Adrastea, starting with what she knew best, herself.

৩৩৩৩

Chapter 7

Chamque sighed at having been woken by Awena so early in the morning. Montrof, a priest of Mor-Lath, sought an audience with her. Would her old bones ever get any peace? When the young priestess told her he had arrived, Chamque did not bother to dress. Montrof wouldn't care what she looked like. She threw her robe on over her nightclothes and shuffled off to deal with him. Awena followed her, complaining about how he had assaulted her as she opened the gates. "He grabbed my bottom and said—"

"Yes, yes," muttered Chamque. "I am well aware of the sort of letch Montrof is."

"So why would you wish to speak with him?"

"It is not what is outside that is so important, than what is inside."

"I heard what came out of his mouth. I doubt his inside is much cleaner than his outside."

Chamque pinched the bridge of her nose. "Off you go, Awena. Leave him to me." He'd receive more than the sharp side of her tongue, for his unwelcome assault on one of her priestesses.

"Gladly," she muttered, and slouched off as only a young adolescent can do.

The high priestess' office occupied a sizeable room in the back of the temple. It had the added luxury of a glazed window facing eastward, so the morning sun shone in, illuminating the motes of dust with silver light. The wooden desk and the shelves took on a gleam as if they were lovingly polished, instead of simply worn.

Awena had left Montrof in her office unsupervised. No doubt he'd already rifled through the desk and the shelves. She wondered if he'd found anything of interest.

Montrof, being a priest of Mor-Lath, was a solitary creature. Priests did not belong to any temple but roamed as will and ministered as they would, if the price was right. It didn't always have to be coin.

Montrof was no longer young. He'd never been handsome, as men go. As time continued its relentless pace forward, it dragged what little advantage he had with it. His belly paunched out beneath his filthy brown robe and bags had settled themselves under his eyes and along his jowls. He carried a satchel so grimy that even he did not remember the original color. His once-dark hair hung in silvery strands, which he only sometimes bothered to brush. The scraggly look suited the stereotype of the lonely, brooding priest, inspiring terror in children and second thoughts in grown men.

Montrof liked to wheedle. He'd attempt to solicit favors or goods without needing to pay for them. Chamque learned to keep her coffers, her kitchens and her doors closed. At least she didn't have to worry about anyone not keeping their legs closed.

So why did she tolerate him? Because of all the priests roaming the city, he had the most talent. He'd also had a fair bit more education than most. It was for these two reasons alone she ever let him pass between the temple doors. Still, she would have something to say to him regarding his lack of respect toward the younger priestess.

"Get your filthy feet off my desk," Chamque scoffed as she came into the office. He had helped himself to her chair and was leaning back in a most undignified manner. "I ought to beat you senseless for what you said to

Montrof, whose shabby sandals had knocked sand and worse on the top of the desk, lowered his pasty legs and let his unwashed robe fall to cover them. "I hear you have a priestess who claims she bears the Sign."

Chamque folded her arms. "That waits to be seen." How did he know? Had he read it in the Lines of Deeper Power? Chamque herself was not yet sure it wasn't a trick.

Montrof swiped most of the detritus off her desk before leaning his elbows on it. "I am of a surety it is genuine."

How? How could he know such a thing?

"It may even signify more than you think."

"Oh, why?"

"You found her four days prior, didn't you?"

"Everybody knows that, who listens to gossip." Despite her best efforts, the priestesses of the temple had put two and two together to come up with juicy little tidbits for rumormongering.

Montrof inclined his head. "As I do, for while the majority of gossip is incorrect, it has its root in truth somewhere. Additionally, we are a people who believe in prophecy."

"So? Most of the time prophecy doesn't make sense until after it's been fulfilled."

"That's my point. Why don't you go confirm the second mark and I shall explain further."

"Don't need to. I saw it the first day." Her fears grew in her belly. Montrof was not one to pursue something as trite as temple gossip. "She is not the first Chosen, nor will she be the last."

Montrof chuckled, showing his decaying teeth. "Ah but she may be more than that."

Chamque felt left out of the loop. "You want to explain?"

"Ever hear of the "Bride of Mor-Lath"?"

Chamque sighed. "Of course." All priestesses had. It was a euphemism for being Chosen. "You want to tell me something I don't know?"

He wagged a finger at her. "What if I told you "Bride of Mor-Lath" was to be taken literally?"

Speech left her for a moment as the potential ramifications flooded her mind. "You are jesting me. You are."

"I'm not. Several years ago, I came across some obscure Glasskisser prophecies speaking about how His Holiness once desired a bride. How he would claim her, and it would come with a great price of sacrifice."

"Believe me; many women would consider the marks of the Sign no great sacrifice."

Montrof laughed and wagged a finger at her in chastisement. "Oh, you are a lazy woman, Chamque, to spend your evenings with your ear to the pillow and not to the walls of the alehouses."

Chamque had had enough. "Will you just tell me what's on your mind instead of playing these games? Otherwise, get out of my chair so I may attend to more interesting business." She still owed him for Awena.

He steepled his fingers and gave her a very pointed look. "Believe me, you shall find this most interesting. Last night news came to the city of the end of the war in Feown."

That got her attention. "So, the Cithrans are turning their focus on us now?"

"Nope," he replied with a smug grin of self-satisfaction.

Her jaw dropped. "You don't mean the Feowans won?"

He chortled. "I don't know if I'd call it a win."

She stamped her foot then regretted showing her irritation as a child would. "Just get to the point."

He rose in his excitement. "The Cithrans," he exulted, "every single one of them, are dead." He cackled at the thought.

Chamque watched him laugh and wipe his tears away. He laughed himself out then settled back into her chair, which she was sure she'd have to clean later. He gave a sigh at the end of his amusement.

Chamque shook her head. "You mean every single one of them is dead?"

"Well," he capitulated. "I don't know if every single one of them is dead but certainly all that dwelt in Feown. And I have confirmed here in Avelia. More Cithrans hiding here than we thought. I have people out there counting all the mysterious deaths of people who failed to wake up a few days ago."

He waved his hands with histrionic flair. "One morning, they all dropped. No explanation, no marks, nothing. One moment alive, then all dead." He leaned across the desk.

Chamque sighed. "Why?" she intoned in an impatient voice, wondering why he had to play these dramatic games. Perhaps he'd spent too much time alone.

"Rumor has it there was great power wielded that day, far more than any priest or priestess I know could ever do.

"Maybe the Glasskissers—"

"Not them either. Few Glasskissing priests survived what the Cithrans called the Purge. Believe me, if they had that sort of talent at their command, no doubt they would have attempted to wipe us out long ago." He leaned across the desk even further, until he was nigh prone across it. "Think, Chamque. What one being do you know wields enough Power to kill thousands, maybe even tens of thousands, at a single blow?"

Chamque stood there silent for a moment as her head ran through all the possibilities. She didn't know of a single mortal who could do all that.

"Oh, come on, woman! And there you stand in his temple and profess ignorance?"

A cold shiver ran down her back. "His Holiness?"

Montrof sank back to the chair, it creaking under him as he sat back rather hard. "His Holiness."

She shook her head. "Why would he save Feown?"

"He didn't save Feown. That was an accident. What he did was sacrifice the lives of Cithra."

So Montrof saw a connection between the unexplained deaths and...?

"Those of us with a real god, we know true prophecies. We know how to read the Lines. And I hear that all those deaths had to do with the Bride of Mor-Lath. Not a euphemism but an actual bride."

It was all too much for Chamque. Her head buzzed. "What does Desmone have to do with it?"

Montrof shook his head. "You are one of the daftest women I know. How did you get to be high priestess of this temple, I'll never know."

Chamque hissed at him. "It's too early in the morning for me. Your riddles are too obtuse. Are you saying Desmone is *the* Bride of Mor-Lath?"

"It all fits."

Her head ached. "No. It's all speculation."

"You are unaware of the other prophecies, perhaps?"

Chamque had had enough. She strode around the desk and, risking her health, grabbed Montrof by his greasy locks and hauled him up out of her chair. "I've been too busy keeping a temple running to spend my days in searching obscure texts. That's your job, as I recall. So, stop playing the mysterious priest and just tell it straight. What leads you to believe that our Desmone is the Bride?"

After he put himself to rights, he ticked off the points on his fingers. "First, the sacrifice. One prophecy speaks of His Holiness giving a great sacrifice for the sake of his Bride. Every source puts the date of the great slaughter about four days ago. And if I recall my gossip, that's when you discovered your Desmone sprawled across the altar."

"Yes." Another shiver ran down her back. In the back of her mind, she entertained the notion of Desmone being the true Bride of Mor-Lath. If so, she would probably be gifted, if not with great power, at least great influence. And here was Chamque treating her most shabbily.

"The timing is too close together to be anything else."

Chamque grasped at straws. "Perhaps there is another Bride?"

Montrof snorted his derision. "I don't think so. What sort of man would marry a woman one hour, then bed another one the next?"

Chamque gave a weak sort of chuckle. "Yeah, that would be

ridiculous... But—There is the prophecy of him marking his Bride."

"Which has been attributed to the Sign and the Chosen. That has already been fulfilled." Montrof leaned back. He was going to put his feet on the desk but Chamque moved forward and knocked them off the moment his dusty heels touched the wood. He gave her a rebellious sneer.

Surely not Desmone. Of all the people? Desmone was shallow and selfish. Why would His Holiness choose her, of all people? Chamque could not turn her belief to that. "What if we were wrong?"

"About that prophecy? I don't think so."

"I seem to recall you saying that most of the time prophecy doesn't make sense until after it's been fulfilled. We may have been misinterpreting the prophecy until this point."

"We can't have. It fits what we know already." He lifted a finger. "But the sacrifice doesn't."

"That's unconfirmed."

"That they all died is confirmed. How and why they died is yet to be shown." He shook his head. "I know what I know. I believe I have the right of it. There are far too many close coincidences for me to dismiss them as you are wont to do, old girl. I say there's a chance that great things are afoot. We may be near the heart of it."

She folded her arms. "And if we're not?"

He rose to his feet and came forward. "I think the consequences of not believing when it's true will be much, much worse than believing when it's false." He came close enough for her to smell his rancid breath. "Think upon't, Chamque. Don't think I don't know what's in your heart. Play the girl right, play everyone else right, and you would become a powerful woman indeed. Isn't that what you want?"

He strolled to the door. "I trust you are treating her well? No doubt the Bride of Mor-Lath will reward those who have served her well from the beginning."

As he slipped out, before he closed the door, he stuck his face back in. "I do believe I smell breakfast. Do try not to be late."

T he embroidered blouse was far too fancy for what Adrastea was used to. Under the embroidery, the blouse had a see-through quality that bothered her sense of modesty. The jade-green skirt, pilfered from a gown that would have suited a patronesses' assembly room, would never have been ideal for work. But after Desmone and Berengaria raided the whole of her wardrobe, Adrastea determined nothing else suited her purposes.

Desideria fiddled with the lay of the blouse on Adrastea's shoulders. "I cannot think you would blame His Holiness for your wardrobe selection. These are the costumes of a lady, which you are. We never expected to need to clothe you as a stillwoman."

Adrastea conceded the point. Beyond saving her village, she never thought past the moment of pledging her troth. No, these would not do, not until after she'd taken to them with a thread and needle.

Finally, she gave up and requested they find something suitable for day wear. "I am going calling instead," she had announced, "so try to keep things simple."

Berengaria pointed to the clothes Adrastea wore. "That's the simplest we got."

Adrastea sighed. It would have to do.

Ari would forgive her.

Berengaria had brought a few items that Adrastea had requested, not sure what her mistress wanted with a sheaf of unbound paper.

Time to go home. She drew on the Deeper Power and focused where she wanted to go.

Shift.

Moments later, as Adrastea stood awkwardly on Ari's porch, she had no idea whether or not Ari would forgive her her clothes. Her knock on the door was soon answered.

"Adrastea!" Ari gave her a big hug. "Are you all right?"

"I'm fine."

Ari held her old apprentice at arm's length. "That blouse is rather indecent," Ari commented, after she got over her moment of shock.

"And I'd rather the villagers didn't see me in it."

Ari invited her in. "Your husband didn't come with you, did he?" she said, looking around carefully before she shut the door.

"No. He's busy at the moment."

Ari snorted. "Doesn't mean he won't pop by when you least expect it."

Adrastea felt awkward, like she was the apprentice again. "I have to apologize for earlier," she said. "We shouldn't have squabbled like that in front of you."

"So, I take it the honeymoon is over?"

Moving to a chair at the table, Adrastea seemed to wilt into it. "Didn't get much of a honeymoon." She dropped the paper onto the table.

Ari scooted the other chair next to Adrastea. She took her former apprentice's hands. "I hope he wasn't too harsh with you. I—" she squeezed Adrastea's hands. "Your marriage was so sudden. We really didn't expect you to marry him until you did." Ari licked her lips and looked away. "When a couple announce their intentions to be married, there are certain, ah, premarital rituals for the bride—"

Adrastea felt as awkward as Ari looked. "I know about that. I'm a healer too, remember?"

"Yes." She still clutched Adrastea's hands. "The point I wanted to make was that the reason for the rituals are to spare the bride any unnecessary discomfort on her wedding night. It should be a time of joy, not..." Ari looked up. "Mor-Lath doesn't strike me as the sort who would be gentle."

Adrastea gave a small shrug. "I wouldn't know. He hasn't touched me."

Ari didn't say anything for a while. Adrastea wanted to pull her hands away, for the healer's gaze was penetrating.

Ari hmphed. "He hasn't? Why not?"

She hadn't thought about it, not really. "We've been too busy, I guess."

Ari snorted. "I don't know if I believe that. I can't think of a man who is too busy to satisfy his own pleasures. Don't tell me he isn't interested in the marital bed. I saw the kiss he gave you at the wedding."

He'd given her several over the course of their courtship. She remembered them all. She pulled her hands from Ari's. "I am not here to discuss my intimate life. I came to apologize to you and to pick up a few things." Adrastea plucked at her blouse. "I've more clothes than the whole village put together and not a single item of practicality. Oh, and I'll need my note book, and copies of your other books. I'm setting up my own stillroom. After all, I am a journeyman healer.”

“Oh.” Ari gave her a nervous sort of smile. “I know this is silly but where do you live now?”

Adrastea sighed. She wasn’t quite sure of the location but, “There’s a temple to the west, carved out of a solid mountain. There we are served by several dozen priestesses who are utterly devoted to His Holiness.”

Ari looked as if she hadn’t heard right. “His what?”

Adrastea couldn’t help but smile. “That’s what they call him.”

“His Holiness?” Ari laughed. “That doesn’t fit him.”

“I know. That is how one addresses a god. But to me, he’s just...”

“...Mor-Lath,” Ari finished. “You know, I know he’s a god and all, but he doesn’t quite strike me as, well, godlike. To me, a god is some obscure, distant being to whom we direct our prayers and to whom we hope is listening to us.”

Adrastea leaned forward. “You’ll never guess what. I’ve met the God of the Light.”

Ari’s jaw dropped. “No! What is She like?” The curiosity in her burned brightly.

“She is very tall and extremely curvy. He is likewise tall, with a white beard and rather slim.”

Ari thought about it for a moment. “Wait. There are two gods?”

Adrastea shook her head as she chuckled. “No. A god is a dual being, male and female. Two halves of a whole.”

Amazement filled Ari’s breast as she realized the implications of this. “That’s why Mor-Lath wanted to marry you! He needed a female half.”

Adrastea nodded in confirmation.

A chill settled about the room as Ari backed away. “Does this mean you’re a god?”

Her former apprentice sighed as her countenance fell. “No. Immortal, yes. But not yet a god.” She held up her hand. “Please don’t ask me about the immortality. It’s not something I can talk about yet.” Instead, she rose and checked the fire in the stove. “Perhaps we could have some tea while I make copies of your notes?”

Ari didn’t rise. “I never thought of the gods as dual beings. That would explain a few things, though. I wonder if Chloe knows. Carles might.”

Adrastea took the kettle into the stillroom to fill it from Ari’s water barrel. Did the healer still haul all her water from the creek, upstream from the village. It was not a task Adrastea enjoyed during her apprentice days.

The handcart had to be loaded with the casks and wheeled to the watering spot where they were filled, then lifted with some effort back to the cart before being wheeled back. Adrastea had begged Ari from time to time to dig a well, but Ari claimed well water as inferior.

The Innkeepers had a well, as did several others. Adrastea could never taste the difference.

She returned with the kettle. Ari was still at the table, riffling through the paper. "My notes are quite extensive. How long were you planning on staying?"

"Not long, I don't think." Adrastea had been entertaining an idea on how to make copies quickly. "It shouldn't take me much time."

Ari rose and fetched her notes and home-made books containing all the healer lore she knew. "I don't know where your copy is," she confessed.

"I think it's still with my belongings. I left them up in the house."

"Oh," Ari replied. "I don't think it's a good idea for you to go traipsing through the village. Maybe while you're copying, I could have Mikal bring it down for you."

"I don't plan on being here that long."

Ari eyed the stack of paper on the table. "If you're using all that, you may be here a long time."

Adrastea gave her a small smile. "You leave that to me."

As Ari fetched Mikal, Adrastea rummaged through Ari's stillroom for a bottle of ink. Then it was a simple matter to lay a piece of paper over Ari's notes. She requested Creation to match the ink to Adrastea's sheet so it patterned the ink on Ari's notes. It even duplicated the accidents and splotches. It took her longer than she expected, doing it sheet by sheet. Ari was not wrong; there were quite a few notes and entries.

She had not yet finished when Ari returned, helped by Mikal in carrying a trunk between them.

"There is no way I'm going to be carrying that back up the hill," he complained, "so you'd just better get used to having—" He saw Adrastea.

"Bloody Light," he yelped. "Adrastea."

At the mention of her name, she rose. Adrastea offered him a sheepish smile. "Hello, Mikal."

He took a step back. "What happened to you? You look different."

She turned away from him. "Long story."

Uninvited, he sat. "I've got time."

Ari grabbed him by the scruff of his shirt. "No, you don't. Natan will be wanting you back soon."

"But Ari, I never got to hear the whole story." He appealed to his sister. "Please?"

She looked at his eager face. "I promise I'll tell you someday. Just not now. It's too soon."

"Aw, come on."

Ari warned him. "Not now." She shoved him out of the house, to let him protest outside. He howled for a moment then there was silence. Ari opened the door but there was no Mikal.

Adrastea returned to her seat. "How much have you told him?"

Ari checked the kettle on the stove; it boiled, so she decanted the water into the tea pot and let it steep. Adrastea smelled peppermint and chamomile, as well as a few other familiar herbs. "We haven't told much of anything to anyone. There were those on the hilltop who saw what happened but still aren't sure who Mor-Lath truly was. There are others who deny he is the God of the Dark, because after he claimed you, the barrage continued for another five minutes."

"But it wasn't that long."

"Five minutes is a long time when you're under attack. Then the army dropped dead, literally. We had no idea what to make of it. Some people claimed it was the Light, some thought it was the Dark but didn't dare voice their opinion aloud. Those in the know are not pleased they owe their lives to Mor-Lath. It is believed that the Dark will extract a price for salvation."

"He already did. I was the price. All he wanted was me. And it wasn't him who killed all those people, it was me."

Ari fell into her chair with an audible thump. "Did you say you were..." She put a hand to her mouth.

"Oh, he tricked me into it, but it was by my hand they all died." She leaned back in her chair. "Half a million people dead, because of me." The guilt was gone from her heart, but the seriousness of the crime would never leave her memory.

"No way!" came a voice outside the back door.

Adrastea, startled, commanded the back door to open. It opened a little harder than she meant, for it hit against a shelf behind it. Mikal stood there, frozen in his eavesdropping, both hands clamped over his mouth. By the Deeper Power, Adrastea hauled him into the house and slammed the door behind him. Ari jumped with the sound of the door.

"Mikal," Adrastea warned. "You shouldn't eavesdrop."

He stood there until the shock of the moment thawed. He shook. "By the Light, who are you?" he whispered.

Adrastea didn't know how to answer that question. "I don't know." Mikal trembled so hard his teeth rattled. "Please don't be scared. It's just... I'm, I..." She sighed. "I've had a bad week."

"Haven't we all?" he squeaked at her in his breakable voice. He let out the breath. "Did you really kill half a million people?"

Adrastea dropped back to the chair. "I didn't mean to. He tricked me."

"But why?" her brother asked.

Adrastea was still figuring that one out. "It was the only way to make me immortal."

"That's a high price," Ari commented. "I don't think he values life very much."

Mikal let out another squeak. Adrastea studied the figure of her brother the mayorpentice, standing awkwardly in front of the door. He twisted his hands and wouldn't meet her gaze. "Mikal, you've got to promise not to tell anyone."

Now he looked at her, a frown beetling his brow. "What is it with you and promises?"

"Everyone will think I'm a bad person. But I'm not."

"Well you bloody married Mor-Lath, didn't you?"

That stung. "I did it to save you and everyone else."

Mikal folded his arms. "Well," he said, trying to think of something to prove himself right in the argument. "You didn't have— Why did— Oh!" He turned and fled through the door, slamming it behind him.

Adrastea dropped her head into her hands. That didn't go right. "Now he'll tell everyone, and they'll hate me."

After a moment's hesitation, Ari put her hand on Adrastea's shoulder. "They won't hate you. They don't know what to think of you right now, but I can assure you Mikal won't tell them.

"Natan made Mikal promise that he would tell him everything and tell no one anything about anything unless Natan cleared it. Mikal's been true to his word. You're in the clear."

Adrastea rose. "I ought to go. I really can't stay here. I'm sorry." She scooped up the copies of Ari's stillroom books and hugged them closely to her.

Ari stood by, feeling useless. "What are you going to do about your trunk?"

Adrastea laid a hand on it. "Good-bye, Ari. I don't know when I'll be back." She looked up to her former healermistress. "Please don't think bad of me."

Ari swallowed her heavy heart. "I won't." Then she watched as Adrastea and the trunk disappeared, leaving only a faint swirl of air.

Adrastea sighed in comfort. Nothing like her good old country clothes to make her feel like herself again. Now she could work.

Desideria led Adrastea deep into the bowels of the temple, past the kitchens and storerooms to an unused corridor. In her hands she carried two of those strange glowing balls. "I confess we have not used this room for years. I hope it has what you need." The door had no lock and creaked open under exerted pressure from Desideria's shoulder.

The stillroom was a large cavern, dusty and quiet. Nothing lurked here, not mice, not spiders. The light of the globes, one of which brightened with a word from Desideria, illuminated the space.

As Adrastea entered the stillroom, her senses opened up, pulling in new information. Memories of healers and herbalists brushed along her awareness, telling her of ancient brews and herbs, tisanes and decoctions. The room may have been empty now but it never forgot its history.

Even without the benefit of memories, the room impressed her with its size—easily three times larger than Ari's. The depth of dust that had coated various surfaces offered testament that it had not been used in several years. As soon as she cleaned that up, she would fill the room once more with every good thing she could—herbs and medicines, lotions, potions, and maybe a few brews.

With a whispered word, Desideria sent the globe up to float over the room and illuminate all corners. Adrastea promised herself to figure out how those globes worked. Ari would love to have one.

"Oh," sighed Adrastea. "Look at this." Wooden cabinets, shelves and drawers lined the walls, once upon a time the repository of decades of experience. Adrastea explored these. She found little of interest remaining, other than empty wooden boxes, glass jars and old pottery. They remembered long-ago contents, the hands that touched them and nothing else. If there had been chairs or stools in this room, they were long gone, possibly taken for use elsewhere. Didn't matter, as they couldn't have told her much anyhow. At the far end was a longstove Ari would have adored. As Adrastea ran her hand across the top, the blacking flaked off. "How long has it been since anyone's been here?"

Desideria shrugged. She ran a hand over one of the three long benches that occupied the middle of the room. Under these benches were more cabinets. "Maybe ten years?"

"Ten years? Where did the priestesses go if they need something?"

Desideria drew a finger through the thick dusk on a marble bench. "There are plenty of doctors and physicks in town. If His Holiness is about he will answer requests for healing." She rubbed at the dust. "To be honest, we rarely encounter illness. Another way His Holiness blesses us."

"Ah." Adrastea studied her own hands. She remembered how Mor-Lath taught her to heal Master Mason's leg. "I guess you don't have much need for a stillroom, then." She closed her fingers, feeling rather useless. What would the priestesses need with a country healer if they had a god who could heal at a touch?

"If I may ask, Mistress, why do you want the stillroom?"

She sighed as she tapped her fingers on the stone top. "Before I was married, I was a country healer. A stillroom is all I know."

Lines of surprise radiated from Desideria. "You mean, like proper doctoring?" She licked her lips. "Or were you one of those herbwomen who thinks she can brew love potions?"

"Doctoring." Now there was a word she hadn't heard in a while. Only Ari used it in the village. She had spent her journeymanship in Feown where she said she'd learned a few things from the 'city doctors'. A few of her techniques like lancing boils or stitching up cuts she called 'doctoring'. Anything to do with medicines was 'physicking'. Everything else—icing bruises and relocating shoulders—was 'healing'. "I do a little bit of everything, from mending broken bones to birthing babies."

Desideria made a funny noise. "Not much use for that skill here."

"Not much use for any skill, really." The words escaped out as disappointment filled her. She sank back against a cabinet. "I feel useless."

"Hmm," said Desideria. "You said stillroom. I assume you know how to use one?"

"Yes, and?"

She paced the room. "You make your own medicines?"

A few, like poppy tar oil, Ari bought from Crossroads but lots of others were easily created—cough syrups, headache powders and more. "I can but I don't know what you'd want with them."

Desideria stopped pacing, thought for a moment, then laughed. "I have an idea." She came before Adrastea. "The reason we have a stillroom in the Temple is because long ago we used to make medicines and other things. They weren't for us; we'd give them to the poor."

That got Adrastea's attention. "You help the poor?" Since when did Dark priestesses help the poor?

"Of course. We're priestesses. It's our job to help others." Her eyes lit up as the idea took root. "I confess we've not been as diligent in all our good works." A frown wrinkled her forehead and disappeared as quickly. "When Caerolie died, we never found a replacement. She was the last one to use the stillroom. But now we have you." She grasped Adrastea's hands. "Not only are you a healer but could teach us how to make for ourselves."

Desideria opened her mouth but paused. "I think," she began slowly, "we have lost our way. Maybe you are the one to put us back on track?" She still held Adrastea's hands.

Surely this was not her whole purpose.

However, it was a start. And if she could get his priestesses on her side, perhaps she could truly figure out what it was she was supposed to do. "I will do this thing." She cast her eye over the filthy room. "We start with cleaning this up."

Chapter 8

Mor-Lath sat on the top of his mountain, seeking as much solitude as he could. His being called to accounts by the Light and his losing discussion with Lucea had left him feeling bitter indeed. "We have given you all you have asked for," Lucea had told him. "There is aught else you may want." Then she proceeded to chastise him for mistreating Adrastea. While she was now his bride, They still considered her a daughter of the Light. No matter how he argued, he couldn't convince Them that she belonged wholly to him now.

Has it been any other being but the Light, he would have dismissed Their words as lies. But the Light never lied, not even by omission. However, They could choose not to answer the questions he didn't ask.

They had tricked him, in so many ways. He had married her, she knowing exactly who he was but here he sat, a demi-god still. There had to be something more. He pressed Lucea, but she continued to state that marriage was the key. "It is not My fault you don't know how to be married."

His parents had been married. He refused to dwell too often upon his childhood and his pre-god days. Nothing glorious there. Well, there were a few young women with laughing eyes and open legs, all too easy, and who left as quickly as they came.

No matter how hard he tried not to think about it, his thoughts kept coming back to his wife, or his bride, rather. That was another thing that irked him. The whole reason for her creation was to raise him from a demi-god.

He had sought answers from them: "How do I become a full god?"

"You need a wife," They had replied. "Your other half." Then They had gone one step further to design a resonant soul that would someday be born into a mortal body.

That had pleased him at the time.

As soon as the premortal soul was created, prophets read the Lines of Deeper Power and had come up with a few prophecies that disturbed him greatly. There were several versions but they all boiled down to the same, as far as he was concerned: The Son of Mor-Lath shall destroy him. In Their designing of Adrastea, They had given her the capacity to birth a mashiah.

Interesting creatures, mashiahs. Here were mortals with an extraordinary power to affect Creation in significant ways through their choices. Most mortals followed the patterns of Creation. They stayed in their stations but mashiahs were different. They had the potential to bend Creation to their will, to change their destiny. They even had the potential to destroy a god. Wild cards, they were.

A mashiah had killed a god before.

Thank the Light Adrastea was not a mashiah herself. While she had the potential for great power, she still remained subject to her destiny, even if it contained the potential for birthing a mashiah.

Mor-Lath had brought up this issue with Lucea as well. She never directly confirmed nor denied that this was intelligent design—but had he actually asked the direct question? No. They had played him and his anger against him, something which riled him even more. He dared not go back and ask Them again, because he knew They'd work against him. He would not come back with the answer he sought. Yet he had enough of an answer to curse them and damn his own foolish self.

"We know your selfish practices," She had said. "If your lust of the loins is greater than your lust for godhood, then by all means, risk damaging your bride and alienating her. If you do so, you shall never achieve your greatest desire." Now that he thought about it, that all but confirmed her mashiannic-generating potential.

So, make sweet love to his wife and risk a son who would destroy him, or never touch her and burn forever. Damn Them, for condemning him to keeping her at arm's length. Yet every time Adrastea drew on the Deeper Power, his soul sang to join with her. His body yearned for it as well. At least he could slake his thirst elsewhere and maintain his bride in a virginal state. Terribly unfair. She was so passionate.

Then She went straight to condemning him for how he had brought Adrastea to her full potential. "You have disrupted the Balance," She had said, "when you took those many lives before their time. You nearly destroyed the world."

Yes, there were other ways, slower ways but because they held onto her soul for so long, nearly until the end of time, he didn't have the luxury of doing things the slow way anymore.

They had a huge discussion about that—or rather, he tried to convince Her that They had tricked him again. She insisted that it was his own fault.

Always back to how everything was his fault. "We gave you your bride. How you treat her is up to you. Remember, she is not a toy, nor a possession. She is an immortal, sentient being just like you, with the potential to allow you both to become greater." Then Lucea said no more, even though he felt She had plenty of smug things She itched to tell him.

"We feel the turning of the clock," She stated. "You're running out of time."

Again, They tricked him. They denied it, but he still maintained that They had deliberately waited as long as possible before letting Adrastea be born, to give him as little time as possible to achieve full godhood. They had hidden her birth from him and had dissuaded her from using her talent, so he couldn't find her. They had to have done.

Because They were a god and he was not, he had lost the battle of words, sent off with an admonishment and even a commandment(!) that vexed him. Mor-Lath did not do well being commanded, especially with a commandment by the Light. What twisted the knife even further, he knew that if he obeyed Their commandment, They would bless him. He couldn't stand Their condescension. He was the bloody God of the Dark!

And the Light still had the advantage over him.

If They could be believed, then Adrastea was the key to his success. They gave her to him. They wouldn't take her away.

Didn't mean he couldn't lose her. That terrified him more than the Light's machinations angered him.

Mor-Lath dragged Mydala's soul out from his pocket. "Now," he said, holding her terrified intelligence up, "are you going to tell me who your master is?"

When Mor-Lath arrived outside the walls of Feown, he found Tanat, the immortal who Judged all souls, harvesting the dead. There were quite a few, as the occupying army had been large.

Around the walls of the city the white tents of the Cithran flapped in the air, their stakes and guy ropes loose. The unclaimed souls floated about, lost and confused.

The remaining citizens of Feown also roamed the fields, stripping the bodies of weapons, armor and anything else of use before disposing the bodies.

Tanat moved among them, sighing. The hearts of the living were heavy, some dark enough to weigh them down to damnation. War was not conducive to righteousness and good morality, even among the best of men. Let her moan about the lack of balance. Mor-Lath had a job to do.

The late summer breeze ruffled the hair of the corpses. It was not enough to blow away the stench. Firearms of various sizes, war engines, the quartermasters' wagons, the officers' signets and more were appropriated by what was left of the Feowan military. After they went through, the poor came out in force. The Feowan treasury had been authorized to pay each worker a tenner a day for the disposing of bodies. Timepieces, foreign small coinage, medals buttons and other items considered militarily useless were left as a bonus for the scavengers. Meanwhile the buzzards, ravens and rats feasted on the fallen flesh. When nothing remained of interest for anyone or anything, the Feowans rolled the putrid bodies into the trenches. When the trenches were full, they scattered lime over the bodies and then a heavy layer of dirt. No greater insult could the Feowans offer the Cithrans than the refusal of a funeral pyre. Off into holes they went, like the trash they were.

Not that it mattered to Mor-Lath. Bodies were fleeting. Dead was dead.

Their mortal remains gone to poisoning the water table, the Cithran souls wandered about. Their thoughts shone transparent to Mor-Lath. How they had died so suddenly, they asked one another. Why did they die? Every one questioned their death.

Let Tanat answer them. She had the time. His was running out.

He culled through the souls as quickly as he could, resisting the lure of those whose life works had tilted their balance towards Darkness— granted, that was most of them. As soon as Tanat got around to judging those souls, they would be sent to him. He could enjoy their sorrow at his leisure.

Meanwhile, he had to find one particular soul. His name was Paedep. He had been the one to tell Mydala about the mark of the Bride. Mydala didn't know much more. All she knew was if she found a woman whose face bore the scar as described, she reported back as soon as possible.

It was how she said it, "the scar as described," that bothered Mor-Lath. Was he getting so predictable that the patterns of Creation showed the smallest of his actions to any prophet who had half the talent to read them? He'd never marked anyone like he did Adrastea. In that, she was unique. No wonder she'd been spotted. But who had received the prophecy first? Who had put the order in motion to watch for her?

And if they were watching for her, why? There were plenty of other signs that presaged the end of this cycle of time; why was this one so important?

For that was how Mydala had seen it—important. Paedep had considered it important too and had impressed its magnitude upon this lesser priestess.

Paedep was nearby. Whenever Mor-Lath touched upon the Line that connected him to Paedep, it echoed his presence.

So why couldn't he find it?

He felt a pair of not-eyes on the back of his head. "Mor-Lath, I have issues with you."

He sighed before turning around.

"Hello, Tanat." He came face to face with her. "So nice to see you again."

Tanat gave him a cold look. "You have disrupted the balance. I hate that."

He snarled in her face. "I don't care. I think my need for a bride outweighs your nitpicky little compulsion to keep everything in order."

She stared at him, her jaw open. "Nitpicky..." Her brows furrowed over her not-eyes. "You nearly destroyed the world!"

"But I didn't." He flicked away another unwanted soul. It would come back his way again. "The power was pulled through her. Last I checked, she was not a mashiah. She can't destroy the world."

"But you are. And you nearly did."

He drew a breath. It would not do to let Tanat provoke him. "I needed her immortal."

"There were better ways. Safer."

"But not quicker. If the Light had cooperated sooner, this would not have been necessary." Then he noticed what she possessed. Ah, he might have found his lost soul.

The sentient force that comprised a soul clung to her fingers. She cradled it close to her grey robe. There was Paedep. He held out his hand. "Give me that."

"No."

"Give it to me now."

"Ha," she scoffed. "You cannot command me."

He grabbed her by the arm. "I need that soul. Give it to me."

"I'll Judge you later," she said to the soul tucking it in her pocket.

"You heartless bitch. I only want the answer to one question." He held a finger up in her face. "One question only."

She looked at him with her not-eyes. She didn't bother to hide her smile.

While he fumed, Tanat snatched Mydala's soul straight from his fingers. She judged her quickly and tossed her back to Mor-Lath. "Here. The sins on this one aren't so bad but enough to weigh her down. Purge her and send her to the Light."

Instead, he stuffed Mydala's soul into his pocket and held out his hand. "The only reason you have for holding Paedep is spite. I expected better than that from you."

"You're a fool, Mor-Lath, to think that I would aid you now."

"You never did," he spat. "All I ask is that you stand out of my way."

"What? And let you tip the balance? The Light may let you do what you want, for They know you are your own worst enemy. I cannot stand by and let you destroy the world in the process. I will have balance."

Must she be so vexatious? "At least answer my question for me: who instructed him to look for my bride?"

Tanat laughed at him. "Why, his master, of course, and his master before him. You could roam the fields of death questioning each soul. The chances are good I've collected the ones you want, judged them, and have sent them on their way." She leaned closer to whisper, "And I'll bet each one has gone to the Light." The humble often did. These lesser Cithran priests, for all their misdirected faith to a non-existent god, had remained true to their own moral codes, their actions striving to do Good, despite their circumstances.

He looked across the field, where too many ghosts roamed as they tried to sort out their new existence. To ask them all would take a long time. On the other hand, no other task pressed him for completion.

Two fights and two losses in the same day. So, was he going to go home to his bride? No way. Bad things always came in threes.

Tanat pulled out Paedep's soul. "Such a pity," she said. "The intentions of this soul were good. The evilness of society failed to nurture it to its best potential." Just like that, she Judged him and tossed him to Mor-Lath. "Don't let your obsession with your new bride obscure your true purpose in Creation."

Yeah, right. No way was he purging this soul until he had the answers he wanted.

Adrastea's visit with Ari lifted her spirits. The fact that she could come and go as she pleased comforted her. She didn't need to sacrifice the village she knew and the family she loved for the sake of her new life. Because of that, perhaps her new life wouldn't be so bad.

Desideria encouraged the priestesses to take an interest in their new mistress, not so much for His Holiness' sake but for theirs. Adrastea didn't know what the high priestess had whispered into their ears, but it worked. Each priestess of the temple came and helped her clean, whether for an hour or until sleep tugged at their eyelids. By the time the last priestess left, the room was as sparkling as mortal hands could get it.

Long after the priestesses abandoned her for their beds, Adrastea remained in her new stillroom. Her country clothes were comfortingly familiar and better suited for work. Berengaria was shocked that the Mistress would prefer such simple clothing over her more elegant trousseau.

The thought of her working also scandalized the priestesses. Only Desideria did not mutter in surprise that someone so exalted would think to engage in something so menial. "As we serve His Holiness, do not forget that he serves us. One could not expect any less from his bride, if she be true and worthy."

Adrastea wasn't sure if she should be pleased or insulted.

Still, she and the priestesses had worked side by side to get the stillroom clean. That was the easy part.

Adrastea looked about her new work space. It would take years to restock and redesign. And she'd have to get new equipment. Other than the longstove, the room lacked any tools like a still, or even a single copper kettle. Also, by being inside the mountain, where was one to toss the grey water? Adrastea did not like the thought of having to haul water in and out by hand.

She thought of the warm bath in her rooms. How did the water get in there and how did it get out? She pitied the poor priestess who had to carry it in, if that was how it arrived. There had to be a better explanation.

Adrastea picked up a smooth glass ball that glowed from within. These were all over the temple providing light. She could sense the Deeper Power that allowed it to shine. The ball itself felt warm but not overly hot. "Cease glowing," she commanded it. It dimmed to complete darkness. "Glow." It relit to order. What amazed her most was not the ingeniousness of the item but how easily command of the Deeper Power came to her. It was as if Creation wanted her to order it about.

Holding the ball before her, she returned to her bedroom and to the bath room that lay within. Laying down on the warm floor, she stretched out her hand to dabble in the water. After calling the Deeper Power to herself, she asked the water, "Show me where you come from."

A system of pipes and drains kept the water fresh, summoning it from deep within the earth, cold and pure, first to the kitchens where lingering Lines of Deeper Power encouraged it to pull the heat from the storage rooms, chilling them. Once heated, it could be used anywhere, from the kitchens, to another bathing chamber far off in the priestess' quarters, or along to here, Adrastea's bedroom.

What a resourceful system. Mor-Lath's doing?

If water could be brought and taken away from her rooms, it could be brought and taken away from the stillroom. While she could figure it out on her own, perhaps it was better to consult with Mor-Lath before she made any changes to his temple.

His temple. Shouldn't it have been *their* temple? This would have to be another thing she would ask him. But not any time soon. She did not want to risk angering him again. She never got answers from him when he was angry.

She cleared her mind of her husband. No good would come from dwelling on him.

Let Creation talk to her. The water told of where it had been but also where it was to go. The mountain spoke also of flowing, though much, much slower. So slow Adrastea would never have noticed, had it not told her.

While Creation sang to her about the patterns it followed, she sensed something else, not of a pattern. Somewhere someone—for it was a someone and not a something—called her.

She sorted through the many Lines until she found one full of anguish and grief. Her own heart ached in sympathy.

Was there anything she could do? Adrastea laid her hand on the Line and closed her eyes.

Shift.

Morning couldn't come soon enough. Saraym, Duchess of Feown, laid a hand on the glass panes of her closed casement. She stared at the stars moving through the dark firmament. Every time she closed her eye, she'd relive again the horrors that General Miniver had visited upon her.

Sleep stole in only when she could not fight it off. She slumbered in fits and starts, only to be woken by her own screaming. Eventually, she dared not close her eyes. Would the horrors ever go away?

She sat in the window nook, more alone than she'd ever been in her life. She stared out at the navy-blue sky with its brittle stars. Her heart broke with the weight of it all.

"Oh, Grey Lady..." she murmured. "What do I do?" She laid her face against the coolness of the glass.

A glow filled the chamber behind her. She sat up in surprise.

The Grey Lady stood in the middle of the room, a glowing orb in her hands. "Your Grace?" She took a tentative step forward. Her country garb made her look more real, less... noble? It made her look more like a country woman named Adrastea, rather than the all-powerful Grey Lady.

Saraym hastily rose to her feet. She looked around, fearful the Dark One would appear. "I— I did not mean to call you." She fiddled with her hands. "Prayer has become too much of a habit. It's just..." the tears of abandonment, rage and sorrow filled her soul and spilled out her eyes. "I cannot sleep." The despair that filled her was so strong, she was sure the Grey Lady could feel it. "Something so simple, that comes to even the tiniest baby. I cannot sleep."

The Grey Lady—Adrastea—laid the globe aside. She came to Saraym and took her hands. "I'm sure the Light hears your prayers."

But Saraym shook her head. "If She did, why hasn't She answered them?" A rage grew within her. "I spent years praying to the Light. I thought She answered them in the subtlest of ways. Even my priests and priestesses ensured me that She listened." She spat on the floor. "Even in the moment I lose my faith, my heart yearned to pray.

"And who succors me? The Dark God and his wife."

Adrastea gathered Saraym into her arms. "Does it matter who comes to your aid?"

Saraym's body shuddered. She gave over to her grief. Who could be a Duchess when all she wanted to be was a child.

Adrastea simply held her. A warmth spread from her hands through Saraym's back and into her heart. There was a knot in there, one so big, how could it all be contained in one little broken heart? She no longer had the strength to hold it together on her own. "Has the Light forsaken me?" Saraym cried, her voice high-pitched and childlike.

Adrastea shook her head. "I do not know." The knot loosened. "I might be able to ask..."

But Saraym shook her head. "I don't know if I want Her help anymore." But she wanted someone to help. No, she wanted someone to take her entire burden. She wanted to run away, to let someone else deal with the grief, the pain. Where was a god when she needed Her?

"Don't give up on Them." Another tendril of grief unraveled and evaporated.

"Why not? They have given up on me."

Adrastea sighed. "So, what do you want?"

Saraym clutched at Adrastea's blouse. "I simply wish to sleep." How she craved that blissful oblivion for an entire night.

Adrastea said nothing for a moment. "That's all?"

"What more is there? You healed my body. I am grateful, though I shouldn't be. Can you heal this pain in my heart?"

Even more of the knot unraveled. "For now. The Light hasn't forsaken you. He taught me broken hearts can be healed."

The anguish in her heart loosened. The anger and pain evaporated away. Peace flooded in.

She was free.

Raising a hand to stifle a yawn, Saraym relaxed. Adrastea released her and held her hands once more.

She looked Saraym in the eye. "Feeling better?"

She nodded. "Thank you." She glanced over to the window seat and its comfortable cushions. She had to sit down, then lay down. As she looked out the casement, she saw light touch the sky and the stars begin to fade. "Thank you." Dawn had arrived at last, as had sleep. Saraym shoved away the little niggle of guilt over her changing allegiances.

Anything for sleep right now.

Chapter 9

Jonathan should have listened to the angels. His regret grew as the boils on his skin had increased. For the past few days Jonathan had been unable to sleep, his joints ached so. Now he'd lost feeling in his fingers. A tight little niggle in his heart whispered that it might be leprosy.

And it served him right, for hesitating when angels commanded.

Digging through the box under his modest bed, he brought out the last of his bandages and wrapped his hands tighter. His feet he did not dare wrap anymore, lest they not fit in his shoes.

Thus prepared, he made his way to the secret door in the library of Pennexter House.

He pulled the library bellpull in code: three rings, two, one. Then he retreated to the hidden corridor and waited for his sister to arrive.

But Dessie never came. Instead, a footman, too old for war and looking like he'd been newly wakened, knocked on the door.

Jonathan peeked out.

"Forgive me," the footman offered. "Lady Pen is indisposed and unable to meet with you."

Indisposed? "What do you mean?"

The footman yawned and scratched at his unruly hair. "She does not wake up for several hours yet."

Jonathan sighed. At least someone got some sleep. He licked his dry lips. "Tell me, is it safe outside?" He scratched at his face. Flakes of skin sloughed off.

The footman shuddered and stepped back. "Yes. Thought I doubt there will be too many out at this hour."

It was safe to leave the house. "Please inform my sister that I shall be going out. I have a pressing matter. I.. I don't know when I shall return."

The footman hesitated then offered, "Would you like an escort, sir?"

Jonathan shook his head. "I shall be fine."

"Very good, sir," replied the footman, not bothering to hide his relief. Was it the going out, or the accompanying of a clearly ill priest that discomfited him the most?

Thus, Jonathan departed the house pre-dawn to make his way to the palace and hopefully, towards forgiveness from the Light.

Jonathan Pennexter hauled his creaky old body through the corridors of the ducal palace. His feet burned terribly despite their wrappings. As long as they hurt, then he could pretend that it wasn't leprosy but merely broken boils that ailed him. He'd save his panic for the numbness.

He studied his hands. He'd been cursed for his hesitation—he and the whole family. The angels had warned him. Would the Light lift the curse once he had delivered his message?

Jonathan had not spent much time in the palace. He preferred small groups to large crowds, the smaller the better. But as he walked the marbled corridors, he wondered where everyone had gone. An occasional lone courtier hurried along, staring at him but keeping her distance. The few servants, all female, likewise skirted around him, after pointing him in the correct direction.

Their avoidance made him squirm. Why had He chosen him as His prophet? Wasn't it enough he was a priest? But if the news that his sister, Lady Pennexter shared was true, then few priests, Light or Dark, survived the Cithran's Purge.

It had been years since he'd walked through the palace. He remembered it as opulently decorated, as the home of the ruler of a rich and powerful duchy should be.

Now, nothing was left but stone-floored corridors, the occasional gaslight, burning as a bright patch in an otherwise dark hallway. Dawn had come outside but inside retained the gloom and stillness of the night.

After he reached a second floor, natural windows allowed in the brightness of the newly-risen sun, making him squint. Third floor and the fourth, the light growing even brighter.

He reached Her Grace's chamber. Fighting the knot of nerves in his stomach, he knocked politely.

"What?" came a startled woman's voice.

He entered.

The room had two deep windows, their curtains drawn back, letting in the morning sun. Cushions filled one window seat while the other remained bare. Otherwise, all furniture had been removed, save a plain table shoved up against a wall and an occupied chair in the middle of the room. A woman, dressed in country clothes and looking oddly familiar, rose from the chair. "Who are you?" she asked in a country accent.

He wondered the same thing. "I have come with a message for Her Grace."

While the woman's accent held a touch of country drawl, her voice rang with authority. "Don't wake her. She only just fell asleep."

Jonathan looked again at the window ledge full of pillows. Among them lay a woman, a blanket draped over her form. He didn't notice her before. She blended in quite well with the cushions there.

Jonathan wrung his hands. "I must speak with her."

The country woman planted her fists on her hips. "Well, you're going to have to wait." She fixed him with a firm stare.

Why did other people never let one do what one had to do? They had to contravene. "I think I come with a higher authority than you."

The country woman tilted her head to the side. A smug smile played her lips. His sister used the same expression when she knew a secret he did not and was about to rub it in his face. "I doubt it."

"I am a priest of the Light. I bring a message of prophecy, as revealed to me by His angels."

The country woman straightened, the smugness replaced with surprise but not fear and certainly not doubt. Could it be she believed him?

Then she frowned. "Well, you're too late. Why weren't you here yesterday?"

He opened his mouth, but she rushed on.

"And why weren't you here the day before that. Or the day before that? And where were you when the Cithrans were here, torturing and raping and killing?"

He knew exactly where he had been—cowering in fear behind stone walls. But then, if he had not been hidden, he would have died like the rest. No. His true cowardice lay in that he was the last of priests, preserved to save a family, or a nation, and he had hesitated after being called by the

Light. He looked at his painful hands and clenched them. The country woman was right. He should have been here days ago.

She wasn't finished. "Do you have any idea what she's gone through?"

Jonathan shuddered. "I know everything that happened to her. It was shown me in a vision."

The woman lost some of the wind from her sails. "Did They really show you that? I mean, everything?"

Another chill of dread ran up his spine. It had been so real it could have been his own memories. "I am not here to discuss the vision. I am here to bring her a message. The sooner I deliver it and leave, the better." He started to the window.

The country woman blocked his way. "She's had a hard night. Let her sleep."

"Just let me do my job," he snapped.

"Why? What's so important in your message you must disturb her?"

Jonathan didn't want to push past her. She would create trouble if he tried. "That is not your business."

She stood her ground. "If you won't tell me why it's so important, then it's not that important. You can wait until she wakes up."

Jonathan sighed in frustration. "Just let me tell her. Then she can go back to sleep."

"If it's not disturbing enough to keep her from returning to sleep, then it's not important enough to wake her with."

Jonathan tried to sidestep her. She countered. He tried again and again, found his way blocked. "Oh, step aside!"

"No." The Deeper Power flared within her.

Jonathan swallowed and stepped back. "Who are you?" he whispered. The angels had told him not to delay. He'd disobeyed.

Had the Dark beaten him here? His heart thumped. Never again would he disobey the Light, even a little bit.

The country woman controlled her temper. She showed genuine concern about waking the sleeping Duchess. "I am a Healer." She licked her lips and toed the floor, her hands tucking into the back folds of her skirt. "I've been caring for Saraym. They didn't treat her well in the cellars."

Jonathan's own memory flashed back to the vision he'd seen. Yes, a healer was exactly what Her Grace needed.

Meanwhile, what to do about this country woman? She had drawn on the Deeper Power, most likely for defense? That she had talent was clear. Who that talent served was still in question. And if the sheer amount of Power she'd drawn on was any indication, Jonathan Pennexter had no desire to be seen as an enemy. "So, if you're a healer, what healing have you performed?"

The woman relaxed. "She suffered some pretty bad—" she cleared her throat. "There are some things that don't get discussed in front of men." She'd released much of the Power but not all. "I couldn't do anything about her eye."

Jonathan nodded. Keep her talking and she might not ask questions. Jonathan had seen the whole of Her Grace's sufferings in the angels' vision.

"What did you do? Poultices, stitches?"

She shook her head. "No." Holding out her hands before her, she studied them. "I've got a talent for healing others with the Deeper Power."

Jonathan had never heard of this before. The scholar in him sat up in interest. "Really? How do you do it?"

She shrugged. "I just... ask the flesh to return to how it used to be, and it complies."

He had to sit down. He groped back to the nearest chair. "That's impossible!"

The woman shrugged. "I wouldn't know. Impossible's a word I've stopped using."

He trembled at the thought of using the Deeper Power to heal. There were stories of Dark Priests who commanded the elements of Creation to do their selfish bidding. No doubt the Light Priests of sufficient talent could do the same, were they not bound to subject their wills to the Light; one did not use the Deeper Power for one's own ends.

But to heal? Miracles of healing often came after sufficient prayer, according to the Will of the Light. But to heal of one's own will? While healing was a noble act, to do so without sanction of the Light had to be a misuse of the talent. Those who served the Light had to be objective in their use of the Deeper Power. Subjectiveness was of the Dark. "Why did you heal her?"

The woman resumed her seat. "She asked me." She licked her lips. "Nobody else helped her, so I did." She turned away.

"Who sent you here?"

The question puzzled her. "I came of my own accord."

"And she let you in?"

"She called for me and I came." Her voice rose at the end, making it sound almost like a question, or that she doubted her own words.

Jonathan frowned. "How did she know about you?"

The country woman didn't answer for a moment. She scratched her head, looking sheepish. "Ah, that would be my husband's fault. He insisted I come meet Saraym."

That was the second time she used Her Grace's given name. Had this country lass no manners? What would Her Grace say if she knew? Clearly this was the first time the country woman had been to Feown. When he asked her, she confirmed it.

"The first time I saw Feown was about a month or two ago... I think. A lot has happened since then. I'm a little shaky on time of late."

"Who's your husband?"

The woman stiffened. "It's best you not know."

Jonathan's heart hammered. "He's not Cithran, is he?"

"Oh no." Then, possibly to cover her discomfort and to lead him away from what was clearly an unpleasant subject, she said, "I don't know who you are."

He studied her for a moment, she now uptight and guarded. "I am Jonathan Pennexter, scholar and Priest of the Light. I daresay one of the few remaining priests in Feown, or you would not see me here."

"What?" Her voice squeaked. "Are all the rest of them dead?"

Jonathan nodded. "The Cithrans saw to that. I survived."

She looked genuinely concerned.

"I serve the Light," even when it's difficult and He asks one to do things one does not want to do. "Who are you and who do you serve?"

"Oh." She blushed. "My name is Adrastea Healer, journeyman."

"Adrastea?" He straightened up. "My mother's name was Adrastea." And so was his sister Dassie, Lady Pen and a great-niece. "It's a family name." A city name, a noble name. "I'm surprised they use it in the country. Where are you from?"

Her forehead wrinkled in puzzlement. "Sacred Spring. It's near Crossroads, on the way to the Great Western Pass."

Jonathan could not recall it. Must be a piddling little nowhere village. "How did you end up here?"

"I told you: my husband brought me. And before you ask, I don't know where he is, nor do I care." She said it with such force that Jonathan didn't press the matter. But he kept that question tucked into the back of his mind. What sort of man is her husband that she would be ashamed of him?

That she had a husband was the biggest sign that if she served any god, it was the Dark. Light priests never married, having dedicated their lives to the Light.

His eyes looked over to the Duchess, sleeping peacefully in the morning light. "Please let me deliver my message. It is important."

Her eyes narrowed. "If I let you wake her, and you deliver your message, will you go away?"

"Gladly." Didn't mean that he would. He had a nasty feeling that the Light had dragged him into a bigger mess than he would ever have willingly entered into by choice. Even if he wanted an end to the matter after delivering his message, he felt that this was only the beginning.

The vision warned that the Duchess had reached the extent of her endurance and could give out at any time.

Or give in. Jonathan studied Adrastea Healer even closer, trying to get a sense of her from the Deeper Power she clung to. He drew on his own and tested her boundaries.

"Stop that," she warned.

He inhaled in surprise.

She had to be of the Dark. If she was of the Light, then the He would have given the vision to her to deliver. That she prevented him from delivering it at all was another strong indicator that she was, at best, not serving the Light. Perhaps it was best to come right out and ask, "Are you a Dark Priestess?"

Adrastea wrapped her arms around her. "I don't know how to answer that. I'm not a priestess of any sort." Then she amended her statement. "Well, I was apprenticed to Mira—our priestess—a few months ago but then she was killed."

Who killed the priestess? Had the Purge reached to the backwaters? He restated his question. "Who do you serve? The Light or the Dark? You must serve one or the other. Those with talent are never allowed to sit on fences."

She frowned. "No, we are not." Her eyes narrowed again. "Why has the Light compelled you so?"

"The salvation of Feown."

"And it can't wait until she's had some sleep?"

Jonathan's feet hurt. "There are things more important than sleep."

"Not this time. Can't you just give her one good night of sleep?"

He wrinkled his nose. "It's daytime."

"That doesn't matter! She's got to have some sleep. She's only human. Nobody has to be asked to endure what she's endured."

Jonathan felt he was getting nowhere. "The Light did. Now, I must deliver my message."

A new voice spoke. "What message?" Her Grace groaned then pushed her tired self to her elbows. She squinted against the light coming through the window, let her bleary one-eyed gaze linger on Adrastea for a moment before settling it on Jonathan. "Who the hell are you?"

He genuflected before her, ignoring his knees' complaints.

Adrastea hastened to her side. "I'm so sorry. I tried to stop him waking you."

He kept his head bent, though Adrastea's moving to the Duchess' side concerned him. "I am Jonathan Pennexter."

Her Grace squinted at him. "Lady Pen's brother. I know you now. How did you survive?"

He ignored her question. "I bring you a message from the Light."

"I don't want to hear it," Her Grace said. "I'm not interested."

His head shot up. "What?"

The Duchess stared at him with blood-shot eyes. "I want nothing more to do with the Light."

Jonathan's heart sank. He was too late. The Light had warned him. Why didn't he act sooner?

What did this mean for the significance of his message? What of his hands? He clenched them. Was numbness creeping in already? "But still, I must deliver my message."

Her Grace grasped Adrastea's arm tightly. "I don't want to hear it. Go away, priest."

His knees cried out for him to stand or lie down or move into some other position than where he was. He ignored them. "Not until I deliver my message." He would stay there until he died, for if he left, death was almost guaranteed.

Adrastea rolled her eyes. "Are you always this stubborn?"

Stubborn. It was not a word he could remember being applied to him, especially of late. "All I know is that if I don't deliver my message, bad things will happen to me."

That caught the interest of the two women. Her Grace leaned

forward. "What sort of bad things?" Did she wish him to suffer?

"Wait." Adrastea laid a hand on Her Grace's arm. "You're awake. You might as well hear what he has to say."

Jonathan looked at Country Adrastea. She wanted to hear the message. Why?

Her Grace's wrath turned to the woman at her side. "I don't care who you are, you don't dictate to me."

Adrastea withdrew her hand, looking hurt.

The Duchess didn't notice or care. "Where was he when the Cithrans were torturing me in my own cellar? Where was he when they used my body again and again like I was a common whore? Where was he when I bruised and bled, and they laughed and mocked me? Where was he when I begged for death? If the Light truly cared about me, She would have sent him then with a sharp knife!" She inhaled sharply in anger. "Well, priest? Where were you?"

Here was the opportunity to deliver his message. "The Light has reason for all you have suffered. You were spared the knife for the Light wishes you, Saraym, to be the knife."

Her Grace folded her arms. Her eyes narrowed. "She wishes what?"

He drew a breath. "The Light allowed you to suffer to the edge of reason so that when the time came, you would act with sureness and swiftness, never wavering with doubt."

"I'm not doing the Light's bidding. She never came when I begged Her to come. Why should I dance to Her tune now?"

He repeated what the angels had told him. "You are to be the Hand of Justice, to destroy the Cithran nation." He drew a breath at this. He did not doubt the source of the message but why would the Light, a god of benevolence, wish the destruction of an entire nation?

Her Grace snorted most ungracefully. "A little late for that, old man. They're already dead."

Adrastea pressed her knuckles to her lips. "Only the army. The rest of them live."

Jonathan gave her another glance. Just how much did the country woman know? "And they will rise again to sweep forth across your land, bringing more death and destruction."

"If the Light wants them dead," Her Grace mocked, "Why doesn't She simply kill them Herself."

Jonathan said, "That is not how the Light works."

Saraym frowned. "If it was not the Light who delivered us from the Cithrans...?" She looked over to Adrastea with puzzlement. "Then who?"

A cold pit opened in Jonathan's stomach. Queasiness roiled about. He had been cast into something far greater than he ever could imagine. He sent up a silent prayer to the Light. *What have You gotten me into?*

Her Grace sat down on the window sill. "So, Deliverance was— was—"

"I'm sorry," said Adrastea.

Until now, Jonathan had assumed that the Light had caused it. Could it be the handiwork of the Dark? How? And why?

Too many questions and not enough answers.

She claimed she was but a country healer. Jonathan suspected Adrastea was far, far more than that. A priestess of the Dark? Most likely. But she looked Feowan.

Jonathan shuddered. The angels had not warned him of this. Deliver the message, they said. He would obey. "The Light desires you to be the knife that removes the Cithran nation from the world."

"What if I have no desire to do this?"

"There is an evilness driving the core of the Cithran Empire." He glanced at Adrastea whose face betrayed nothing. "If you do nothing now, they shall rebuild before you can recover. They will invade again. This time, there will be no Deliverance."

Adrastea bowed her head. Jonathan vowed to discover more about this strange woman.

Her Grace was not touched. "Feown is weak, old man. Do not think that the Avelians will not take advantage of my weakened position and invade. That is my bigger worry now. It has only been the strength of my army which has kept them in check all these years."

"Your army will be strong again."

Her Grace snorted. "There are not enough men to breed enough sons. Even if there were, there is not enough time to raise them to fight."

Jonathan sighed inwardly. He thought a woman who inherited her position would be above such limited thinking. His sister would certainly agree. Nobody told Dassie Pennexter what to do, or rather, what she couldn't do. The financial empire the Pennexters ruled certainly did not suffer under her leadership. Lady Pennexter was strong, like their father, their grandfather, their great-grandmother had been. Jonathan remembered her, also another Adrastea. She ruled with a fist as iron as the color of her hair.

And then he understood. What his family had been doing for generations to strengthen their family is exactly what the Light had proposed for Feown. Is this why they sent him?

Too late now to back out.

Might as well get on with it. "So, build an army of women."

Saraym blinked. "Women? Women can't fight."

Adrastea begged to differ. "They fought at Sacred Spring. You fought in the cellars."

"I was angry."

Adrastea spread her hand to the window. "So are they. They're not fighting for money, or even their country. They're fighting for their families."

Jonathan looked sideways at her. The country healer Dark priestess was on his side now? "The world is changing. Lead that change and you will survive. Crawl into a corner and you will surely die."

She sniffed. "You say that as if death was a bad thing."

The words popped into his head—surely not from his own mind. He uttered them before he realized what he was saying. "Only to those who have reason to fear death."

"I don't." Saraym waved a hand dismissively. "I am tired. Leave me, both of you. I have much to think about."

Jonathan bowed, his relief at a message delivered easing his heart. "As you wish."

But Country Adrastea hesitated. "Are you sure you'll be all right?"

The Duchess gave her a pointed look. "Nothing a bit of sleep can't fix."

Chapter 10

Nyabern, the Cithran capital, had changed since Mor-Lath had been there last. How many decades had it been since he walked here? He stood in a narrow street in the Manufacturing Quarter. The wood framed buildings with stuccoed walls and slate-tiled roofs towered over the narrow streets, giving the impression of a warren teeming with rodents. The sewers were enclosed and hidden from view, but the stench did not let one forget their presence, rising up through grates in the middle of paved streets. It mingled with the ever-present smell of smoke and human sweat. If the breeze changed, the rot of the river did not let itself be forgotten. How could mortals live in such squalor? No Tredan city would ever let itself fall this far.

Industry had not been kind to the sprawling metropolis, for a pall of smog darkened the skies. The wastes of Progress spoiled the river that flowed through the city and out to the eastern ocean. No wonder he preferred the western lands.

But what he wanted was here, so here he came. The paved streets of the city twisted every which way, thus betraying their country track origins. Carts and horses and humans pushed and shoved as if there was not enough room for them all.

On every street corner stood wrought-iron gas lamps, some of which were kept lit even during the day, so dark and close were the buildings. There were doors aplenty along the street front but no windows until the second or third story. These were kept tightly closed, for the quality of the air outside was not much better than inside.

Here in the poorer quarters of the city, the narrowness of the streets pressed the population close together. They pushed and elbowed their way through, heedless of whom they hurt. Instead of taking umbrage, the bruised masses passed the favor forward to the next poor person who got in their way. Mor-Lath let himself be buffeted about, for the people ignored each other and him. It was the only way they could achieve any form of privacy in such a crush of humanity.

Such unordered closeness. While it provided the perfect setting for those whose activities were best kept clandestine, he found it oppressive and annoying. He pulled Paedep's soul out of his pocket. "You chose a pretty miserable place to live."

Paedep cringed. He'd been a junior priest of the One Faith, young and not very *au fait*. "It's not my fault. Not everyone lives well."

Mor-Lath delved into the soul's memories of the place. "No but if one has the wit to stay a step ahead, one can improve one's lot. You should have."

The soul had thought he'd done just that by joining the local barracks as a spiritual advisor. He knew better now. Besides being fed every day, not one thing had improved. So far, death itself had not been much of an improvement either, except one no longer needed to eat or sleep.

But the soul still yearned. Mor-Lath ignored Paedep's longing for a kind word and stuffed it back into his pocket with all the other souls. "Let's go have a look at your parish."

Mor-Lath found the pathetic little chapel down an alley and across a square with a fountain green with slime. Unlike the large cathedrals of the well-to-do, this was a small stone building with no glass windows, only slits towards the peaked roof to allow in some light.

Mor-Lath pulled up the hood of his cloak to blend with the others in the square. He could sense the darkness in their souls, put there by a society and a faith that favored the rich who could pay to lighten their sins. The rich were burdened by pride while the poor were burdened by bitterness and anger. Mor-Lath cared only because it meant more souls from which he could draw strength.

He slipped in the open wooden doors into the darkness within. The heat of day was no less in here than it was on the streets, but the stench of mankind was not as strong. Instead, the old smell of wood and dust resided here. Unlike the temples of Light and Dark in Feown, there were no altars. A pulpit faced outward, flanked by two unlit candles. Two pews stood in the front, for those who'd paid their exorbitant tithes and gained their Rest. The rest of the congregation had to stand. Or, if one's soul was so weighed down with sin that it would be cheaper to pay the non-attendance fines, then one could stay at home and sit on one's own comfortable chair.

No worshippers or criminals occupied the chapel, leaving it quite empty. Behind the lectern was a door leading to the office of the parish priest. He was more facilitator than shepherd, turning a blind eye away and an open palm toward those who used the parish chapel for activities other than worship.

Mor-Lath knew how the priest had treated the soul in Mor-Lath's pocket. To that, he objected. This reminded the god of how another apprentice had been treated by a selfish master once long ago. He buried that ancient memory back where it belonged and stepped through the door without knocking.

The office was unoccupied. It was a small, dusty room, the only light coming through a paned window high in the wall. Had the window ever been washed? It's coating of dust clouded it to a dull translucency. The sun might attempt to shine in of a morning but would have to be strong to fight the clandestiness of the room. It sported little furniture, namely a dark wooden desk, with a large, comfortable chair on one side and two small, uncomfortable wooden stools on the other—presumably for guests.

The walls held old pictures of irrelevant subjects, framed by once-elegant carved frames. Low bookshelves lined the room under the pictures, two shelves high but not as full of books as bookshelves usually are. One particular bookshelf under a largeish picture had a notable absence of dust on top of it. There was the hidden door. Beyond that were two other men, keeping each other occupied with a bottle of something alcoholic. With a brief word from him via the Deeper Power, they both sank down into sleep.

The entrance and the hidden door were not the only ones in the room. In the corner stood a smaller door, suitable more for a child than an adult. One could almost not see it, so well-designed to fit into the panel work it was. It was the door to a water closet, occupied by the person he sought. The embarrassment of being discovered would further discomfit the priest. Discomfiture served to activate the mind, bringing thoughts and secrets to the fore. While a mortal lived, their thoughts belonged to them alone. Only the Light had the authority to know them fully. But once dead, the thoughts and memories of the soul were no longer exclusive. Anyone with the power to hold a soul could see those thoughts. The Light, of course, could do it. Tanat, as judger of the dead, could do it. Mor-Lath could do it. Maybe Adrastea could as well. He saw no need to tell her that.

Mor-Lath arranged himself in the cushioned chair, feet propped up on the desk in a most disrespectful manner. He waited while the man on the other side of the small door finished urinating.

His name was Tammas, not that Mor-Lath cared much. He'd followed the trail of similar men, each one holding a secret connecting him to another. Each one a step closer to the answers Mor-Lath sought.

The small door opened inward and out came Tammas. He was a tall man, proportionately built, dressed in the usual somber robes of the One Faith. A white fringe of hair decorated his uncovered head. He had the large nose typical of the Cithran people and his eyes had bags underneath them. Tammas had to crouch to fit through the little door.

When he straightened, he jumped in surprise to see someone else in his chair. "By Holy, who the hell are you?"

Mor-Lath didn't move. "'The hell' indeed. By your reckoning, I am the devil."

Tammas tucked his arms into his sleeves. He kept knives there, and a small firearm strapped to his waist. It was a dangerous profession, dealing in other people's secrets. Wariness took place of surprise in the priest. "I meant, what are you called?"

"My name is Mor-Lath."

Tammas said nothing but waited for him to get down to his business.

"I am the God of the Dark." Mor-Lath gave Tammas a look, daring him to deny it.

"The God of the Dark is a foreign myth." Tammas frowned at Mor-Lath's boots still on the desk. "Kindly put your feet down."

Mor-Lath continued with the same even tone of voice. "I will do as I please, for I am who I say I am. I know you serve me."

Tammas objected. "I serve the True Faith."

"Unless you can prove otherwise, there is only one Dark God in this Creation. Whoever your True Faith is, it is not he."

Tammas let out a breath of impatience. "I don't care who you are, but I am not in the mood to discuss trite points of blasphemy. Tell me your business—buying or selling—then get on your way."

"Taking."

Tammas frowned. "Taking what?"

"Everything."

Tammas grinned an ugly grimace. "You get nothing from me." He didn't bother to hide the knives but unsheathed them. "There are five other priests on the other side of that door. You can't abduct me, nor can you torture me here without them hearing. You could kill me, but you can't get secrets out of a dead man."

The god yawned. "There are only two drunken priests on the other side of your secret door, fast asleep. And yes, I can get secrets from a dead man."

Mor-Lath rose and let his awful glory radiate. Tammas inhaled and took an involuntary step back. His grip weakened on the knives.

Mor-Lath pressed forward. "I am the God of the Dark. You will tell me of the True Faith's search for the Dark's own Bride."

Tammas' knees weakened before his panic ebbed and he drew himself straight. "The Bride? The foreign sorceress?" His voice wavered.

"You have knowledge of her. I want to know how you came by it. Have you any missives from your superiors, obscure books of prophecy, ancient writings?"

The priest's heart thrummed harder. A vein in his forehead pulsed. "I know of nothing."

"Sure you do. And now those secrets will belong to me." He stretched forth his hand and ended Tammas' life, like he had done the others.

Tammas shrieked at the sudden rending of his soul from his body. The body slumped to the floor. He howled a long denial of his death while Mor-Lath settled back into the chair at the desk.

Setting the soul before him, he removed all the memories that had been foremost in Tammas' mind. Yes, there were missives, filed away with other non-important papers in the drawers of the desk. Mor-Lath drew them open and found what he sought. It was not like the search for the "Bride" was any great secret among the priests. As far as Tammas and any of the others knew, "Bride" was simply a title, the high priestess of the foreign blasphemy and sworn enemy of the True Faith. They had not her name, nor knew where to find her. There were prophecies and clues to identify her should they encounter her. Mor-Lath knew all this, for the previous priests were all forthcoming.

The Cithrans had collected the same prophecies that had led him to find Adrastea in the first place. Unlike the Cithrans, he could recognize the resonance of her soul once he found her.

But what he hadn't known before his search is that while the Cithrans would kill any and all "foreign priests", the Bride they wanted alive. What for?

"Anything else?" he demanded. The search frustrated him.

Tammas denied there being anything else. Mor-Lath believed him.

"Who is your superior? Who sent this letter to you?"

Tammas gave up a name, whereas Mor-Lath stuffed the soul into his pocket.

Unlike the other leads, the name Tammas gave Mor-Lath was one of status and influence.

He felt like an idiot. He'd spent an entire day killing men and torturing their souls, when he could have saved himself some time and went straight to the top. He dragged all the souls out of his pocket. "You've all wasted my time." He slammed his fist on the desk, causing the souls to howl.

"Mor-Lath" came a woman's voice in front of him. "You will give me those souls."

Mor-Lath looked up with a frown. "Go away, Tanat. I'm busy."

Tanat, Judger of the Dead, put her hands on the desk and leaned over. She straightened a ledger book lying at a slight angle. "You've disrupted the balance too much already. Personally, I'd love to see you fall, for all the trouble you've caused me this past week—"

"Oh, your precious balance," Mor-Lath spat. Then he deliberately skewed the book again.

"Stop it." She moved the book back. Mor-Lath stuck out his hand to annoy her further, but she slammed her palm on the book. It disappeared as she lifted her hand. "Give those souls to me. They are not yet yours."

Mor-Lath stuffed the souls back into his pocket. "They will be soon enough."

She shook her head. "Not all."

He rose from the chair. "I know this people. They've twisted truth to serve themselves and have sent the whole of their people spiraling downward. They are dark and evil. You know it, I know it. Give up on the formality already."

Tanat snorted and folded her hands. "You know it doesn't work like that. Some of their souls can be saved. Not all have forsaken goodness. Alas, for those whose souls weigh them in your favor."

She shook a finger at him. "You are neglecting your duties, God of the Dark. Once they're dead, who know how long it will be before you shrive them?"

Mor-Lath said nothing. He turned his gaze from the depths she called eyes.

With a chuckle, she leaned over the desk further, until she could cup her chin in her hands. "You know how far you've gone," she vaunted. "You'd love to kill them all, but you can't."

He did not meet her gaze. "I killed a half million. I could kill the rest."

She straightened, shaking her head. "No, you couldn't, and you know it. Oh, you could go about killing them one by one but each one is the drop in the balanced bucket. You know how close you are to tipping it.

"Tip the bucket, and you lose, long before the final battle."

"Why should you care?" he snarled. "Throw your balance off so much you'll never achieve equilibrium again?"

Her smile faded. "I doubt it."

Mor-Lath stepped over Tammas' body and walked around the desk. He raised a finger at Tanat. "You're annoyed with me because of the half million."

"Do you realize how much work that's caused me?"

He nodded cheerfully.

Tanat folded her arms. "Your little stunt has tilted the balance far out of your favor, possibly more than Adrastea is worth."

"You don't know how valuable she is to me."

Tanat sniffed. "You don't know how valuable she is to you. You know, there are easier ways of becoming immortal."

Mor-Lath turned away. "I don't have time."

"That's your problem."

He shrugged. "Yours too."

"Give me the souls." She held out her hand as if wearied.

He handed them over. She was more than capable of taking them from him by force. As she seemed rather irritated at the moment, he didn't want to risk her wrath. She was not a mashiah; she could not kill him. But she could cause him a great deal of pain.

He returned to the dead man's chair while she sorted through the souls. Tammas' soul she tossed back to Mor-Lath, it flapping like a handkerchief. "He's yours. Have fun purging his evil."

Mor-Lath snatched the soul out of the air and deliberately did not thank her.

She took her time weighing the souls, for many of them were old and had accomplished many deeds. Mor-Lath exhaled in impatience several times but all that earned him was a glare. She did this to annoy him. She could judge a soul in a blink, should she so choose.

When she was finished, she had claimed only one for the Light. "You know, there is a way to correct the imbalance."

He knew. "I won't do it."

"Why must you continue to neglect your province?"

He snorted in mockery. "What? And leave myself weaker than I am now?"

She pursed her lips. "Suit yourself. I will not miss you when you are gone."

"Yeah, whatever. Don't you have some other souls to collect?"

She pointed a finger at him. "I know this was your fault. I'm not going to forget this. The Light will curse your name, for leaving so many ghosts to walk the earth."

He turned a shudder into a shrug. Yes, the creation of so many dead all at once, as well as the natural death rate of humanity had left plenty of unjudged souls to walk the earth. Unclaimed ghosts disrupted the web of Deeper Power. If there was anything to regret, it was the creation of so many ghosts. That could interfere with his and Adrastea's path.

But there had been no other way—not one that would ensure Adrastea was ready before the final battle. His own path had taken far too long. He'd had no choice.

"I've got work to do," he declared, before Tanat could get in another word. She always had to have the last word.

He left without saying goodbye. No doubt Tanat would bring back the ledger and set it to rights on the desk, centered properly. For someone who liked order, she had left him rather off-balance.

⁂

Jonathan fled Her Grace's presence. He'd delivered his message.

Also, the presence of Country Adrastea discomfited him. The more he thought on it, the more he believed she was of the Dark.

He had nearly escaped the deserted corridors of the palace when he ran into a young noblewoman. Their impact knocked them both back. "Sorry." His hands and feet hurt at the sudden stop. He'd done as He asked. When would the Light heal him?

"Oh, I beg your pardon," she exclaimed as she stumbled to the wall.

She was a young thing, handsome in her own way. She looked like a Yustibar, a noble family closely allied with the Duchess. The Duke's mother had been a cousin to the Yustibars.

She grasped him by the sleeve. "Wait." Her voice made her sound younger than she appeared. "You're a priest!"

He was not acquainted with the young lady in question. At least she recognized his robes. What did she think of his boil-ridden face?

She looked back down the hallway from whence he came. "You've been to see her, haven't you?" She did not waste time on pleasantries. "You must come to the court."

Before the fall of Feown, Saraym held a glorious court of nobles selected neither for their titles nor their riches but for their strength of mind and ability to rule. As her court, they assisted Her Grace in governing Feown.

After the fall, there weren't many of them left. The Cithrans killed those of high rank, no questions asked. The middle and lower ranks might have survived, if they capitulated their power and loyalty to the invaders.

Panic teased at his guts. "I can't." He backed away.

"You must." Her quick little footsteps made her skirts rustle. She reached out for him.

"Somebody," she called out. "I need help!"

Jonathan ran. His bandaged hands lifted the hem of his priest robes. He dashed down the hall.

The lady gave pursuit, her own skirts bunched in her hands.

He might have escaped, had he not run into a pair of liveried women, of the burly washerwomen type. Their strength and bulk must have recommended their elevation to palace guards.

"Stop him," the young lady called to the guards.

He couldn't outrun them; they caught him with ease.

The guards followed the young lady, dragging Jonathan behind them, to the doors of what was once the council room. The precedent office was empty of secretary and the desk. No longer did footmen stand outside the door to open them nor to announce the guests. The young lady knocked on the door before opening it herself. She held it open while the burly guards escorted him in.

Chairs and settees and smaller tables filled the room, more like a lady's salon than a council room.

As he expected, there was no one but a bunch of women present. They sat in clusters of three or four, their heads close together. There was about two dozen, all dressed in the dark clothes of mourning, with grey or black dominant. Several of them stood when he entered the room, the better to sate their curiosity. He recognized several high-ranking ladies as having served the previous court. How had they survived? Others turned away and lowered mourning veils over their faces.

No doubt the others, of lower nobility, would never have been invited, had Feown not fallen. As for the modest ladies, he couldn't say. He didn't recognize them.

The young lady who captured him seemed to have forgotten any sort of protocol. "Look what I found roaming the halls of the palace. A priest!"

An exclamation rose from those gathered. Even the veiled ladies turned at this.

Jonathan wanted to retreat from their gaze. He was here as nothing more than a curiosity. But the guards had not relinquished his arms. At least they let him stand on his own two painful feet.

He recognized Lady Jeratigue, possibly the highest-ranking lady here. She and his sister Lady Pennexter occasionally paid visit to one another. She came forward, her eyes shrewd and sharp. "How did you survive the Purge?"

Jonathan shrugged best he could. "Same way you did. When the Cithrans were killing our people, I tried not to be where they were."

He watched her as closely as she watched him. She was an older lady, austere and firm, though never as bitter as Lady Pen. One respected Lady Jeratigue. His young lady—he was certain she was a Yustibar—moved next to Lady Jeratigue.

Lady Jeratigue studied him well. "I know you. You're Jonathan Pennexter, Lady Pennexter's priest brother."

"The same." He attempted a small bow, as much as permitted. With a motion of her head, the guards dropped his arms. The other women, especially the unveiled ones, drew closer. No way he could escape now.

"The palace is forbidden to men," Lady Jeratigue. "How did you get in?"

"The Light provides a way for His servants." He had not heard anything about the palace being forbidden to men. He had walked right through its unguarded front doors. Didn't Her Grace fear looters? Then again, there was nothing left to loot.

Lady Jeratigue gave it to him straight. "I don't believe in the Light anymore." Lady Yustibar dropped her gaze but said nothing.

Did she believe in the Dark? Had the whole court turned their face from the Light? Jonathan didn't have time for this. "Your belief or lack thereof does not mean the Light does not exist. It is in His name I come to the palace today."

"Get to the point," Lady Jeratigue groaned, as if he were a wearisome child.

"As one of the few surviving priests, I was given a vision for the benefit of Her Grace. By the authority of the Light, I am compelled to deliver His words."

Lady Jeratigue sniffed. "How about you give me those words? I shall see them delivered to Her Grace."

A superior smile played his lips. "You are too late. I have already appraised her."

This caught everyone's attention. One of the ladies, a rather large lass who didn't wear a corset, strode up and jerked off her veil.

Only she was no lady. Jonathan swallowed in surprise. General Tropeter, head of the Feowan army, in a dress? General Tropeter was not a small man. His stomach had spread as his rank increased over the years. Jonathan doubted greatly whether he could defend himself adequately with a sword, should it come to that. "You've seen her?" the General demanded.

Speaking of defense, how did General Tropeter escape the Cithrans? If he had thwarted death, who else had?

"I thought the palace was forbidden to men," Jonathan murmured without dulling his point.

General Tropeter attempted to stick his thumbs in his belt, only to discover he had none. He tugged at his gown in frustration. "What Her Grace doesn't know will serve her better than her overwrought delicacies."

Jonathan's jaw dropped. By now, everyone had gathered around. Out of the corner of his eye, saw every single 'woman' in a veil was really a man. Some were the General's circle. Others, he didn't recognize. They gathered around General Tropeter to form what could have been an intimidating wall if they weren't all in women's clothing.

Something in Jonathan snapped. "'Overwrought delicacies'? Do you have *any* idea what she's been through?"

A lady Jonathan didn't know spat on the floor. "She should be thinking about her people. Not herself! You know what I suffered? I was dragged from my house into the street, stripped naked and beaten for nearly an hour." She balled her fists as her voice crescendoed. "How dare she sit up there day after day, moping about. She needs to think about somebody else for once."

Jonathan's eyes narrowed. "You stupid woman."

She took umbrage at that, her eyes widening, her mouth an Oh.

He balled up his fists, welcoming the pain. He deserved his punishment. The Light had tasked him, he balked and look what happened.

"You've suffered nothing compared to what she's been through." He shook in anger. Was it bad form to put his fist through a lady's face? "The Duchess was forced to watch her children's heads bashed against stone pillars. She watched her ladies-in-waiting raped and killed, then her husband also raped and killed. Then she was stripped down, dragged to the cellars, where she was beaten and tortured and mocked and raped for three weeks." He held up as many disease-ridden fingers and shook them in her face. He really wanted to shake her instead. "*Three weeks*! Nonstop. But did she complain? No. She stood her ground and defied General Miniver while you," and his gaze swept the room, "all of you, hid away like the cowards you are." He hung his head, for he was as guilty as they. "And when she stared him down, he plucked out her eye. I see you still have both of yours, madam."

The lady gasped and put her fingertips to her lips. "She's lost an eye?" she squeaked.

Didn't they know? "What? You haven't seen her?"

Lady Jeratigue took the news better than the others. "Few of us have seen her," she snapped. "She tolerates no company, driving out even the maids, takes little to eat. She has the most awful temper, should you attempt to press her."

Jonathan pointed an accusing finger at Lady Jeratigue. "But you've seen her."

"I saw her a few times after the morning of Deliverance."

"You know the extent of her injuries. Why have you told the others nothing?"

Lady Jeratigue drew in a steady breath. She didn't answer him, withstanding his accusing glare with coolness. "There is more at issue here than one woman. She has been allowed her time to grieve and to heal." She pointed a finger up towards Saraym's sanctuary. "There is still a duchy to be run. It was raped and beaten just as much as she was."

"She has been allowed...?" Now he got the lay of the land. Lady Jeratigue had shown ambition. She took a terrible situation, with everyone confused or hurt, and stepped forth as the voice of reason amid the chaos. She gave them leadership and focus.

And as long as Saraym wallowed by herself, with no support and no diversion, Lady Jeratigue had free reign. While one may wish to be alone during great sorrow, it is best they not remain so for long. It did things, strange things, to a person. They never healed right. They withdrew even more while their soul twisted in pain.

Lady Jeratigue knew this. Saraym may have wished to be alone and Lady Jeratigue encouraged this, in her opportunistic grab for power.

Was Adrastea her creature?

Another thought occurred to him. Was Lady Jeratigue Adrastea's creature?

Jonathan tucked these thoughts away for ponderance another time. He drew himself up. "I have said all I need to say to those who needed to hear it. Your duchess will return to you soon. She will have a plan. Heed it well. It could very well mean your own survival."

He stalked to the door without looking like he was fleeing, for that was what he wanted to do. He wanted to hitch up his robes and sprint out of there. The air felt too close.

He fought back the fear that he'd been too late. He dreaded that the Dark had gotten there first, a coup of one of the strongest nations of the Light.

"Wait!" Lady Jeratigue called after him. Before he could reach the door, it opened.

Her Grace, Saraym, Duchess of Feown entered. No guards, no attendants, not even Country Adrastea. She moved into the room, slowly, carefully. She wore a dark dress, clean and loosely laced. Her feet were bare. About her head she wore a white silk scarf that covered her missing eye. The other eye scanned the room, taking the measure of every person there.

The men hastily drew on their veils, but Her Grace gave out a snort of derision. General Tropeter let his veils slide to the floor, his eyes also casting down.

"Well, I see you all found a lovely new place to hide." She sniffed.

Lady Jeratigue came forward, genuflecting as was proper. Out of habit, she reached for Her Grace's hand to kiss it.

Saraym didn't offer it. "I see you've met the priest. Did he have much to say?"

Oh, how Jonathan wished he could escape. He backed away from the advancing duchess but not far enough that he would be able to skirt by. As far as he knew, she was still likely to bash his head in with a chair.

"Your Grace—" began Lady Jeratigue.

"What a coincidence that you are all here." Saraym's voice was low and dangerous. She might have been healed of her physical wounds but how was her hold on her temper? "Good." She continued her measured, stately pace into the room. "We have work to do."

Jonathan edged toward the door.

"Stay, priest."

Jonathan froze. "Yes, Your Grace." Why did he not run? He had delivered the Light's message. Having obeyed in the end, couldn't He have let Jonathan get back to his peace and quiet?

Even as he wished for it, he knew it was never meant to be.

Saraym moved carefully to the middle of the room. She selected a nice, soft chair and gently lowered her body down. No one else dared sit in her presence. "I have spoken to the Dark and the Light has spoken to me. I am not quite sure who to believe." She raised her voice. "Priest."

Jonathan froze. He folded his scabrous hands before him and gave her a little bow. "Your Grace?" So much for escape.

"I do believe you're the only person to offer any kind of solution to our current situation. Nobody else, not even the Dark, has come up with even the remotest whiff of a plan."

Jonathan swallowed. "I cannot claim credit."

Saraym's mouth twitched. "I am not going to believe it came from the Light."

Lady Jeratigue made a small noise. A few others squirmed.

Her words tightened in Jonathan's chest. He fought them. "I hope I may convince you some day."

"You may try, priest but do not let your missionary zeal get in the way of a good idea. Let us save Feown while there is still a Feown to save. I'm sure you'd agree it is much easier to save souls while they are still living."

Her attention turned from Jonathan, but he knew she was not done with him. Feeling rather sore, he made his way to an abandoned seat, closer to the door than to Her Grace. A few nervous eyes glanced his way at this obvious breech of protocol.

Saraym either didn't notice or didn't care. "General Tropeter. Good to see you're still alive. That color suits you, though the cut does not flatter your figure."

General Tropeter, fiddling with the veil in his fingers, gave a man's bow. "Yes, Your Grace."

She regarded his couture. "You are hereby ordered to continue dressing in that manner until I see fit to change your wardrobe."

A few members of the court made little noises. One of the younger ladies coughed to cover her laugh.

Jonathan's heart cringed. Surely Her Grace couldn't be so cruel as to punish General Tropeter with humiliation. Surely, he could not be completely at blame for surviving the Purge. Someone had to remain in command.

General Tropeter's face held a stony expression. "As you wish, Your Grace."

Saraym waved her hand dismissively. "You may dictate the nature of fashion for the other men here in this room, should you wish, General. I leave that in your capable hands."

The General inclined his head. Would he be merciful?

Jonathan looked at his own priest's robes. Other than a few minor pattern differences, the holy vestments of priests and priestesses did not differ. He only hoped General Tropeter would not see fit to place him in some frothy confection even the silliest of his nieces would not touch.

Saraym ignored the low rumblings of discontent and speculation. "I am hungry. It's going to be a long afternoon." She pointed her finger to young Lady Yustibar. "You. Head off to the kitchens and arrange something suitable to feed me and my war cabinet." She spread her arms to include the population of the room.

Lady Yustibar curtseyed. "Yes, Your Grace."

One of the older ladies—Jonathan didn't recognize her—gasped. "What?" she cried.

Saraym turned her one remaining eye to her. "Lady Bettane. As you saw fit to consult with others in my absence regarding the future of Feown, I believe you are willing to consult in my presence."

Jonathan watched Lady Yustibar take a surreptitious head count. At least she would obey, even if she considered such tasks beneath her.

Saraym noticed Lady Yustibar had not yet departed. "A moment," she said to her. "I have another task for you as well." Saraym looked about the room. "Is there anyone else still living, who you all believe should be here?"

The assembly looked about. People shook their heads, consulted with each other, then looked to Lady Jeratigue. "None," the Lady reported.

"I disagree," Saraym replied. "But I thank you for your opinion."

She beckoned Lady Yustibar over. "Order food. Then find a secretary, if any still exist. Otherwise, pen these yourself: send one letter to every major family, and any minor ones of good connexion. They are to immediately send the highest-ranking member here."

Lady Yustibar nodded her head. "Even if they are men?"

Saraym considered this. "Even so. But all men must come dressed in a lady's gown or they will be denied entrance."

A few people groaned at this. Otherwise, they kept their opinions to themselves.

"Replies are expected." Saraym looked Lady Yustibar up and down. "I do hope you can find a secretary. I don't want this messed up."

Lady Yustibar's young cheeks burned in embarrassment. But she tendered her curtsey. "Yes, Your Grace."

Saraym waved her away. "That will do. And next time, bow. It's more dignified."

With Lady Yustibar making her relieved exit, Saraym turned to the business at hand. "I'm glad all of you could make it today. We have some important business."

A few people squirmed. Saraym waved her hand. "You all may as well sit. This will take a while. Hmm," she mused to herself. "I should have told everyone else to bring a chair. I don't know if we'll have enough."

Jonathan volunteered. "I am happy to vacate mine, if you don't require me anymore, Your Grace."

"Oh, no. This was your idea." He wasn't getting away that easy. "You're going to help us form it."

General Tropeter had found a seat rather close to Saraym. "You keep speaking of this idea, Your Grace."

"I do indeed. As you know, Cithra has been dealt a severe blow. Now, I believe, is the best time to strike back."

"But our army was slaughtered. We lost more than half our men. If we strike Cithra now, we'll leave Feown completely defenseless."

Saraym considered these figures. "Half our men, hmmm? A quarter of our population." She looked to Jonathan. "Well, then it's a good thing we have the other three-quarters of the population from which to pull."

The General sat up. "Your Grace?"

"It has been brought to my attention by the only priest left in the city that we have been neglecting an important part of Feown—an untapped resource, you could say."

All eyes turned to Jonathan. He squirmed. "I cannot claim credit—"

Saraym waved away his protest. "Therefore, I put this to you all. How many of you are angry that you have lost brothers and sons and husbands?"

Many women raised their hands, some quickly, some tentatively.

"How many of you wish to pay the Cithrans back?"

More hands rose.

"And there you are, General." Saraym pointed to all the women. "There is your new army."

He fiddled with his skirts. "Are you saying we recruit... *women* into the army?"

"Yes."

"But the army's always been men."

"I know. But you said we were low on men."

He swallowed. "But an army of women?"

"An army of angry women." Saraym leaned forward. "Tell me, General." Her voice dropped low and dangerous. "Can you think of anything scarier than an angry, bitter woman?"

Jonathan looked at the fierceness on Saraym's face. Knowing his sister, and knowing other women throughout his life, he could not think of anything more frightening.

Chapter 11

Mor-Lath regretted not paying more attention to Cithra earlier. Oh, he'd glanced in every once in a while, as necessary—for he was the God of the Dark—but on the whole, he only kept half-an-eye on them. They were not as fascinating as the peoples of the West. The Western peoples had drama and intrigues aplenty.

And the Cithrans?

They were a practical people, lacking in senses of humor and imagination. They had discovered the riches of the earth—all of which belonged to him—and they sought to increase their wealth. Technology and manufacturing boomed. As their factories belched black smoke into the skies, their production lines turned out useful good—steel, cotton, ceramics and more. Their philosophy: the better one conformed to society and did their part, the better for all.

Perhaps he should have kept a closer eye on them. At first, they had not been an overly religious people, as the people of the West had been. While he'd have loved to see his faith creep in and consume, the Cithrans tended to favor money as their god. That was how they measured their worth. Do your part, get paid your value.

Ah well. Their souls all came to him in the end.

As long as his demons reported the people dwindling and perishing in wickedness, he was content to let them go their own way. The more dark souls he could collect, the more powerful he became. The last time he paid any sort of close attention to Cithra, they had developed as a society. They had a working government of the people and by the people.

They had even developed some weak-handed form of religion. Interesting that no matter what, the mortal heart turned toward the divine.

The Cithrans had created a High Council of governmental

ministers—almost like a parliament—that combined wealth, religion and politics in one conglomerated whole.

And it was to this High Council that Mor-Lath's path for the Cithran's rumors of the Bride led.

Of course, they weren't gathered together that evening; that would be far too convenient for Mor-Lath. But he had located each member of the High Council. They weren't too far from each other within the affluent quarter of the city.

The Cithrans were like that. Artisans gathered to one quarter, while fine craftsmen to another. The military quarter was all but gone. The manufactories and their woefully paid wage slaves kept the city in smog and goods while the more affluent—those with power and money—claimed the best lands.

One by one he gathered them up, these affluent ministers. He kidnapped them from their tables, their beds, their mistresses, their gold and dragged them along to their parliamentary council room.

The High Council met in the Rotunda, a grand stone building in the middle of Nyabern. A large, round forum of granite topped with a shiny copper dome loomed on the highest hill. It dominated the city. Hundreds of workers must have labored constantly to keep it white and sparkling. An unending job, as the smog of progress darkened all the other buildings around it.

A few unskilled maids kept it clean inside.

The center of the Rotunda was a large, circular room. A ring of ornate, padded seats of various colors surrounding the dropped floor. Bewildered men occupied those seats, all those who had been snatched from their evening's diversions.

Only two seats remained empty. The War Minister, alas, was rather dead. He would not be joining them. As for the final seat, the High Council did not have to wait long. Mor-Lath returned with the last member, Caralman, the Merchant Minister, fetched from his bed.

He'd gathered no one else—only the ministers. The back benches and the secretarial desks were vacant, making the Rotunda feel very empty. The voices of the bewildered men echoed about as they muttered in confusion.

Mor-Lath dropped Caralman into his seat, somewhat rather hard. The older man grunted as his pajama'd bottom met the wooden chair despite the cushion there. Mor-Lath strode to the center of the chamber. With a flick of his hand, he commanded the gaslights to brighten.

"I'm glad you all could make it." He paced before them, the edge of his black cloak flicking back and forth with his every step. "We have some important things to discuss."

Thofferson, the Speaking Minister of the High Council rose to his feet. He fidgeted and kept looking over his shoulder for someone who wasn't there. His age-white hair enhanced the paleness of his skin and his eyes burned bright with experience. "You have no authority over us." As one, the rest of the Council rose.

Mor-Lath felt smug. He loved this game. He loved the drama, the thrill of making his opponents feel stupid or cowed or humbled, if not outright humiliated. He loved the look on their faces when they discovered who he really was. "On the contrary. I am surprised you don't recognize me; I've had a hand in your works for a very long time."

But Thofferson did not give off a scent of doubt. Caution, certainly, and his heart rate had increased, only he was a man who spoke with surety. "We know what you are, sorcerer. We will not stand for these parlor tricks."

Parlor tricks? Mor-Lath turned to face his accuser. "I am no sorcerer. I am the God of the Dark, the god you have been praying to. The god you've—"

"You're no god," Thofferson said. A few others nodded in agreement. Several of the Council had moved their hands to where they had hidden weapons within their clothes. Most Ministers' clothing had been finely tailored from high-quality cloth as befitted their station, including hidden pockets in their design. The presence of various weapons, from knives and darts to firearms gave many of them confidence in a situation that should have been at the very least, perplexing. But not a single one of them felt disconcerted.

Mor-Lath expected their doubt but not their confidence. "You have much opinion of what is and what isn't." With a touch of the Deeper Power, Mor-Lath bade Thofferson to sit. The minister did so, though not nearly as hard as Caralman had. Usually a demonstration or two of his talent, at least, would ruffle most people's confidence.

"Your tricks will not change the truth, sorcerer. We follow the One True god. He has shown us the truth of all things."

Mor-Lath folded his arms. "Oh really?"

Thofferson leaned against the wooden arm of his chair as if reclining on a throne. "Nothing you say, nothing you do will ever convince us you are a god, because of one simple fact: you have a body. The One True is beyond this mortal realm. He has no need for a weak mortal body."

"Let me guess. He told you?"

Thofferson's eyes did not shift, yet they seemed to grow colder. "Do not mock the One True, blasphemer."

Now, this sounded like the philosophies of men, a religion twisted beyond its origins to include doctrines as different from the primitive faith as to be virtually unrecognizable from the original beliefs. These men and those who followed them would never find the Light again. He'd enjoy their foundering in Darkness if he didn't have more important things to deal with.

What did they want with Adrastea?

"I hear you seek a woman called the Bride."

Thofferson considered his words. He looked behind himself. For a moment, he seemed at a loss, for no one was there. Did he miss his staff to prompt him? The others, seeing their leader hesitate, settled to their seats around the Chamber. "That is none of your concern."

"It is if I am her husband."

These people were quickly losing their novelty value. Perhaps he should risk the balance and kill them as well.

Thofferson simply nodded at the information as if he already knew it. But an emotion welled within the man. It certainly wasn't fear or even doubt but anticipation. He gave a few meaningful glances to the other men in the room.

Mor-Lath knew it was coming. At once the men pulled their secret weapons and attacked him. They leapt forward, knives and stilettoes and small firearms drawn.

As if they could overpower a god. With a flick of his wrist, the Deeper Power obeyed him and as if with a mighty force, the whole of the council was knocked back to the floor. They all gasped for wind. Their weapons, as one, all disappeared.

Thofferson, who had remained seated during the attempted capture of the "sorcerer", had been pushed over backwards by the force. He lay on his back, still in his toppled chair, catching his breath as well.

Fun time was over. Mor-Lath strode over and squatted next to him. "You may or may not believe that I am Mor-Lath, God of the Dark but believe that I possess the Power to destroy you all." He called upon it until it filled him to overflowing. Even the chairs of the Rotunda vibrated with it.

Even flat on his back, Thofferson retained some shred of dignity.

"That you call yourself Mor-Lath I can believe. That you are a god?" He shook his head slowly. "Impossible. You are deluded."

"If I killed you and claimed your soul, would that be proof enough?" He said it harsher than he meant to, for he did not want to be seen losing his temper with these men.

It was habit, more than anything that brought him to this situation. Had he not been so used to playing his role in the melodrama, he would have simply gotten to the point and not bother with all the histrionics. He drew a breath. "Enough of these games." And bedamned Tanat's precious balance. Surely one more soul—two dozen more souls—when compared to the prior half-million would not be enough to push him past irredeemability.

He tugged harder than normal to free Thofferson's soul from his mortal remains. Thofferson's will was strong. But in the end, he came free, leaving his mortal body on the floor, where the light of life went out in its eyes.

Yet Thofferson remained nonplussed. "Yes," he said. "Enough of these games."

"You're dead, man!" Mor-Lath snarled at him. He turned the soul so it could see the body. "Look."

Thofferson's soul shrugged. "You don't fool me. It's an illusion."

Mor-Lath gave up. He delved into the soul's memories to find what he sought when a voice startled him.

"Mor-Lath!" Tanat called out, shocked. "What have you done?" She appeared in the middle of the chamber. A few of the nearer councilmen scooted back from her sudden appearance.

Mor-Lath sighed in frustration. "Must you follow me everywhere?"

The Council had recovered, mostly. They clustered together in groups of four or five, but none were so confident as to resume their chairs. Some murmured quietly one to another, unaware of the new soul Mor-Lath held. Instead, they stared at the newcomer, a grey-robed woman.

Tanat's angry not-eyes were for Mor-Lath only. "I told you not to kill again." The low murmuring of the crowd rose to a buzz. Now he could sense their puzzlement and possibly some concern bordering on fear. They retreated back from him and Tanat to consult with one another, wondering whom the sorcerer had killed.

Mor-Lath waved Thofferson at her. "One more isn't going to make a difference."

"Every soul makes a difference. Every single one."

He capitulated on that point. "All right, perhaps this one has value to me. He has the answers I seek."

Tanat held out her hand. "Then depart, Dark One. Leave these mortals alone."

When all but Thofferson had risen to his feet, a murmuring rose among the remaining councilors; they knew which one of them had died. Mor-Lath caught words such as 'murderer' and 'sorcerer' then other words that sounded like prayers. These did not concern him. He knew there were exactly five immortals, two of them a god, the other two of them that should have been a god, and the last one who maintained the balance. Mor-Lath wondered if Tanat would do what she could to ensure her precious balance was kept, even at the cost of Creation? What mattered most to her?

He looked at the soul in his hand. Thofferson wondered why the illusion hadn't ended, despite his denial and his faith. No matter. Mor-Lath didn't need Tanat to tell him that this soul's debt weighed in his favor. He would have plenty of time to convince this dead man of the truth.

But first things first. To Thofferson he asked, "Does anyone else know more than you concerning the Bride?"

The answer was clear in Thofferson's mind: no. Nobody knew more than the High Council, except for the One True. It was that god that told them to find the Bride. Only then could the One True finally defeat evil.

Mor-Lath raised his gaze to Tanat, meeting hers. "I'll leave these alone if you leave me alone."

She twitched her mouth once. "I'll leave you alone if you leave." She held out her hand. "But first, the soul."

Mor-Lath flipped it to her as one would toss a coin. Thofferson would be coming back to him soon enough.

He opened the gates of Dom-al-gol and called forth several demons. They rushed forth, eager to be free from the darkness and imprisonment.

Tanat sighed. "This one is for you," she said of Thofferson. "Though I mourn the futility of giving him back."

Mor-Lath snatched the soul back from her. "That's my business."

"I wish you'd do your business," she muttered.

After a brief moment of instructions to the demons he would attach to each Council member, he departed.

H is temple was such a warm, comforting place to return to after that stone-cold Rotunda. How good to be home. Here he could indulge himself in his meretriciousness should he so choose.

The main chapel was empty this morning as all his priestesses were off on tasks or other occupations. Perhaps Adrastea was good for them after all.

His bride—it took him a moment to locate her—was in Feown. He could feel a puzzlement coming through the connection between them. This gave him a moment of satisfaction; he was not the only one wondering what was going on.

Mor-Lath shook his head in disappointment of himself. Had he been so caught up in his own pursuit of Adrastea that he failed to keep an eye on the rest of the world? He often forgot mortals were far cleverer than he gave them credit for.

Anyhow, he had a whole hell of demons eager to do his bidding, if only to buy themselves some time out of that dark and lonely place. He would send them out into the world to bring back news. Just how far had the Cithrans gone when he wasn't looking?

He sat on his altar as if it were a throne and pulled out Thofferson's soul. "Welcome to my temple," he told it. "Did I mention you were dead?"

Newly-dead souls retained an echo of their body's mortal shape. Thofferson shook his head. "I'm not fooled by your illusion, sorcerer." Indeed, he believed he was not. Mor-Lath could see every single thought that drifted through Thofferson's consciousness, no longer obscured by the complexities of mortality. Thofferson had this solid belief he would be freed from the illusion eventually. He had this unshakeable faith in his god, the one he called the One True.

Unlike other misplaced beliefs, this was no delusion but an actual memory of a manifestation. Mor-Lath forgot the questions he was going to ask. Instead, he delved into Thofferson's memories of the One True god.

Thofferson had first witnessed the manifestation when initially called to the Council. The One True had an appearance like unto a man but with vague form. He had pale hair or perhaps a halo of light, indistinct eyes—nothing at all like Tanat's—in a somewhat humanlike face. What passed for his body was wrapped in pale robes of ethereal mist. He had a low and gentle voice that sang as if in chorus. No wonder Thofferson and the Council were impressed. Mor-Lath was impressed. It was a very good illusion.

For that was all it was, all it ever could be. When Mor-Lath studied the Lines connecting Thofferson with this One True god, they faded away. If he were anything more substantial, there would be a Line.

There was no such thing as an incorporeal god. There were angels and there were demons. All served one god or the other according to their natures.

The One True god was not a god and not truthful. Someone had to be behind the illusion.

"So," Mor-Lath asked. "Who is the One True god?"

Thofferson sprouted some sort of philosophical "he be who he be" and other such poetic appellations.

"Yes, yes," Mor-Lath cut him off with a wave of his hand. "But who is he? How do you summon him? I want to meet him."

Thofferson laughed. He spoke. "One does not summon the One True. We are his servants. He comes to us when he wishes to speak."

"Well, I wish to speak with him."

Thofferson grew smug. "He does not appear to unbelievers."

"Oh, I believe in him, all right. Maybe not the way you do, for I do not fall for his tricks like you. But I certainly won't deny his existence. Now. Tell me how to speak with him."

Thofferson did not use spoken words. But his thoughts mocked Mor-Lath, calling him a fool.

"At least, in that we are well-matched," Mor-Lath replied. Perhaps Thofferson did not know so much about the One True as Mor-Lath supposed. Whoever was behind it was the puppeteer pulling Thofferson's strings. He snorted at the irony of the Council calling him a sorcerer.

He changed tactics. "At least give me his name."

Thofferson's tone turned wry. "The One True has no name. He be who he be."

Mor-Lath gave the soul an extra hard squeeze. "Oh, come on. Everything in Creation has a name."

Thofferson continued the habit of trying to shake his head. He would probably keep it up until he realized he was dead. Mor-Lath hoped that was imminent. As soon as Thofferson broke, the easier it would be to extract the answers. Until then, he said, "Names are labels to compartmentalize us lesser beings. By having names, we recognize our place in the universe. The

One True has no name, for he is the all of the universe."

Oh, please! "Even the universe has a name."

"No, it doesn't."

"It does so. It is called Creation."

"That is merely the label you gave it."

The game wore thin. "No, it is the universe's true name. You doubt the word of a god?"

Thofferson grew smugger. "Why do you continue to insist you are a god and then continue to give me evidence you are not."

"You have no idea what a god is, do you?"

The fool soul honestly thought he was winning. Mor-Lath had to admire Thofferson's stubbornness, if for a brief second. If only his own followers had such dedication.

"The One True had made the truth manifest to me. A true god has no beginning and no end. He is everywhere and nowhere."

Ah ha, Mor-Lath thought. Got him in his own logic. "Then why does your One True have a face like a man?"

Thofferson sighed.

Mor-Lath thought he had him in a logical corner.

But only for a moment. "He manifests himself in a manner so that we can comprehend him."

This guy was good, whoever he was behind the pretty One True illusion. He must have thought for a very long time to come up with such a solid bunch of deceptions. For all his being the God of the Dark, Mor-Lath more-or-less stuck to truth. It was much easier to remember. Lies were not for elaborate deceptions, just for little moments, for hazing the truth, creating half-truths, bending things ever so slightly so that they continued to resemble the truth without actually being so.

It would take him quite a while to unravel this pretty little puzzle.

On to other things.

"Am I safe in assuming that among the many truths the One True has revealed to you, he has spoken of the Bride?"

Thofferson could have rolled his eyes. "Not this again."

"Answer the question."

"The One True has revealed many things to us—"

"Answer directly, please. Has he or has he not mentioned to you the Bride of Mor-Lath?"

Thofferson did not use words. Lying was a sin, apparently but if he didn't open the mouth which he no longer had, it couldn't really be considered a lie. It's a shame his thoughts were transparent. The One True had spoken of a Bride. "I cannot say if she is the same 'Bride of Mor-Lath' you seek."

"You used the name "Mor-Lath".

Thofferson, to Mor-Lath's amusement, had translated the Dark god's name as "Evil One" or "Dark One." Well, he was half-right. Yet for Thofferson, the term was not of a name or a person but a general concept of evil.

Thofferson shrugged. "It is not a name but a foreign word, used to describe a foreign darkness."

"No, it's my name."

Thofferson gave him a look as if the very fact of Mor-Lath having a name was proof enough of him not being a god.

Mor-Lath disliked being doubted. "My mother gave me that name."

"Again, you are not a god. You had a beginning."

And he'd probably have an ending until he sorted out the whole mess with Adrastea. His stomach clenched at the thought of her being hunted by this One True. Cithrans killed foreign priests, calling them sorcerers. Did that extend to Adrastea? "Why does he want her destroyed?"

"Destroyed? No," he uttered before he could stop himself. One True did not want her destroyed.

A cold knot formed within Mor-Lath. At first, he didn't recognize it, so long had it been since he felt true fear. "So, all sorcerers and sorceresses, as you call them, are to be killed?"

Thofferson confirmed it. "They work against the One True Faith. They seek to bring down the true believers and destroy what is Truth."

"But not the Bride?"

"No. Her coming had been foretold."

The Dark God was familiar with many of the prophecies that went through Thofferson's memories. He had followed them himself to find Adrastea.

"So, what is so special about her?" Mor-Lath asked. "Why keep her alive, the antithesis to your One True person?"

Thofferson was silent for a moment as he contemplated the question. His first thought had been, I don't know.

The other souls in Mor-Lath's pocket—he had forgotten about them—also mulled over the question. Until now, they had been listening silently, learning as much as they could, not that this knowledge would avail them aught. In life, some of them had wondered about the order passed down from above. If they should come across the Bride in their holy crusade, she should not be destroyed. Instead, they were to report her whereabouts. In death they wondered about why the greatest evil to walk the world was to be spared. Was she being reserved so the One True could destroy her himself, thus ridding the world of evil once and for all?

They didn't know. Newly-hatched doubt filled their hearts. Those souls knew for a surety that they were dead. All they were taught in the One True Faith about what happened after death had not come to pass. While there had been a god there to greet them, it was not the glorious rest they had been led to believe.

While the other souls pondered upon their unexpected new estate, one soul made a connection. His thought, in its brilliance, rang out. "I think I know."

Mor-Lath dropped Thofferson and fished out the brilliant little spark. It was Paedep, the young priest the god had found among the disembodied troops outside the wall of Feown, the first Tanat did not steal for the Light. This was the one who had led him to Tammas, who then led him to the Council. He held up the little soul between finger and thumb. "What do you know?"

"There is a prophecy..." he began, unsure of himself.

"There are lots of prophecies." Mor-Lath frowned as the soul's thought flitted about in nervousness. He couldn't get a fix on just one.

After he gathered his thought together, the soul said, "The son of Darkness will destroy it."

This was nothing new to Mor-Lath. There were few prophecies that occupied his thoughts more than this one. It wasn't even an original variation. "I know that one."

The soul wished he could swallow. How could one get a lump in one's throat when one was dead? "Perhaps the One True means to spare her, for the offspring of her womb may be the one to conquer all evil?"

Mor-Lath also knew of this aspect. That is why he had left Adrastea alone in that manner. Did the One True also believe that the fruit of her womb would destroy Mor-Lath?

A new fear blossomed in his stomach. Mor-Lath knew how he himself had come to the power of the Dark. He had not been the first god. Was there another who sought his mantle of authority, who sought to destroy him? A mashiah?

He sent out his senses along the Lines. Surely the name of one powerful enough in the Deeper Power to be a threat would impress its essence on the Lines. But he heard nothing.

Maybe there was something more to it? Something he had not yet sussed out? "You're a clever bit of spirit. I think I'll keep you around for a little while longer," Mor-Lath told Paedep.

With a wave of his hand, a great gateway opened into the endothermic abyss known as Dom-al-gol. Into this he tossed the other souls he'd pulled from his pocket, Thofferson included. He closed the gateway without a second thought.

His pet soul he shoved back into his pocket, to be forgotten while he thought some more.

So, someone else had their eye on Adrastea? Who could it be? It certainly wasn't an immortal, so someone somewhere had pretensions beyond his place. Well, Adrastea could hold her own against a mere mortal, so he did not worry too much about her.

What he learned today disturbed him. The religious sheep of the Cithrans hid sharp teeth under their wooliness. No doubt the Feowan faithful, whether Light or Dark—as it was all the same to the Cithrans— would be blamed for the deaths of the Cithran army.

Mor-Lath's thoughts strayed to all his priests and priestesses. He was rather fond of them, as a crowd.

Perhaps the killing was not yet over. He would have to warn them, of course. Possibly teach them how to defend themselves better.

Forget about destroying the Cithran army; perhaps it was time to conquer the whole nation.

❧❀❧

Ever since Adrastea returned from Sacred Spring with her copies of Ari's books, she'd discovered a thirst to know more about the healing craft. She'd found more than a few books in the library on herbal lore.

Armed with these, she studied and experimented in the stillroom. The priestesses were more than happy to come along. She'd ask them what they knew about local herbs, told them stories from Sacred Spring, and showed them how to set up a proper still. She'd even ventured out from the temple into the Tredan capital, properly escorted by Radelisa, to see what she could find.

The variety of herbs and medicines available to the Tredan peoples gladdened her heart. Here were plants she'd never encountered before. She returned to the temple with so many she and Radelisa could barely carry them all.

After her fruitful field trip, she went to the library for more books on Tredan medicines.

The library was not empty. As she turned a corner, she saw Mor-Lath scanning a shelf. His left arm cradled several books. He selected another.

"You come and go without warning," she remarked.

He didn't look at her. "I did not know I needed your permission." Mor-Lath had been gone for many days.

While it was an easy enough task to keep track of his location, his apparent abandonment of her was not sitting well in her heart. "No. You don't. But you should inform me. That's what married people do." She felt empty inside. She had a sudden desire to call upon the Deeper Power if only to fill that empty spot. That could be a mistake. She didn't want to alarm him. Instead, she filled the silence between them with words. "You were not here for me to tell you I was venturing out." She laid a hand upon his arm.

He sighed and bowed his head. "Adrastea, I know where you are at every given moment."

She drew closer. "You married me for a reason," she murmured. "Spoken vows begin a marriage but there is so much more to being married."

He settled his books against his chest. "So, you've come to terms with your state of matrimony?"

Caution. That's what she was getting from him. Why did he need to be cautious? "I'm not going to bite."

"You came here to read. And I'm distracting you." He hefted his books. "I've got a bit of reading to do myself." He moved away from her, his attention a little too firmly on the shelves.

Had she been dismissed? She followed him. "The Light would have us succeed." Maybe that would get a rise out of him.

A small flutter of annoyance touched her lines and disappeared. "Only after we figure out a few things. Why don't you read up?"

And off he walked, leaving her very much alone. Occupied. That's how he felt.

What was that about?

Disappointed, she resumed her original task—books on Tredan medicine. Perhaps if she focused on her task she could forget how it stung to be ignored. She gathered as many books on the subject as she could carry and headed back to her stillroom to read. Maybe it would take her mind of the strange behavior of her husband. How unlike him to ignore her thus.

She didn't see Berengaria until she nearly tripped over the young priestess who slunk along the wall. Adrastea's books flew from her hands, to flap away like awkward birds. Berengaria's dropped something, it hitting the floor with a thud, coming to rest against the hem of Adrastea's skirt. A book, a rather small one.

Berengaria let out a small shriek of surprise then fell to her knees, forehead to the floor. She was too far away to snatch back what she had dropped without coming in range of Adrastea's hand.

Adrastea stooped down and picked it up.

"Oh," gasped Adrastea as she received the powerful memories the object held. Images of desire, of lust and building tension rushed forth from the leather cover. The book of intimacy burned in her hands. It slipped from her fingers. "Berengaria! Where did you get that?"

It hit the floor again. Berengaria snatched it up, secreting it in her bosom.

"I'm sorry, Mistress," she bleated, then said something else, her voice muffled to near incomprehensibility.

"Sit up," Adrastea snapped. "I can't hear you." She then regretted her sharp words. Berengaria did not deserve her temper.

Berengaria raised her face from the floor, but she did not look up. "Please don't tell Desideria, please," she whispered. "I know I'm not supposed to read it but I," she swallowed, "I was just curious." Berengaria babbled on. "I promise I was putting it back."

"You don't want to do that," Adrastea advised. "*He* is in there." She held out her hand.

Berengaria dropped her face to the floor. "Oh..." she moaned. Berengaria's embarrassment radiated off her in waves of heat. She held out the book to Adrastea.

Adrastea took it. The memories stored within the book were incomplete. Most of what it remembered was of things that Adrastea did not want to investigate too closely. Adrastea fought a blush as her own memories came to the fore. She'd nearly walked in on Ari and Natan a few times. She had caught Rop and Jira Storekeeper out in the woods before they were married.

That was nothing compared to the images she got off the book. A wave of desire rolled through her nether regions. She was married. But her marriage hadn't been consummated. Why not?

As the strange memories flooded her once more—they were quite powerful, possibly due to their passionate nature—the awareness of her naivety and inexperience irked her.

A moment of self-realization came to her. What if Mor-Lath's lack of interest was because she was inexperienced? This book shared fragments of memories with her, memories of a thousand—a million—moments of sexual experience? And here she was, as green as the spring wheat. Her fumbling and hesitation must be some kind of turn-off for him. What if the frustration she sensed from him was not sexual frustration but intellectual frustration? What if he found her tedious and uninteresting?

Her hands closed about the book. "I have a better idea. I promise I won't tell, and I'll put the book away for you." After she had a read.

Berengaria exhaled her tension and she relaxed, her arms flopping out to the side, before she sat up.

Adrastea studied the book. It was small enough to almost fit into the palm of her hand. Surely small enough to slip into a pocket or under a pillow. "I wonder if he's read this?"

The girl on the floor began to squirm. "Oh no! His Holiness would never— well, maybe. It's not like the—"

"Like what?"

Berengaria knocked her head to the floor again. "The stories," she admitted. "Forbidden stories."

Adrastea's heart chilled. "Of what?" Iciness frosted her words.

Berengaria sat up. "Oh, not with us. I mean, he's never had anything to do with us. He's made that very clear. And, well, with you here, I don't see why he'd, um, you know." she trailed off. "Well..." She seemed to be thinking. "Perhaps in the past there have been others—not other wives," she added hastily. "But I think Desideria's had had questions with that in the past. Not that she's said anything to me. But the others talk."

Adrastea's countenance took on a full blush.

Berengaria's eyes cast down and her voice dropped to a whisper. "So, is he—" She touched her fingertips to her lips when she saw the confused expression on Adrastea's face. She fell to her knees. "Forgive me. But since you showed up, we've all wondered."

Wondered what?

Berengaria chewed on her lip for a moment. "Sometimes the others speculate what he's like, you know, in bed. All on the quiet, of course. Desideria forbids us to speak of His Holiness thus."

Of course, they wondered. One could not live and serve the Dark God personally without wondering about the various aspects of him. And then there had been the earlier conversation with Desideria. That "His Holiness" had a laissez-faire policy concerning his personal priestesses had comforted her. But that left plenty of other women in the world. The book in her hands confirmed her suspicions.

The thought of him in the arms of another woman piqued her. In the time she'd been here, he'd not made a move in her direction. He was all hands and kisses when they were betrothed. Once she married him, that all stopped. Why? Surely if he were celibate, he would have told her. She could have accepted that, quite cheerfully. (Or maybe not. No. Definitely not.)

Desideria did not expect him to be. Did the High Priestess know something Adrastea did not? Oh pesk, of course she did. But if Mor-Lath was not interested in Adrastea sexually, then why the whole courtship thing? Why the whole marriage thing? How irksome.

"You know," she said to Berengaria, "if you are curious, why don't you ask him?" More bitter than she meant.

Berengaria didn't have an answer for that. "It is not my place to question His Holiness."

"Does anyone question him?"

The priestess thought about it. "No, I don't think so."

Adrastea thought back to her earlier conversation with her husband. More to herself, she replied, "I think I'll start."

A few days later, Adrastea discovered her husband in the library. She had not seen him recently—a bit of a relief, come to think of it. It had given her room and time to think.

They had unfinished business. The sooner they got it out of the way, the more at ease she'd be. In the pocket of her skirt rested the little book she'd recovered from Berengaria. She hadn't opened it, for the waves of lust it radiated intimidated her. But its mere presence gave her courage.

Now it was time to confront him, or perhaps persuade him.

She found him at the great carved table, poring over a dozen books.

He read quickly, turning the pages every moment or so, sometimes back and forth. Then he'd consult other tomes.

She leaned against a bookshelf and watched him. He looked so casual in his plain cotton shirt with no vest or coat. Every once in a while, his forehead would crease for a moment and his lips would twitch. He seemed almost mortal. A small twitter of regret fluttered in her chest. If he had been mortal, would things have been different between them?

What would their marriage have been like, mortal him and her? Would there have even been a marriage, or would she have been simply another convenient body to warm his bed until he moved on to the next woman? Would she have fallen for his charm then? Or had his casual ways developed after years and centuries watching everyone he ever knew grow old and die?

He stopped reading, laying his hands on the table while he drew in a deep breath. Then he turned to look at Adrastea. "You're looking at me."

Her heart rate accelerated. She shrugged.

"I'm busy," he added.

"All right," she replied but did not move, nor make another sound.

That too-familiar frown flitted across his face. "I don't need you watching me."

"Hasn't bothered you for the past half hour."

He pushed the book away. "You haven't been there for half an hour."

She folded her arms. "So, how long have I been here?"

"Five minutes. Do you mind? I'm busy."

"My presence didn't bother you before."

He sighed. "But do you have to watch?" He looked at her again. "You want something, don't you?"

"It is time we discussed our consummation."

She felt a frission of fear emanate from him. The impression was so strong the lines on her face grew chill. He pushed it back down as quickly as it arose.

That was something new. Of what was he afraid?

His face was neutral. "I'm busy." He spread his arms, indicating the books. "Do we have to discuss it now?"

"Yes. We do." She moved towards him, her fingers brushing the surface of the table. "You moved heaven and earth to win my hand." She held out her palm. "Yet you show little interest in the rest of me." Her fingers played with the low neckline of her blouse, stroking along her gently swelling décolletage.

She felt more tension of a different kind through the lines, one that warred with that undercurrent of fear. He swallowed. "I don't know what you mean."

Ah, that was not entirely true. She took a step closer.

He sat up straighter. "I don't have time for this now."

"Make time." She ran her fingertips over his shoulder. He caught her hand with his.

The moment their skin touched, he drew in a deep breath. But he did not let go of her hand. She let the faintest hint of Deeper Power buzz along in her blood. "According to my 'quaint country customs', we are not yet completely married. For someone who pursues things single-mindedly, I do not understand why you'd quit half-way."

His hand tightened on her. He refused to look at her. "I am familiar with your customs." He nudged her hand away and pulled a book closer to him. The tension did not leave him, though. "What I don't understand is why you spent all that time denying my troth and now you're saying yes?"

"When I agreed to marry you, I didn't just agree to say the words. I agreed to everything."

He wrapped his arms around the edges of the book and turned his focus to the pages. "Can we discuss this later?"

"Why? Am I making you uncomfortable?"

A ping of truth came through the lines. "Your... timing is poor," he replied. He held a book out to her. She took it. "Spoils of the Cithran war."

The book weighed heavy in her hands. Disappointment weighed heavy in her heart. "You prefer to sit and read rather than—"

"The book is about you." He spread his hands over the whole table. "They're all about you."

Adrastea drew more on the Deeper Power. This elicited a small reaction of alarm from Mor-Lath, one he quickly suppressed. Her attention was not on him but on the book. Treatises and essays on a various number of topics. "This book is not about me."

With a wave of his hand, the pages turned, startling her. Oh, why didn't she see that coming? It flipped open to a certain page. He jabbed a finger at a passage. "There. It speaks of the Bride."

"One passage."

He shrugged, turning back in his seat. "Just an example."

She let the book fall to the table with a negligent thump. "So, you're going to read all these?"

"I've already read all these. I'm putting the pieces of the puzzle together."

Why was he being difficult? "What puzzle?"

"Why the Cithrans are interested in you." He lifted her hand and pressed it to his lips. "They want you. Why, I don't know."

A tendril of untruth echoed between their touch. He did know, or at least, suspected.

She was getting nowhere. Time to be bold. She slipped into his lap and pulled his arm about her. "I don't care what the Cithrans want. What I wonder is why don't you want me?" Her heart thumped. She draped her other arm over his shoulders and pulled his head closer to hers.

He drew in a shuddery breath. His hands settled about her waist. He hesitated, while the energy flowed between them. She leaned her face in closer.

In an unexpected move, he lifted her up and off his lap. "I told you I don't have time for this." His chest heaved. He pushed himself up from the chair and went to the other side of the table.

She'd been rejected. "What? Why not?"

"There are more important things to do than to waste time dallying."

The sting of his rejection fueled anger in her heart. "This isn't just 'dallying'. This is important."

"Then it can wait."

She folded her arms and drew on the Deeper Power. That always got a reaction out of him.

He straightened. "That's a pretty poor attempt to manipulate me."

She did not go of the Power. "If I've learned one thing, it's that I can't manipulate you. Oh, you're very good at manipulating me. In the end I'll only end up doing what you wanted, because you've put me in such a tight spot that my only choice is a bad evil and a worse evil." She promised herself she would later think upon what other things he would ask of her and what their consequences would be.

"But in the past few days," she said, "I realized something." She looked at him. "You need me. You really, really need me. But has it ever occurred to you that I don't need you?" Those words sprang from her bitterness. She followed him around the table.

She ran her fingers over the books. Discourses, essays, prophecy, even a book on science. Why were these more enticing than a willing woman?

"What do you want?" He was not in the mood for games. He stood his ground as she drew near.

She answered swiftly. "I wanted my dreams to come true. Shame they're gone now. You've taken those away."

He folded his arms. "Your... dreams?" he scoffed. "What pithy sort of little dreams could not be satisfied with the wondrous gifts you now possess?"

She stopped, her fingers lingering on some governmental report. "Oh, I know I lack not for anything material. I doubt you suffer the pain of poverty. Your priestesses provide me with more than enough companionship. Should I ever grow bored of them, I can travel anywhere in the world I wish, even back to Sacred Spring." Her voice rose in pitch and her words tumbled out. "Any thing I want I can get. There are more than enough interests to keep me occupied. But none of it fulfills the dreams I've grown up with."

Adrastea drew a breath. Anger fueled itself. It did not assuage her pain.

He sniffed. "Like what?"

If there was never a Mor-Lath, what would her life have been like? She let all the possibilities flow through her mind. Finish her Journeyhood, leave Sacred Spring and seek her fortune elsewhere. She could have been a great healer. Maybe she could have made her way to Feown and studied at the university, like Ari had. Skills, knowledge and respect through her own actions.

She might have met someone she could love. Family. Children.

"We can start by completing our wedding." It irked her to see the priestesses give her coy glances and subtle knowing nods whenever they were together. As far as they were concerned, the marriage had been consummated a thousand times over. They found it all romantic. "Everyone believes we have." She pushed herself back into his arms.

"Let them believe." He drew her closer. He buried his head in her hair and inhaled. His hand slid down her waist.

What about what she knew, what she believed? She wanted love, like her parents had enjoyed, like Ari and Natan had. She wanted someone to share everything with her. Her heart ached with longing.

His hand slipped into the pocket of her skirt and withdrew the little book. "This isn't about propriety. This is about curiosity." A self-satisfied grin spread across his face. "You want to know what I'm like in bed. You've listened to the priestesses and their speculations. I know Ari's wondering."

"Ari is not." Ari had never said anything of the kind.

"Every woman wonders." He whispered in her ear, his own core filling with the Deeper Power. It washed over into her and she swayed. Oh, the power was sweet! "You do not think I do not know of the furtive stories told in the wan hours of the night?" He shook his finger at her. "You've been listening to stories too. And now you want to know if they're true or not."

He stroked her cheek, sending the line singing. He pressed his forehead to hers and sent her quick images. Partial memories of powerful intimacy, enough to leave an impression and make her limbs buzz, flowed over her like warm water.

Then he pulled back, leaving a cold emptiness inside her. "There. They're true. Curiosity assuaged. Now go away and let me be." He thrust the book back into her numb hands.

Her emptiness consumed her. What? That was it?

Mor-Lath would never see her as a true companion. She served one purpose only—make him a god. Ever since he'd learned of her existence, ever since she displayed talent that fateful day when young Peter fell into the water barrel, he'd pursued her until he got her.

And after that, what was there for her?

The sorrow wrestled with her will and won. She didn't mean it to. She released some of the pressure of her sorrow with a small sob then steeled herself once more.

He was watching her. She would not let him see her cry.

"I don't need you, Mor-Lath. You would never give me what I need."

"It's all about you, is it? You ever think to ask what I need?"

She wrapped her arms about her chest. "You've already got what you need. I will not shame myself with begging. You're only wanting me to tell you, so you can mock me and belittle me and shatter my dreams. As if you haven't done that already.

"You want me, Mor-Lath. You need me. But you can't love me." Adrastea fled the library, the little book still clutched in her hands.

He didn't bother to follow her out.

She ran down the corridors. Once she was well and truly away from the library, only then did she slump against the wall and allow herself to cry. When her tears had taken the edge off the pain in her heart, she dashed their remains from her face. If that's how he wanted it, then she would go make her own way in the world. Really, why did she bother staying?

⚜

Adrastea took to the bed. As an immortal, Adrastea didn't require as much sleep. It still claimed her from time to time. However, she discovered she could go for days without feeling the need to seek her bed. But now, the bed became the place to cry.

She had little other reason for the ornate piece of furniture. Despite its soft mattress, feather doona and silken sheets, it was the lack of something, or rather someone, that made it cold and lonely.

She sank down into its softness, deflating as she went. She threw the little book at the headboard. It slid down behind the pillows as if it knew where it belonged.

Her earlier conversation with Berengaria got her to thinking. Did she really wish the Dark God in her bed? A need ached within her. Was it for him?

Before she sacrificed herself for the sake of Sacred Spring, there were times when she almost gave in to her passions. Her blood and the Deeper Power had rushed hot through her veins and her lips had sought his as if to draw more from him. He gave his attention to her as willingly as she was to take it. Mor-Lath had seemed interested in those sorts of things, at least that was her impression during their courtship.

But now, he had spurned her. Why?

Before their marriage, there were greater things at stake for her, such as her immortal soul and what little she had left of her reputation. Not that reputation mattered any more. Her body had joined her soul in immortality, so that was no longer an issue either. As far as she knew, she was free. She even had the benefit of matrimony.

She would have the Dark God. Why wouldn't he have her? Could it be that he was not physically attracted to her?

No, that wasn't it. He'd touch her, he'd slip his arm about her waist, he'd kiss her. She'd felt his blood burn as much as hers. If he simply wanted her for her power, he wouldn't have bothered with that sort of attention.

Was it her ignorance and her lack of experience? He'd made it clear she was to educate herself in all manner of things. He'd given her free reign of the library, all the books she could cram into her curly brown head.

Her gaze moved sideways to the little black book. It was a library book, so Berengaria claimed.

Little good it had done her.

She wanted a reaction out of him. His uncaring attitude earlier in the library, which originally drove her to tears, now raised anger in her heart. How dare he ignore her? She was his bride. So why wasn't she his wife?

Her hand reached under the pillows and hesitated over the book. She slid it towards her, palming it guiltily. Images of many hands having claimed it, sequestering it in dark, hidden places filled her mind. She pushed away the experiences of others and looked at the book. It had no title on cover or spine. She opened it to a random page. There was text, but the illustration drawn in ink drew her attention.

A rather graphic depiction of a man and woman seared itself into her mind. Once it sank in what she was looking at, Adrastea slammed the book closed. Heat suffused her cheeks. What would he say if he knew she was reading this?

She realized she had no idea what he would say. She honestly didn't know if he'd be angry or titillated or would go on ignoring her as per his latest policy. Or would he simply tell her she could do what she wanted as long as she left him alone?

No. That was the last thing she wanted. She'd given up her life as she knew it. She should get something pleasant out of it in return.

Her fingers stroked its spine. Had he read this particular book?

She nearly dropped it when it radiated an answer: yes. And he'd enjoyed it.

Huh. So, Adrastea opened to the first page, driven more by the potential to stir her husband, rather than curiosity.

Goodness. Her cheeks suffused with so much heat she had to fan herself with the pages of the book simply to cool them down. Of course, she knew about the act, or she thought she did. The techniques in the book made her feel like the greenest of virgins.

The more she read, the more it seemed she would have to take matters into her own hands. Mortal husbands and wives enjoyed each other's intimate company. She thought back to the subtle courtship of Natan and Ari and the more obvious interactions of her own parents. And then there was the rest of the village. Young courting couples teased and flirted and touched.

And the women talked. According to them, men weren't that hard to convince into sex.

If they could do it, could she?

As Adrastea read, she tossed the beginnings of a plan around in her head.

Chapter 12

Chamque chafed at Desmone's new status. After a month, the third sign had proven itself. Desmone failed to bleed as a woman. Grudgingly, she acknowledged Desmone as one favored by their god.

Montrof, who had wrangled a permanent sleeping cell within the temple, encouraged Desmone in her role with one hand while steadying Chamque with the other. So far, he had not done anything to raise overt suspicion in Chamque's mind. But she continued to observe him and questioned all.

The only advantage to Montrof was that Chamque did not have to deal directly with Desmone. She turned her attention to the rest of the temple.

"Chamque," he called out as she left her office for evening devotionals. Chamque cringed when she heard his voice. Montrof hurried up and matched his pace with hers. At least he availed himself of the baths and his robes were clean, if worn. "I have news."

She sighed. "Go ahead."

"I have learned that it was not the whole of the Cithran population that was killed. Only the army. The rest of the nation still lives."

"I knew that," she said, more to annoy him than anything. She's heard unconfirmed reports, having stirred up her network since her first conversation with Montrof.

He didn't rise to her bait. "You know this means they will be sending a second army."

"That's Feown's problem."

He held up a finger. "No, that's our problem. But that wasn't what I wanted to talk to you about." He paused, then said, "Well, it is but..." he waved his hands. At least he didn't send a stench of unwashed human around anymore when he did that. "I digress. While we know the real truth, as far as the Glasskissers are concerned it was a miracle of their god. The Cithrans also believe this. They will plan their attack differently this time. We have got to take advantage of the situation before that happens and before Feown rebuilds its army and their faith recruits more priests."

They reached the door of the main chapel. Montrof waved his hands excitedly. "It's the perfect opportunity to invade Feown."

"What? Invade Feown? Are you mad?"

He grinned widely. What teeth of his hadn't rotted away were now clean. He had a few gaps where a dentist had free reign. How much of her coffers had paid for that? "But instead of sending a regular army with a few priests, we send an army of nothing but priests, to destroy the temples of the Glasskissers and rid us of our enemies forever.

Her hand dropped from the door. "You forgot one thing: the True Faithers aren't just killing Glasskisser priests. They're killing ours as well. They don't care that we worship different gods."

Montrof chuckled. "Are we so different?"

Chamque couldn't believe he said that. "Yes! We serve the glory of the God of Wealth. In turn, he rewards us. They have to give all the reward to their god before they believe He'll pay attention to them. Not a good way to earn the faith of followers. Who thought of the daft idea in the first place?" She raised her hand to open the door but Montrof put his hand on it to keep it closed.

"It's a rather backwards way of doing it, especially since they have no guarantee that He'll bless them. Certainly didn't bless them a few months ago when the Cithrans descended." He leaned in closer. Chamque leaned away from him but did not step back. "Speaking of the Cithrans, do you even know who their god is?"

"No. He has no name."

"That's right. Has no body either, apparently. Anyhow, I digress. What I meant to say is that if I can come to the conclusions I've come to, no doubt the Glasskissers will have well. They're expecting a second wave of attack."

"So?"

"So, what happens if we get there first?"

Chamque snorted. "Attack Feown while they're weak? Saraym's

doubled her patrols along the borders. She's expecting us to take advantage of her weakened state."

Montrof held up a finger. "No. I'm suggesting that we don't attack as Avelians. Certainly not in the name of our god." He chuckled for his benefit. "Oh, this is brilliant! Instead, we dress up as Cithrans and finish wiping out the Feowans."

Chamque did not hide her scorn. "Right. Nice plan. What if we lose?"

He laughed. "Don't you see? We win no matter what. Either we will defeat them, or not. If we don't, they won't know it's us, They'll mount this great big campaign against the Cithran empire. Then, depending on how the wind blows, we wait until the Feowans lose, then wipe out the remains."

Chamque moved his hand from the door. "Your plan has a few holes in it."

"Give me time and I'll improve it." He followed her through the door and ran into her stopped form. "Chamque? Wha—"

He glimpsed over her shoulder and saw what she saw.

A rather annoyed god looked up from the priestess he was kissing. "You have poor timing," he growled. Mor-Lath stood up from his bent position over the altar.

Desmone, still pinned against the altar, turned to look at a surprised Chamque and Montrof. She frowned. "What do you want?" She had gotten uppity since her change in status. Her current position didn't humble her much either.

It took Chamque a few moments to let it all sink in. Then she lowered herself to her knees, ignoring their aged protest. "Apologies, Holiness." It was the first time she had seen her god. So many times she'd come close in her life but had missed him. She'd always had been a room or a moment away.

She'd been a devoted priestess her whole life. It had stung that Desmone had not only seen him first but... She shook that thought from her head. She did not want to waste what little time she had in the presence of her god trying to ponder why Desmone had been chosen and she never was.

She did not hear Montrof fall to his knees. "Could have been worse, Holiness," he said, as if he conversed with the Dark God every day. "We could have walked in five minutes later."

Mor-Lath made a sound of annoyance and released Desmone. Desmone let out a whimper of disappointment. She plucked at his clothes.

He ignored her. "Now, you lot. Listen. I know what you are planning, Montrof. While I would normally encourage you in your plans, I must have you forgo them for the time being."

"What do you wish of us, Holiness?" Montrof asked.

Mor-Lath abandoned the altar and its contents. "You will heed my words and you will carry them to Wacifice. You tell Wacifice to withdraw all his troops from the border. And I mean every single one. Any left behind shall have the honor of meeting me personally. Wacifice will obey. If he doesn't, remove him from power."

Chamque blinked. Montrof lifted his eyes. "But Holiness, Feown is ripe for—"

"Leave Feown alone. I have plans for them. It doesn't include you invading them. Bad Montrof." He pointed at Chamque. "Rise and heed me."

She obeyed.

"If Wacifice does not do as I say, it falls to your hands to remove him from the throne." A subtle smile crossed his lips. "I know you have ways, Chamque."

Chamque swallowed at his words. Wacifice, corpulent king of Avelia, was not going to like Montrof's message. He had this obsession about the northern border. Chamque never understood it. Already she started going through her mind the best way to deal him. "Even if it means his death?"

"There is no need for death if he's obeying me. Make that clear to him. Otherwise I'm sure his heir will understand that if he doesn't."

When he put it that way, Chamque's tasks did not seem so onerous. She never did like Wacifice—fat, greedy, sacrificing competency for self-indulgence. While his sons looked they might follow in their father's footsteps, they were young enough to influence in the correct direction. Perhaps Desmone could be persuaded to encourage the lads. She needed something to do other than indulge herself.

Montrof spoke. "But what if Feown discovers our unpatrolled borders? What if they attack?"

Mor-Lath smiled. "They won't. Feown belongs to me now. I have an important task for them." His expression darkened. "Leave Feown alone."

Chamque did not need to ask what would happen should they disobey. While Mor-Lath gave further instructions to Montrof regarding the Cithrans, Chamque watched Desmone, who stood to the side, ignored. Interesting that the god did not have any instructions for her.

When Mor-Lath was done with Montrof, Desmone approached him, clinging. "And what would you have me do?"

He patted her on the head like a good puppy. "There's a good lass."

In the blink of an eye, he was gone.

Chamque remained on her knees after he'd left. Convince or remove the king. Nothing too difficult there. Montrof had a whole host of tasks given to him, mostly concerning uniting the scattered priests to hunt down any True Faithers in Avelia. It would give the troops who no longer patrolled the border something to do.

As for Desmone? It seems their god had not given her anything, not even the chance to warm his bed. The jealous ache in Chamque's heart eased a bit.

What did this mean for the "Bride of Mor-Lath"? Chamque had a feeling she and Montrof were going to have another conversation about her soon.

Mor-Lath cursed himself. What had he been thinking? His encounter with Adrastea left him unsettled. Where had she found that book? His little country girl had discovered her courage. Her boldness in asking for consummation both frightened and excited him. Had it been anyone else who'd made him such a bold offer—in his lap, nonetheless—he would have taken her across that table in a heartbeat.

But this was Adrastea. The risk was too great.

He could not let her get to him.

Without calculating the risks, he had left his books and fled to Avelia, his only thought on slaking his lust.

He should have realized there would be a bit of fuss around Desmone for a while. Ah well, no big loss. She was not the only one in his stable.

In the lands the Feowans called the East Bank sat a small, tidy cottage. The owner, Lanne Saponer, a woman of lush figure and frustrated passions, lived alone. She often clashed with her neighbors who envied her her fertile land and scorned her for her forward opinions.

Today, Mor-Lath didn't care what she opined—on the whole, he quite liked that she had a mind of her own. But today, all he cared about was how she felt, in every pleasurable way.

Large trees bordered her property, to break the sweeping winds of the plains. Between the trees she'd erected a simple wooden fence, more to keep anything out, rather than in. Her modest home, while bigger than one would expect for a family of one, still looked like any other thatched cottage.

Here he found her, gathering potatoes from the newly-turned earth with help of a trowel. Wisps of sun-faded hair stuck to her face under her wide-brimmed straw hat. Her little button nose crinkled with the effort of her work.

Mor-Lath leaned over the wooden rails of the fence. "Good afternoon to you, Mistress Saponer."

Mistress Saponer paused in her work then raised her head. "Milord," she uttered with some surprise. "What a surprise." She stood in a slow manner, awkward, even. She wiped her hands on her dull brown skirt like a child who forgot to wash.

But there was guilt in her voice. "You can't come in. I'm married now."

He raised his eyebrows. "Married?" he said at her honest disclosure.

"I'm Mistress Farmer now."

He allowed disappointment to cross his face. "You married a farmer?"

"It wasn't like I could marry a lord."

Disappointment colored her voice. Surely the woman hadn't been so foolish—and she was the least foolish of the women of his intimate acquaintances—as to hope for something more than a tumble from any lord, much less the likes of him. "I see your point," he conceded, deliberately mistaking her meaning.

"Anyhow," he continued. "I offer my best wishes and hope for the same from you. I, too, have been recently married, though I confess it was of a political nature." He rested his arms on the fence. "I assume you are more fortunate as to have married for 'less noble' purposes?"

Mistress Farmer sank back to her knees, picked up her trowel and grubbed through the dirt for potatoes. "No. My marriage was as political as yours. I don't love him," she confessed.

Mor-Lath visibly brightened. "You don't?"

She shot him a warning glance. "But I do respect him."

Respect, huh? What wasn't she telling him? "Of fine character, is he?"

She didn't say a word. A brief pause in her hands told him enough.

"For a farmer, that is," he added, as an afterthought. "He must provide for you well, keep you company and, I hope, pleases you in bed."

He knew he'd hit a point of contention. No mortal could compare with him when it came to the erotic arts. No doubt that husband of hers was rough, uncouth and uncaring as to her needs. Yes, she was ripe for the picking.

He sighed. "I'll admit when it comes to the pleasures of love, my wife... Well, let us not talk about her." He dismissed Adrastea with an effete wave of his hand. "Do tell me about this paragon of a man who has captured your heart."

Mistress Farmer drubbed harder, damaging the spuds she threw into her basket.

Mor-Lath prodded her further. "I can understand why he, why any man, would want to marry you," a little flattery never hurt. "But why did you marry him?"

She dug even harder then stopped. "Because I was lonely. He made me an offer I would have been a fool to refuse."

"Oh," he sighed. "We are so much alike." He hoped he put just the right touch of wistfulness in his voice. Soothe her anger, play up her loneliness, which remained dulled but not sated. Comfort her while igniting her passion. Easy but would take time. So why did he choose her? He could think of at least three others who were, in all likeliness, quicker marks. So why Mistress Saponer? Before a certain reason could rise up, he pushed it down and distracted himself by asking a question.

"What did he offer you?"

She rested her hands on her knees and looked out to the horizon. "He was a younger son."

"So am I."

She glanced back at him with narrow eyes. "I know. You've told me."

She scanned the horizon. Mor-Lath noticed she was looking away from town. Looking for her husband? Oh, there he was, occupied with the earth. "His father, nasty old man that he was, died last year. Each son got a parcel of land with which to support their families." She took off her hat and fanned herself. "Well, not quite enough. Not that it matters now..."

He could sense a sorrow that surprised even her. But he didn't care about that. "Let me guess, being the younger son—"

"Youngest actually, though he is not considered a young man." He heard the faint echo of her voice, *and I am not a young woman...*

"The youngest son," Mor-Lath amended. "So, he got the smallest parcel of land?"

She nodded, still looking to the horizon. "Bordering mine. Mine's been too much for me to farm. I kept Bess there until she dried up last year."

Bess? Oh yes. Her cow.

The fields were no longer fallow. Master Farmer had done his job. Master Farmer worked out in the fields of wheat, quite a way down. He would be occupied for quite some time.

"So, he offered marriage to you, hoping to get your land as well as his, enough to grow a large enough crop to support you both. Is that it? So, between your lotions and potions and his farming, you should be turning a tidy profit."

Mistress Farmer colored deeply and turned from him. "I... don't do much of that anymore."

"What?" Was that enough shock in his voice? "No more soapmaking? But you enjoyed it so much."

"I have other duties now. More important ones." Regret flavored her voice.

"But you were such a good soapmaker."

"And how would you know?"

He sniffed. "I am a lord. I know about quality." Subtle flattery would do for now. Anything overt would sound fake.

She glanced back over her shoulder at him. "I dare to ask: where is your horse, Milord?"

With no guile on his face, he answered, "Why, back at the inn with the others."

"Why didn't you bring it? It is a long walk from the inn."

"What? Should I request my saddled horse to be brought around, the others of my party would demand to know what I was up to. They'd insist on coming. I didn't want to bring them out here to visit you."

She huffed her scorn and returned to the earth. "You are ashamed of me, not that I should be surprised."

"Not at all. The reason I wanted to come visit you alone is because I simply wanted to talk about things they would never understand."

"Well, I can't talk. I need to get all of these potatoes out of the ground and stored before my husband comes home."

He put some pleading into his voice. Some of it was genuine. "But I need to talk. Of all the people I know, you will understand. You'll listen."

She did not stop her potato harvest. "And who will listen to me when I explain to my husband that our potatoes are still in the earth because I had to idle away my time comforting—"

With a negligent wave of his hand, Mor-Lath pulled all the potatoes out of the earth, including the ones she'd missed. They stacked themselves in her basket.

Mistress Farmer shrieked and jumped back. Her heart thumped, causing a vein in her neck to throb. She stared at the basket before turning her fearful gaze to him. "Milord?" she whispered. "You never told me you were a priest as well."

"I'm not." He climbed to sit on the fence. "Please don't tell anyone, or they will draft me."

"They who?"

"Well, the Cithrans killed all the priests, didn't they? The temples are empty. Now the Feowans are looking for anyone with smidgen of talent. They force them to take holy orders."

"But you're married."

"They won't care." He inspected his fingernails.

She stared at him. "Is this what you wanted to talk to me about? You're afraid of being drafted?"

"That, among other things."

Her eyes darted back to the fields beyond where her husband worked, well out of sight now. "I can't talk with you. I'm married now, don't you understand?"

"Talking is not a crime."

"Everything else is." Her words were heavy with meaning.

Indeed, they never 'just talked'. A few memories of her soft flesh pressed against his sent his blood rushing to his loins. "Ah, yes." He put a bit of embarrassment in his expression. "How does that happen?"

"Well, you show up on my doorstep with some excuse or another. You say you mean only to talk, and then..."

"And then you seduce me."

That lit her fire. He watched, with inner glee, as the sparks lit her eyes. She worked up a temper to deny any spark of desire within her. "I seduce you?"

"Is that so bad?" He jumped off the fence. She took a step backwards. Instead of pressing his advance, he changed his tactics. "Remember the first time we met? I'd fallen off my horse and had done something to my ankle."

She folded her arms. "I remember."

"You're a kind soul who would take in an injured stranger. How would I know I was to fall victim to your charms? Your hands were so soft as you tended to me... Oh," he concluded, waving his arms in exasperation. "You were meant for better things, Mistress Saponer." He knelt to run his fingers through the turned earth. "Not grubbing around in the dirt like some..." He, still in his genuflective position, looked up at her. "You're a woman of great knowledge and skill. And now you're a common farmer? Does your husband know what you are capable of? Or are you just some convenient body on which to sate himself without a thought for the person underneath?"

She winced. He'd hit a nerve. He rose and took a step forward.

She bowed her head in sorrow and bitterness. She missed him, of that Mor-Lath was certain. He put his arms around her shoulders.

But at his touch, she flinched, shrugging her shoulders out from his touch.

"Come now," he besought. "We are old friends. I am not asking to go inside. We can stay out here. Let us talk, like we always intend. Your heart is heavy. Mine is too. Let us seek comfort on each other's shoulders, not in each other's arms." He held out his hand in invitation.

She looked at it, then at him, then to the potatoes stacked and back to him. She hesitated a moment before placing her hand in his.

He had her. He sent a small thrill of passion through her that got her heart beating again. Then he did what he knew would win over any woman. He attentively listened to her sorrows.

She tried to defend her husband, for he was a clever farmer, well-respected in the community. But what about love?

"He doesn't thrill you," Mor-Lath prompted.

"No." By now, she was enveloped in Mor-Lath's arms. "It's like there is a wall between us. I get no sense of passion, of..." she drew in a sharp breath. From the tension in her shoulders he knew she fought tears. "I don't feel anything."

"Did you expect to?"

"Yes."

"Why?"

She thought of this. "I thought I was supposed to."

"Because... we did?"

She didn't answer.

He stroked her face, making his touch leave a trail of excitement on her skin. "I thought you would have, even with him. You are such a passionate woman."

She brushed away his hand. He enveloped her hand in his then kissed her. Just as she was to deepen the kiss, he pulled back. "You kissed me," he said putting surprise in his voice.

But he had succeeded. Her blood burned with desire for him. Her other hand grabbed his head and pulled his face to hers.

The rest was easy.

Chapter 13

Adrastea strolled along the shelves of the library, her fingers lightly brushing their spines. She'd paced like this for some time now, letting the rhythmic thrum of her fingers across the books relax her and allow her to think without distraction.

He'd rejected her, the one woman he should have been free with. If he couldn't bed his wife—and those memories he'd shared proved he wasn't impotent—then why choose celibacy?

She'd spent the past week giving herself a rather embarrassing education in the acts of love, with all the techniques and tricks the book contained. Then she'd snuck it back to the library, to find others there on similar subjects.

The sensual arts were simple to master, to draw a man into desire, if the books were to be believed. How one stood, how one spoke, how one moved were powerful tools. She'd practiced in the mirror, standing, back arched, arms uplifted, to display her bosom to perfection. Then slide a foot to the side, tilt the head just so... At first it looked a little silly but as she grew used to the movements, she improved her technique. Not bad. Smooth enough to seduce a mortal man. Could she seduce a god?

Before she put her plan into action she had to make sure he was seducible. That his heart pumped and his blood raced, of this she was certain. She thought of the times during their courtship when she had weakened under temptation. He'd taken her to the wall of Feown and tempted her with power. Instead of killing the half-million then, as he had intended, she'd succumbed to its sweetness. Her desire had rolled over to him; that kiss was not one-sided.

Then later he'd tempted her with Power again and she'd failed to control it. Its raw creativeness spilled over into her instinctual need to mate. He'd shared her ardor for a moment, then stopped her.

Then there was the time on her mother's porch, when she pushed all the Deeper Power she had into him. Her original intention was to destroy him, but it had the opposite effect, his senses overwhelmed. He'd said, "We're not doing that again without the benefit of matrimony."

Well, here they were, married, and no advantage had been taken.

He'd stopped her every time. He could have besmirched her and then claim to do the "honorable" thing by marrying her. That would have been simple.

But then, that wouldn't have been fully willing. That would have been serving duty. He'd made it very clear from the beginning that he needed her willing.

Why? Was it so she would not regret her choice? Or was there some other reason?

She'd reached the end of the row. She turned the corner of the shelves and ran her fingers along the next aisle of books. Thump, thump, thump. She matched her pace so her fingers thrummed three books per step.

In the end, he'd threatened Sacred Spring and she gave in. How willing what that? Seduction would have been neater, easier and quicker.

But he didn't.

And that brought her back to her original question: was he or wasn't he celibate? He was the sort of man who enjoyed the sensual side of things. He was passionate. He was melodramatic. He was selfish from time to time. But try as she did, she couldn't come up with a single shred of evidence that supported his being currently sexually active.

So, what if he was celibate? A tendril of disappointment wrapped around her heart. Was it out of choice, or necessity? It couldn't be because he felt no desire. That kiss on the parapet at Feown was not the kiss of an uninterested man.

He chose celibacy? Why?

Why? echoed a book. *Why what?*

She snatched her fingers away in surprise, then replaced them on the leather spine. "Why would the Dark God choose celibacy?"

The book didn't know.

Adrastea continued her promenade down the aisle but instead of being lost in her own thoughts, she fixed the question in her head and addressed the books as she walked.

No answer, no answer, no answer. At the end of the row she moved to the next aisle and tried again. She expanded the question: Mor-Lath and love, Mor-Lath and sex, Mor-Lath and virtue... No luck.

She ran out of patience before she ran out of library. "Is there anything in here concerning him?"

The books on craftsmanship didn't have a clue. But he handled them once, if that was any help. It was a long time ago, though.

What about prophecy? Adrastea went back to the section containing books of prophecy. Her fingers skimmed spines. Prophecies of Mor-Lath?

One book thought it might have some, then another. Then several, then lots. There were a few books that remembered being taken off the shelf many times, to be deeply perused.

She selected a few of these to read at the table. Reading came easy now. Had she tried to tackle these books pre-immortality, it might have taken her all year. Still, this would not be a short task.

No sooner had she cracked the cover than she heard a voice in front of her.

"There you are. Put that book away and come on," said Mor-Lath. "I've got something important to show you."

Adrastea looked up. She hadn't heard him enter the Library. Before she could open her mouth to say something, he had disappeared. His presence lingered, for he left faint ripples along the threads of the Deeper Power.

Was he paying attention to her now? Did he want to share something with her? Adrastea dropped her book in her haste to follow. She didn't want to risk him changing his mind.

He hadn't gone far. By pressing her hand to her cheek, she sensed him close by, possibly out in the temple courtyard. As she left the library, she saw a pair of priestesses hurrying far ahead of her.

Adrastea closed her eyes and imagined herself within the great courtyard of the palace.

A touch of Power and she was there.

When she opened her eyes, she saw half the priestesses gathered in a loose circle around Mor-Lath and more joining them.

He looked up, his hazel green eyes singling her out. "You're late."

She blushed and turned away. If he knew the goal of her research, he didn't show it. Any thoughts she had fled the stage of her mind when she saw what Mor-Lath had in his hands. Adrastea pushed forward through the priestesses. They let her pass with slight dips of their knees.

Mor-Lath held a firearm, similar to the one Natan owned. This one looked newer and not as long in the barrel. Still, its length reached Mor-Lath's shoulder. Uncle Natan never let her touch his gun. Her hand hesitated now, several inches shy of the gleaming barrel. Yet something about the weapon drew her.

"This is a breech-loading rifle." He hefted it up so they all could see. "It's a new kind of firearm."

The priestesses oohed and murmured in excitement. Who could blame them? She wanted to hold it in her hands. She'd watched Natan fire his gun once, shoving gunpowder, wadding, lead bullet and tamping it down before firing it, making her ears ring with its loud report. How would she fire one and hold her hands over her ears at the same time?

"There may come a time when you need to use one of these, so I'm going to show you now." He pointed to the far end of the courtyard where he had set up several bales of hay, with bullseyes on cloth, like the archery targets during fairetime.

Wasting no more words, he lifted the rifle to his shoulder and squeezed the trigger.

The report echoed in the courtyard, as loud as she remembered. Most of the priestesses shrieked in surprise. Somewhere beyond the walls of the courtyard, she heard a dog bark.

A few of the younger ones started running towards the target.

"Stop!" he commanded. All the priestesses dropped to their knees in obeisance, leaving Adrastea the only woman standing.

He fired the gun again, startling everyone. Even Adrastea let out a shriek. How did he load it again so fast? Everyone scuttled back.

Then Adrastea saw what he did. There was a little knob on the side of the gun. With great speed, he moved this knob down, inserted a small object, then moved the knob back. He lifted the rifle to his shoulder and fired a third time.

When the echo of the explosion faded from the walls of the temple, did he speak. "Do not run before the end of a rifle. Because of this swift repeating action, is a more dangerous weapon than its predecessor. You wait until it is safe, then you may inspect the target."

Desideria sat up and watched him expectantly. The rest of them kept their faces pressed to the ground. He gave a nod to her. She gave the order. Now they could go look.

All but the few who had disobeyed rose and rushed to the target. Adrastea didn't bother. She knew he had hit it straight on.

The acrid smoke of the barrel made her nose twitch. She'd smelled something similar during the attack of Sacred Spring and later Feown. Guns were weapons of war. She knew their scent. Natan had shot small rabbits from time to time and even wounded the occasional deer, allowing fellow hunters to catch and dispatch the animal.

Did this rifle, like Natan's muzzle-loader, leave bruises and even crack bones like stones from a sling, or did they pierce the body like arrows? She and Ari had dealt with arrow injuries. For all the war they hadn't faced, neither one had ever treated a gunshot wound.

While the priestesses exclaimed over his excellent marksmanship, he reloaded the weapon. A flick of the lever, a new bullet.

"Where did you get this new rifle?" Adrastea asked.

He watched his priestesses as they cleared the target area. "The Cithrans have them, though they are not practical in hand-to-hand battle."

"So why teach us how to use them? Wouldn't arrows be more efficient?"

He leaned on his rifle, resting his chin on the top of the barrel. "The world is progressing. Industry and inventions that didn't exist ten years ago are now commonplace. Right now, Tredan inventors are developing an even better weapon, one that you load up with all the bullets you mean to shoot. Then you can fire as often as you can pull the trigger." He stroked his hand down the barrel of the rifle.

"We can either stay in the comfortable ignorance of sticks and stones or we can move with the dance of Creation and apply men's novel ideas. Believe me, if the Cithrans are going to be using these, we should be using something better."

"Who are 'we'?"

He held out the rifle. "You first, then."

She took it. It was far heavier than she expected. Mor-Lath moved behind her to help. His arms came around her to help her steady the rifle and position it properly. The warmth of his body pressed into her back. The question of his potential abstinence rose in her mind. She quickly stuffed the thought back into its corner. This was no time for distraction.

"Don't tuck the stock under your arm," he instructed. "It rests against your shoulder."

It fit there but the rifle was awkward to hold. It wanted to dip down in the front. She drew on the Deeper Power to lift it up and steady it.

He drew in a slight breath. "If you must cheat."

He supported her left arm with his hand, sliding his palm slowly down her elbow. "Put your finger on the trigger and sight down the barrel." As he did that, thrill of excitement flowed to her through the lines on her face. He enjoyed this, possibly too much.

"See that nub at the end? Align that between the two closer to you, and match them up with the target," he murmured in her ear. She felt his warm breath on her skin and she nearly dropped the rifle. "When you're ready, squeeze the trigger."

His arms were around her when she fired. The rifle had quite a kick, to her surprise. He braced her against the impact and then caught the rifle as she let the end drop. "You couldn't even hit the wall."

"Well, it was my first time shooting a rifle."

"Now it's your first time to load it as well."

Adrastea took the proffered bullet. It was a long shape, the top the familiar lead but the shank was a tubular case of brass. She'd watched him load it the first time. Adrastea copied his motions of levering open the bolt, ejecting the spent cartridge, inserting the bullet, and closing it up again, all before he could instruct her.

He only grunted his reluctant approval. He helped her hold the weapon. He needed to touch her. His desire seeped through the lines on her face. Not so cold then.

Again, he wrapped his arms around her to help her hold the rifle properly, steadying it against her.

She drew in a breath. She had to relax. If she let his feelings distract her, she would lose her aim again.

And there was nothing wrong with cheating. Adrastea called upon the Deeper Power and felt it fill her. Behind her, Mor-Lath gasped. "What are—" Adrastea sighted and pulled the trigger. She did not need to inspect the target to know her shot was true.

"Cheating," she murmured.

The sillier priestesses yelped again because they had not covered their ears. Radelisa exclaimed, "I do believe you hit the target." The others murmured their admiration as well.

Putting down the rifle, Adrastea said to the priestesses, "Go on. See how well I did." She held the Deeper Power around her, to give her confidence. She'd done well. She did not want him taking away her glory.

A smile of satisfaction lit her face. She did it. She'd fired the weapon and struck true.

He didn't say anything but looked at her. She met his gaze. He drew in a deep breath.

Something within her sang, whether it was the triumph of her aim, the Deeper Power within or simply being close to him. She enjoyed his presence next to her.

An impulse possessed her. Adrastea slid her free hand up to his head and kissed him. Her lips brushed his. She broke contact for a moment before his lips descended on hers, returning her kiss and deepening it. His hands slipped to her waist as if they'd always belonged there, pulling her closer. For a moment, she melted into him. Her awareness of the courtyard faded as the sweetness of the kiss sang to a yearning place within her soul.

"I wish I could aim like that," a priestess commented to her companion, studying the target.

"I wish I could kiss like that," came the reply. Her companion's attention was on a different target.

Both Mor-Lath and Adrastea heard that. They broke apart. Their eyes met for a moment before he turned away. He took the rifle from her hands and stepped around her. The loss of contact was so abrupt, she hadn't time to blush for being caught in the act.

"Desideria, you're next." If the priestesses' comments irked him, he didn't show it.

Feeling snubbed, Adrastea stood to the side and watched as he instructed the others. She lost her interest in the new weapon. She drew on the Deeper Power to fill the empty space that cropped up within her. Mor-Lath frowned at her. She'd distracted him. Leaving him with his priestesses, she returned to the Library and to her books.

Only once she was there, she could not concentrate. The problem of Mor-Lath intruded upon her thoughts. She left the table and began to pace.

Celibacy, or not? It didn't make much sense. Why did he spend all that time wooing her before the marriage, only to push her away once he got what he wanted? Other than her transformation to immortality, she hadn't felt any different. He certainly wasn't any different from before, other than the new emotional distance. If he'd wanted her, he could have had her. That first day, she would have been curious, maybe reluctant, surely bewildered but would she truly have told him no?

It wasn't like he was ugly. Glory, no! Had he been a mortal man she would have quite enjoyed the thought of him in her bed.

She had to admit, reluctantly, that her mind had not exactly been free of impure thoughts in that direction where he was concerned.

Even if he was a god.

Upon further thought, she was not ugly herself. Even as a mortal, she'd been one of the better-looking girls of Sacred Spring. No doubt if it wasn't for her mother's reputation, several young men might have approached her, possibly catching her wandering off beyond the village green on Council night to watch the stars. Only none of them had taken her fancy, then.

Now, here she was married, and her husband wouldn't touch her.

He hadn't been expecting that kiss. Adrastea put her fingers to her lips. She wanted it to happen again, only this time, no snub, no being ignored. That had hurt.

She wanted to hurt him back but how does one hurt a god?

Her eyes fell on the five books she'd brought to the table. They contained prophecies, possibly reasons as to why her marriage had not been consummated yet.

Resuming her seat, she drew the top volume towards her.

It was written in Feowan, her first language. While she had picked up the knack of reading other languages, the conversion of the words into understandable ideas disconcerted her. Foreign words might have had similar meanings to Feowan words but then they could also mean something else. In older dialects words sometimes have the altered or even opposite meaning than their modern counterparts. She couldn't always discern when it meant one thing versus another unless she was really concentrating.

Good old Feowan. There was little doubt what a word meant when she read it.

The book wanted to fall open to a certain page. She turned back a page to see if the chapter started there. It didn't start until several pages back. But before she completely turned over the pages, a phrase caught her eye.

Mashiah. Amarice's baby had been a mashiah. Mor-Lath had feared him so much not only did he kill the baby but saw Amarice and Marlon dead as well, so they could not have another. Poor Amarice. She had wanted a baby so much. Adrastea sent up a little prayer to the Light that Amarice had found comfort after death.

A mashiah, according to the book, was an individual, whose feet were *"planted firmly in Creation. He lives to salve or spoil the world. He holds in his hands the power to destroy the gods if he must and shake the foundations of Creation."*

That went a long way to explaining why Mor-Lath feared a baby; the baby could grow up to be a man who could "destroy the gods if he must".

Adrastea firmly pressed away the memory of Mor-Lath's vision given to her of Amarice's son as a man. Perhaps that image was the result of the god's own fears projected.

It didn't explain the celibacy, though.

Unless...

She stared at a line at the bottom of the page. She let the words tumble about in her mind, forming and reforming. It seemed as if her mind wanted to make them mean something else. Then she shook her head and looked at them again.

"For if there should be one, the son of Mor-Lath should destroy him."

So that was it! His compelling reason for his reluctance to consummate their marriage.

She slumped back and lifted her gaze to the ceiling. A tiny little line within her heart snapped. All the eagerness of finding an answer, an undefined hope, and her vision of the future drained away. It flowed down and out her limbs until they felt heavy.

Always the bride, never the wife. That couldn't be right. She didn't want it to be right.

She closed the book so no more bitter words could escape its pages and torment her further.

There were four other books in the pile she brought to the table. "Do you all speak of the Son of Mor-Lath?"

Three affirmative, two no.

Oh. "Do you speak of the Bride of Mor-Lath?"

All claimed they did.

Alas. Then, "Do any of you speak of the Wife of Mor-Lath?"

To her surprise, all five books responded in the affirmative.

She selected one of the books that did not speak of the Son of Mor-Lath and opened it. To her dismay, it was written in Avelian. In pique she slammed the cover shut.

That kiss was not the kiss of a celibate man.

So, what if she was not experienced in this area? Had he been as inexperienced as she, no doubt their first few kisses would have been awkward affairs.

But they hadn't been.

Adrastea traced the leather pattern of the book with her finger. She cupped her chin in her hand. Even if he did not believe in full consummation, at least he had no compunction about kissing. Surely, he could engage in a bit more of that with her.

But then her heart ached. She remembered the few times they had kissed, deeply and passionately. To her dismay, it hadn't been enough. She'd wanted more. He'd refused.

She cried out in frustration and knocked her forehead on the table.

So. There was this prophecy, about a son of Mor-Lath who would kill him. Now, it could have been taken figuratively, that the "son of Mor-Lath" could have been not a son of his body but something else. A high priest, perhaps? One who would betray him? Maybe that was why he kept only priestesses?

Yet it seemed he believed the "son of Mor-Lath" to be a literal son. He was taking the best precautions he knew how.

If that were true, then that was that. At least he could have told her from the beginning. She might have accepted a celibate marriage.

Well, no, she wouldn't. A little niggly voice deep in her head refused the idea. A celibate marriage was not a real marriage.

Ever since the kiss in the courtyard, she'd felt a frission of sexual tension in the lines of her face. Oh, how hard it must have been for him to resist.

A sudden rush of passion ignited the connection between them. What on earth was that about?

She pressed her hands to her cheeks to silence the lines.

No matter how hard she tried, she couldn't get them to stop. Tears filled her eyes and spilled down her face. Even they could not quench the awful fire.

A frightening thought threatened her control. She fought it and pushed it away, for if it was true, it would surely break her heart.

Jonathan picked at a scab on his hand. His leprousness had faded as soon as he'd obeyed the Light. But how was his heart to heal? And how would he cope with Saraym's? He trailed behind her as she inspected General Tropeter's military grounds.

What had once been a parade ground at the palace was now given over to the recruitment, training and housing of hundreds of women. Tents, purloined from the Cithrans, lined the walls of the palace. Weapons—also 'gifts' of the Cithrans—were used in drilling and practice. Many of the women had a type of firearm Jonathan had never seen before. Would he have been able to use one? He'd never handled a gun in his life. Neither had most of the women they'd recruited. Yet here they were, aiming and firing with a rapidly-improving accuracy. They also trained with knives and in hand-to-hand.

Their anger had driven them to recruitment tables in droves. It was the promise of the Duchess' shilling and regular feeding of them and their families, that kept them there. Men went to war because their blood sang the song of violence. Women went to war in defense of their loved ones.

The few surviving male soldiers ensured these new female soldiers were brought up to scratch.

If Jonathan squinted, he could have sworn every soldier was a man. Each one wore the uniform of a soldier and trousers. They didn't look right on a woman, bunching up in all the wrong places. However, it did provide for easier movement. Skirts did hamper one.

Saraym still wore skirts, albeit greatly shortened. Underneath, she wore pantaloons like a little girl. The hue of her costume reflected her deep mourning. "Lord Pennexter," she addressed him. No matter how many times he'd told her priests were never addressed by any titles they held in civilian life, she insisted on it. "I have been pondering."

Jonathan's stomach flip-flopped. Whenever Saraym announced she had been thinking, it meant something unpleasant. "Yes, Your Grace?"

"As a priest, don't you find it odd that both the Dark and the Light wish to see the Cithrans destroyed?"

He stumbled a few steps. "I beg your pardon?" She did not stop her pace. He had to scramble to catch up.

"Adrastea and her husband are most interested in my restoring my fortunes to strengthen Feown. And then you come along, telling me to tap into hidden resources and strike when I have advantage. I wonder what could be so powerful to get the Light and the Dark to work together."

"Is that what she said?" He wondered about this Country Adrastea. Her Grace's statement all but confirmed that Country Adrastea was indeed a Dark Priestess.

"What? That you are working together?"

Jonathan waved his hands. "No, no. That she had Feown's best interests at heart?"

"Something like that."

"You believe her?"

Saraym stopped, her boots sinking into newly-churned dirt, the turf long torn up by marching feet. "I don't believe either one of you. I will do as I see fit. The Dark has a reputation for not being trusted. The Light has a reputation for not being there when I need Her. The only wisdom I can trust is my own."

Jonathan spotted one of General Tropeter's colonels. He wore a dress, like all the men had when they'd hidden out in Her Grace's salon. Unlike the frilly things they sported that day, they now wore something very similar to Saraym's own clothing—namely, shorter, less-full skirts, and some sort of pantalet underneath. How much longer was Her Grace going to insist on this feminine uniform?

Jonathan looked at his own priestly robes. "If your faith is waning, why do you keep me close?"

She didn't answer at first. When she resumed her walking, he followed but didn't dare disturb her. When she thought, her brow furrowed, her attention turned inward, and she paced, hands behind her back.

A century of trousered young women marched by, double-time, kept pace by an angry-sounding man in a skirt.

Saraym said, "You believe you server a higher power, one who supports benevolent goals. Therefore, anything you suggest is because you believe is for the greater good." She held up a finger. "Doesn't necessarily mean it will be. In the past many have committed great atrocities in the name of Greater Good. After all, the Cithrans believed in their One True, and a purity of doctrine."

That took him aback. "Surely you don't think—"

"I think what I will. While the Cithrans' devotion to the letter of the law can achieve great results, they're very much into the violation of the spirit of the law." She frowned again. "They're very much into violation of all kinds, aren't they?"

Jonathan's breath caught in his throat. What under the Light was he supposed to say to that?

"Therefore, I will judge by that which follows both the letter and the spirit of what I think is best for Feown." She gave him a sideways glance. "What are your thoughts on mercy?"

Was this a test? "Generally, I am in favor of it."

"And should we show mercy to the Cithrans?"

Yes, it was a test. What was the best answer? What would be too weak, what would seem too hypocritical? Cryptic would look pathetic.

He sent a silent prayer to the Light: *guide my words.* "I would suggest showing them the mercy they didn't show you."

She took these words in. He could see her rolling them around in her head. If she came to any conclusions, she did not share them with him. Instead, "Answers like that is why I keep you around."

She continued her tour of the grounds. "You know, the more I think about your idea of an army of women, the more I like it."

Jonathan sighed. It wasn't his idea.

"Albeit, there are many who think this a ridiculous idea. They think I'm hysterical, that I'm ridiculous, and that warfare is best left to the men." She ran her tongue over her teeth. "What should I do with them?"

At least Jonathan had an answer for this: "Prove them wrong." After all, if the Light believe this was the best course of action, naturally it would succeed.

Her reply was low and full of raw promise. "Oh, I plan on it."

$\backsim\!\circ\!\!\circ\!\!\infty\!\!\circ\!\!\sim$

Chapter 14

A man dressed in the livery of a High Council secretary knocked on the Intelligence Minister's office door.

"Come," said an unfamiliar voice, young and only just broken.

The secretary brushed his lanky blond hair out of his handsome eyes and entered the office.

Inside, it seemed he'd entered a jewelry box. Thick red carpet covered the floor and maroon curtains, tightly closed, of course, draped the windows.

Another secretary, a junior one, if the lack of insignia on his shoulders was any indication, stood near the door. "Ah. You are not who the Minister is expecting."

The Minister himself had been pacing behind a giant, ornately gilded desk. He'd paused when the doors had opened but when he saw it was but another secretary, he resumed his pacing.

"The Minister is very busy." The junior secretary hastened after him.

"I know," the blond secretary replied. "I bring him further reports."

The junior held out his hand. "Give them to me. I'll see he gets them."

The blond secretary stared the junior down. "Or I can hand them to him myself."

A shiver ran up the junior's back. He took a step away. "I..." He hastened out of the office.

With a flick of his hand, the doors closed, leaving the secretary alone with the Minister. "Have you acquired the final volunteers?"

The Intelligence Minister kept pacing. "I am not ready to report to the Speaking Minister."

"That is a no, then?"

"He needs to give me more time. Half my network perished when the army died. I've lost contact with most of my foreign agents. I don't know if they're dead or captured." He shook his head. "I can't send inexperienced agents out in the field. None of them speak those foreign languages." He shuddered at the thought. To poison one's mind with obscene, foreign ideas was a shameful thing. To be able to speak the language of a foreigner, unheard of. Only properly trained spies, with the absolution of One True, could ever hope to carry out what this secretary was asking.

The secretary came forward. "You know how important this is. Thanks to your network, we were able to ascertain the existence of the Bride and where she has been seen. But we must hurry. She plans to destroy the world. Neglect of one's duty would shame you. Do you wish to face the One True god with such sins on your soul?"

The minister stopped his pacing. "It may be a sin to neglect one's duty. It is also a sin to act rashly. Invading Feown was rash. I advise caution this time. I will not risk another direct confrontation with the Bride."

"Perhaps you are right," the secretary conceded. As he opened the door, he offered his final opinion: "Do as you see fit. Get your spies in place as quickly as you can. I would not wish to stand before the One True having not done my best."

Adrastea pressed her hands to her face. The powerful emotions of lust and fear that radiated through her lines had eased but not dissipated entirely.

What was he doing? The lines also told her he was nowhere near the Temple but far away to the east.

A sense of satisfaction tinged with bitterness finished off the experience.

She laid her head on the table. Sorrow welled within her and threatened to spill out her eyes.

Mor-Lath appeared in the library, smug and self-satisfied. His back was to her. He didn't know she was here.

He flung his jacket onto the table and held out his arms as if to an appreciative audience.

Adrastea lifted her head. "Mor-Lath, where have you been?"

He turned to her, his relaxed expression dropping into wariness, then moving to contempt. "Nowhere of interest to you." His defenses went up. He radiated annoyance, not guilt.

That offended her. She stood and moved around the table. Adrastea reached out to grab his shirtsleeved arm. "Tell me where you've been!"

He pulled his arm from her grasp. "None of your business."

Too late. The moment she requested knowledge, the fabric of the shirt remembered. In a moment her senses were overwhelmed with its memories, the dark temple she had seen earlier, a dusky-skinned priestess, her grasping hands pulling the shirt away, and then skin upon skin. Images of the whole scene burned themselves into her mind.

Every kiss, every touch, desperate and needy, the total surrender to lust until it was satisfied. And the familiarity. This was no awkward fumbling of a first time but the practiced habit of repeat offenders.

Adrastea put her hands over her eyes but that only pushed the vision deeper into her mind. Instead, she covered her mouth to hold in the ache of betrayal.

Mor-Lath had been with another woman.

He snatched up his jacket and strode away. "My business is none of your concern. You may be my wife, but I'll be damned if I'll let you turn into a shrew." He ran from the library, letting the door slam behind him.

Adrastea battled against the memories, as fresh as if they were her own. The chit was young, more girl than woman. She opened her arms and legs far too easily.

Oh, how she wanted to deny it. But one cannot deny truth. "By Creation, I will not be turned into a cuckold either." The tears welled up hard and fast and full and spilled down her face in a hot torrent.

It seemed he was not a celibate after all. Quite the contrary. He had no problems indulging himself.

Just not with her.

A drastea fled to the darkest corner of her stillroom. She bawled until her eyes were sore with dryness and her throat thick with sorrow. When all her self-pity had bled out, only a hard knot of anger remained. Her limbs felt numb, as did her head.

She'd sacrificed her life and her dreams to marry Mor-Lath. Was she not to get even the least benefit out of a marriage?

Who was this woman he so freely gave his attentions to? Adrastea closed her eyes and focused on the memory given to her by the shirt.

She felt the change in the air around her, from slightly cool and still, to warm and oppressive. The humidity enveloped her skin. When she opened her eyes, she saw the flickering of lamps that did little to dispel the darkness.

This was not her stillroom.

She was not alone. She heard gasps of surprise. Several people shuffled away from her. Worshippers on their knees.

Adrastea looked about. She had arrived at a temple with stone walls, narrow windows and altar. She had not expected an audience of people. Her resolve wavered momentarily but she steeled her nerves. Her rage still burned, a hot little lump in her chest.

As one, they all stood, about twenty of them, backing away. Only one man remained seated. Dressed in a simple brown robe, he was not of this crowd but occupied one of the benches along the wall.

His long hair had been scraped back from his dusky-skinned face. His robes had seen better days. He did not radiate fear like the others but intense curiosity as he stroked his lower lip. The others may have been worshippers, but his aura said 'priest'. He studied her as she studied him. So. Mor-Lath had priests as well.

"Who are you to disturb our worship?" a feminine voice demanded. Avelian.

Adrastea turned. It was her, the woman of the vision. Instead of sprawled naked across the altar (he took her on a sacred altar?) she stood behind it, clad in a dark robe. A priestess? So much for his policy. A scowl distorted her dark, elegant features.

For a brief moment, the memory of the woman's face in ecstasy flashed before her. Adrastea's guts knotted up.

No. Breathe. It took a few inhalations, but she kept a reign on her temper.

She strolled forward, each step a study in measured casualness. "I should be asking you who you are. You're just a priestess, aren't you?"

The woman's scowl deepened.

A murmur rose from the crowd, which shushed when Adrastea scowled back. She was on to something. "I assume you are a priestess, as well as a whore?"

The woman's voice dripped with arrogance. "I am more than just a priestess, stranger. I am The Priestess. I am the Bride of Mor-Lath." Her fingers lingered at the opening of the robe, just above her breasts. "And you are interrupting me."

Adrastea's mouth gaped. She shook her head. "You're not the Bride of Mor-Lath."

The woman drew in a breath of indignation. "I am. I bear his mark."

But her face was clean. She had no black scars marring her cheeks. Adrastea's hand slipped up to her own face. She stopped before touching her lines. She did not want Mor-Lath to know what she did here. If he favored this priestess, she did not want him interfering.

Interfering in what? Her stomach clenched in anticipation. A dark thought niggled in the back of her head. "I do not see any mark on you."

The woman sneered as she undid her robe. She flung it open, displaying her nakedness not only to Adrastea but to the others present. A sigh of awe rolled through the congregation. The man on the bench whistled in amazement. But was it for the appreciation of a woman's body, or for...

On the woman's lower belly was the clear mark of a man's hand, almost black against her dark skin.

Adrastea did not have one of those. What did it mean?

This woman was dramatic, rather like Mor-Lath. "I assure you it is real."

Did he mark all his priestesses in this manner? Did Desideria have the same handprint?

Adrastea thought fast. "You can't be. He hasn't married you." Had he? A whole slew of possibilities threatened to gnaw at her self-confidence. She shoved them back. She needed to stay strong. But for what?

The arrogance in the woman's face slipped a little. She regained control. "I have His Holiness' personal favor."

"Personal favor? What's that supposed to mean."

A smug smile crossed the woman's lips. "I mean, *personal*."

Adrastea felt sick. The shirt's memory flooded back. Only this time, as this priestess strove against his naked body, her face turned towards Adrastea as if she knew she was looking. Her smile of triumph was an ugly one. She mocked Adrastea.

Adrastea snapped. The anger and the shame she held at bay spilled out of its tiny prison. It washed her soul of doubt and restraint.

She thrust her hand up to Creation. Let the Deeper Power flow into her!

The self-satisfied expression on the priestess' face wavered. The walls of the temple hummed with Adrastea's effort.

In front of everyone, Adrastea ripped the soul from the priestess' body. It came away like a gossamer web, clinging to Adrastea's fingers. Panicked cries rippled through the crowd. The priestess' lifeless body tumbled to the floor. Their agitation grew as they pressed back against the walls.

Adrastea's anger burned hot in her heart. "Listen to me, you idiots! I am the true Bride of Mor-Lath, not this pretender." She jabbed a finger down at the dead body. "I am and no other. I will not be mocked!"

In panic, they fled, crowding the door at the back until nearly every soul had gone.

Only one person remained. The man on the bench in the back sprang to his feet. "I believe you. I believe you." He held out his hands as if to calm a skittish colt.

Could she trust him? He was a middle-aged man whose body reflected a life free from physical labor. Lord, perhaps? His skin was shiny. His hair looked like it could have used a wash. His voice sounded the same.

"Forgive me, great lady. Only a true Bride of Mor-Lath can control such Power."

She wrinkled her nose. "Who are you?"

He sketched a bow and remained low. "Only a humble priest and servant of His Holiness."

Adrastea held up the priestess' soul by the scruff. She could see through the soul as if it were a shimmery veil of falling water. Now that the priestess was free from the obscurity of mortality, Adrastea could see her every thought and emotion. The priestess was named Desmone. Yes, she did have the favor of Mor-Lath. Adrastea's fist tightened on the soul. The priestess, knowing what had happened to her, cried out. But nobody reacted to her pain. Could it be only Adrastea could see her? The priest watched her with great caution. Perhaps he could see the soul as well.

Adrastea scowled at him. "And you knew about this, this blasphemy?" Yes, that was exactly what it was.

He inclined his head. "I am but a humble priest—"

"Don't give me that! If you aren't good for any answers, I might fail to see why I should keep you around."

His Adam's apple bobbed. "I had no knowledge of you, high lady. I knew that a Bride existed." He extended his hand to the corpse on the floor. "She bore signs."

"Now you bear witness." She shook Desmone's soul at him. "I will not tolerate this nonsense."

"Mistress, do not allow me to keep you from your business. I see you have much on your mind."

This was true. Then Adrastea realized she was being dismissed. How presumptuous! Her anger swelled once more. "What is your name, priest?" she snapped.

The man avoided her gaze. "I am honored that you would want to know my name."

"Well?" She stretched out her hand, intending to reft him of his soul if he displeased her as well.

"It is Montrof," he offered quickly. He bowed once again and withdrew, moving backwards to the door, punctuating his movements with bows. "I am not a remarkable man. I beg to withdraw from your august presence."

Adrastea looked at the wispy soul of Desmone, who cried in useless regret. She departed, the soul of Desmone clutched tightly in her fist.

❧

Back at the Maiden's Tower in Feown, Adrastea caught her breath. What had she done? When she went to Avelia, to the temple of shame, it wasn't with intent to kill.

Was it?

The soul of the priestess remained trapped among her fingers. Adrastea squeezed her fist and sent the full power of her anger against the soul.

Desmone squeaked, more in anguish than physical pain. She was more an idea than a corporeal being. As a result, not only could Adrastea sense her emotions but could see her very thoughts swirl through the center of her being like smoke. She had her last memory, of offering devotions at the altar. Her emotions were one of pride, yet there was a small streak of shame.

Adrastea didn't care.

When she loosened her grip, Desmone tried to form herself into a personage. That's how she remembered herself. As she looked at what could have been her hands, the rest of her blurred. It took a fair bit of concentration to pull herself together.

"You've been spreading your legs for my husband." Adrastea could not keep the shakiness from her voice. Adrastea held a corner of her soul between thumb and finger.

Desmone leaned back as far as she could get. "I've done no such thing." The confusion resolving to self-doubt said otherwise. "Um, which one was yours?"

Adrastea twisted a corner of the soul around her finger. A breeze blew across the wall of the Maiden's Tower, bringing the smell of woodsmoke. "Do you sleep with so many men you can't keep them straight? Or are they so insignificant to you that you forget about them even before your sheets are cold?"

"I am not a whore," Desmone countered.

"Could have fooled me."

"It's not like that," the priestess shrilled. "I enjoy the special favor of His Holiness. None other."

Adrastea wound more of Desmone's soul around her finger. As twilight deepened across the land Adrastea called forth a small light, just enough to illuminate the soul before her. "See, that's the problem. 'His Holiness' shouldn't be—" A stray thought through Desmone's soul caught Adrastea's eye. "Today was not the first time, was it?"

"I didn't say anything!"

Adrastea gathered the rest of Desmone until she was bunched up like a fistful of shirtfront. "You don't need to. I can see into the depths of your soul."

Desmone whimpered.

"How long as this been going on? How long?"

Desmone clammed up but her memories tumbled through her. Adrastea's horror grew as Desmone sorted through her every memory of Mor-Lath, from today's pleasures back... back to her supplications and his personal answers, back... through the tortures of waiting in a cold room naked. Adrastea had no idea what that meant, back... back to the first day.

Desmone knelt before an altar and prayed for her god's favor. He came to her that day, finally answering what had been a long succession of prayers. He'd granted her, then and there, her specific request. The pleasure of it shuddered through her memories. Even her fear and shock of death could not dampen it completely.

Envy twisted Adrastea's soul. This priestess, no older than she was, had known such great pleasure that it overwhelmed her even now. After the most powerful part of the memory passed, Desmone's soul ached. It was only a memory. No satisfaction to be had. A tiny flare of frustration nibbled at the edges of that memory.

"When was this?" Adrastea demanded. "Show me!"

"I'm not sure."

Adrastea frowned. The glow of the light grew brighter as if to illuminate the darkest recesses of the dead soul.

Of course, it remembered. Some very significant things happened that day. They weren't to know until later but that was the day the mighty Cithran army, which had Feown besieged, had fallen down dead.

"WHAT?!?" Adrastea shrieked. "You took my husband on my wedding day?" Adrastea let out a wordless bellow of rage. She pounded Desmone's head into the stone of the Maiden's Tower. She beat her and beat her. Desmone's shrieks as her instinct caused her to raise her nebulous hands to cover her insubstantial face.

Adrastea whacked the soul as hard as she could, calling it all the names she could think of. "Slut! Harlot! Trollop! Whore! Bitch! That was my husband! He was mine!"

She thrashed the hapless priestess. Adrastea had felt the power of his passion as he, through her, reft all those souls. She remembered echoes of it as she demonstrated her power for the first time for his priestesses. When he took her to her—not their—room, how she expected to consummate their marriage. He'd reached out to her but had withdrawn his hand, then himself. It was not a hard leap to realize that he'd probably gone straight from her bed, to Desmone.

Why? She may have been shocked from the earlier events of the day. She may have harbored apprehension. She had vowed to be his wife, to accept his heart to hers, and him to her body and bed. He turned her down in favor of... this. That insulted her deeply.

She beat Desmone's head against the stones a few more times until the initial rage burned down. Adrastea turned her epithets towards her husband.

She released the soul who, being so newly dead, did not know how to escape. She fled to the far corners of the Tower. The door refused to open to her ethereal grasp, so she huddled as far as she could from the wrathful true Bride of Mor-Lath.

So much for celibacy. Adrastea's whole face burned with shame. She'd been cuckolded—on her wedding night, no less! Who knew how many times since?

Adrastea approached Desmone. "Who else has he been tossing?"

Desmone shook her head. "I don't know." She told the truth. As far as she knew, she'd been the only one. There had been tales of other women in the past. Chamque had known one in her youth—

"Who's Chamque?"

"The head priestess at our temple."

"And she knows of more?"

More truth: "I don't know. Maybe."

Maybe.

Her thoughts turned back to her husband. He'd spurned her. She had been too stupid to realize it. He'd played her naivety.

Adrastea's only thought was of revenge.

Montrof remained obsequious at the door until he was certain she was gone for sure. The priest shuffled forward, one tentative step before the other, enough to see Desmone's body lying at the altar. Then he moved back.

A few of the braver worshippers had returned, peeking furtively through the door.

Behind him, one of the women gave a little squeal of fear. Montrof looked up. Chamque, high priestess, stood in the doorway, the crowd of worshippers behind her.

Chamque was no fool. She appraised the situation before opening her mouth. "What is going on here?" She came into the vacated chapel.

Her voice of authority vibrated through the crowd. All of the followers shrank back. None dared follow.

Montrof turned to her, the oily smile on his face. "A step too late, as always, my dear. You have just missed the true Bride of Mor-Lath."

It seemed she didn't hear right. "Who?" Her gaze fell on the fallen Desmone. She knelt by the body. Desmone was well and truly dead. Nothing to be done but final rites. Caution filled her voice. "What happened here?"

Montrof folded his arms. "It appears the true Bride does not like pretenders. I advise against crossing her."

Desmone's body was still warm. Her heart did not beat, and her lungs did not aspirate. So much for Mor-Lath's favor. "Why do you say the true Bride?"

Montrof barked in laughter. "A woman of great Power, claiming to be the Bride, shows up and kills a priestess without a second thought. Do you want to tell her she's *not* the Bride of Mor-Lath? Certainly not I."

"Hm." It was a sound full of doubt. "Regardless, His Holiness will not be pleased."

Montrof came closer. "You want my personal opinion? No great loss. This does not change his orders to you or me. You still have to deal with Wacifice. I still have to hunt Cithrans." He squatted down near the body. There was not a mark upon her that either could see. "Although this does add some depth to the situation."

"What? Why?" Chamque asked, vexed.

Montrof did not answer but studied the body instead.

Adrastea fled to Sacred Spring, hiding well among the trees in the night. She did not wish to encounter her husband. Who knew what she might do to him?

What did she want to do to him? Her rage burned in her heart. She couldn't keep still. As she stomped through the forest, she considered a suitable revenge.

Physical harm topped her list. The sheer need to pound her fists into his face overwhelmed her. She wanted to pound her husband as she'd pounded Desmone.

Some poor tree bore the brunt of her rage. Her fist stung against the rough bark.

"Now, now." A feminine voice startled her. Adrastea whirled around, ready to destroy whoever it was who had disturbed her.

"That poor tree had done nothing to you," a second voice said.

Adrastea sent out her senses. The Lines did not connect to any living being. "Show yourselves."

From among the shadowy aspen wandered two souls, women, if she judged their forms right. They seemed familiar. They glowed slightly in the darkness.

"Ah, look who we have here," one said to the other.

"I do believe it's the young Healer girl."

To Adrastea, she said, "Now, you apologize to that tree."

Adrastea's rage bled out of her. "What?"

"Trees are living beings. They have feelings just as much as we do."

Adrastea's memory floated a thought to the surface. "You're Crozie." She said to one of the women. "You're dead." She looked to the other. "Who are you?"

Both ghosts looked to each other. "I thought she was brighter than that," said the second. "She recognized us both easy enough when we were alive."

Said Crozie, "However, there was only the one body at the time."

Adrastea fought to keep her rage. "I need to be alone now."

Both Crozie and the... other Crozie laughed. "Alone is the last thing you need to be. We can't have you killing more trees. Next it will be entire forests. Maybe villages."

"And maybe you would destroy the entire world."

Adrastea balled up her fists. "I only wish to destroy my husband. Bastard!"

Crozie and her other looked to each other and sighed. "That will not do."

Crozie came forward and guided her to a rock. "Sit. You have much thinking to do."

The other also sidled up. She poked at Adrastea's clenched fist. "What have we here?"

Adrastea looked at her hand. Ah, Desmone. "It's nothing." She stuffed Desmone into her pocket. "I do mean nothing."

Both ghosts studied the imprisoned soul. The other sniffed. "A foolish girl. She deserved her fate, though probably not like this." The other looked up to Adrastea. "She didn't know."

"Oh, she knew, all right. She even gloated."

Crozie also smelled about the pocket. "Not at first. Not that she would have cared." Crozie inhaled again. "All this one ever cared about was herself." Another sniff. "She was using him as much as he was using her. There was no love here."

Adrastea folded her arms. "That doesn't make me feel better."

Crozie straightened. "What you're planning won't make you feel better either."

She didn't want to let go of her acts of violence. "But maybe it'll make him feel worse."

The two ghosts looked at each other with long-suffering. "Oh, you were always a rather dense girl. I'm surprised you've made it as far as you have." Crozie tapped hard on Adrastea's head. "Can't you string more than two thoughts together?"

She'd had enough. "I don't have to listen to you."

Both ghosts chuckled. "Oh, look who knows so much."

Crozie said to Adrastea, "You want a true solution to this problem? Seek out why you are angry."

"Oh, like that's a mystery. My husband cheated on me." She started to call upon the Deeper Power to take her away from here.

"You must love him, then," said the other.

That stung. "No, I don't."

The ghost shrugged. "You feel something. Otherwise, you wouldn't care about who he beds."

"I don't love him. He doesn't love me either."

The ghosts didn't believe this. "Ah," the other said to Crozie. "Jealousy."

"She wants his love," Crozie replied.

"Stop saying that." Her ire rose once more, possibly because their words rang truer than she wanted to admit.

The ghosts circled her, their footsteps silent on the fallen leaves. "You want his attention, at least. You want what he's not giving you."

A lump rose in her throat. Questions rose in her head. Why does he fear a child of her? Why didn't he fear a child of Desmone? Why take her in marriage if he wouldn't complete the act?

"You are confused," said Crozie. "Perhaps it is best you give it some time. Sleep upon't."

"See with new eyes on the morrow."

The ghosts took her hands and drew her along. "But first, you must bathe in the sacred spring. Wash that taint of anger off you."

Adrastea balked. It was night and cold.

Crozie shook a ghostly finger at her. "Now, now, remember the last time you were told to bathe in the Spring? You failed to obey."

Sorrow warred with the anger in her heart. "Can't anything ever go right for me?"

They had a ready answer for that. "Sure, it can. But you've got to stop waiting for others to do for you. You've got to do for yourself. Be the one who moves the world. Don't let the world move you."

They pulled her to the sacred spring. The night air grew cooler nearer the water. It felt as if the edges of her anger were freezing away.

She removed her clothes and stood there, quite naked, in the marshy bank of the spring. She dipped in a toe. The spring had always been frigid. Every time she'd ever submersed herself, she came up chattering.

"In you go, girl. You haven't got all night."

Adrastea nodded. Arms crossed about her chest, she eased her way in. Each step took her deeper. The coldness seeped into her bones.

"All the way in," Crozie demanded. "Otherwise, you'll give yourself a chill."

Her toes went numb. Perhaps complete numbness wasn't a bad idea. Drawing a breath, she sank to her knees, then fell forward into the water.

Oh! So cold! Her skin prickled and her muscled clenched. But as that water washed over her, it cleansed the anger the fear and the rage from her soul. She wished she could stay longer and let it completely purify her. She shivered.

When she climbed out, shaking, Crozie and the other nodded. "There. Feel better?"

She did. "What do I do now?"

"Dry off, of course. Otherwise, you will catch a chill."

Adrastea availed herself of her skirt to wick the moisture off her skin. She slid into her shift and her blouse and hunched on the grass under the stars. Her heart still ached but it was more a distant memory now, like the buzz when one drank too much of Ari's beer.

The ghosts settled on either side of her. "You are angry with your husband because he will not give you what you want?"

The topic harshed her mellow. "Must we discuss that now?"

Crozie gave another of her infuriating looks to the other. "Didn't we just tell her she needs to take charge of her fate?"

Adrastea groaned. "So, what am I supposed to do?"

"That's obvious," Crozie snorted. "Take what you want. Seems he's been doing an awful lot of taking. I reckon it's your turn."

"I wouldn't know where to begin." Adrastea's teeth began to chatter.

"It's a far more suitable revenge." The other settled next to Adrastea and patted her hand.

Crozie said, "You'll think of something. Figure out the *why* of things, and you can solve your problem. It's not like he doesn't desire you."

A spark of an idea formed in her head. Mor-Lath had his weaknesses as well. He'd succumbed to her spontaneous kiss before he realized what she'd been doing. No doubt if she could catch him in a moment of distraction, she could press the issue further. How far could she take it before he resisted? And how often could he resist before even that wall broke down?

Crozie stroked Adrastea's forehead. "You rest for now. Best thing for you. Head on home. You'll catch cold out here."

Adrastea sighed. She called upon the Deeper Power and with a thought, disappeared.

Crozie tutted over the empty night air. "Your great-granddaughter's not terribly bright, is she?"

"Must take after her father's side."

"Mmm hmm."

Her sister shook her head in disappointment. "And yet we're trusting the fate of Creation to her."

Back at the temple, after a good day's sleep, Adrastea sorted through the vast wardrobe available to her. If she was going to seduce the Dark God, she'd need something suitable to wear. The blue dress was insufficient, as it required a corset. So did many of the others. One could not seduce in a corset, no matter how good one looked laced up.

It was a matter of how one moved, rather than how one looked. Adrastea held up a green velvet gown, considered it and put it back. All of her clothes were nice but none of them were erotic. Whoever chose her wardrobe did not want her displaying, much less using, her assets.

"You know, you could drape a few scarves around your naked body," Desmone offered by way of not-so-helpful advice. Her soul drifted around Adrastea, plenty to say, little of it to Adrastea's benefit.

"I'm not a slut. This isn't a case of tumbling a village lad." Adrastea's hands tightened around a pale linen overdress. "Now I'm sure you've got plenty of experience displaying your charms to such an extent nothing is left to the imagination. I'm sure your common man on the street preferred it that way."

Offense swirled through Desmone's soul. "I am not a whore."

"Of course not. Whores get paid. You gave it away for free."

The dead priestess snorted, insulted. Adrastea flicked her to the far side of the wardrobe with her finger. She drew a black silk gown off the rail and stroked its fine embroidery on the bodice. Shame it required a corset to sit right.

"Better a whore than frigid old cherry." Desmone drifted back from her temporary banishment to sneer in her face. "I got to tumble your husband—several times—and he hasn't even bothered to touch you."

Adrastea threw the dress to the floor and snagged Desmone out of the air. "Look here, you harlot. In case you haven't noticed, you're dead. You're not going to be tumbling anyone, much less my husband ever again." She strode out of her wardrobe, kicking discarded dresses out of her way. She crossed to the dressing table. She emptied a wooden box that held hair pins, hat pins and other notions and dropped in the soul. "Now, why don't you be a good little girl and sit here to think about why you no longer have a future. No doubt the men of the street can find another lay to keep them warm, but your brother'll miss you very much."

She closed the lid on Desmone's rather blue retort and returned to the wardrobe.

Bitch, she muttered to herself. What in Creation did Mor-Lath see in that ill-mannered chit? Other than her fair face and her talent for spreading her legs, Adrastea saw nothing remarkable.

If there had been one slut, there would be more. She vowed she would find them all. She'd make certain that they would not lure her husband away again.

But first, she had to stake her own claim.

Back to the wardrobe. Next to where she dropped the black silk dress, she found an overdress that just might do the trick. It, like the dress, was black. It was a fine gauze, with a transparent quality. Despite its tailoring, it did not require a corset. She slipped it on and stood before the mirror.

Hmm... too much not left to the imagination. If Mor-Lath saw her in that, he'd know she was up to something. He'd raise his guard before she could get even close.

She found a white satin shift, plain and untailored. It suited her, especially with the black overdress, natural and unfettered. She sighed over her unsupported breasts. If her plan worked, support wouldn't be much of an issue.

What was her plan? Walking in all graceful and seductive would work counter to her goal. Demure wouldn't work either. If anything, she'd fade into the background.

She sat down at the dressing table and gave in to introspection and thought. After their marriage, when were the times he weakened? She'd kissed him after she'd hit the target at rifle practice. He'd not kissed her the day of their wedding, when he'd shown her this room. Before that, he'd given in whenever she had called upon the Deeper Power. Also, when he wasn't expecting her to turn on him.

It was only when he became aware of what he was doing, that he stopped. Why did he stop?

Fear.

He was truly afraid. Of what? Of her, of the consequences?

An idea formed in her head. Many things caused fear, but fear was fear. Saraym had suffered fear and Adrastea had fixed that. Her fear had been a tangle of Lines wrapped tightly about her heart.

Could she do the same for Mor-Lath?

If only she could catch him unawares. She dropped her face into her hands and felt the presence of the lines. She closed her eyes, stilled her thoughts and felt for his presence there.

He was in the library. But she couldn't tell what he was doing. It was as if he was asleep.

Did he sleep? Adrastea couldn't recall seeing him asleep. Sure, there were several times when she woke up with him beside her in bed, but did he actually sleep? She focused more on the senses received through the lines. Even sent a tentative prod. No response. How serendipitous.

As an immortal, she only required sleep when she had expended a great deal of energy. What had he spent his energy on? Adrastea pushed the thought of post-coital exhaustion from her mind as quickly as it came.

Immortals may be immortals, but they were still subject to the laws of Creation. Then it only made sense that he would require sleep every once in a while. If so, when did he sleep? She listened carefully to the impressions through the lines. Where did he sleep?

Apparently, in the library.

Chapter 15

Adrastea opened the door to the library as gently as she could.

Mor-Lath had fallen asleep at the library table. His head rested on an open book, with other books sprawled about. One hand was tucked under his chin, the other spread up above his head. Adrastea listening to his breathing, deep and even. Imagine falling asleep on a book, too tired to read any more. She still wasn't sure what he was looking for, in his furious research.

With a soft request, she commanded the globes of light to dim.

He was at her mercy. She placed her hands on her cheeks and sensed him out. Most of his barriers were down. However, there was a knot of fear within him, one that she suspected never unraveled. Was it related to his paranoia, his drive?

She pushed away her nerves. Would this even work?

She had nothing to lose.

Adrastea sought out the knot of fear. With the gentlest of touches, she unraveled it, thread by thread. She did not stop to investigate each thread but let them go. She had to fight them to keep them from knotting back up. Fickle things! Had they been tied so long they forgot how to loosen? It hadn't been this difficult with Saraym's fear.

As the fear released, she called upon the Deeper Power to fill her. She needed its strength and perception. She summoned forth her memories of the secret book and let their influence ignite the passions of her body. If she was to stir his lust, she had to draw from the fount of her own. Oh, how good it would feel to have his hands caress her skin.

The more she yearned, the more she wanted to draw on the Deeper Power.

Creation obliged. Creation itself wanted her to unravel his fears. This time, he could not stop her. She would have her consummation.

As the heat of her passion enflamed her loins, she focused it all and sent tendrils of it to Mor-Lath. She replaced the fear with desire. Once he was adequately suffused, she laid a hand on his shoulder.

He jumped, knocking a book off the table. Adrastea caught it before it hit the floor and replaced it. Mor-Lath sat up, startled awake.

Adrastea didn't give him a chance to gather his thoughts. "Sleep," she commanded. She pushed her will against his half-consciousness until it slipped deeper and he entered a dream state. *Sleep.*

His eyes drooped, and he slumped forward, falling back into that state of in-betweenness.

Immediately, she straddled his lap and captured his lips with her own. She twined her hands through his hair and would not let him go. She sensed surprise. She battled his puzzlement, seeking to unravel it as she had his fear. It kept wanting to reform, not so much as a knot but as a type of armor for the soul.

So much to keep track of. While she battled on those fronts, she continued to feed her emotions through to him. "Dream," she murmured, over and over, "Dream." She had to keep him half-asleep.

At first, he didn't respond to her kiss, more from surprise, than anything. When his fear did not respond, he threw logic and caution to the wind. He responded greedily to her kiss, drawing in her lower lip and running his tongue along it.

As Adrastea's experience of kissing was rather limited, she let him take the lead, and responded to his advances. The passion came easy now. He shared his lusts with her. Lines of Deeper Power twined about them and she welcomed their presence.

She gave as good as she took, letting the raw emotion mount between them. Once or twice, the tendrils of his fear slipped past her guard, but she kept them from knotting up again.

Mor-Lath's hand slid to her bottom. He pressed her closely to him. She felt the heat of his arousal. She knew what she had gotten herself in to, in theory. She also knew there was a good chance it was going to hurt. She'd utterly failed to prepare herself in that manner.

Don't think about that, she warned herself. Instead, she took all the lust that sang in her blood like the furious strumming of lute strings and sent it all into him. She wanted him to be overwhelmed. She wanted him to lose control. She did not want him to stop and think of her. If he realized what she was doing, his fear would come streaming back and she would not be able to fight it.

Focus, she reminded herself as her desperate fingers fumbled at the laces of his shirt. They wouldn't come loose, so she pulled on the Deeper Power to dissolve the laces entirely. They fell like dust under her fingers. She slid her hands onto his bare skin.

Likewise, his hands slid up under her skirt, to press her hard against him. His tongue warred with hers and she found it hard to breathe, so passionate were his kisses.

Every time his awareness lifted from his hypnotic state, she pushed it back down. *Sleep. Dream.*

He lifted her up and set her on the table. His mouth still fastened on hers, he bore her back with the weight of his body. His hands slid up her legs, along her hips and up to the waist of her dress. The form-fitting gown did not last long, as the fabric parted at his unspoken request. His hand played and cupped her breast.

The urgency of his kisses waned. She didn't have much time. Her hands moved down his body to his waistband. They moved along, searching for the fastening. Not finding one and not wanting to interrupt his passion, she willed his clothing to dust.

Adrastea raised her knees and stroked the back of his leg with a foot. This stirred him. The throbbing heat of his erection pressed against her. He paused in his kisses, rising slightly, and then renewed his attack by capturing her mouth as he entered her body.

It wasn't so much a sharp pain as it was a sudden stretching. Still, it surprised her. Her body tightened.

For the briefest moment she lost control. The strands of fear wound themselves around his heart. She fought them and struggled.

It was too late. Her passion evaporated as she focused all her energy on the knot.

His face pulled back from hers. He shifted from the dream state into full wakefulness. His passion, like hers, perished as palpable terror replaced it.

"Adrastea?" he gasped in disbelief. Mor-Lath disengaged himself, pushing away from her and off the table.

Adrastea sat up. His fear bled through their connection.

His anger blossomed. "WHAT HAVE YOU DONE?" His rage filled him and spilled over onto her, terrifying her.

Adrastea scrambled back across the table until a hand slipped over the edge. She nearly lost her balance.

He followed her over the table, knocking the remains of her clothing out of the way. His wordless bellow rent the air as he reached for her. The force of his sheer will pulled her towards him.

Panic jolted through her limbs. She had gone too far. She pushed herself off the table and fled.

She didn't think. Her soul cried out for sanctuary. Creation obliged her.

The air around her changed from the steamy closeness of the library to the cold breezes of a hilltop. The dead grass of autumn crunched beneath her feet.

She found herself back at Sacred Spring. The night air had a nippy quality to it. The stars sparkled at their brightest.

Her eyes adjusted. Shouldn't she be running towards the sacred spring, not away? She paused just long enough to get her bearing and make a course correction. None too soon, for an angry Dark God followed.

Adrastea did not stop but fled to the edge of the Spring itself and stepped in.

Her naked legs shrieked at the near-frigidness of the water, then grew numb as she waded in further, up to her knees, and over.

"Adrastea." The coldness in Mor-Lath's voice rivalled the icy waters. She turned to find her husband, still clad in the remains of his shirt, approaching the edge of the spring.

The iciness hurt her legs. She shivered too much for words. Where was that defiance she felt earlier, to strengthen her backbone? He could not get her here; therefore, he could not harm her.

For harm was what she saw in his eyes. His whole being glowed with the power of his fear and rage. He paused at the edge of the spring.

To her horror, he stepped in! Slowly but surely, he advanced, each step a careful one.

Reason deserted her. She stepped back, slipped and plunged completely in the spring. Its chilliness closed over her. Jolts of electricity flowed through her body. Her panic fueled her enough to scramble out of the spring. Her wet feet slipped on the grassiness of the hill.

A hand grabbed an ankle and pulled her back.

"No!" She turned around to fight him, scratching at his face. Alas, his strength was greater than hers. He pinned her down. Her numb fingers scrabbled uselessly at his forcefully-planted hand. Then he placed his other hand on her belly. Drawing on more Deeper Power than she thought possible, he sent the force of his fear through her in a searing hot force.

Adrastea threw her head back and screamed. It echoed through the meadow and into the trees. Birds startled and exploded from their night perches. Far away, dogs began to howl and bark.

And still, she screamed as the heat scorched her belly. Something within her withered and disintegrated. She fought against the arm that pinned her.

Without a word, he lifted his hand and released her, stepping back. She writhed and wailed on the ground. He shivered and turned his face away before disappearing.

Her pain rolled through her, far greater than anything she had ever experienced before. Regret and loathing flushed her cheeks.

It took a long time for it to subside. As soon as she could move, she edged back to the Spring and dunked her body in, in vain hopes of stopping the pain.

It failed. She pulled herself out of the water as soon as she knew it did no good.

For the longest time, all Adrastea could do was shiver and whimper, curled in a tight ball. Time lost meaning for her as she focused on fighting the pain.

Sometime later, she heard voices. They were not in her head.

She raised her head enough to call out, "Ari?" Then she called out again louder. "Ari!"

The voices called out again and drew near.

"Oh, good glory," someone cursed. A dry, warm cloak settled over her body. Only then, did she sink into blessed oblivion.

A drastea's eyes opened. She sat up in the bed with a cry. For a moment, she didn't know where she was.

She recognized the chest of drawers opposite the bed—Ari's.

The quilts on Ari's high bed were thick for autumn. The heavy curtain over the window ensured the room remained dark.

What a nightmare she'd had. Now that she was awake, everything was going to be fine. The past few months had been not real. Sure, felt like it, though.

Ari opened the door, spreading sunlight across the floor. "Adrastea," she began without preamble. "You're awake."

Her belly started to ache and her head as well.

"What happened?" Ari came in, hovering over the bed.

Cold realization drenched her. That had been no nightmare.

Adrastea brought her knees up to her chest and set her face in her hands. She wanted to cry but nothing came. Had she used up her allotment of tears?

Ari sat on the end of the bed. She wiped her hands on her work apron then touched Adrastea's covered foot. "Adrastea?"

Adrastea gathered her thoughts. "Ari, I made a terrible, terrible mistake."

"Other than agreeing to marry the mongrel?"

She was sure Ari meant it as a joke, but it fell flat.

"Sorry," Ari apologized.

Adrastea gave her a half-shrug. "This was my fault."

Ari pulled her hand away and sat up straighter. "No, no. It was not your fault, whatever happened. No man has the right to abuse his wife, even if he is a god."

Adrastea folded her arms across her knees and rested her chin there. "Even if he's the God of the Dark?"

"Especially then." Ari's anger settled. "So, why'd he do it?" She gripped her hands in her lap. "What did he do?"

Adrastea sighed and looked away.

"You've had us worried for two weeks."

Adrastea swung her head back like a whip. "I've been asleep for two weeks?"

Ari nodded. "Healing, most likely. I'm sure I could have wakened you, but I didn't want to."

She scooted closer and laid a hand on Adrastea's elbow. "You've got quite a pair of lungs on you, girl. You shrieked for a good fifteen minutes at the spring, if not longer. We heard you all the way down here. The Crossroaders got to you first, because they were closer.

"They didn't know who you were, originally. You were calling my name, so they brought you here." Ari's finger traced the curve of Adrastea's elbow. "In my surprise I may have said your name. Now everyone knows you're back. You should hear the rumors flying. Tell me everything's all right. Everyone's worried."

Adrastea gasped. "No, everything's not all right!"

Ari jerked her hand back. "No, I meant—" She sighed. "It's just that everyone's worried you-know-who will come back and wreck vengeance. They—" She paused and shook her head. "Gossip's baseless. Please. Tell me what happened. You were a wreck when they brought you in."

Adrastea sat back against the pillows but gently. Every time she moved, her belly ached like she'd worked too hard in the garden. She laid a hand on the quilt over her belly but didn't dare draw on the Deeper Power to inspect the damage. She didn't want to know how bad it was. Not yet.

"He wanted me as a wife in name only. So, he lavished me with fine clothes, excellent food and even given a stillroom of my own. Then he abandoned me to my own devices."

Ari opened her mouth to say something and changed her mind.

Adrastea continued. "He had little to do with me. If I reminded him I was around he'd brush me off in annoyance."

"Some would say you had the best of a bad situation. It wasn't like you wanted to marry him."

Adrastea traced the quilt pattern with her finger. "Some could say that." She looked up. "But I had dreams too. Long before I ever met him.

"I wanted to be married. I'm old enough to remember what my father was like. And I know how Uncle Natan treats you."

Ari winced.

"I know you two aren't married but he loves you."

"We all have our dreams," Ari replied tightly. "We don't always get them."

"Doesn't mean we can't hope."

Ari sighed in agreement. "It's our foolish dreams that keep us warm at night."

Adrastea nodded. "So, I was married. Wasn't it you who told me that it was up to me to make the best of a bad situation?

"He was... attentive to me before we got married. It was worth hoping he'd be as attentive after. But..."

Ari shifted on the bed. "But he ignored you?"

"Worse." Adrastea drew in a breath that turned ragged at the end. "He cuckolded me."

Ari said nothing. She remained still and offered absolutely no reaction. Ari's heart beat harder, her throat pulsing, betraying her anger.

"Please don't think poorly of me, Ari."

"I never do."

Adrastea chewed on her lip. "Her name was Desmone. She was a priestess in Avelia. And on our wedding day, he..." she drew a deep breath to steel herself, "he chose to enjoy her favor."

Ari gave a little shudder. "You mean he had sex with her?"

Adrastea nodded.

"Before or after he'd been to your bed?"

Adrastea shook her head. "That's the thing. He's never been to my bed. He's never touched me."

"What? Never?" Ari mused on this. "How odd." Her gaze met Adrastea's. "So, you're saying you're still a maiden?"

Adrastea hesitated. "I'm getting to that."

Ari gave her a puzzled look.

"So, I managed to track this Desmone down, where I killed her."

Ari inhaled sharply through her nose. "You didn't!"

"I'm sorry, Ari. I was so angry. And she was so smug. The next thing I knew I had ripped her soul out of her body."

Ari looked as if she was going to be sick. "But to kill someone?"

"What's worse, I don't regret it."

"Oh, Adrastea." Ari shook her head.

"But the story doesn't end there."

Ari didn't look at her former journeyman. She kept her head bowed and listened. "So, then what happened?"

"Well, I got envious. I couldn't stand the thought that he was off tumbling other women while I was being neglected. After all, wasn't I supposed to be the wife? But I wasn't, not really. So, in all my thinking of 'not fair' and 'how dare he?' I decided it was time I seduced him."

Ari pressed a fist to her lips, but she continued to listen.

"I worked the details out. I caught him in a weak moment. And, well..." She let Ari's imagination fill in the rest.

"So, you succeeded in consummating your marriage?"

Adrastea nodded. "And that's when things began to go horribly wrong." Then the words came tumbling out. "I tricked him into it. It took a lot of effort to get past his fears. I'd succeeded until the pain distracted me. The moment that happened, he realized what we had done, and he was so angry. I've never seen him like that before.

"I fled but he caught me and..." A sob shook her. "He pinned me down, put his hand on my belly." She let the smallest tendril of Power into her body. "I think he sterilized me."

Ari's countenance shifted from aunt, friend and confidante into Ari the Healer. She nodded her head and said, "That's explains the rather obvious bruise and the pain."

"Bruise?"

Ari gestured to Adrastea's belly. "Have a look. I dare say it's a lot better than it was a fortnight ago."

Adrastea lifted the quilt. She was dressed in one of Ari's nightgowns. Folding the quilt back, she undid the buttons of the nightgown and peered down to her belly.

There, in splotchy purple and green was the distinct shape of a handprint, with yellow splotches radiating out from it. Of course.

"It was much worse," Ari explained. "Nearly black. I would have used leeches, had I any. Your whole belly swelled for days, with accompanied bleeding, then it settled."

Good thing she was immortal. She poked at her belly, wincing at the increase of pain. Things still hadn't healed completely yet.

"How about we wait another week or so for you to heal more? Then I can have another look." She tucked the quilt around Adrastea. "I'm sure he's done some permanent damage."

Ari sat on the edge of the bed again. "Why would he do something like this? Surely this isn't pure rage over having been tricked. It's premeditation."

"No." Adrastea settled down, though she didn't feel tired. "It was all fear. There's this prophecy: 'The son of Mor-Lath shall destroy him.' It terrifies him beyond reason."

"Not enough to stop him sleeping with other women."

Adrastea toyed with the edge of the quilt. "I considered that. I'm thinking he does the same thing to them as he's done to me." Desmone had a handprint. Had she been seared sterile as well? Adrastea made a note to ask the dead priestess about that.

Ari rose to her feet. "Adrastea, he's not going to come looking for you, is he?"

"I don't see why he should. I have a feeling he'd like to forget all about me."

"Are you sure? Because the last thing we want is him coming here and creating trouble."

Adrastea closed her eyes. "I could leave."

"And go where? You need to heal. You need people you can trust around you. I'm just..." she licked her lips. "I'm concerned about the rest of the village."

Adrastea didn't open her eyes. "I promise if he shows up, I'll leave."

"I'm sorry to ask this of you."

"I understand."

Ari moved to the door. "You are welcome to stay as long as you need. At least, until you figure out what you're going to do next."

Uncle Natan arrived for a visit later that afternoon, accompanied by Mikal. By that time, Adrastea was able to get out of bed. She gently made her way to the kitchen table.

Now that she was awake, Ari felt it safer to give her painkilling drugs. She sipped a chamomile tea laced with something that tingled on her tongue.

Natan eased his large form into a chair at the end of the table. "Well. Nice to have you visit us, though I wish it was under better circumstances."

Mikal said nothing but sat opposite Adrastea. Thoughts tumbled through his head strong enough to ripple the Lines.

"These things happen, I believe," she replied.

"Not in my village, if I can help it."

Adrastea peered over the rim of her cup. "I don't live here anymore."

"You do this week. From what Ari told me, this happened on my land."

Adrastea set her cup down. "And what are you going to do, Uncle Natan? Fine him? Beat him? Tar and feather him and ride him out of the village on a rail?"

Natan gave her a great big grin. "A man can dream."

Mikal spoke, his tone wistful. "He seemed so nice to me."

Adrastea frowned. "He seemed so nice to me too, until he got what he wanted. You didn't think he was truly a nice person?"

"Yes, when he wasn't the God of the Dark."

"Well, he's always been the God of the Dark."

Mikal was frank with his questions. "And who are you, at the moment?"

This gave Adrastea pause. She ran a finger over the edge of her teacup. She hadn't thought of that. Perhaps she should.

"You aren't Adrastea Healer any more. Do you call yourself Journeywoman? Lady Adrastea? Goddess Adrastea?"

She shook her head. "No, not that. Not yet."

Mikal tapped at the table. "I thought that was the whole reason he wanted you in the first place."

Adrastea sat up. "Where did you hear that?"

Mikal looked at Natan. Natan stood his ground. "How could I not know something that important? We are family."

Adrastea looked to Ari. "You told him!"

Ari defended herself. "Of course, I did. It wouldn't be right to not tell him, either as Mayor or your uncle."

Adrastea felt hurt. "And did you tell him everything I told you this afternoon?"

Mikal whooped. "You seduced the Dark God."

Adrastea let out a shriek. "Ari! How could you tell him?"

In her defense, Ari said, "I didn't tell him. I only told Natan."

Natan held up his hands in innocence. "Not me." He warned his apprentice, "Mikal, what did I tell you about eavesdropping?" He pointed to the door.

Adrastea wasn't finished. "He didn't need to know."

Mikal stood up with a rueful look on his face. "Sorry," he said to nobody in particular.

Adrastea had some sharp words for him as well. "Don't you dare tell another soul or I will hurt you. Don't think I don't know how."

Before Mikal undertook his banishment, Natan pointed a finger at him. "Mikal will keep his mouth shut if he knows what's good for him. He knows mayorprentices must, above all else, keep secrets." He shook his finger at his apprentice. "My sister may have brought you into the world, boy, but that doesn't mean I can't take you out of it."

"Yes sir." A contrite Mikal slunk out of the house.

Adrastea wasn't done with Ari. "Nobody needed to know I seduced him."

Ari hesitated before she offered her apology. "I'm sorry. I felt the Mayor needed to know. For everything that happens, there is a cause."

Natan added, "If you're going to live here in the village, even temporarily, I do need to know why. I'm sure you know my biggest concern is the return of your husband. As I recall, he was desperate for you to marry him. Knowing what little I do of his reasons, I don't see why he's going to change his mind."

"I'm not going back."

Natan sighed. "I was afraid of that. Not that I object to you, personally, staying. It's just that I have a whole village to worry about. I don't want an irate husband with vast powers at his whim destroying my village because he's displeased with you."

"Frankly, I don't think he cares," Adrastea muttered.

"That's the problem. He doesn't care one whit about Sacred Spring. He wouldn't think twice about its destruction."

Adrastea hadn't considered that. If he didn't care about the happiness or health of his wife, no matter how important she was to his personal goals, he certainly wasn't going to give two groats about a piddling little village full of insignificant mortals. "But what about the..."

"What? The protection he cast? I doubt it excludes him. However, it has proven its worth. But that's a tale for another time.

"What I'm most concerned about is Mor-Lath's return. As long as he stays away, you can remain. But the moment he shows up, I will have to ask you to leave. I don't care if you leave with him or you run away from him. You're all he cares about."

"But Uncle Natan, he doesn't care about me. That's the point."

Natan didn't reply. Adrastea finished her tea. The drug Ari dosed her with was beginning to work. The pain in her belly had lessened enough that as long as she didn't move, she felt nothing.

"I don't know the finer points of your marriage, Adrastea. I don't know if I want to know.

"However, as a married woman, you are an adult. You will need to make some adult decisions. Stay here if you want but I cannot shelter you completely. If you stay, you contribute just like everyone else. As tempting as it is to avoid the situation, you will have to confront your husband again and deal with him, even if it means seeking a divorce."

Adrastea sat up. She hadn't considered that possibility. Was it possible?

Natan continued. "I don't know how the gods would handle something like that. I doubt it's something he'd accept if the words were spoken by a mere mortal priest.

"What you do is up to you, Adrastea. But do something you must."

Adrastea studied the empty cup before her. "I need to think upon't."

Natan rose from the table. "Do. And for all our sakes, when you encounter the other villagers, please be discreet. You don't have to answer their questions if you don't want to. Don't feel the need to explain."

He laid a paw on her shoulder. "Good luck, Adrastea. I do not envy the choices ahead of you."

Chapter 16

Uncle Natan was right. Adrastea had to do the adult thing. That meant confronting Mor-Lath.

To keep Sacred Spring safe, she returned to the temple. As she appeared behind the altar in the main chapel the lines on her face told her Mor-Lath was here, but she didn't see him anywhere. Who she did see was Desideria, kneeling on the other side of the altar.

The older priestess looked up at her in surprise.

"Where is he?" Adrastea leaned over the altar and with one fist, hauled Desideria up by the front of her robes. "I know he's here. I can feel him."

Desideria wrapped her hands around Adrastea's fist. "It is not my place to say."

Adrastea gave her a shake. "You're his bloody high priestess! Don't tell me you weren't just talking to him."

"I was," Desideria admitted. "He left before you arrived." She kept her calm, all but for a slight wrinkling of her forehead.

Adrastea shook her. "What? Doesn't he dare face me? Do you know what I am going to do with him when I catch him? First, I'm going to cut off his testicles, skewer them and let them roast slowly over a fire. I'm going to scoop out his eyes with a blunt spoon and then do the same." Her voice rose in crescendo. "I will rip open his belly with my fingernails and use his entrails to tie him to my bedpost before I slice off his ears. Those, I'm going to keep in a little velvet box where I shall take them out once a day to tell him," and she shrieked this last part, "what a total and utter bastard he is!"

She released Desideria and shook her fist at the ceiling. "Do you hear me, you mongrel?"

Desideria backed away from the altar, rubbing her stomach where it had pressed against the edge of the stone. She said nothing until Adrastea had vented this peak of anger. When Adrastea's temper had died down to a simmer, Desideria kept her distance. "What has he done to invoke your wrath?"

Adrastea's deep breaths turned into sobs. She sank to her knees. She tried to keep her anger hot so she could vent her frustration on her husband. Why did Desideria have to be so gentle?

She told the priestess about Sacred Spring, his angry pursuit of her and her painful sterilization.

Desideria listened, venturing no opinion. "There is so much I don't know about you. I should know better by now. Every time I assume you are like the rest of us, I learn something new."

"What? You're surprised that 'His Holiness'," she made a mockery of the title, "is not above abusing his wife and searing her belly?"

Desideria did not have an answer for that. "Sometimes I forget you don't know the things we do."

Adrastea's anger was returning. "What's that supposed to mean?"

The priestess lifted her gaze. Caution entered her eyes. "Only that I never realized that you weren't, well, protected, like the rest of us. I had assumed he'd already..." she drew in a breath. "You've been fertile all this time? He married you, took you to his bed and risked his very life by leaving you fertile?"

Adrastea sniffed then blotted the end of her nose with the hem of her skirt. Her sleeves were too short to be of any use. She closed her eyes and willed a handkerchief from her temple rooms into her hand. With this she dabbed her eyes. She climbed up to sit on the altar. Much of the fight had left her. Hurt and embarrassment took the place of anger in her heart. "He..." She hesitated. "He's not exactly taken me to his bed."

Desideria remained standing. "What?" she said, her voice faint and puzzled. She reached out a hand to the altar to steady herself. "You mean to say, never?"

"Why do you think I had to seduce him then? Would that have been really necessary if—" Adrastea drew in a breath that turned ragged and threatened to become a sob. "After he had my hand and my troth, that seemed to be all he wanted. I did expect him to complete the marriage, but he never did.

"Then I spoke with—" she caught herself before she spilled

Berengaria's name, "someone and she made me realized that conjugal rights were also my rights too." She wanted to tell Desideria everything. While Ari was willing to listen and vilify, she didn't understand the god. Desideria knew Mor-Lath, knew what he was like. She knew him in a way that Adrastea didn't, and Ari never could. "Why should I sacrifice myself and everything I ever knew to become his bride and not get some pleasure out of it?"

She hopped off the altar. "And there is that. I'd always been the bride but never the wife." She took a step towards Desideria, who swayed but did not move back. "Do you know the difference between a bride and a wife?"

Desideria nodded.

"Well, I am no longer the bride. I am now the wife. I am going to make certain that my husband never lays eyes on another woman again."

Desideria stepped back as Adrastea drew out a wispy form from her pocket. "Do you know who this was?" She shook the form at Desideria.

She shook her head.

"This poor unfortunate soul was a priestess by the name of Desmone."

Desmone took on more shape. Desideria drew in a breath and stared at the dead priestess.

"She thought to get above herself, only I learned, after her death, that it was not wholly her idea." Adrastea strangled the soul who squeaked in fear. "Did you know that my dear faithful husband has been giving her his favor? And do you know when? On our wedding day!" She hurled the soul to the ground near her feet. Desmone bounced once then tried to scrabble away.

Adrastea stuck out her foot, trapping the faint soul. "I am the wife, not her. I am the Bride of Mor-Lath, not her. And unbeknownst to me—oh, Light forbid he should ever tell me anything important—it seems that I have a greater role than I originally thought."

Her eyes narrowed. "You knew about it, didn't you?"

Desideria took several steps backwards. "About what?" If she tried to keep the nervousness out of her voice, she failed.

"The prophecies and everything."

Desmone, once free from Adrastea's foot, tried to escape. She was too slow. Adrastea snatched her out of the air and stuffed her back into her pocket. "You are going nowhere," she told the soul. "I'm not done with you."

Desideria drew a measured breath. "To be honest, I've never really given it much thought. The term "Bride of Mor-Lath" used to be a euphemism for..." Her eyes glanced to Adrastea's pocket and looked away.

Adrastea formed a fist and slammed it against the side of her pocket. She couldn't hurt the soul this way, but it did make her feel just a wee bit better. There were other, better, ways to torture a soul. She planned on investigating every one of them later. The flames of her temper had died down, but the coals still burned. "We know different now, don't we?

"And what is this with the *Bride* of Mor-Lath? That's what every single prophecy describes me as. Why Bride and not Wife? Is Creation assuming that the Dark God was going to remain celibate for the rest of his—" She stopped as a nasty thought occurred to her. "Oh wait. It's not him, it's me! That is not right. Why do I have to be the celibate one?"

Desideria held up her hands in a calming manner. "I don't think it means it like that. Some of these prophecies are really old. The original prophecies were given in other languages. In Old Avelian, the word for bride and wife are the same. Back then, when you were married, you were married, consummation notwithstanding..."

Desideria was holding something back. "But?" Adrastea voiced the priestess' unsaid word.

"It doesn't matter."

"I think it does, or you wouldn't have thought of it."

Desideria sighed. She lost her train of thought. "You know," she said eventually, "I don't know under which tradition you were married."

Adrastea pointed a finger at her. "You're avoiding the subject."

Desideria inclined her head. "I am simply trying to clarify the situation."

Adrastea relented. "We were married under the tradition of the Light."

Desideria let her jaw drop for a moment then recovered herself. "You mean you were married as *Glasskissers*?" She laughed. "Are you jesting me?"

Adrastea folded her arms. "No."

Desideria drew in a deep breath and wiped the tears from her face. "I should not laugh, or His Holiness may not be pleased." To herself, she murmured, "However, it would explain a lot. No wonder you're so caught up on consummation. Feowans put too much importance on the act of marriage." She sniffed and composed herself. "I do have one question. Why Glasskisser?"

"I was raised in the duchy of Feown under the tradition of the Light." She gave extra emphasis to the name 'Light', a most appropriate label. Glasskisser indeed!

Even though her laughter was over, Desideria retained a wry grin. "Hm. Feowan. Figures."

"It wasn't like we had any other choice. The Cithrans were attacking my village. All we had was a priest of the Light." Adrastea hunched her shoulders. "Anyhow, the Light Themselves blessed our union when we went to see Them later."

The priestess' face froze in surprise. "What?" she said faintly.

Adrastea wasn't sure how to proceed. "He said he accepted Their authority and that the marriage was binding. Why?"

Desideria's knees wobbled. She sank to the ground. "You mean…" she put her hands to her head. "Are you telling me that the Glasskisser's god is real?"

"Of course They are."

Pressing her hands to her face, Desideria rocked slightly.

Adrastea still felt Mor-Lath's presence but the turn of events in conversation pushed her thoughts of vengeance to the side for a moment. "You're surprised? I thought you knew."

The priestess let out a soft sob before getting a hold of her emotions. "I never believed that there really was a god of the Light. Oh, Creation!" A soft sound escaped her lips. "He never said anything about Them being real."

"Well, They are. I've seen Them."

Desideria huddled on the ground. "I always thought they were a false god the Glasskissers made up. The Light never did anything for them."

"Let me guess. He told you They weren't real?"

Desideria sat up. "No. Now that I think upon it, he never mentioned Them. Then again, I never thought to ask."

"Perhaps you should question things more."

She lifted her gaze to Adrastea. "Oh no. It's not my—"

"Yes, it is your place to question things," Adrastea snapped. "You're the High Priestess. Nobody should know more than you." She pointed a finger at her. "If you don't ask the questions, who will?

"You had better ask them quickly, though, because when I get a hold of him, there may not be enough of him left to ask." Adrastea muttered some epithets under her breath, as well as a few promises to do nasty things to his person.

Desideria rose to her feet. "All right. I have one question for you. How many gods of the Light are there?"

"Just the one."

Desideria hesitated. "Then...how come you said 'They'?"

A sudden smile, one of maliciousness, crossed Adrastea's face. She scrambled to her feet. "You don't know, do you?" She crowed in delight. "Oh, this is too sweet." She took great pleasure in revealing, "Mor-Lath is not a full god."

Desideria had a reaction that Adrastea did not expect. The priestess' eyes filled with tears. "Yes, he is," she moaned.

"No. He is only a demi-god. See, a god is a being made of two halves, male and female. The Light are comprised of this duality. That is why there is only one god, but we refer to the Light as They. Mor-Lath is but one half. Don't you see? That's why he needs me. He can't become a full god without me."

A smile shone through Desideria's tears. "You are a god too?" When Adrastea didn't confirm, she lost her bright point. "Aren't you?"

Adrastea simply shook her head.

"Why not?"

"I don't know. The Light's given him everything he needs. They told him the rest was up to him. Humph." She folded her arms again. "Figures it would be his fault."

Silence fell between them. The elation of getting one back on Mor-Lath by revealing his secret to his High Priestess faded.

"What about love?"

Adrastea sneered. "What love?"

Desideria wilted a little. "Oh. But didn't you—"

It took Adrastea a moment to realize Desideria meant the act, not the sentiment. "I wouldn't have called it love. It was more anger and frustration on my part and nothing but lust on his, probably mistaken or misplaced." Yes, she meant it as harshly as it sounded.

"Oh." She ventured an opinion. "Maybe you didn't do it right."

Adrastea took umbrage at that. "Hey. I may have been a maiden, but I wasn't an idiot."

Desideria tried to wipe the tension from her face. "I didn't mean it like that either. I have no doubt you know something about the things you do. I was just thinking there had to be more to it than..."

"Than what?"

"Please don't be offended." When Adrastea didn't say anything, she continued. "It might not count unless it means something."

Adrastea's thoughts grew dark. "Oh, I think this meant something to him. I'm certainly not going to let him forget it." Tiredness overcame her. She sank back onto the altar. "He's got to show up some time. Meanwhile, I have to attend to some business. If you see him before I do..." she wagged her finger at Desideria. "Well, you'll know you saw him before I did."

"I'm glad to see you feeling calmer." A tremor had overtaken her hands.

Adrastea shook her head. "No. I'm not. I don't think I could forgive him for what he did to me." She felt forlorn. "I had my dreams too, you know." She glanced at the priestess. "Was it too much to hope for children?"

Desideria answered honestly. "With His Holiness? Yes."

The sorrow she'd held at bay with her anger welled up inside her and threatened to spill out her eyes.

With little conscious thought, she closed her eyes and went to the place she thought she was safe. When she felt the cold breeze of autumn and smelled the fallen leaves, she knew she'd gone to the sacred spring.

Why did she keep coming back here?

Opening her eyes, she gazed into its cold bubbling water. Contrary to her former beliefs, this was not the safe place she supposed. Where then? She couldn't go back to Ari's; the healer had been right. Adrastea had to fight her own battles, no matter what the casualty.

The Palace at Feown was no refuge either.

The spring would do in the meantime. Adrastea cried until she felt more drained than better.

In the end, there was only one place she could go. Adrastea willed herself back to her room. Mor-Lath would have to return to his temple eventually. When he did, she would be waiting for him.

Maybe after a bit of sleep. It took a great deal of energy to be angry.

No, wait. There was one more task to fulfill before she turned her attention to her wayward, overproud husband.

Berengaria and Radelisa were not there, nor did she expect them to be. No one other than Desideria knew she had returned. This suited her perfectly, as she did not want any of *his* priestesses fussing about her or asking any awkward questions.

As she divested herself of her country clothing, she pulled Desmone out of her pocket. The soul had more form now. Her aura was dark with the sin of pride and selfishness. Adrastea let the dead priestess squirm.

"You know who I am now, don't you?"

Desmone did. She was feeling very sorry, though whether it was because of what she did or because she got caught, Adrastea was too tired to differentiate.

"Do you know what I'm going to do to you tomorrow?"

No, she didn't.

Adrastea gave her a grim smile. "You've got all night to think upon't." She tucked the soul under her pillow and told her to stay put.

Desmone did not dare disobey.

◦◦◦

Desideria stood before the altar unmoving after Adrastea left. She waited and waited in case the irate wife of her god returned. When it looked like she was to be left alone, she let her breath out slowly, her heart sinking with it as well. She fell to her knees and pressed her forehead to the floor, cool and unforgiving.

A sad sigh announced Mor-Lath's presence. "Now you know."

Desideria raised herself to look at him. "You lied to me."

Mor-Lath folded his arms, his expression as cold as his voice. "I don't recall lying."

"Letting us believe one thing when it's not true is the same thing."

"I've told you everything you needed to know. It's not my fault you made assumptions."

Desideria rose to her feet. "Don't you play your games with me."

Mor-Lath watched his high priestess. She stared him down. Disappointment welled in her heart. She had spent her whole life as a follower of Mor-Lath, most of that as a priestess. As his high priestess, he had confided in her, or so she had thought. "Why did you never tell me the Light was real? You deliberately let me believe a lie."

"Why?" The light mocking tone he normally used was gone. "You thinking of converting?" This was his dangerous voice, the one that should have warned her his temper was rising.

She didn't care. Her faith, her trust had been shattered. "You lied to your wife, too."

"She is none of your business." He shifted towards her ever so slightly.

She fought the fear that battled to overwhelm her. It would not do to give in now. She had to stand up to him. Unlike before, she feared death now, for once her soul left her body, where did it go? Before, the promise had been that she would be taken up to dwell among Mor-Lath's own. After seeing poor Desmone in Adrastea's angry clutches, she was no longer so sure. She wanted to be certain she knew where her soul was going before she gave it up.

"She is every part my business." Why would Adrastea lie? She wouldn't. Desmone pointed a finger at him. "You are not a god." The pain of loss and dashed beliefs blossomed in her heart.

"I am."

"Not a full god. Not in the past. Not now."

His eyes tightened. She'd hit a sensitive spot. She risked much in search of the truth. "I don't know if I believe in you anymore."

He took another step toward her. She couldn't help but step back. "I don't," she repeated, more to convince herself.

And she wouldn't cry in front of him. Crying would be a sign of weakness. He would cow her no more. She even went as far as to turn her back on him. That was dangerous. A thousand thoughts tumbled through her head, like who was he really? What would he do to her now that she discovered his façade? Would she survive this encounter? And what about her soul?

Did it matter now? She took a step away from him.

"I guess one of us has to die to prove the other's point," he said too casually.

A thrill of panic ran through her bones. Before she could bolt, he grabbed her by the arm and spun her around to face him. His eyes blazed with fierce passion. Indeed, his whole person glowed with such an awesome presence that her heart skipped a beat. Faintness threatened to consume her. Her knees buckled but he held her upright until the weakness passed.

Tears spilled from her eyes. He was going to kill her for sure.

He did not shout. "Tell me again how much you don't believe."

"Please." The word barely escaped her lips. He stroked her face, his fingers continuing down to her neck.

"Don't you think I'm a god, even if only a demi-god?"

She let out a small whimper.

He released her and stepped back. Holding out his hand, palm up, he presented her a knife. This was no kitchen knife but a weapon of war, double-edged and sharper than anything Desideria had ever handled in her life. "Take it," he ordered.

She shook her head.

"Take it!"

She flinched at the sharpness of his command but her hand, shaking, reached out and closed over the hilt of the knife.

"Now." His tone was deceptively even. "You have a choice. You can either use this knife to end your life, and thus end your doubt and misery, or you can prove to yourself that I am not the god you think I am by thrusting this knife into my heart."

Her hand closed over the knife.

"Frankly, I don't think you have the courage."

She closed her eyes and let the enormity of the situation wash through her. Along one path lay doubt and despair. Along the other lay certainty and the shattering of all she'd ever known.

Desideria thought on Adrastea. She stood up to Mor-Lath and lost. But she lived to fight another day. Instead of killing her, as he so easily could have done, he let her go. Either her value meant he didn't dare kill her, or she wasn't worth as much as he said she was and therefore didn't bother to kill her.

Desideria took a deep breath and opened her eyes. In a single forceful thrust, she jabbed the knife into Mor-Lath's chest. She stepped back in horror.

Mor-Lath recoiled from the force of the blow. He looked down at the knife and coughed. He slowly raised his gaze to his High Priestess. A smile spread across his face. He grasped the knife and, with some effort, pulled it out of his body. There was a dark stain on the front of his shirt, one with a silvery gleam. The knife had what looked like red blood, but it was bright and glimmery as well.

Not the blood of a mortal.

He did not stumble, he did not weaken. He held the knife up for her to see. "Doubt I am a god now?"

Desideria's knees gave way. She collapsed to the floor of the temple. "I'm so sorry," she wailed before burying her face in her hands.

He had no time for pity. Mor-Lath hauled Desideria up by her hair to face him. "Never, ever doubt me again." He held the knife up to her face. Her wild eyes stared nervously at its sticky blade.

"Please," she whispered. "If you ever loved me, kill me quickly."

He laughed—not a pleasant sound. Instead of drawing the edge across her neck, he drew the flat of the blade across her right cheek, leaving a streak of iridescent red god blood across her skin. "I will not kill you, but we must reconsider our relationship. You will never doubt I am a god again. You will never speak of today to my wife, nor any other living person, mortal or otherwise. The Light are real, even as I am real. They are a god. As They are the Light, I am the Dark. We are in opposition. Does that satisfy your curiosity?"

He wasn't going to kill her. The anxiety fled. A stillness filled her heart. She no longer feared him. Something inside her felt numb. "You ask a lot from me. You yourself taught me I should not accept a deal without asking for something in return."

His face brightened in pleasure. "The kitten has teeth."

"The cat knows better."

He released her. She backed away, rubbing her arm. "That sounds like one of my priestesses." He sounded sure, even proud.

She kept a wary eye on him. With the palm of her hand she wiped away the tears from her right cheek. She didn't dare touch the left. "Am I? Because I don't think I want to be that anymore." She did not turn her back on him but retreated from him, her eyes never leaving his face.

He watched her go, his expression unfathomable. His silence discomfited her. She needed to fill the empty chasm between them. "I don't know who you are, Mor-Lath. Not really. Am I seeing the real you for the first time?"

He shrugged. "Who is the real me?"

Her answer was bitter. "Not the god I once knew. You were never cruel. Harsh, if we happened to disobey but never cruel. Not like this. You were patient, you were passionate." She cut off what she was going to say next. Before Adrastea, she only had one issue with Mor-Lath, one she kept close to her heart and never shared with anyone else. Certainly not with him. "Ever since you got married, things have not been the same. I don't know if it's that she's changed you, or she's brought out a side of you you've kept hidden all this time—the real you."

She fidgeted with her fingers and shifted her feet. She wanted to run away from this place, from him, and forget all of this.

He listened to her. The silence descended between them once more. He let good humor spread across his face. "You're jealous."

"I don't know how to answer that." Perhaps yes, she was a little jealous in the beginning. After her recent conversation with Adrastea, that had changed. He had treated his wife shockingly.

Before his marriage, Mor-Lath had a laissez-faire policy concerning his personal priestesses at his temple. He gave them no restrictions with whom they dallied. As for himself, he left them alone. Desideria could see the wisdom in this; why introduce the potential for favoritism and politicking? This way, no one priestess would get above herself like Desmone had.

Still, she would be very surprised if she was the only priestess who had not wondered, at one time or another, what his personal favor was like.

Then the complete opposite happened. The one woman to whom he should have been giving his favor was denied it to the point where she had to take it from him and suffered for it.

"You are jealous," he insisted.

She shook her head in all honesty. "I would not trade places with Adrastea for all the Power in Creation."

His face lost its benevolence. "She has nothing to do with you and me. We're talking about you right now."

"There is nothing about me worth talking about right now. I served, I honored, I never questioned. And shall I guess my reward?"

Mor-Lath considered those words. Then he let out a visible sigh, his shoulders collapsing. "I'm sorry."

That she was not expecting. "You? Sorry?"

His eyes met hers. "Yes. I..." he hesitated, waving his hands to find the right words. "I must confess my marriage surprised me as much as it did everyone." He began to pace. "Oh, I've known for a very long time it would come about. It was foretold. I wanted it but," he tapped his hands on his chest. "I'm the God of the Dark. I'm supposed to be this vast powerful being, nothing surprising me." He looked forlorn. Lost even. "I guess I don't know as much as I should."

She kept her arms folded tightly against her chest, but she let him speak.

"Please don't tell anyone else but I was scared."

Now she reacted. "I don't believe it." Was he playing her?

"Well, yes. What am I supposed to do with a wife? I've never been married before."

Neither had she but at least she knew how to treat a wife.

"I never meant it to change me. I never meant to treat you, any of you, so shabbily." He advanced on her, arms open. She didn't move towards them but neither did she move back. "I've done several things wrong by you, Dessie," he said, using her familiar nickname.

She didn't thaw to it. The change in his behavior was too abrupt for her to completely believe it was genuine.

He gathered her in his arms. She did not respond. But instead of holding her, he slid his fingertips down her arms and then took her hands in his. She had little choice but to let him take her hands. She did step back so she wasn't too close to him. He had this aura about him that she found disconcerting. Any other time, she would have let herself be swayed by its insistence of attention and comfort. Was this a trick of his? Was he aware of what he was doing?

"Was I wrong to keep you at a distance?"

She looked away. "I don't know what you mean."

He chuckled softly. "I think you do."

She returned her gaze to him. "I don't want to think about that. What's past is past. It's too late to consider something like that now."

He shook his head. "Oh, never."

Her jaw dropped. "I can't believe you said that."

"I can't believe you don't want to talk about this."

"There is nothing to talk about." She extracted her hands. Every time she slipped her fingers away, he recaptured them. She frowned. "What? Do you think this is some sort of game?"

He tched at her. "Game is such a tawdry word, implying interplay that isn't to be taken seriously. No. This is not a game. I want you to take me seriously."

"How?"

"I need you to be my high priestess."

Desideria looked away. She'd discovered too much. She could have sworn the one she had believed to be a god was going to kill her. Now he sweet-talked her? Surely, he wouldn't be doing that if he still planned on ending her life.

But did she want to be a priestess of his, even a high priestess?

"You know me best, of every soul living. You know my quirks, my preferences..." he licked his lips. "My fears." He stepped back, holding out her hands so he could get a better look at her. "Look at you. You even stood up to me when you thought I needed it, not that I need standing up to that often. Actually," he went off on his own little thought tangent. "I haven't needed standing up to for a very, very long time." His glance returned to her. "Not since long before you were born."

He brought her hands up to rest upon his chest while he went all pensive. "I've become too complacent, enough so to forget what's really important. No wonder I'm on edge.

"Please, Dessie. Say you'll remain my high priestess."

She bit her lip and didn't answer.

"Let me grant you a boon."

In this she didn't need to think. "Do right by your wife."

For a moment, his expression froze. "I meant for you."

"This is for me."

"I meant something personal. Isn't there anything you've wanted for yourself, just you? Any mysteries of Creation, hidden knowledge," he inhaled ever so slightly, "personal desires?"

"No," she said, quickly and without thought. Of course, it was a lie. Probably one he would see through. Maybe a season ago, she would have hesitated, before Adrastea. There would have been a few things she would have been curious about, things she would never have known. Now they were beyond her forever.

She knew and liked Adrastea, despite the temper. She feared her strength, too, she admitted deep within her. She remembered the first time she met Mor-Lath's bride, how she glowed with the Deeper Power, as bright, if not brighter than he did. How she called upon Creation to serve her. Before she could pull the very earth apart, he stopped her.

He must have been afraid as well, though that consideration never crossed her mind until now.

There was no way she would poach this husband away from this wife. Desideria saw what she did to priestesses who overstepped their bounds.

Yet Mor-Lath continued to tempt her. "Not even a token, a taste?"

"No." Her hands began to tremble, and she tried to pull them away. "I can't."

"Just once," he purred, "and then things will go back to the way they were."

She managed to extract her hands from his grip. "No, I can't."

Instead, he stroked her face. "You're adorable when you act missish."

She flinched away from his touch. "Please. Go. I want nothing from you."

He guided her face back with a tender hand. Then he captured her mouth with his in a kiss that was as fierce as his touch had been gentle.

She had been unprepared for the force of his emotion. It swept through her like a warm tide, battling her will. She felt her resistance sliding away and she clung to his shirt. Inside, something screamed at her to break away, to pull back. She didn't listen. Instead, she found herself feasting hungrily on the passion he offered her. For too long she'd wistfully dreamt of this moment. She'd entertained thoughts of him offering himself to her. She wanted to sacrifice her body to him.

Then as suddenly as it began, the kiss was over. He broke off their contact and lifted his head as if to listen to something far away.

Immediately, the good feeling was gone, leaving nothing but shame. His expression changed from one of indulgent lover to attentive guard.

He released her completely. "I have something I must take care of." The next moment, he disappeared.

Desideria fled. She sought out the company of the other priestesses and vowed she would never let him catch her alone again.

Chapter 17

Adrastea couldn't sleep. Her blood buzzed too much after her conversation with Desideria. She fetched Desmone out from under the pillow. Over the millennia, he'd probably had thousands of women. They did not concern her. She wondered about all the ones he'd had since they were married, maybe the ones during their courtship as well. It would be poor form if he was courting her by day and tumbling another at night.

But how to find them?

Mor-Lath had done the best thing he could have done; he laid low. She hadn't heard even a whisper of him. The only vibe she could get through the lines on her face were ones of wary caution. Oh, he knew she was angry. Did he know why?

At least he wasn't bedding other women.

While she considered this, she idly twisted Desmone's soul up into a tiny knot.

How did she find Desmone? By the memories of a shirt. Adrastea had no idea where he kept his clothes, or if he just willed them into existence whenever he wished to change.

But did she need an item, or did she only need a memory?

She held up the mournful soul. "Give me your memories of my husband."

Desmone didn't have a choice. The moment Adrastea spoke, the associations ignited Desmone's memories like flushing birds out of the scrub.

Adrastea chose one of the more powerful ones and connected to it. With a trickle of Deeper Power, not quite enough to alert her husband, she explored the emotion behind the memory. She compared it to hers, or rather, the images she fed her sleep-induced husband, and the resonance between them.

From the two memories, she found a sympathetic vibration that echoed along the Lines of Deeper Power.

She sent her request along. Were there any others out there?

From a distance came a very definite yes.

"Well, Desmone. We're going hunting." She shoved the deceased priestess into her pocket and translocated herself to where that positive echo originated.

Shift.

Cold, thin air touched Adrastea's skin. She shivered as goosebumps rose on her arms. She stood at the mouth of a small cave. It was not a deep cavern, possibly carved by the hands of men. Floorboards lined the cave, making it homely.

Adrastea moved deeper inside, for there seemed to be a warm light coming from within.

"Who are you?" came a startled voice. Adrastea jumped.

On the far side of the cavern, next to a fire in a fireplace, stood a woman dressed in a simple robe. In the dim light, Adrastea was not sure of her age, but the Lines of Deeper Power spoke of several decades. Her dark hair was ratted into dreadlocks. She stood next to a plain pallet. Other than that, and the fireplace, the only other furniture was a shelf of books.

The woman clutched a knife to her chest, possibly in hope of defending against the intruder.

He was interested in this? "I should ask who you are."

The woman kept her wary distance. "I am the anchoress." Her eyes narrowed. "You're intruding on my holy meditation."

An anchoress? What was that? No matter. With a flick of the Deeper Power, Adrastea sent the knife flying from the anchoress' grasp. She laid a hand on the frightened woman's head. "Give me your memories of Mor-Lath."

The anchoress cried out. She tried to resist. "My Lord!" she wailed. Images of him coming to her, of taking her in this very cave, were strong.

Adrastea had seen enough. She tore the life from the anchoress. As the soul separated from the physical body, Adrastea felt a dizziness surge through her. She shook it from her head.

Once free, the anchoress' memories were far more vivid. Yes, he had visited this woman, more than two months ago, if her reckoning of time was reliable. Adrastea doubted the anchoress even knew if it was morning or night.

She pulled out the two souls and compared them. Such different women, one thoughtful and introverted, the other rather narcissistic and shallow.

Now that she had them both, she could compare their memories. Between them, she found a certain vibration of the soul. "Who else feels like this?" Adrastea focused on the vibration and sent out her request to Creation.

A few positive pings confirmed there were other women out there. One was faint, the other two stronger, and then one that hummed rather loudly.

Adrastea chose the loudest to visit first.

Shift.

The air warmed somewhat but remained just as dry. Adrastea stood in the back of a temple, where several priestesses and a couple of priests chanted. Adrastea looked up to the woman before the altar. Her back was turned to the congregation. Adrastea studied the Lines that connected this priestess to Mor-Lath.

The anchoress recognized her. "Udevrien."

"You know her?" Adrastea asked her, quietly.

"She is the high priestess of my order before I retreated to the cave."

"Did you know he was tumbling her as well as you?"

The anchoress shook her head. "My devotions are private. I see no one."

"Except for him."

The anchoress conceded. "He never said anything about you."

Adrastea stuffed her back into her pocket, where she and Desmone could commiserate together.

While the priestesses continued their chanting, Adrastea strode up to the altar. One by one, the voices stopped.

The high priestess turned around. Adrastea's presence baffled her. "Who are you?"

"Mor-Lath's wife."

The blood drained from Udevrien's face. "What?" she asked, her voice faint.

Adrastea answered her by refting Udevrien of life. Creation tilted, and Adrastea stumbled.

The body fell at the foot of the altar, startling the congregation.

Shift.

The more souls she collected, the better Adrastea got at finding the rest. With Desmone and the anchoress and Udevrien, the other pulses along the Lines became clearer, easier to find. The third soul, a merchant's unmarried daughter, had no idea who Mor-Lath was. Adrastea took her anyhow.

Likewise, the fourth woman farmed cattle. Adrastea found her all alone out on the prairie, her fellow ranchers too far on the other side of the herd to notice she'd died. The dizziness Adrastea felt from this death brought her to her knees.

Like the merchant's daughter, the rancher had no idea who the dark stranger was, who appeared to her on lonely, starry nights. She never thought to ask, so desperate was her need for company.

Out on the plains, the dust stirred by cattle provided a cloud of isolation. Adrastea regarded the souls she'd harvested. Desmone looked bored. The anchoress kept trying to escape. The two others clung to each other and wept. Udevrien looked thoughtful. "Creation will not stand for this."

Adrastea's voice was low and dangerous. "Creation put me here. I gave my life and risked my eternal soul to save every single person I cared about. I completely gave myself over to the Dark God, all for what he wanted. The moment I agreed, I'm abandoned and forgotten. No one likes their sacrifice to be tossed aside like the core of an apple."

"How many more lives will you end?"

"How many more are there?" She sent a pulse of Deeper Power through all of them and listened for the familiar harmonies.

Only one sang back along the lines. One more.

A feeling of disquiet rolled in along the lines on her face. Adrastea had to act quickly. Mor-Lath knew she was up to something.

Shift.

Adrastea studied the little farmer's cottage on the edge of a field. Such a simple home, even simpler than Natan's.

The front yard was given over completely to garden, with one corner being newly turned. The residue of Deeper Power lingered here.

Vivid memories rose from the earth as she placed a hand to the dirt. She jerked her hand away from the garden bed, but the memories did not stop burning in her head.

Adrastea eased the door open and stepped in. This was the last one. There were no other women in the world whose guilty harmonies, inadvertently set there by the Dark God's lust, hummed along the Lines of the Deeper Power.

The farmer and his wife sat at the kitchen table, silently eating their supper. Adrastea didn't care about him. It was the woman she had her eye on. Adrastea saw nothing beautiful or uncommon about the farmer's wife. She was average of feature, wider in hips than a lady's vanity would desire, with faded hair and faintly mottled skin from too much sun.

He had preferred this drab little creature over her?

She saw Adrastea first. "Who are you?" Surprise raised the pitch of her voice. The man turned around. His voice was gruffer. "What do you want? How'd you get in?"

Adrastea didn't bother with words. The drama lost its thrill after five such killings. She stretched forth her hand to snatch the soul out of the body, but a male hand descended, stopping her.

"No," said Mor-Lath. "I will not let you kill her."

Adrastea's rage flared up. "You tumbled with another man's wife and you can't even approach your own?"

The woman popped to her feet. "My lord?" she squeaked. Her glance briefly touched her husband. She had to look away. "My lady," she said, with more surety in her voice and also dread.

Adrastea snatched her hand away from Mor-Lath. "You can't stop me."

He grabbed her by the shoulders and shook her. "I will."

Meanwhile, the farmer rose to his feet. "You had this man in your bed?" His hands slammed the table. "You're cuckolding me?"

Adrastea reached out her hand for the woman's soul.

The husband also reached for his wife. She backed off, knocking her chair to the side. "It's not like that. This happened long before—" His palm found the side of her cheek. The stinging slap rang out. She recoiled from the slap, tumbling to the floor.

Adrastea's body sang with the Deeper Power as she reached for the farmwife. Mor-Lath had drawn on his own to counter hers. He used his superior weight and pushed Adrastea to the ground. She wrestled with him, refusing to let him pin her.

The farmer's attention turned to the struggling couple on the floor. His aimed kick caught the Dark God in the ribs.

Mor-Lath noticed enough to push the man away with the Power. So great was the force, it had been strong enough to send the man across the room and into the wall, breaking his arm.

However, he lost enough advantage that Adrastea pushed him off. She reached for the woman, the Deeper Power dragging her forward.

The woman panicked. She sprawled on the floor as Mor-Lath broke Adrastea's grip on her.

The farmer cradled his arm, his pain strong enough to be felt by Adrastea. She fed his wisps of pain into her fire of anger.

Unlike before, the farmer didn't dare interfere now. "Who the hell are you?"

Mor-Lath gained advantage over Adrastea, finally pinning her down. "Stop that," he said as she drew on more Power. "You're going to pull down the whole house."

"Good!" she shrieked as she increased her struggles. Physically, he was superior. But when it came to the Deeper Power, they were evenly matched. At least, Mor-Lath had not yet been able to overcome her strength as they pushed against each other through the Lines of Power. Every time she sought an advantage, he'd have to counter it. It kept him busy enough he couldn't do much else.

The farmer sidled closer to his wife, giving a wide berth to the couple on the floor. "Who are they?"

The wife had a hand pressed to the red mark on her face. "He's a lord from the city. A friend of the baron's." She let out a small noise. "You know, I don't even know his name."

Adrastea mocked her husband. "Too much of a coward to give her your real name?"

Her effort to speak gave him a slight advantage. He lay his forehead, a little harder than necessary to hers. "*Sleep...*"

"No!" Adrastea fought the suggestion. Alas, that moment was all he needed to gain advantage. Adrastea's struggle turned to a losing battle to keep from falling asleep.

He repeated the command. "*Sleep.*"

Adrastea relaxed. Her arms ceased pushing against his, her legs stopped thrashing. But instead of succumbing to his will, she gathered her own and focused it in one big push. His forehead was still next to hers. She knew exactly what lay in his heart.

"*Fear...*"

Dread exploded within him, depriving him of focus. While his strength turned inward to fight the fear within, Adrastea pushed him off. She rolled away, stretching her hand towards the woman. "Mine!" She ripped the woman's soul from her body.

As she was still huddled on the floor, the woman only slumped forward slightly. The farmer remained where he was, cradling his broken arm. He didn't realize that his wife was no longer of the living.

Creation rippled. Adrastea fought the waves of nausea.

Mor-Lath reached out his hands to steady himself. Frustration rang in his voice. "No!" He reached for Adrastea, but she scooted out of his way.

"Oh," she cooed. "Was this your pet?" She swallowed to keep from throwing up.

Mor-Lath's eyes burned with anger. He hefted himself to his feet and slammed Adrastea against the wall, making everything on shelves around the house jump. "You didn't have to do that."

"Why not? You do it all the time."

"Lanne?" The man touched his wife's limp arm.

She said nothing. Her soul, trapped between Adrastea's fingers, whimpered. He, being mortal, could not hear. Her thoughts were transparent. *Who are you?*

Adrastea didn't answer. Her focus was completely on Mor-Lath. "Did you really think I would be such a naïf to sit around in your little temple while you roamed the world seducing other women? Did you think I would never find out? I will not be ignored, Mor-Lath. I might have married you because I had no better choice but that didn't mean I would play the lapdog for the rest of eternity.

She pointed a finger at him. "You will never touch another woman again. I have killed all your little playthings. You will not take another. I will know if you do." She stroked the lines on her cheeks with her hands. They sent out a sharp warning through them. "And I will kill her before her bed is cold. I will hunt down every single woman in this world before I let you shame me again." She closed her fist around the soul and brought it near her heart.

Mor-Lath said nothing. His eyes filled with cold bitterness as he looked over his jealous wife. With measured calmness, he held out his hand. "Give me that soul."

"No." Lanne's soul was still trapped between her fingers. No matter how much she twisted in fear, she could not free herself.

"It is not yours."

"Nor is it yours."

He would not be drawn into an argument. "Release her to Tanat. She will judge, and she will deliver."

Adrastea clenched her fists. "Ha! I think not. These souls belong to me until I am done with them."

He drew in a breath. "Souls? How many do you have?"

"All of them."

His gaze turned inward. Of course, he'd have a way of keeping tabs on his little playthings. Then the lines around his eyes deepened in severity. "You bitch. You jealous bitch."

He snatched her arm and pulled on the Deeper Power.

The farmer yelped, falling against the wall as a large hellish doorway into nothingness opened in his home. Beyond the veiled darkness, the voices of countless souls howled within. Mor-Lath hurled his wife through the opening to Dom-al-gol and sealed the door behind her.

He spat on the spot where the doorway had been, as if to bid her farewell.

Then he closed his eyes and pinched the bridge of his nose as he realized something. "She took the souls with her."

Chapter 18

Adrastea's stomach lurched as she flew over the threshold Mor-Lath had opened. Before she could orient herself, it closed behind her, shutting off the clear yellow light of day.

Where was she? There was no ground that she could detect, nor any sky. Which way was up? The lack of connection with anything solid disconcerted her. Adrastea was alone in darkness.

Well, not exactly alone. The darkness resolved itself. It was not with her eyes she saw but rather her inner eye that she could see. Sort of how she could be looking at an empty room, then blink and the next see it full of angels.

There were no angels here. There were other souls, locatable by the pull of their emotions on her. They surrounded her every which way.

Who were the others out there? "Hello?"

That got their attention. The souls drew closer. Adrastea could at least sense distance. As they approached, she could sense the Lines of Deeper Power that connected each one to Creation. She reached out to grab them, more for something to hang on to, rather than try to bring the souls closer to her.

The souls slid along the lines towards her. "Hello, hello!" one of them chimed. "What tender new morsel do we have here?" Some of the others echoed the sentiment. Others were not so eager to examine her. "She feels different," they told each other.

"She's powerful." They came closer, quickly now, as if drawn by her.

One slid along its power so fast it slammed into her, flowed through her and came out the other side. "Merciful Creation! She's alive!"

None of the souls paused. "Life," they chimed, over and over.

Adrastea felt a hunger blossom within them. It had been present before but only as an afterthought. They all yearned after something, whether it be satiation of lust, empty bellies, curiosity. One soul, for some odd reason, felt a tickly itch in the unscratchable spot of what it perceived to be its back. All he wanted was for someone to scratch it for him.

Nobody had. Nobody would.

Their momentum carried the souls through Adrastea and beyond. For all her solidity, they couldn't touch her.

In the beginning, Adrastea threw up her arms to protect herself from the assault. When she saw they couldn't hurt her, she dropped her arms. Souls howled in frustration. Their itches would not be scratched. Their thirst would not be quenched. Their lust would not come. Most retreated to nurse their dissatisfaction. Some remained, for of all the desires, at least curiosity might be satisfied.

By now, Adrastea had a sense of where she was. She floated in a vast nothingness crisscrossed with Lines of Deeper Power. Each Line connected to a soul. The other end of the Line travelled down (for that was how it felt it was going) until, eventually, they all joined together in one knot.

All the souls she had with her were huddled in her pocket. Their Lines did not join the others but remained tethered to her.

They stuck together and did not dare show themselves. Would Death come after them, as she did for all souls?

"Where am I?" Adrastea asked aloud.

The closer souls had mixed reactions to her question. Some couldn't believe she asked it, others simply shrugged with indifference. But one couldn't resist answering. "You be in Dom-al-gol, the Home of the Demons, the place called Hell by some, the Darkness Beyond by others. It is one and the same, for we all come here when we die."

"But I'm not dead." Of that she knew for sure.

"I know," the soul replied. "You are one of the immortals. But who are you? You certainly aren't the Light, nor Love. Nor Judgement, for what would she be doing here? Nor are you the Darkness. Who are you?"

She drew in a breath surprised that she could still breathe. It would not harm her to tell the truth. "I am Adrastea, Bride of the Dark."

"Huh." By now, the rest of the souls seemed to have retreated, leaving only Adrastea, this one that spoke to her, and two others who hovered in the background, watching intently but saying nothing. "And you are here for...?"

Good question. "Let's just say I'm the victim of wrath."

"Surely not the Light. It is not Their aim to damn souls to this place." Its voice turned wistful. "Quite the opposite, actually."

"What? They steal souls from here?"

The soul sighed. "Steal? No. It— We are luminous beings with a destiny." To Adrastea's senses, the soul began to take a form, vaguely resembling a man. "We were not supposed to spend forever here."

This was new to Adrastea. "But I was taught that when you died, you were judged. If you lived a righteous life, you ascended to serve the Light as angels. But if your soul was weighed down by sin, you were sent to the pits of Dom-al-gol."

"So, it is. But why?"

"Why?" She had not been expecting that question. "Why what?"

"Why is a soul burdened by sin sent to Dom-al-gol?"

She had to think on this one. "Uh, to be punished?"

The soul shook its head. "No. To be purged. Dom-al-gol isn't a prison—well, it is but not a permanent repository. Dom-al-gol is a purgatory, where the sins acquired in life must be purged before moving on. Only..." The soul went opaque with suspicion. "You're here for him, aren't you?"

"I'm not sure what you're asking."

But the soul had finished talking. It departed for a farther point in Dom-al-gol from her, leaving her feeling deserted.

The two silent souls ventured closer. "You're not going to let us out either, are you?"

Adrastea wished she could close her eyes to shut out what she saw. The souls couldn't be ignored. They huddled together as if for warmth or comfort. "He promised us he'd let us out, but he hasn't."

"I assume 'he' is Mor-Lath?"

They acquiesced. "We've given up on waiting for him to keep his promise."

"He's like that." Something they said caught her attention. "How long have you been here?"

They didn't know. "Time doesn't flow here the way it does for mortality. When one doesn't have the clock of a heartbeat, one tends to lose track."

An ache that felt like impending boredom—not that these souls had bored her yet—tugged at her ribs. "So, what do you do?"

"Seek knowledge," said one.

"Reflect," said the other. "There is lot of room for dwelling on the sins of one's past."

For a moment, Adrastea thought they were going to expand on what sins they had committed but all they said was, "We're rather sorry for what we did. But we've had no promise here."

"There was supposed to be a promise," one added wistfully.

"What sort of promise?" The more she knew about where she was, the better she might be at coming up with a solution to her problem. Could she will herself out of here?

"We don't know. Some of the souls do but they don't always share their knowledge with us."

"Knowledge is all we've got. Sometimes you've got to guard it closely."

Adrastea wasn't listening. She'd closed her mortal eyes and focused on a place in the mortal world. Her mother's house, on the front porch, looking over Sacred Spring. She called upon the Deeper Power.

But it wouldn't respond the way she wanted it to. It was there, present in the Lines that connected the souls to Creation, but it lacked form and structure.

"What did you just do?" one of the souls asked.

"Just testing things."

The other soul drifted closer. "What kind of things?"

"Just things." It was better to play cautious. After all, these souls were the demons who served Mor-Lath.

The souls began to cling. "Please tell us."

"No." She pushed them off.

"Please?"

The tone was so plaintive Adrastea hesitated for a moment. "How do I know you won't go tell him?"

"We wouldn't," one said. "We promise." The other agreed.

Adrastea did not take them at their word. Instead, she changed the subject. "So, who are you? Or rather, who were you before you died?"

One answered, "A faithful follower of him. Or was. So much for fidelity."

"Not me," the other said. "I was a follower of the Light."

This puzzled Adrastea. "So how did you end up here?"

The soul shrugged. "I wasn't that good a follower. I wish I had been. I wouldn't have ended up here. Now I don't know how to get out."

"I don't think they'll let you out." Adrastea retained her hold on the Deeper Power. She let her consciousness slide along the Lines. That they ended here was something to ponder on. If they had one end, they could have another. What if she followed the lines until she climbed out? Could it be done?

"No. There should be a way out but there isn't. Unless you can find a way."

The other soul nodded. "If anyone can find their way out, it'd be you, Bride."

She regarded the two souls. "I'll have to think about it. You didn't think it would be easy, did you?"

No, it wasn't. With the two souls in tow, and the occasional curious other, she explored the nadir of the Lines of Deeper Power. They joined at the bottom of Creation. There was no more after that. She followed the Lines up as far as she could. No matter how far she travelled, she couldn't find the border of Dom-al-gol.

With no sun nor moon, nor any other way to tell time other than her own heartbeat, Adrastea had no idea how long she'd taken to travel the Lines. During her journey, she gave much thought to her relationship with Mor-Lath.

A few more souls joined her entourage. The evil, snakey ones that she knew accompanied Mor-Lath in mortality were either absent or avoiding her. The souls that gravitated to her here were drab little grey things, more sorrow than anger. Each one wanted to tell her their story. Soon, she was willing to listen, as there was not much else to be done here.

Their sins varied from grossly evil to just enough minor peccadillos to tip the balance of their soul over. The one thing they had in common was that they were thoroughly sorry for what they had done.

One time, when one sorry little soul was explaining how he had cheated his brother in business, Adrastea saw the Lines of Power twist and congregate somewhere in the distance. "What's that?" She indicated the direction of the convergence.

"What?" The soul felt annoyed that it had been interrupted.

"Something's happening over there." Adrastea headed towards it. All the other souls followed, adding a steady stream of commentary. As she followed the Lines to their junction, she listened to the souls. They couldn't see what she saw. They all had their own opinions on what it could be. What struck her is that not a single one of them doubted that she saw something.

They trusted her. It touched her somewhat.

The Lines pulled together, opening into a gateway very much like the one she had been thrust through earlier. It shone into Dom-al-gol as a bright patch of sunlight, illuminating all within. Adrastea squinted against the sudden light. As one, the souls shouted, an overwhelming roar of emotion. They streamed to the gateway. Adrastea remained where she was for a moment, stunned at the sudden exodus attempt. Before any of the souls could make the dash to freedom, the gateway shut. They howled in sorrow before fleeing to the distant corners of Dom-al-gol to deal individually with their disappointment.

This left Adrastea alone with her own brand of loneliness. Had he opened the gateway? If so, he wasn't coming for her. How disappointing.

She wanted him to find her. Why? He didn't love her; he made that very clear. He only wanted her so he could become a full god. So why did she want him? If he wished, he could give her anything she wanted.

Not that he had any desire to grant her anything further than what he had. She'd given her hand in marriage in exchange for the safety of her village but had asked nothing for herself. More fool her. She saw now that he got the better part of the deal. The safety of some insignificant village was an easy price to pay for godhood. Now that she reflected upon it, he had given in a little too easily. How smoothly he had played her.

Sorrow, not anger, filled her. Why had she been so naïve to not think that he would never have entered into a bargain in which he did not have the advantage? She should have held out longer.

But would it have done any good? It would not surprise her if he had let the Cithrans destroy her village. He would have carried her away. Her life would have gotten worse until she gave in.

Upon further reflection, perhaps her end of the bargain was the best she could have gotten. If she gave in earlier, would the protection have been cast over her village? Probably not. Would her mother and Mira have been saved?

Maybe.

When she thought of her mother, she found a guilty little spot in her heart. She didn't mourn but wished she had done something. Was it a sin to feel closer to Ari than to Lillybet?

Adrastea reflected upon the stories she heard from the dead souls here in Dom-al-gol. She hadn't come across her mother or her father here. Was that simply a matter of not having encountered them? There were millions of souls here. Or had her parents been delivered up to the Light? She hoped it was the latter. Perhaps her mother was happier in death. Life hadn't been too kind to her.

Would she recognize anyone here—not that she knew many people who had died.

On the whole, Adrastea had no desire to remain in Dom-al-gol any longer than she had to. How to get out? Mor-Lath wasn't going to come rescue her. She pressed her hands to her face and listened. She could feel him, but he was far, far away. It would do no good to call for him.

Anyhow, she didn't need him. Not really.

Now, these condemned souls, they needed her, if only as an ear. They wanted to tell their stories. They had to share. It was as if they wanted to unburden themselves of the sins they had collected in life. More souls had gathered around her, listening, waiting, mourning. With nothing else to do, she listened to their tales and took her own personal notes.

She reflected upon her own life, the things she'd done right, the things she could have done better or differently. Being a living being, an immortal even, she did not belong here, but it gave her time to reflect.

A cold thought occurred to her during her lengthy ponderance. The Light had created her especially for Mor-Lath. Why would They do that? Why would They give their greatest enemy his heart's desire?

Well, They didn't give him his desire. They gave him the tools. She smiled then laughed out loud. A tool was only a tool if you knew what to do with it. A tool could work both ways, wielded by the hand of another. The Light knew this. They created her not so Mor-Lath could triumph but possibly to bring about his downfall, should his pride and selfishness get in the way.

Light! Was her true destiny not as the Bride of the Dark but the one well-placed tool to bring him down? Had the Light been counting on his character weaknesses? Creation knew she had incensed him enough to be banished here. She hadn't yet figured out to get out. From time to time, a gateway would open but never close enough to reach it before it closed.

She couldn't do much good down here.

Or could she?

Mor-Lath needed another half to become the full god. Her marriage hadn't been enough. Did he realize this? She wasn't sure. As long as she was down here, whatever it was that would make him—them—whole wasn't going to happen. When the final battle came, he wasn't going to be ready.

He would be defeated.

Was this the Light's plan? And what would happen to her?

She didn't want to be destroyed. If he was destroyed in the final battle, would she be as well? Or, as the tool of the Light, would They spare her?

A flush of guilt filled her. She'd been here in Dom-al-gol for who knew how long, and she hadn't thought once of calling upon the Light.

I'm sorry, she sent to them in silent prayer. *I should have thought of You sooner.*

She received an answer but not in words. A steady feeling of warmth and comfort.

She would be all right.

"Why am I here?"

No answer.

"How do I get out?"

You have the power to free yourself.

An answer! "How?"

But They offered nothing further. Even though Adrastea felt better, the steady feeling had faded. She was alone once more.

I can do it, she told herself. I just don't know how yet.

One time she asked one of the souls, "Do any of you ever leave here?"

It shrugged. "For a time. He will call upon the more desperate of us to do his bidding in mortality. He will set us to watch the living and report back what they do or say. Other times he will set us tasks."

"So, you've been. You've escaped."

The soul shrank in sorrow. "I would not call it escape. In the early days after my death I discovered that while I no longer had a mortal body, I still suffered the hungers. I wanted to taste wine again. I loved it too much when I was living. It was what killed me." Adrastea already knew the tale of the soul when it had been a man. If only the living knew what it was like to be dead, they would straighten up their lives instantly. "I thirsted here in Dom-al-gol. I would have done anything to leave, even if momentarily."

Adrastea understood.

"Out there, you can experience a shadow of what it was like to live. You can't experience it fully. It's like licking the mouth of an empty wine bottle. It tastes like the wine, but it doesn't satisfy your thirst.

"In the end, we would be returned to Dom-al-gol. The hungers would come back with no way to assuage them. It felt worse. Soon, I learned it was better to remain here. The only way to ease the hunger was to forget about it.”

How long had she been here? It must have been longer than she thought. Her stomach growled. The hunger would fade and be forgotten but would return every once in a while. She even felt sleepy from time to time, closing her eyes for a moment.

At least, she thought it was just a moment. She always felt better when she opened her eyes. The same souls would be gathered about her. Their stories rotated and changed as several of them shared at once.

She missed food and a clean bed. She even missed the pretty gowns that had become her new wardrobe.

“Tell me,” she asked the soul. “Do you know if angels feel these desires?”

The soul thought about this. “They say they don’t. They say our desires are the last vestiges of our sin, haunting us. Angels have been purged of their sins. They are clean beings. Thus, they don’t feel any of the longing we do.” The soul snuggled closer to her, seeking comfort. “I wish I could be purged. Could you purge me?”

“I don’t know,” Adrastea replied, hesitantly. “I wouldn’t know how.” The other souls pressed closer. She could feel their yearnings as well for deliverance from the hungers that plagued them.

“The Light can do it. So can the Dark,” the soul told her. “Surely if you are the Bride of the Dark, he will have shared his power with you. You could do it.”

Is this true? she asked the Light, but she received no answer. Were They listening?

To herself, she mused, “How would I do it?”

Alas, they souls didn’t know. They gathered around her and waited. They had all eternity to wait.

Sin was a slippery thing. It was woven in to the Lines of Power that connected a soul to Creation. To purge it from the souls meant its untanglement and removal. It reminded her of the skeins of thread with which her mother wove. The thread of Creation was spun of several fibers. Linsey-woolsey was made from two different fibers but once spun up, they looked the same.

Sin was no different. It twisted through the Lines. But whenever she tried to pluck it out, it evaded her grasp.

"Oh, I give up," she cried one time when the sin of one soul evaded her grasp. A thousand tries and not once could she separate the sin from the soul. "I don't think I can do this."

The souls pressed desperately around her. "You have to," they pleaded. "He won't do it and the Light never comes here."

"But I can't."

The souls pressed around her and pleaded. They clamored and clung as if she was their only hope. Their presence suffocated her.

"Leave me alone." She extracted herself from them.

"Oh, free us," they begged.

She drew on the Deeper Power and pushed them all away. The souls scattered like droplets of water. Adrastea fled. Their neediness sucked her patience. She had to have some time for herself.

Down in the bottom of the nothingness, where the Lines of Deeper Power met, she huddled at their juxtaposition and focused on her own heartbeat. It was the one thing that told her she was still alive. She may have been forgotten by the mortal world and spurned by her husband, but the Light hadn't forgotten her. She would not forget herself.

Souls forgot things. Often when they recounted a tale from their lives, a detail would evade their memories. They'd skip over it and continue but Adrastea would wonder what it was they forgot. The longer the souls had been in Dom-al-gol, the more they forgot.

Would she forget things, the longer she was here?

As she fretted in the depths of Creation, she heard a faint murmuring. It came from her pocket. Oh, no. She'd forgotten the souls she had harvested, the souls that had been the reason for her banishment to this abysmal place. They had been with her the whole time and never said a word. If the other souls knew of their presence, they didn't mention it either. How odd. The souls were very forthright about plenty of other things.

Adrastea drew out the dead ex-lovers of her husband and gave them close scrutiny. "So, what have you been doing all this time?"

"Put us back," said Desmone. "We don't belong here."

Adrastea had no sympathy for them. "You're dead. You're sinners. Of course, you belong here."

Desmone disagreed. "We haven't been judged."

"Oh yes you have."

"But it's not our fault," another pleaded. What was her name? Oh yes. Udevrien "We didn't think we were doing anything wrong."

"Really, now. How many of you knew he was the God of the Dark?" Half did, half didn't.

"Shame on you," she told the collective.

Another soul, the anchoress, said, "When I had him, he was not your husband. You cannot blame me for something that happened before you showed up.

This may have been true, but she was not going to admit that to them. Instead, she singled out the two who could be blamed: Desmone and Lanne Saponer. "How about we discuss your sins?"

Desmone stood her ground. "I did not know you were his wife. You can't sin in ignorance."

"How convenient of him to not tell you." Adrastea turned her attention to Lanne. Lanne shrank back. "You, on the other hand, have no excuse."

"But I didn't know he was the God of the Dark."

"But you did know he was married. You were married."

"It was just the last time. He seduced me. I never meant... Oh dear." Despair flooded the little grey soul until she was murky. "It all makes sense now."

"You mean, he raped you?"

Lanne didn't answer for a moment. "No," she admitted with some reluctance.

"The Dark god does not need to rape," Desmone retorted hotly. "Women flocked to him willingly. And who would blame them? He is very skilled in the love arts."

Murmurs of assent rippled through the souls.

"Please understand," Lanne said. "Until my husband came along, he was the only man I'd ever known. I thought he was some guest of the local lord's..." She hesitated. "I guess you know all this?"

Adrastea's impatience grew. "Just get on with it." It was one thing to pluck someone's memories. It was another to hear the tale from their lips.

Desmone exulted. "He made you feel alive. Your blood burned under his touch."

Lanne didn't deny this either. "It was like waking up. When I was with him, I didn't mind that I had no husband. I... found myself waiting for his return. Sometimes it would be months between visits. Then, one year, he didn't return. That same year a neighboring farmer offered me marriage. Know that it was not a marriage of love but one of business."

Sounded familiar. "I'm listening."

"You're very good at that, aren't you?" quipped Desmone. Adrastea ignored her.

Lanne continued. "It was not a bad marriage, as far as arranged marriages go. We prospered somewhat. But..."

Desmone finished Lanne's thought. "Your husband was a mortal man."

She didn't fault him his good points but, "He left much to be desired in bed."

"Don't worry," Desmone said to Lanne. "All mortal men are like that. Only the gods are the good lovers."

The rancher laughed out loud. "What kind of louts have you been bedding, little priestess?"

Desmone frowned. "What? Are you saying he's not the best lay you've had?"

The rancher recovered herself. "Oh, I didn't say that. I'm only stating there are mortal men with, let us say, sufficient skill in the love arts?"

Adrastea felt left out. The whole of her experience had been once, and a very unsatisfying once at that.

Mor-Lath was the only man to have paid attention to her. Now he wanted nothing to do with her. She had reacted jealously when she found out about the others. But if she had turned around and sought out other lovers, would he have been justified in killing them as she killed these women?

How stupid was she? Stupid, young and ignorant. Had she just let these women be, had she let Mor-Lath do what he wanted with whom he wanted, perhaps she could have been free to seek out other lovers unhindered.

What a mess she'd made of everyone's lives.

No, this was not her fault; this was his fault.

He could have said nothing about the women in his past. She would never have known. His mistake had been the women of the present, namely Desmone and Lanne.

She ignored Lanne for the moment and focused her attention on Desmone. "You claimed to be the Bride of the Dark. That's a bold assumption to make."

Fear and thoughts whirled through Desmone's mind. Adrastea could see how much Desmone was thinking. "Don't bother lying," she told the soul. "I can tell when you are."

Desmone believed her. "I wasn't going to say anything."

"Perhaps you should."

"Uh-uh. I'm saying nothing." But the thoughts continued to tumble.

Adrastea reached in and plucked one out for examination. "You thought you were the one foretold by prophecy?"

Desmone defended herself. "The timing was—oh." She'd said too much. The thought related to that came forth. Adrastea plucked it out.

As she looked at it, her hand tightened around it. Tension rose within her. The anger that had remained dormant for so long flared into her heart. "That bastard!" Releasing the thought, she grasped Desmone's soul between her hands and twisted. Desmone shrieked.

The other souls tried to flee but every one of them were tied to Adrastea through the Lines of Power. They would never be free until she released them. They strained at the ties that bound them, keeping as much distance between them and the angry immortal as they could.

Desmone couldn't flee. "What did I do?" she begged between wrenchings and cries of pain.

Adrastea wished she had a rock to bang Desmone against. "You are an insignificant nobody." She gave the soul an extra hard twist. "You are just a toy to him. A convenience. You don't mean anything." She tried to tear the soul in half, but it wouldn't tear.

"Stop it, please," the soul named Udevrien begged. "It isn't her fault. Please leave her alone." The soul attempted to grasp Adrastea's hands but her ethereal fingers passed effortlessly through the mortal flesh.

Adrastea had no problems with laying hands on the souls. With a flick of her fingers she knocked the soul away and continued her torture of Desmone.

Udevrien was undaunted. While she did not attempt to touch Adrastea again, she tried words to break through the red haze of rage. "If you are going to punish her, at least tell her what she did wrong."

Adrastea tightened her fist, causing Desmone to squeak like a kitten. "Do you know what she's done?" she shrilled at Udevrien. "She was seducing my husband on our wedding day. It was not my bed he sought but hers. Then she has the arrogance to boast about it. What sort of slut lures a husband away from his wedding?" She held up her fist with bits of

Desmone hanging out. "This one does." She strangled a woman already dead.

Udevrien tried to lay a hand on Adrastea's arm. It passed through. "You might feel better after hurting her. Or you might not."

"This is not our fault," added Lanne. "Not really. Who you should be mad at is him."

"I'm already mad at him," Adrastea spat.

"So why punish us?"

Her words pricked at Adrastea's soul. Why had she done it? Was she so blinded by rage she couldn't think straight? Or did she feel powerless compared to him, that she'd taken out her rage against these women?

Lanne was right. It wasn't their fault.

Udevrien laid a hand on Adrastea's arm. "I think you feel more for him than you wish to admit. If you didn't feel anything, you wouldn't care who he slept with."

Perhaps this was true. And maybe if he had taken her in the beginning, not being terribly gentle or thoughtful, she might have been grateful for his current lack of attention.

But then... he kept kissing her. When he did, her soul yearned.

"This is the only way I had of hurting him."

Udevrein inclined her head. "Assuming we meant anything to him."

Adrastea looked at the priestess whose soul twirled with all sorts of ideas that she tried to suppress. Udevrien had believed Mor-Lath had cared for her. She honestly thought there was a connection. She still did. Also, in her plethora of thoughts was a new one—disappointment. Like Desideria, like Berengaria, Udevrien had believed in a benevolent god. Upon learning Adrastea's story, she questioned his treatment of Adrastea.

She also questioned Adrastea's behavior. "Why were you never forthright with him?"

"I've always been forthright with him. When he asked me to marry him, I said no. And I meant it."

Udevrien didn't accept that. "No is our natural state, until we say yes. Then yes becomes our natural state. Once you say yes, you can't go back to no."

Adrastea groaned. "I'm not the one who went back to no. If he had no intention of bedding me, why didn't he tell me from the beginning?"

"What?" scoffed the rancher. "You definitely would have said no, then."

Adrastea's memory flitted back to their wedding day. The smoke, the cries, the grief and bewilderment, the terror of war. "Sex was the last thing on my mind when I said yes to marriage."

The rancher's astonishment rolled through her. "Are you sure we married the same Mor-Lath? Are you telling me you never considered the possibility of a physical relationship—even if you rejected the notion—with a god? I can't believe he never tempted you once."

If she could have found her fingers, Adrastea felt like flicking this earthy little rancher to the other side of Dom-al-gol. "Of course, he tempted me. But it was only a ploy to weaken my resolve and get me to say yes to marriage."

Lanne shrugged. "Many a marriage has been contracted because of such a thing."

Udevrien, who had been mostly listening the whole time, shared her thoughts. "And you would think it the easiest way to convince a woman to agree to marriage."

Adrastea shook her head. "Except he needed me willingly."

"So, one of the most skilled lovers to have ever existed bestows his attentions on you in a night of unsurpassed passion. As you lay in your tumbled bed, panting with effort in the afterglow of ecstasy, he promises you you can have that for the rest of your life if you marry him. What self-aware woman would say no to that?"

Shame over her own naivety rolled over her. As a country girl, if he had sweet-talked his way up her skirts she would have considered herself all but betrothed and would have stopped at nothing to drag him before the priestess before her belly showed.

She ran a hand over her too-empty belly. If she had been even worldlier, she might have—

It all made sense now. She had realized something was not right when he was courting her even though she couldn't put a finger on it then. He didn't court her the way a country lad would have courted her. True, he plied her sensual side, but it was only a ruse to weaken her resolve, not an actual interest in herself. She didn't get the 'keep your skirts' down lecture Ari so often gave to other courting couples who ignored her completely. Never even considered she might be worth the lecture.

The clues were there, and she never noticed.

"He never intended on bedding me," she confessed. "I am so stupid not to have seen it before."

Lanne ventured her opinion. "I don't believe that's true. Why don't you do something about it now?"

"I can't do anything about it."

Lanne didn't have an answer to that.

"I don't believe that," Udevrien replied. "You are not powerless, Bride of the Dark."

"Uh, I'm trapped here."

The priestess shrugged. "So, get out."

Adrastea let out a noise of exasperation. "Don't you think I've already tried to get out?"

"If there's a way in, there's a way out. You simply haven't found it yet."

Adrastea hmphed. "He would choose intelligent women." She pointed a finger at Desmone, still trapped within her fist. "Except for you. You're an idiot."

Udevrien tched. "That was uncalled for."

"Well guess what? You're all dead, so I shall do as I please."

"Including getting out of Dom-al-gol?" Udevrien responded wryly. She folded her arms, what there was of them. The habits of mortality were hard to break.

Adrastea paused, then, "Yes. I shall get out of Dom-al-gol. When I do, I'm going to make Mor-Lath, God of the Dark very *very* sorry."

Udevrien nodded. "I think we all have some desire, more or less, to get him back for what he's done. I, for one, am willing to aid you in your revenge."

Adrastea let her anger simmer down. "For a head priestess, you've got a nasty streak in you."

Udevrien shrugged. "Look who my god is."

"He's not my god," Lanne said. "Except for my one weakness, I've been a good woman who walked in the Light." The thoughts began to whirl in her head, the different shades of logic and memory. "However, I am not too sure if She shines on me."

Should she comfort the soul or not? "The Light is one to stand back and watch what the rest of us do. They may seem a bit distant but...hmm."

"What?" Lanne asked.

"They are waiting to see what I do. I can't rely on Them to help me out of every mess. On the other hand, They are not going to interfere when I start taking bits off my husband."

Lanne voiced her concerns. "You aren't going to kill him, are you?"

Adrastea let out a bitter laugh. "Me? Kill him? I'm not a mashiah. Say, are any of you?"

They all denied it. "Oh well. It was worth a try. I don't know any others. He killed the last one I knew of."

"What's a mashiah?" Lanne asked.

"It's a man with the power to kill a god," Desmone said.

"Alternatively," added Udevrien, "it is a man with the power to save humanity."

Adrastea hadn't heard this one before. "Save humanity?"

"Yes." Udevrien lost herself in thought. "I'm not sure how but it's about the final battle and freeing mankind from the yoke that binds them. What that yoke is, I'm not sure. I'm starting to think that it has something to do with him after all. He hasn't been honest with me, with any of us. For all my learning, I realize there is so much I don't know."

"You'd like the library back at the temple," said Adrastea.

Udevrien perked up. "You mean the one at *the* Temple?" She sighed. "Oh, I would give my life to see that library."

The unsatisfied hunger typical of all damned souls rose in Udevrien. "Promise me that you'll take me with you when you leave. Please?"

Adrastea sighed. "I can't even get myself out."

"You will. If anyone could, it would be you. You're an immortal."

"That just means I can't die."

"Yes, but that also means you don't belong here," Udevrien insisted.

Lanne's wish was as plaintive as Udevrien's. "Take me too? I don't want to be left here."

"I don't know," replied Desmone. "I'm starting to like the place."

Adrastea shoved Desmone back into her pocket.

Udevrien had a plan. "It is not enough to just figure out how to get out of here. You must also figure out what to do once you're free."

Adrastea wasn't sure what Udevrien was asking. "Well, set things right, of course."

"Yes, but how?"

Adrastea hadn't given it much thought.

That wasn't good enough for Udevrien. "You've got to have a plan."

"But I can't kill him, even if I want to," Adrastea complained.

Udevrien gave Adrastea a smooth smile. "There are fates worse than death. Since we all of us know something but not everything, I say we pool our knowledge together and come up with a plan."

That suited Adrastea fine.

T here." Adrastea pointed to where she saw the Lines bending. Experience said a gateway would open there. None of the dead souls in Dom-al-gol could see or sense the gates before they opened. Only Adrastea could.

The moment she pointed, they streamed toward the spot. Sure enough, the light of day spilled in, giving a beacon for all the souls to follow.

And like every time, before anyone could reach it, it slammed shut, leaving them all in darkness. Every soul groaned in disappointment. They echoed the discontent in her heart. It was no good. Every time one opened, they could never get there soon enough.

Other souls, the ones that wanted nothing to do with Adrastea, had a different view of the doorway. They did not go rushing up to it but waited until their master summoned them. Then, quicker than light, they were whisked through the doorway to serve him and possibly scratch their itches. Inevitably, they were shoved back through the hole, to howl and writhe in the agony of lost opportunity.

One in a while they would seek to take their frustrations out on Adrastea. She just flicked them away. Now that she noticed, she had plenty of power over these souls.

She spoke often with Udevrien and Lanne, finding she had a great deal in common with the saponer.

"So why didn't he marry you?" Adrastea asked her.

Lanne shook her head as if the answer should have been obvious. "Lords don't marry commoners."

"I'm not exactly of noble blood either."

Lanne tapped her finger aside her ear. "You don't know that. Who is your father, then?" She added. "As far as you know, he," meaning Mor-Lath, "may not be of noble blood either."

Adrastea did not talk to Desmone at all.

Other souls, the penitent souls, gathered to Adrastea, many of them asking to be bound to her. "For when you go," they said, "we want to go too."

Adrastea agreed, not so much for the salvation of these souls but because she knew it would annoy Mor-Lath.

After another fruitless pursuit of a gateway to mortality, the soul Adrastea knew as Wineman asked her, "How is it you know when the gateways are going to open?"

"I see the Lines of Deeper Power. Just before a gateway opens, they bend, they converge, then they bow out and the doorway opens."

"You can use the Deeper Power, can't you?"

She could.

"Why don't you open a gateway yourself instead of waiting for one?"

Weary disappointment colored her voice. "I've tried. Something's got to happen on the other side. I don't know what."

"Can't you see through the gateway to the other side?" It sounded almost like a whine. Could he be as desperate as she was to get out?

Because she didn't want to answer his question and look weak, she changed the subject. "Why do you want to get out?"

"I don't belong here," he sniveled. "It's not like I've done anything wrong in my life." Then while he went on to bleat out his ignorance of his sins, she studied the others as well.

They were all here at the bottom of Creation because they were weighed down. If only they were lightened of their burden, they could go soaring up to...

To the Light.

It all made sense. Those who died with their souls burdened by sin, had to wait here in hell until they were redeemed. And who was the one to redeem them, to shrive them of their sins?

Mor-Lath.

But he hadn't been doing his job. Why not?

Did Tanat know this? Did Lucea and Phyl? If so, why didn't they do anything about it?

Why didn't they do anything about Adrastea's current predicament? Or did they mean for her to remain here, helpless, powerless, and by that token, weaken Mor-Lath himself?

Adrastea would have smacked her forehead if she knew how to find it in the dark oblivion of hell. Mor-Lath's selfishness and anger had injured him far more than he realized, or perhaps more than his pride would let him realize. He would never be ready for the final battle at this rate.

Not that she had any desire of contributing to his chances of success.

Then again, she did not want to remain down here.

Oh, what a quandary he had put her in. Then and there, she vowed to find her way out, if only to wreak vengeance.

He would probably kill her for it. (Was it possible for him to kill her?)

Was that so bad? Well, death, as the souls that surrounded her knew it, wasn't so bad, even if it wasn't so good. They still had their consciousness, their memories, their self-awareness.

But what happened when an immortal died? Did they die like mortals? Or were they destroyed to oblivion, as Mor-Lath feared? He was of the firm opinion that should a mashiah catch up with him, it wasn't mere death but utter destruction of him.

Maybe that would be what would happen to her. Would even a glimmer of herself exist after that?

While Adrastea pondered that, Wineman continued his litany, unaware of Adrastea's inattention.

She weighed whether condemnation for an indeterminate amount of time here in hell was worse than obliteration.

Hard to say. She'd never been obliterated before. Whole life? Half a life? No life?

"You know," said Adrastea, when she realized Wineman had taken a figurative breath, "sometimes the one sin weighing us down is a reluctance to admit the truth to ourselves. How long have you been here?"

Wineman had no answer for that. "I don't think time has much meaning down here."

Adrastea conceded that. She had lost count as to how many days she'd been here. For the first time in a while, she thought about the markings on her face. Could she sense whether Mor-Lath's anger against her had cooled? She'd sensed very little from them during her sojourn down here—mostly brief flashes, moments of moments when she thought he'd thought of her. They were so fast, though, she couldn't be sure if they were real or not.

"I've been counting your heartbeats," said Udevrien. "It has been a long time since the last gateway. Isn't one due to open soon?"

Adrastea exclaimed, "What? You mean they can be timed?"

"Well, not really. They have no discernible pattern that I can fathom. But if my memory serves me correctly, this is the longest interval we've had between gateways."

"Oh." Adrastea hadn't thought of that. She'd been too busy with her thoughts and the stories of others. "Perhaps we've missed one. Perhaps it opened elsewhere."

Udevrien denied that. "Dom-al-gol is not a place, per se, where distance has much meaning. Haven't you noticed that wherever we roam, the gateway never opens near us? It only opens far enough away that we can come within a fingertip's length before it shuts. I think distance is merely a limitation of our minds, and not our—" Adrastea sensed Udevrien regarding herself and her lack of body. Did she miss it? "—our selves."

"So, you'd think," Adrastea replied, "that if I willed it, I could be in the place where a gate opens."

"In theory."

"Could I will it to open near me?"

Udevrien sighed. "That I don't know. Maybe. If your will was stronger than he who opens the gate."

Adrastea didn't know. The anger that fueled her strength had long since died down. Maybe a glimmer of it still flickered within her but she'd given up on it recently.

"I see doubt in you."

Adrastea let out a small snort. "I thought it was you who was transparent."

Udevrien gave a shrug. "In the while I've known you, I've learned to read you somewhat."

Adrastea hadn't thought about that. She'd been so busy reading and learning from the others that she never stopped to consider that they may have been observing and learning from her.

Udevrien continued. "Adrastea, you amaze me. How can someone with so much strength be so vacillating? You can do what you want. Why don't you? Why do you hesitate in the presence of others? Why don't you stand on your own?"

"Because doing what I wanted was what got me banished here."

A new voice spoke. "Adrastea?" It was a female voice, familiar and strong. "Is that really you?"

Adrastea reached out to the newcomer. "Who are you?" she asked as she drew the soul to her.

"Oh, glory," the other cursed. "It is you! He killed you! That snakelicker."

Adrastea's mind placed the voice. "Desideria?" Oh no.

Desideria's soul let out a small sound of acknowledgement. "I don't know who's more surprised: me or you." Sorrow filled the ex-high priestess, a palpable grief. "I'd hoped you had—" a sob cut her off.

Adrastea gathered her close to comfort her. "I'm not dead. He didn't kill me. Listen: I have a heartbeat."

Desideria's soul curled up close to Adrastea. Her grief lessened as she heard Adrastea's rhythm of life. "So, if you're not dead, what happened?"

Adrastea shared her whole story with Desideria, leaving out no detail. She even displayed the six souls that had led to her damnation. "I think he was too angry to kill me."

Desideria made a noise that explained perfectly how little she held Mor-Lath in esteem.

"So," Adrastea asked. "How did you get here? You were too young to die."

Bitter disappointment flooded through Desideria's soul. "Not too young I can't reft my life by my own hand."

"What?" The shock of Desideria's suicide rippled through her. "Why?"

Desideria shared the same full honesty Adrastea had shared with her. "Because I couldn't stand being his high priestess anymore.

"He changed, Adrastea, after you left. It wasn't for the better. He started breaking rules."

Adrastea scoffed. "Since when do rules matter to him?"

"I meant his rules. Rules he normally wouldn't break. I didn't know who he was anymore. I couldn't trust him anymore. Soon it got too much. I couldn't stand it and the Light wouldn't heed my prayers."

"*You* prayed to the Light?"

"I certainly wasn't going to pray to him. He'd become unreasonable, temperamental and..." she seemed reluctant to say it, "evil.

"So, in the end, I chose to end it all. As I contemplated taking my life, I was so afraid he would come and stop me. I thought he'd sense my fear. But then, I'd had a great deal of fear in my heart for the longest time. So, when I stood there, a loaded gun in my hand, I knew he'd stopped caring even for me.

"Oh, in the beginning, he promised me a great many things, including protection. But that turned out to be selfishness, not magnanimousness." She let out a bitter chuckle. "He thought he could control me the way I think he wanted to control you. But you wouldn't let him control you. You went out and did exactly what you wanted, knowing it was contrary to his wishes."

Adrastea pulled the dead souls out of her pocket. "Everything has consequences." She gave Desmone a nasty tweak, "I might have forgiven him for his past but to go spend one's wedding night in someone else's bed is a little unforgivable. I will not be cuckolded."

Desideria sighed. "Then I guess when you get out, you have more women to kill."

Adrastea's heart froze. "What?"

"You didn't think after his despicable treatment of you that he would suddenly gain morality? He's never abstained before. You really didn't think he'd start after you disappeared, did you?"

"Bastard," Adrastea muttered. "He works awfully fast."

"I wouldn't call it fast."

"Adrastea," Udevrien came forward. "Stay focused. It is not these others who you are angry with. It's him. Don't get distracted." She turned to Desideria and offered a curtsey. "I know of you, most high priestess. I am sorry to hear of your death."

Desideria flinched from her words. "I do not deserve such sympathy."

"Still, I have always admired your leadership."

Desideria turned away. Shame and guilt washed over her small thread of vocational satisfaction, obliterating it. Then Desideria drew in a breath of exclamation. "Adrastea, do you know how long you've been down here?"

A nasty niggle babbled in the back of her mind. "No. How long."

"Adrastea, you've been gone at least ten years, if not longer."

Her head spun. How many heartbeats had she been down here? "No. It can't be. Ten days, maybe but not ten years." Her voice rose in pitch. "It can't have been ten years."

She wanted to pull her hair out. She wanted to rent her clothing. She wanted to scream to the high heavens and wail over ten lost years. Her family, her village. Ari and Uncle Natan. The priestesses she knew. Saraym and Feown. The Avelians, the Cithrans. The impending war. "No. It can't have been that long."

"At least. I'm sorry."

"More than ten years?" Lanne echoed.

"More, possibly. Maybe a dozen," Desideria confessed.

Adrastea couldn't stand their presence any longer. With a lingering shriek, she abandoned them and fled to the nadir of Creation, where the Lines of the Deeper Power met. She tried to throw herself beyond them, to fling herself off into nothingness. Creation wouldn't let her. It held stubbornly on to her and would not let her go no matter how much she fought the Lines.

Ten years. More. Ten long years he had abandoned her down here. As far as she knew, he had intended her to stay here forever.

Her newly-kindled flame of anger served as a pilot light to ignite her rage. How dare he? Did he think that he was the only one who mattered? She abandoned herself to raw fury. Let it consume her.

She'd discussed what she would do once she escaped this place with others but now her plans changed. She didn't know how but she would kill him.

No, she did know how. She would take an axe and cut off his head. She would dismember his body and scatter them all across the universe. She would cleave his skull in two, put one half in hell, perhaps, and maybe lay the other in heaven.

Even if that didn't kill him, the two halves would be so far apart, there would be no way he could gather a whole coherent thought together. He would never plague her again.

So, what if he banished her to hell again? If she got out once, she could get out again. He would have to destroy her. Would oblivion be so bad then?

Eventually, she gathered enough of her presence to return to the others. They huddled together, clearly worried about her, although they didn't voice it. She could see it in them, as one would see the emotions on the face of a child. Her heart softened. Some of them genuinely cared about her as a person. Many of them cared because they knew she was their only way out of this infernal place. She was fine with that. They were bound to her. As long as she got them out of there, they would do her bidding.

"I believe I can open a gateway," she announced.

Joy, relief and exultation rippled through these souls who had allied themselves to her. Not a single one harbored any doubt.

So be it. Manipulating the Deeper Power was purely an act of will. If they had enough faith in her, then she knew she could do it.

The Lines of Power lay before her, like the warp on a loom. She grasped them and pulled them, forming them to her will. In her mind she focused on the one place she wanted to go. She did not think beyond what she would do once she stepped through the doorway; that would be too distracting.

Her destination firmly in place, she willed Creation to open before her and let her step through.

A gateway, bright and yellow with true light, shone forth, to the awe of the other souls.

Adrastea stepped through, followed by all who had tied themselves to her.

The gateway opened into the library at the Temple.

Mor-Lath sat at the large wooden table, his back to the gateway. A moment after it opened, he sat up in surprise.

Adrastea stepped through, accompanied by all the penitent souls of Dom-al-gol. Before she could draw in a breath of real air into her body, the souls, as one, rushed the Dark God.

It was like the night the angels rushed him, the night he killed Amarice and her new baby.

He never got time to utter a curse. The souls tackled him, the force of their impact thrusting him up onto the table. He slid half its length before struggling uselessly against their collective attack.

All the plans Adrastea had discussed with the others fled her head. Udevrien's caution evaporated. One thought remained. She wanted to cut out his cheating heart.

The first weapon to come to mind was Ari's big butcher knife. As a child, Adrastea had feared this mighty knife. Now it seemed most appropriate for her task. In a request fueled purely by emotion, she willed it into her hands. Adrastea leaped up to the table, straddled Mor-Lath, who still contented with the damned souls.

"Wha—?" he started to say, before Adrastea drove the knife, with all the force she possessed, into his heart.

The knife passed through his sternum, through his heart, past his spine, to embed its tip in the wooden top of the table. Mor-Lath was truly and thoroughly pinned.

Her sudden act of passion surprised him. Whatever else he was going to say remained unsaid. All the souls, who moments before, had been gabbling angrily at him, fell silent.

Adrastea said no words. Her face said it all. Her eyes burned. Her very being glowed with all the strength of the Deeper Power she could call forth. Slowly, she stood up to tower over him. She held out her hands. In an instant, the axe Ari had used to chop wood appeared in her hands. She lifted the axe above her head. "You cheating bastard."

With all her strength, she swung the axe downward towards his neck.

Chapter 19

Mor-Lath panicked. Where did his wife come from? Where did she get that axe? "Adrastea! No!"

But the axe in her hands never completed its descent. Behind Adrastea, a familiar Light brightened the library, far more intense than the light of the sun. A pair of hands, whose Love was stronger than Adrastea's rage, stopped the axe and removed it from her angry grip. All the souls that held the Dark God pinned, fled to the farthest corners.

The knife in his heart ached. His pounding heart beat against it, slicing itself with every desperate attempt to pump blood through his panicked body. He wasn't dead, wasn't going to die, at least, not by his wife's unmashiannic hands.

Not today, anyhow.

But as Lucea and Phyl brightened the room, he fought his first instinct to rejoice. At the least, he conceded they saved him from a very nasty blow.

The axe was gone, no doubt returned from wherever Adrastea had called it.

The knife remained.

Adrastea growled in frustration at the loss of her weapon. She wrestled with Phyl until His calming influence won over, draining her of her anger. Phyl put His arms around her and guided her down from the table. The rage Mor-Lath felt in her, the passion, the fury, melted into sorrow and penitent tears as Phyl forgave her sins. Over the edge of his chest, he watched as a rival god guided her away for a bit of a talk.

Mor-Lath reached a hand up to the hilt of the knife. It was not a knife of war but a common kitchen utensil, old and oft-used. The wooden handle had been worn by someone's hand. The blade, while regularly sharpened, had worn down along the edge. He wrapped both hands around the handle and pulled but that only caused him more grief. He fought the pain. He had to remove the knife.

It wouldn't budge.

Lucea approached Mor-Lath, still pinned on the table. "Well, dark lad. Here you are."

"Bugger off." He tried to get a hold of the knife. He kept failing. It couldn't be that hard, unless... "Let me up, Lucea."

Was She was holding the knife down by Her will?

She shook her head. "No."

"Let me up."

Again, she refused. "No."

In frustration, he collapsed back to the table. Phyl still had Adrastea off to the side. Adrastea had collapsed onto Phyl's shoulder, sobbing like the country girl she really was. With Lucea so close, he had a hard time holding on to his pride. The guilt, on the other hand, had no qualms about nagging the edge of his conscience.

All the souls Adrastea had freed from Dom-al-gol stood on the periphery. Silent. Observant. Intense. Their emotions whirled inside them like smoke in a glass bowl.

"Damn it! Unstick me and let me up."

She let him fight against the knife for a while longer, then, "No."

"Why not?" he asked.

Lucea sat on the edge of the table and arranged Her white robes about Her. "Your wife put it there. Your wife can remove it."

That was not what Mor-Lath wanted to hear. He attempted to pull it out again. Then he risked the integrity of his body (he'd already lost some blood) and lifted himself up against the knife, hoping to move it that way.

All he got for his troubles was more pain.

"Worry not. You won't die. Your wife is not a mashiah. Lucky you. But she is an immortal, worthy to be a god. And yet you treated her shabbily. If she hadn't spent the past fifteen years wallowing in pity and self-doubt in Dom-al-gol, I'm sure she would have done this much sooner."

Mor-Lath turned his head away from Her. "If all You're going to do is gloat, You can leave."

She didn't. "I give you a beautiful gift. This is how you treat her? What came over you, Mor-Lath? If I didn't care so much about her and you, I would have been content to see you both spiral towards destruction. It will save Us the sorrow of having to deal you later."

"Somehow I don't believe You would suffer that regret."

She sighed and traced Her finger across the wood grain on the table. It reacted joyously, arching up as a cat would, to meet Her loving touch. "You were born a child of the Light."

"Not news."

"You had ambition, drive and a cleverness rare in humans."

He said nothing. Once upon a time he would have been proud for someone to acknowledge those traits in him.

"Look at all you accomplished, all you became. And then, to come to this? What happened? Do you truly want to be destroyed?"

No, Mor-Lath did not. He had realized at a young age that he had talent. He had learned how to use it, so much so, he had attracted the attention of the then-Dark demi-god.

He had made the perfect disciple, willing and eager. That was how he learned it took two to make a god. As soon as he was strong enough, he convinced the Dark God to share his mantle of authority with him.

But two men do not a god make. Not that Mor-Lath cared. As soon as the mantle of authority was granted, Mor-Lath destroyed the Dark God, assuming all that god's authority for himself. Mor-Lath's fear of being destroyed by a mashiah came from first-hand experience.

He had been born a mashiah and had taken full advantage of that fact.

More than a thousand years ago he had gloated to the Light, "You did not think I would not form my own destiny?"

Now that he reflected upon it, the Light had never been forthcoming about Their opinion on his betrayal and subsequent assumption of power.

Mor-Lath had been a most powerful god, even more powerful than the one before. He had ambition. He had drive. He studied and learned about the prophecies, and what it meant for the end of time. Didn't that frighten the Light even a little?

Then there was the foretold final battle, between Light and Dark. The confrontation was inevitable. Creation demanded it. Balance demanded it. In the end, there would be only one god, one to rule Creation.

Mor-Lath wanted to be that god. He'd gone so far to request a worthy bride from the Light and They complied.

Lucea put her hand back on the knife. "Mor-Lath." Her voice was low and dangerous. He'd never heard that tone from Her before. It chilled him to the core of his soul. "I could destroy you now, forever."

His heart thumped, slicing itself over and over against the knife. "What?" His voice caught in his throat. Spots appeared before his eyes as terror washed over him.

"You have mistreated your wife. Because of this, you are more vulnerable now than when you were a newborn babe." She caressed the knife. Her hand tightened about its handle. "Right now, I could end your life and existence."

A tear fell from his eye. "Lucea... please."

Her eyes flickered to Adrastea. "Start treating her well. If you do not, she will never let you up. The next time My hand rests upon this knife, I will end you. I promise."

He swallowed. More tears streamed to the table.

She reached out and ran Her fingers through his hair. He jerked his head away, but She did not stop. He found the tender gesture disconcerting. Lucea sighed, a sound full of sorrow. "You asked for her. We gave her to you, no tricks, no hidden agendas, nothing. We have given you everything you wanted, everything you could possibly need to succeed in the final battle. The rest is up to you and you alone." After a moment's pause, she conceded one point: "Well, up to you and her. After all, if you wish to triumph, you both will have to become a complete god.

"There could never be a better wife for you than Adrastea. Do not make her wish she could have had a better husband." Her words sank into his core: *Do not make her wish she could have had a better husband.*

"This is your final warning. Ignore that, and you will be on a path of no return. Nothing you say or do will redeem you. You will have lost all chance at becoming a god."

She leaned over and gave him a motherly kiss on the forehead. "Dear boy, ponder upon what Our thoughts would be should you succeed in the final battle. It could very well help you win."

He closed his eyes. Anguish filled him.

And regret.

Oh, so much regret.

Adrastea's hands went numb. She'd swung the axe back, fully intending to bury it in her husband. Whether it severed his neck or cleft his skull in two, she didn't care.

The axe stopped. She voiced her opinion in raw emotion. *Let me kill him,* her voice raged in her head. *Let me rid the world of him.*

Her anger flared but her arms felt useless. Someone stood behind her. Adrastea knew who He was.

"Peace, daughter of the Light. This is not your way." Phyl's hand held back the axe.

She fought Him and His calming influence. She did not wish to relinquish her anger, her oh-so-justified anger. She needed that anger to exact revenge. She had to give all her pain back to Mor-Lath.

Phyl took the axe from her hands. Adrastea's anger bled out into the incoming tide of sorrow. Her breath caught in her throat and she began to cry. Helpless, like a child, she let Phyl put His hands about her waist. He helped her from the table. As she gave herself over to tears, He pulled her into a comforting embrace. "Dear child, what happened?"

Adrastea couldn't speak she was sobbing so hard. She clung to Him and cried and cried. All of the anger, the frustration, the confusion, everything she had ever felt because of Mor-Lath she howled out onto Phyl's chest. He simply held her, not speaking with her but sharing her emotions.

She felt helpless because Mor-Lath had thrown her into Dom-al-gol and she couldn't figure her way out for fifteen years. (Fifteen years!) She felt hopeless because when he first came to her, he'd offered her a sham of a choice, then simply tightened her options until there was little left but to acquiesce. Then after she'd agreed, he'd tossed her to the side, a pretty toy the child wanted, begged and whined for, only to be discarded five minutes after being granted it. He'd abandoned her.

Yes, Mor-Lath had gotten what he wanted. What about what she wanted? "He never stopped to think I might be a real person, did he?"

Phyl shook his head. "No, he didn't."

"Why did You yoke me with him?"

Phyl didn't answer right away. "Don't you want to be a god?"

Adrastea had her answer ready. "God of the Dark? No."

"What if he were God of the Light?"

"I don't care if he's the god of little fishies. He's still Mor-Lath."

"What if he'd been a mortal man? If he'd wooed you then?"

"Certainly not then," came her too-hasty answer. It was true, she told that deep down niggly voice. The niggly voice disagreed.

He had been charming during their courtship. Her body ached for him then and now. "I'm sick of this. I'm sick of his games and him using me and... and everything."

Phyl pulled her into a spontaneous hug. "I am so, so sorry. We honestly did not believe he would treat you this way. He surprised Us. We expected him to cherish you more than anything, to honor your value and potential. We never expected his fear to warp his ambitions thus. As strongly as he feels ambition and passion, he feels fear." Phyl glanced at his wife then back to Adrastea. "He fears you, not so much who you are but of what you are capable. See, We gifted you with complimentary powers and abilities to what he possesses. Otherwise, you could not be his true half. Then again, being a woman, you have power he could never have. For that as well, he is terrified."

She was about to ask him what he meant but she knew—her barren belly. "It's that stupid prophecy, isn't it? A son of Mor-Lath will destroy him."

Phyl opened his mouth but reconsidered what He was going to say. "Yes," He said, eventually. "The son of his body would indeed have the potential to destroy him. Such a son would be a mashiah."

Adrastea pressed her hands into her belly. "Heal me, then. We need not let Mor-Lath know. Let him believe I am as barren as he made me. Surely I would know I was with child long before he would." Adrastea raised her hands to cling to Phyl's snow white robe. "I could leave, go far away where he couldn't find me. I'll bear the child then hide him. Mor-Lath would never know until it was too late. Please."

Phyl did not disengage her hands. "You would destroy your own husband?"

Her eyes grew hard. "I do not love him." That niggly voice came back. She told it to shut up.

Phyl laid His hands over hers. "Could you learn to forgive him?" The weight of His touch weighed heavily in her heart.

"What? Why?" That baffled her. She wanted nothing more to do with Mor-Lath, didn't she?

"Because forgiveness is the true path to greatness."

"I don't want to be great." Was that entirely true? There was a tug at her heart when Phyl had said those words.

"Learn to forgive your husband. Let go of your hatred and anger. He, too, must learn to forgive."

But Adrastea shook her head. She withdrew from Phyl's touch. "I wish a divorcement."

"A divorcement?" Phyl's countenance fell; she had surprised him. "You know he will not agree to that."

Adrastea's anger rose in her again. "It's always about what he wants! It's never about what I want. I want to divorce him. I want nothing more to do with him. He's beastly, he's cruel," she continued her tirade, not needing to stop to find words to describe him. They all came so easily. "He's selfish, he's abusive. I hate him. I want to be free of him."

"Mmm-hmm." Phyl sniffed as if fighting back tears. His sad expression darkened the whole world. "We had thought him truly ready."

Adrastea wrinkled her nose. "He isn't." Then, "What do you mean, ready? Ready for what?"

Phyl sighed. "Mor-Lath has two very important tasks. He's not fulfilling the first as he should. The second will never happen if he does not do the first. This is the saddest part of all. We have always meant him to fulfill this second task. It is why We have tolerated his vagaries for so long, hoping he'd go back to who he was meant to be. Only when he truly believes, and accepts what he must do, will he succeed."

As she was about to ask, Phyl explained. "His first task is the role of the God of the Dark. This is to free souls from the burden of sin. That is the purpose of the Dark's existence." The sorrow rolled of Phyl in palpable waves. "It needs to be done, more than you know. Alas, We cannot force him to do it. Of all who have ever been born, only you can make Mor-Lath complete the role he must do."

She exhaled sharply. "I've never been able to make him do anything."

"I beg to differ." His hand hovered over her seared belly. "You've been able to force him to face things he's been avoiding. Granted, his reactions..." He withdrew His divine hand. "It is an easy thing to coerce someone into anger. It is harder to inspire regret and a desire to change."

She wrapped her arms about her. "He'll never change."

"He will." He gave a subtle gesture to the god pinned to the table. "He's realized he's met his match. He's also realizing that unless he changes, he has already lost the final battle. He must let go of his pride and must forgive. Until he does, We are more than content to let him remain stuck."

Her gaze turned to where Mor-Lath laid pinned on the table. Lucea sat next to him, conversing gently. "I'm sorry about that. I was so angry."

"Oh no. He thoroughly deserved that." A smile tugged at his lips. "That's not what he has to forgive."

"But I haven't done anything else."

Phyl inclined his head. "You tricked him. You took advantage of him. You seduced him when he was not yet ready to give that gift to you."

Her expression darkened. "Oh, but it is all right if he gives it to other women?"

"No. The moment he married you, even the moment he proposed, all that he is, is indeed yours by rights. But a gift can only be given. It can never be taken.

"A marriage also requires respect. He respects you more than you think."

Adrastea studied Phyl's eyes, even though there would be no guile in them. "I find that hard to believe."

"Remember what I said about power? You are as strong as he is, if only you stop to realize it. Stop thinking like a mortal. Think more like an immortal. Creation will answer your Will. Granted, We must think more of the consequences of Our Will. If We truly wish to accomplish something, there is little beyond Our grasp."

Adrastea released His robes and let her hands slide down to her belly. "Could I heal myself, then?"

Phyl dropped his gaze. "Sometimes there are some things that..." he hesitated as if not sure how to proceed. "Let us say that what one god does, sometimes another god may not undo."

"So, I can't heal myself? And you can't either?" The bottom fell out of her world. "So that's it, then?"

He inclined his head. "It is for Mor-Lath to undo."

"That's not fair!"

To her surprise, Phyl chuckled. "Funny, for that is how Mor-Lath feels at this moment. See, you pinned him to that table through sheer force of will. Neither I nor Lucea can remove that knife. Mor-Lath can't do it. Only you can release him."

Until that moment, all Phyl had been saying about her having equal power had been nothing but words. Only now did the actuality of her potential strike her. "You mean I could leave him pinned to that table forever?"

"I recommend you not. If you wish his good will, especially if you are to convince him to lift the veil of sterility from your womb, you will have to release him."

"But I don't want to let him up."

"Nor should you if you don't want to." He released her. "Give yourself the chance to want to. If he is truly penitent and has earned your respect, you may feel differently later."

"I doubt it. I want to see an end to this marriage."

Phyl sighed. "While I understand, I wish you did not feel that way. You retain the greatest power over him if you are his wife. This includes compelling him as God of the Dark to shrive all those souls he hoards." He picked up her hands once more, pressing her fingers to His lips as if in prayer. "Please help Us in this penultimate matter. Make him do his job. I confess it will take some time. But when the task is completed, if you still desire it, We shall see your union dissolved, whether Mor-Lath agrees to it or not."

Phyl laid His forehead against hers. "Adrastea Healer, *Are you a daughter of the Light*?"

His question rumbled through her soul like nothing ever had, not even the Deeper Power at its full capacity. Its resonance rang through her so loud she could think of nothing else.

More tears streamed down her face. Fear of the correct answer seized up her throat. With all her effort she answered her god: "I... I am."

"*Then behave like it.*" No admonishment could have been truer.

Guilt over her behavior flooded in. Mira had educated her enough to know right from wrong. Even now, when faced with the God of the Light, she had behaved in a shocking manner.

She had become the very creature she despised. She may have been Mor-Lath's wife but that didn't mean she had to behave like him. What really stung was that she knew what she had to do. She didn't like it.

Still, she had to do it. If she wished to be free, she would make her husband do his job.

"It is time for Us to depart." He led her back to where Lucea and Mor-Lath waited.

Lucea slid off the table to greet Her husband. "All better now?" She asked both Phyl and Adrastea.

Phyl turned to the Bride of the Dark, waiting her answer.

Adrastea gave a half-shrug and half-nod. The enormity of change she would have to make rattled her. To let go of her anger was a hard, hard thing. To live with her guilt was even harder.

Her gaze fell on Mor-Lath. He had turned his tear-dampened face from her, but she could feel the anguish that emanated off him in waves. What had Lucea said to him? She'd never seen him cry before.

Well, that was too bad. He'd damned her for too long to Dom-al-gol. She was not going to let him up any time soon. Perhaps not ever. He could stay pinned to that table until he lost—they lost—the final battle.

Phyl whispered in her ear, "Do not let anger and revenge dominate your thoughts. These will drag you both down. You will be miserable for the rest of your days. Find it in your heart to treat him well. The most one can expect from anyone is no more than what one is willing to give. You want his respect? Give him respect. You want his love? Love him."

"Love him? After what's he's done?"

"Love him for what he will do."

"And what is that?"

Phyl shrugged. "That remains to be seen. Give him a chance."

She fought the doubt in her heart. Phyl had commanded her.

At least Mor-Lath was going nowhere. How far his reach extended, pinned as he was, she didn't know. But at least she knew he would not be bedding any other woman.

Not even you, a little thought niggled in the back of her head. It was her own thought, and not one from Someone Else.

Phyl pulled her in and gave her a hug. "Your forgiveness will last as long as you are willing to be forgiving. You have the strength and the will. Develop the desire." He planted a fatherly kiss on her forehead. It spread through her, warm and comforting. It didn't assuage the guilt. He released her so Lucea could embrace her and bestow Her own blessing as well.

"You have a great destiny, my dear," Lucea told her. "Be true to yourself. Be strong."

The god stepped back. They joined hands and with a final benediction, departed.

Their departure filled Adrastea with emptiness. The room was definitely dimmer, despite all the glowing balls that bordered the perimeter of the room. Under those lights stood thousands of souls, all bound to Adrastea. They watched and waited, silently but their eyes were not on her. They all gazed at Mor-Lath.

She didn't blame them. Not a single one felt terribly benevolent towards him at the moment. She fought joining her opinions to theirs. Phyl had just forgiven her her sins, thus lightening her soul and easing her pain. If she wanted to keep it that way, she would have to work hard.

It was so easy now to see how her own spiral into darkness and misery had trapped her, very much how Mor-Lath was trapped now.

The thought that he was completely in her power sent a flush of dizziness through her head. For the first time, she had the upper hand in their relationship. As long as she did not let him up, she would always have the upper hand.

Adrastea strolled over to the table. She let her finger trace the grain of the wood, polished by hundreds, if not thousands of years of use. For the first time since she returned, she noted her clothing. She wore the same country bodice she'd donned the morning she went hunting for souls. Even her skirt felt as fresh as the day she'd put it on. She shook the farm dirt loose. Had nothing changed?

She hoisted herself up to the table, straddled his body and settled back onto his thighs, so she could look at him straight in the eye. "You know I'm not going to let you up," she told him as calmly as she could. She felt all cried out. "I am terribly upset with you right now."

He said nothing.

"I will be honest with you. Phyl and Lucea wish me to forgive you. They wish me to treat you kindly. I'm finding that a hard thing right now."

"So?" His reply came out flat. The lines on her face told her something completely different. Regret. Desperation.

"Phyl said that if we cannot make our marriage work, He will grant me a divorce."

An icy chill ran through Mor-Lath. Even Adrastea shivered, so strong was his reaction.

"No." Panic snuck into his voice. "They can't do that." He grasped at the knife.

"Oh, yes They can."

He sniffed and wiped at his face. His voice came out cold. "What do you want?"

She paused to consider this. "I don't know. When I have settled on something I will share it with you."

"There is no such thing as a woman who does not want something."

She shrugged as she conceded his point. "I didn't say I didn't want anything. I simply didn't know what I want now."

His eyes strayed to her belly. "What about...?"

She knew what he was thinking. She placed a hand over her belly. The pain he had caused her was no longer present. She hadn't checked in the past fifteen years, but would there be a mark, as the other women claimed they had? "I will not ask for something you may not grant. What happens if I request something else later, something incompatible with your piddling little fears? Will you then deny me that request as well?" She leaned forward until her chest touched the hilt of the knife. If she pressed her weight on it, would it tilt forward, to grate and grind against his sternum? That would hurt.

She fought the impulse for revenge. Phyl had to be right; her only chance of success was to play by the rules; she was a daughter of the Light. Still, she could not resist one last verbal jab: "The Light forbid I should ever bear a Son of Mor-Lath."

The souls bound to Adrastea stirred. *Someone comes*, they warned her.

Adrastea straightened as the door to the library opened. A diaphanously-draped priestess, bearing her own globe of light, entered. She saw the couple on the table. "Oh, I'm sorry." She backed out as quickly as she could, her embarrassment vibrating through the Lines.

"Wait." Adrastea beckoned in the priestess. Having spent so much time in Dom-al-gol with disembodied souls, she'd forgotten about how bodies worked. The Lines of Deeper Power pulled the priestess back through the doorway. Instead of floating the rest of the way on its own inertia, as a soul would have, she fell to the floor hard enough to knock the wind out of her.

The priestess struggled to her knees. "Forgive me, Holiness. I mean no—" she gasped, still breathless.

"Oh, get up," Adrastea snapped, not in the mood for her groveling.

"At once— what?" The priestess lifted her head. She had not been expecting a female voice to be ordering her around. She looked at the woman on the table, her eyes growing wider. "Mistress!" she gasped, then knocked her head back down to the floor. Her scantily-clad back heaved as she sobbed.

That wasn't quite the reaction Adrastea had been expecting.

Desideria's voice whispered in her ear. "That's Berengaria. Your disappearance broke her heart."

It was? My, how she'd grown. No wonder Adrastea hadn't recognized her.

She sighed. Was there no one anywhere who was not in need of soothing? She spoke the priestess' name as gently as she could. "Berengaria." But Berengaria continued to cry. "Please sit up," Adrastea asked. "You know I don't like that."

Berengaria sat up. Adrastea could see the child she knew in the face of the woman. Berengaria had indeed grown. Her face was gaunter, her form more graceful. The pain of a dozen years dwelt in her eyes. How much of it was for her and how much of it was due to Mor-Lath?

Adrastea had learned from Desideria that no one was safe from his selfishness. After he banished his wife, he had availed himself of his priestesses and any other woman who had taken his fancy. The most Adrastea could hope for was that he had waited until Berengaria had come of age. As precocious as the priestess was, Adrastea hoped Berengaria's first time with Mor-Lath had been better than her own.

She turned the full fire of her glare on her prone husband. "You have much to answer for."

He turned his face from her. Tears streamed down his temples to splash dark upon the table.

Adrastea climbed off the table and approached Berengaria. "Stand up so that I may see you."

The priestess obeyed. Her eyes remained downcast. Adrastea allowed her her shame.

"Have you no questions?" Adrastea asked as gently as she could. "Or will you continue to tremble like a leaf?"

Berengaria clenched her hands tightly in front of her. She did not answer. She did not dare leave either.

Desideria hovered over Berengaria's shoulders. "She's too afraid of him. I don't blame her."

"Was it really so bad?" Adrastea murmured back.

"I killed myself, didn't I?" Then Desideria told her something she hadn't revealed to Adrastea before. "I was not the only one. I was not the first."

Adrastea wanted to cry. "I'm sorry." Why had she wasted all her tears on herself? Here were others who needed them more.

Desideria's presence settled on Adrastea's shoulder. "Just make things right, will you?"

Adrastea nodded. To Berengaria she said, "It's all right to look at me." She said it with surety. It was not quite a command but more than a request.

Berengaria lifted her eyes then risked meeting Adrastea's gaze.

Adrastea saw sorrow there and weariness. Instinctively, she held out her arms.

Without a second thought, Berengaria threw herself into them. "It's been so long," Berengaria asked, *sotto voce*. "Where have you been?"

"I promise I will tell you." Then she turned to point to the god pinned to the wooden library table. "Look."

Berengaria leaned past Adrastea to see what she had done to him. She gasped, and her hands flew to her mouth. "You killed him!"

"I'm not dead." Mor-Lath's voice made Berengaria jump.

She fell to her knees. Adrastea wouldn't let her complete the kow-tow. She caught Berengaria's arm and pulled her back up. "Things are going to change around here, starting with him. You do not need to fear him anymore."

Berengaria rolled her eyes to Adrastea. She did not believe her mistress.

"I promise," Adrastea insisted.

Mor-Lath spoke. "You are awfully free with your promises." Ah, his bravado had come back. Despite his brave face, she felt the tension and sorrow in his heart.

She released Berengaria's arm and strolled up to the table. "You wouldn't want me to break my promises, would you?" Then she yawned. "I've had a very tiring fifteen years. Berengaria, see that a nice hot bath is run for me, followed by a substantial dinner. And I want fresh linen on my bed. I'm going to sleep."

Berengaria hesitated.

"What?" demanded Adrastea. "Have you forgotten how?"

The priestess shook her head. "No, mistress."

"Oh, and do keep this," she gestured towards the table, "to yourself for the time being."

Berengaria gave another worried look to Mor-Lath before hurrying off to do her mistress' bidding, leaving Adrastea alone with Mor-Lath.

Adrastea ran a hand over the hilt of the knife. She touched her fingertips in the stickiness that marked the cut edges of his shirt. "Things are going to be very different around her, dear husband."

He said nothing. He refused to look at her.

"Tomorrow, unless I find something better to do, you and I are going to have a little talk. Meanwhile, I hear my nice, soft bed calling me."

He clenched his hands over his belly. "And what am I supposed to do in the meantime?"

Adrastea spread her arms. "You're in the library. I'm sure you can find something to read."

Chapter 20

Adrastea sank into the bath. The warm, warm water enveloped her body. A sigh of luxury escaped her lips. To her relief, there was no mark on her belly. Its skin was as pure and smooth as the day of her wedding.

The more she thought of it, it did seem like she had been in Dom-al-gol for fifteen years. She touched upon all the conversations she shared with the damned souls. So many. She had learned more about the human condition than she would have in a whole mortal lifetime, especially if that lifetime had been spent entirely at Sacred Spring.

Berengaria had been the priestess to organize her bath and her other requests. She had danced constant attendance on her. Adrastea didn't mind. The souls bound to her also remained in her presence. They lined the walls and explored the apartments as well as they could, being disembodied, gazing at the giant bed and surveying the wardrobe.

However, the six women Adrastea had punished for Mor-Lath's infidelity did not have such freedom. They were placed in a small box and told to stay put. Desmone protested, as she always did but the others accepted their lot.

The freed souls reported back to Adrastea little things they had discovered. As she soaked away in the bath, she learned that not only had the linen required changing but the whole mattress had to be removed. The priestesses couldn't find a suitable replacement. Perhaps they could make do with two smaller ones?

Meanwhile, the state of the contents of the wardrobe was dire. The clothes had been handled from time to time as the occasional priestess came exploring but not enough to prevent them from growing stale. Some of the finer fabrics had perished. Others moldered. As two of the younger priestesses sorted through, they discussed how old-fashioned the clothing was. They would have to consult with Garsinda about the possibility of a new trousseau.

Why Garsinda?

She gestured to one of the priestesses genuflecting nearby. The elder of the two rose and hurried to Adrastea's side, dropping to her knees again. "What is your bidding, Mistress?"

Adrastea nodded to herself. Berengaria had clued them in as to her identity. "Tell me about Garsinda."

"Um," she started, clearly not expecting such a request. "I don't know what to tell you, Mistress."

"Why isn't she here?"

The priestess swallowed audibly. "I don't know." She leapt to her feet. "I shall fetch her at once."

Adrastea lifted a hand clear of the water. "No. That is not necessary."

The priestess hesitated at the door before returning to her place next to the other priestess. "I'm sure she means no insult, Mistress. The high priestess has much to do. Perhaps the news of your arrival hasn't reached her yet."

So, high priestess, huh? Adrastea mulled this over. Desideria, who had been out keeping an eye on Berengaria, must have heard this. She returned forthwith. "Garsinda?" She swirled around Adrastea's head. "How did she end up high priestess?" The news agitated her enough she couldn't keep still.

"Why? Wasn't she supposed to?" Adrastea murmured softly, so the two young priestesses couldn't hear her. As the words were meant for Desideria, the former high priestess understood them clearly.

"No. Iocaste was supposed to be high priestess after me."

"Perhaps she was. Maybe she killed herself too. Then Garsinda moved in."

Desideria shook her head. "No. Something's not right."

"A lot of things aren't right."

"I blame him."

This last comment of Desideria's surprised Adrastea. The living Desideria would never have uttered something like this. "We'll learn what's going on in due time."

The souls in the other room reported someone new arriving. Garsinda?

Another dark-haired priestess came into the bathing chamber to stare. She was older, possibly thirty summers or more. She gazed upon Adrastea with a wistful expression on her face before she fell to her knees. "You have returned." She pressed her forehead to the floor.

"Radelisa," Adrastea exclaimed.

Radelisa sat up and smiled. It was not a smile of pure joy but tainted by sorrow and forlorn hope. "You are staying, aren't you?"

"Yes, I am. Things are going to be very different around here."

"Do you promise?"

Adrastea sensed a desperation in the request. Her first instinct was to make the promise. Was she going to stay? "I have every intention of staying. There is no one who can say different." Would that do?

Radelisa accepted this. "Please don't leave again. Things changed after you left."

Adrastea sighed. "Would you like to tell me about it later?"

She nodded, glancing quickly at the two young priestesses, the ones who could not remember a time when Adrastea had lived here.

Berengaria popped her head in. "Mistress, we're having a little bit of trouble. Would you be terribly offended to sleep on straw?"

Adrastea let out a small chuckle. To think, someone was concerned over what she slept on. "Seeing where I've been for the past decade, I would be happy to spend this night on straw."

Berengaria let out a breath of relief. "Your bed shall be ready soon."

"And supper?"

"Forthwith. We did not have anything ready. It is only the afternoon."

Adrastea sat up. "Is it really? Huh. I am out of time." Then she yawned. Indeed, she was tired.

Berengaria drew close to Adrastea. She, too, sank to her knees, not out of supplication but to be closer to talk. "Where have you been?"

"I promise I will tell you later." She glanced back to Radelisa. "Both of you." Then she gestured Berengaria closer. Her voice was low. "But only you two. I will not disclose this to anyone else, nor will you."

"As you wish," Berengaria whispered back. She rose to her feet. "I'll see how your supper is coming." As she passed Radelisa, she laid a hand on the other priestess' shoulder. "Attend her until I return?"

Radelisa nodded. "She will not leave my sight."

Nor did she. Radelisa watched as Adrastea finished her bath. The priestess dried her then wrapped her in a large bath sheet of the softest terried cloth. She followed them into the main bedchamber, where Lamicia and Efanda finished preparing the bed. They greeted her but kept their opinions to themselves. Adrastea could see their unasked questions in their eyes.

Berengaria soon returned bearing a tray of food and a trail of followers, younger priestesses who had heard of but had never seen, the Mistress.

"Tell me," Adrastea requested of Radelisa, "how many priestesses are currently in the temple?"

"Not quite thirty."

Adrastea sat on the edge of her newly-made bed. The sheets had a fresh scent to them, reminiscent of summer. The straw of the tick crunched beneath her body. "But there were more than sixty when I left."

Radelisa sighed, as if she did not want to hear the reminder. "Things changed. Fewer candidates were chosen each year. None were selected the past two years."

Was it coincidence that and the death of Desideria?

Radelisa added, "And there is the laity."

"The... what?"

"There is an order of beguines. After you," she hesitated, "um, disappeared, there was no one to tend the stillroom. Instead of letting it fall into disuse, we, well, Desideria brought in a stillwoman. She was nowhere as good as you, of course. But it was comforting to have her there." Radelisa twisted her hands. "We, you could say, started losing, um, not quite faith... but..."

Adrastea shook her head. "What?"

"Well, before, you know, we always sought out His Holiness' blessing for illness or injury. I guess we lost our trust in him."

As Desideria had.

What did Garsinda, as new high priestess, think?

Interesting that Garsinda had not shown up. Why? Did she fear her position of power, now that the Mistress had returned? Knowing the reason would reveal itself with time, Adrastea tucked this bit of knowledge into the back of her mind. She focused on the food set before her.

Two priestesses had brought a small table over by her bed. Berengaria had set down the tray. There was warm bread, with small crocks of butter and jam. A light sauce glazed the steamed vegetables accompanied by the thinnest slices of cold chicken and salami. One of the priestesses held a jug of watered wine and made sure Adrastea's cup remained filled.

"Will you require anything else?" Berengaria asked, as Adrastea reveled in the taste of the food.

"No." She swallowed and waved her hand to dismiss the priestesses. "You all can go." She pointed to Berengaria and Radelisa. "You two stay. We need to talk."

From the lines on her cheeks, Adrastea felt a rush of frustration. The Dark God was not enjoying his sojourn in the library. She took pleasure in that.

As the other priestesses left, no doubt they would gossip. The two younger ones who had attended Adrastea in the bath didn't wait until they had cleared the room before their dark heads bent close to whisper.

Berengaria closed the door. "Are you going to tell us where you've been for the past fifteen years?"

Fifteen? Desideria had said ten, maybe twelve. But fifteen?

"Yes." Adrastea patted her bed. "Come sit here and I shall answer your questions."

Radelisa and Berengaria looked at each other for a moment, then complied. They kept their distance from their mistress, however.

"So," Berengaria repeated, "where have you been?"

Adrastea had been expecting this. "I did something which displeased my husband, so he damned me to Dom-al-gol. I have been languishing there this whole time."

Both priestesses drew in sharp breaths. Radelisa put a hand over her mouth. "He wouldn't do that," she whispered between her fingers.

Berengaria rolled her eyes. "Sure, he would."

Adrastea spread her arms. "As you can see, I have returned, no thanks to him." Her eyes flickered over to Radelisa. "Did you tell her about 'His Holiness'?" she asked Berengaria.

The priestess shook her head. "You told me not to."

This pleased Adrastea. "All I tell you here in confidence must remain in confidence. I have a feeling you two are the only ones I can trust." She turned to Radelisa. "It was not by Mor-Lath's will I returned. If he could have had his way, I would have remained there forever.

"He was quite surprised when I showed up. We had a bit of an altercation. Currently your Dark God is pinned to the table in the library by a rather big knife." Adrastea pointed a finger at the two priestesses. "I put that knife there. Only I can remove it. Anyone attempting to remove it will not only fail, they will invoke my wrath. Mor-Lath made me angry; look what happened to him."

Radelisa looked to Berengaria, puzzlement on her face. Berengaria nodded. "It's true. I've seen him."

Radelisa still entertained doubts. "But what if he frees himself?"

Adrastea smiled. "He can't. That's the beauty of it. Only I can release him."

The two priestesses mulled over this.

Radelisa could not look Adrastea in the face. "Forgive my impertinence, Mistress but what did you do to get damned?"

"You really want to know?"

Radelisa hesitated, then nodded. "I feel I should know. For my own safety, of course."

Adrastea fought the impulse to laugh. "I killed all the women my husband had sex with during our courtship and marriage. I stole their souls."

Suddenly both Berengaria and Radelisa had elsewhere to look, their faces flushing. "Oh," they murmured, unsure what to ask next.

Adrastea sighed. "Don't worry. I'm not going to kill you, nor any of the others now."

This startled the two. They looked at each other and leaned away from the other. "What?" squeaked Radelisa. "You mean..." she glanced over to Berengaria. She covered her face with her hands. "I thought I was the only one... he told me to keep it a secret because..."

Berengaria shrugged. "I knew he was tumbling several of us."

Embarrassment stained Radelisa's cheeks. "I didn't."

Berengaria also retained her blush, but courage fueled her words. "Yes, he broke his own rules." She looked up to Adrastea. "We... that is, I, I thought you were gone for good. You disappeared without explanation for years. Whenever any of us asked after you, His Holiness would refuse to talk about it if he was in a good mood and if he wasn't..." She didn't finish her thought. "Truthfully, we didn't know what happened, and soon nobody spoke of it, not really. I mean, there were always the tales, told on the sly to the newer priestesses.

"Some of the others blamed you for the change to His Holiness. He was strict before but fair. After you came, things were different. But once you were gone, it was as if the good in him died." Berengaria sniffed and dabbed at the tip of her nose. "He was not the Mor-Lath I knew.

"A lot of priestesses lost their..." She hesitated. "Faith? Trust?"

Radelisa nodded.

Berengaria continued. "Anyhow, their vocation was gone. They left, whether it was departing out of the gates or departing the mortal realm." She grew still. "However, I have a suspicion none ever left his service and lived. I think the moment they walked out that gate, they had sealed their fate."

"I'm sorry." More deaths on her conscience? "When I was in Dom-al-gol, several souls sought me out. Desideria was one of them. She told me much of what happened here while I was gone." She reached out and took the hands of the priestesses. "I'm sorry you suffered. I'll see if I can set things right again."

"How?" Berengaria asked.

Adrastea didn't have a ready answer for that. "Well, by fixing what is wrong here in the temple, for a start."

Radelisa and Berengaria didn't reply to that one. This baffled Adrastea for a moment. "What?"

Neither one inclined to answer.

"You've got to tell me. Is there something else I don't know about?"

"Not exactly," confessed Berengaria. "The only thing wrong with the temple is... well, *him*."

"Ah, yes. He was first on my To Do list."

"What are you going to do?" asked Radelisa. "You can't leave him there forever."

Adrastea gave her a very pointed look.

Radelisa swallowed. "Can you?"

The next day Adrastea woke to a morning free of pain, both in her belly and in her heart. Phyl had something to do with her heart. Time had taken care of her belly.

Despite feeling better, she was in no mood for dealing with her husband. He could remain pinned to that table for a lot while longer.

What to do? Adrastea's first thought was of Ari and Natan. No doubt they would have been worried sick about her, disappearing for ten—no, fifteen years. Berengaria said fifteen last night.

Had it been so long?

No, she would not go visit them. She couldn't bear the emotional reunion at this time.

Fifteen years was a long time to be gone. She knew nothing of the current situation in the world. Last she knew, Her Grace, Saraym, Duchess of Feown was considering the possibility of war.

Would Her Grace even remember the Grey Lady?

Without calling for a priestess to assist her, she rummaged through her wardrobe until she found a grey dress—extremely unfashionable. Adrastea had little choice. She found a cotton shift that hadn't perished too much, unlike the silk ones, and pulled it on over her head. She hooked herself into a corset and employed the Deeper Power to tighten the strings. She wriggled into the grey gown, its satin rustling as she pulled it on over her head. The shoes were wearable, if a little stiff.

Adrastea ran a hairbrush through her curly tresses then declared herself suitable for noble company. Standing up from the dressing table, she closed her eyes and sifted through her memories for the Maiden's Tower.

She called upon the Deeper Power to take her there.

Shift.

When she opened her eyes, she looked down on the wretchedness of Feown from the Maiden's Tower. The grey light of dawn showed the vague shapes of buildings far below. The sun would soon rise, yet the city hadn't seen fit to stir itself too much. A cool—but not cold—breeze ruffled her skirts and kissed her skin. What season was it? Possibly spring?

Adrastea entered the palace.

As she walked through the corridors, it looked as bare as she remembered. Surely Her Grace would have replaced the pilfered treasures by now. It had been so long since the war. Adrastea's feet took her to the salon where Saraym had sequestered herself after her ordeal.

It had changed, with a few newer chairs and small tables but no Saraym.

Of course, she wouldn't be there. Perhaps she was still abed?

Should she should disturb the duchess?

In the end, she decided a quick peek wouldn't hurt, just to see how she was doing.

Adrastea closed her eyes and focused Saraym's Lines. She shifted through space.

"Wha—" called out an alarmed female voice, followed by a thump. Adrastea's eyes shot open.

She stood in an antechamber, lit by a warm lamp on a desk. On the other side of the desk was a very surprised young woman—not Saraym—picking herself off the floor. She'd fallen backwards on her chair.

Adrastea's fingertips flew to her lips. "Oh, I'm sorry. I didn't mean to startle you."

The young woman stood up and straightened her chair before dusting herself off. She had dark curly hair like Adrastea. Her light brown eyes were of a shape that tickled Adrastea's memory. Her nose was aristocratic, and her puppy fat made her seem like she was barely out of adolescence. She wore the oddest clothing. She had a short-sleeved fitted blouse of a soft green color—with no bodice—and a matching not-so-full skirt that ended just below her knee. Below that she wore full pantaloons that ended in lace at the ankles. She had a knife strapped to her hip.

"No, accept my apologies." The young woman put the chair to rights. "I didn't hear you come in." The young woman looked Adrastea up and down. Her gaze dwelt on Adrastea's floor-length hem. Her eyes also lingered on the lines on Adrastea's face.

Adrastea looked around the antechamber. It looked more like a small office, than a sitting room, with the desk and the shelves and the young woman looking like a secretary. She yawned and covered her mouth with delicate fingertips.

"I'm... sorry it's so early?" She didn't mean for it to come out as a question. "I wasn't aware of the time."

"Why? You up late?"

"Up early." She looked at the solid wooden door that lay between the antechamber and the bedroom. "I guess it's too early to seek an audience with Her Grace?"

"You could say that. Her secretary should be here soon. You can make an appointment with her."

Adrastea nodded. Saraym slumbered deeply in the other room. Did she dream? If so, Adrastea sensed nothing. But she could sense exhaustion. Perhaps it was best to let Her Grace sleep.

She looked for somewhere to sit. There were no other chairs but the one upon which the young woman sat. She contented herself with leaning on the desk. "If you're not the secretary, who are you?"

Her question surprised the young woman. "My name is Dassie—Adrastea—Pennexter. Yes, of those Pennexters."

Adrastea disregarded the family name. "Wait, your first name was...?"

"Adrastea. But everyone calls me Dassie. There's so many people called 'Adrastea'."

"Really?" This was news to Adrastea. "It's my name too."

"No!" Dassie gasped and leaned across the desk. "What's your nickname?"

Adrastea shrugged. "I never had one. I was the only Adrastea in the village."

Dassie nodded. "Yeah, I thought you sounded country. What part?"

"I'm from a village called Sacred Spring. It's near Crossroads, on the road to the Great Western Pass."

Dassie came around the desk eagerly. "Are you? I've had friends go there on pilgrimage."

People other than the locals have heard of Sacred Spring? "When?"

"About eight years ago. You might have met them. The Chartrelaines? Amalthea and Robesperre?"

"Oh, no, we wouldn't have met." Adrastea wondered how much of the truth she should tell this young woman. "I was a journeywoman healer at the time and out of town."

Dassie shifted to a more comfortable position. "If you're from there, perhaps you could clear up a rumor I've heard."

Adrastea gave a little shrug. She didn't know how much help she'd be, for her news was a dozen years out of date.

"They say the Dark One came to the village, during the Cithran invasion."

Adrastea sighed. "That much is true. I was there."

"Really?" Dassie inclined her head towards Adrastea. "Did you see him?"

Adrastea folded her arms and looked away. "Everyone saw him."

"So, is it true that they sacrificed one of the maidens to make him leave?"

"What?" Adrastea turned back to look at him. "What do you mean, 'sacrifice'?"

Dassie shook her head. "I don't know. That's why I'm asking you."

"If you mean, did one of them give up herself so he would leave them alone, then yes. They disappeared, and no one ever heard from her again." Her tone said she wanted no more of that particular tidbit. "I thought you were going to ask about the Innkeepers or something."

"Well, yes, I was."

This surprised Adrastea. "Why would you want to know about the Innkeepers?"

Dassie gave the back of her head a quick scratch. "Well, it is part of the story, one of them, anyhow.

"They say that not only did the Dark One leave, but he took all evil with him. He left this circle of protection so that no one with evil intent can enter the village proper. They say Mistress Innkeeper had left the village before the troubles. When she tried to return, she couldn't get back in." Dassie chuckled at that. "Now there's a tall tale for you."

Adrastea perked up. "Marta couldn't return?"

"Oh, I'm sure it's all hearsay, for there was a rather formidable dragon of a woman who ran the Inn. If it was her, she figured out how to get through."

Adrastea couldn't help but giggle. "Oh, I will have to hear about that one."

An awkward silence fell upon them, as their conversation lapsed. "So," Dassie asked, after a moment, "when did you arrive? This morning, I assume?"

Adrastea nodded. How did she know that?

"You don't know much about court etiquette, do you?"

Adrastea wasn't sure where this was going. "What do you mean?"

"Your dress. Why didn't you alter it before you came?"

Adrastea looked down at her dress. "I know it's old-fashioned but other than that, what's wrong with it?"

Dassie pushed herself off the desk. "Where have you been?"

"What do you mean?"

"Your hem is too long. I recommend you go take care of it or you'll get a fine."

Adrastea sighed. She hitched herself up to sit on the desk. Dassie cleared her throat but Adrastea deliberately didn't take the hint. "Pretend I've been asleep for the past ten years and I know absolutely nothing. Now, please tell me what's wrong with my hemline?"

Dassie picked it up. Adrastea squeaked and batted her hand away. Dassie scowled at her. "Why are you so missish?"

"I don't make a habit of having others lift my skirts."

"What?" she teased. "Can't afford pantaloons?"

Adrastea's face grew hot. "I beg your pardon." One did not talk about pantaloons with new acquaintances, even if they shared the same name.

Dassie's smile faded. "You... really can't afford—" She blushed and turned away. "I'm sorry. I didn't mean to insult you."

Adrastea folded her arms. "It's not my fault I don't have anything suitable to wear. I've got a few country things but they're just as old-fashioned. Hardly suitable for court."

Dassie gestured to her dress once more. "Is that why you dug that old thing out?" She looked closer. "Are you wearing a corset?"

She looked at the young woman looking at her. This Dassie was awfully forward. "It's the only way I would fit in this dress. And please, you still haven't told me what's wrong with it."

Dassie stepped back and folded her arms across her chest. "It's the sumptuary laws. No dress hem can be longer than the knee, though pantaloons can go to the ankle." She pulled out a fold Adrastea's skirt. "This is far too much fabric for one dress. You could make four sets of clothing from what you're wearing."

"Oh." Adrastea plucked at the tucks and folds. No long, full skirts? She'd feel naked in anything higher than her ankle.

"How about you run home and change before the guard awakes. I won't report you because you're new to Feown. By the time you get back, the secretary should be here. You can make your appointment. Don't worry about needing to dress up for an audience with Her Grace. That sort of thing went out after the second war and all."

Adrastea felt a small thrill of hope, but it wasn't her own. The sensation came from the lines on her cheeks. She frowned. What was her husband getting all hopeful for? This wasn't good.

Dassie continued. "Her Grace isn't that much of a stickler for court protocol as long as practicality is observed. She won't condemn you for dressing common clothes as long as they're neat and clean."

Adrastea looked up from her reverie. "No, really. I don't have anything practical at all." How could she be dressed in as much cloth as she was yet still feel so naked? "I mean, if I had a pattern..."

Dassie pushed herself off the desk. "Look, how long are you in Feown?"

"Well..." What to say? "I'm here until my business is finished." She felt another twinge in the lines of her face. She'd to have to see what was going on back at the temple.

"So, you'll be free later? I mean, like, this afternoon or something?"

"I could be."

"Okay. How about this: you leave a message here with the secretary letting me know when you're free. I'll be back and forth anyhow since my uncle's not well enough to come himself. I'll skip out and take you to the best tailor I know." Dassie eyed her dress once more. "Don't worry about the cost. She owes me a few favors. If you're willing to part with that gown as-is, I'll swing you a deal with her. She'll cut it down to something suitable for no cost, as long as you let her keep the spare fabric."

That sounded good. If Adrastea could get her hands on a single outfit, it would be a simple matter for her to copy it. The Deeper Power made it so easy. She ran her fingers down the front of this one. Was this dress stitched by tailors, or did Mor-Lath create it himself?

Speaking of Mor-Lath, she felt yet another twinge. "Look, I need to go. I've got something I need to take care of."

Dassie laid her hand on Adrastea's. "Promise me you'll leave a message. Even if you can't come, let me know. Otherwise, I'll wait and keep my eyes open for you."

"I will."

"Okay!" Dassie replied.

Oh-Kay...? Adrastea wondered what that word meant. She made a note to herself to ask the young woman later. Later. She did want to meet up with this creature who knew nothing about her. It made her feel almost—normal.

"I don't know if I'll be back any time soon. Could you pass a message to the secretary for Her Grace from me?" Without waiting for Dassie's acknowledgement, she said, "Simply tell her that the Grey Lady has returned and will wait upon her when she can."

When Adrastea appeared in the library, she found a priestess pulling uselessly on the knife that pinned Mor-Lath to the table. "What are you doing?"

The priestess startled and cut her hand on the edge of the exposed blade. She cringed and scurried back.

Mor-Lath let his head fall back to the table. "Damn." He gave Adrastea a dark look.

She ignored him. Her attention was on Garsinda, the current high priestess.

Adrastea approached Mor-Lath. Garsinde scurried away, keeping the table between them.

She reached out and caressed the hilt of the knife. "I'll have you know," she told the priestess, "that I put this knife here. Only I can remove it. You can pull and pull, but in the end, you will fail. So, don't bother." Her voice was even. "If I catch you attempting to free him again, we shall have more than words."

Garsinda didn't reply. She stared at Adrastea, as if trying to suss her out. She wrapped her bleeding hand in the edge of her veil.

"You can go now," ordered Adrastea.

Garsinda looked to Mor-Lath, then back to Adrastea, who frowned at her.

"Don't look at him," Adrastea spat. "I gave you an order." Without giving her a second chance to obey, Adrastea drew upon the Deeper Power and propelled the priestess as hard as she could towards the door, willing it open. She threw Garsinde out, slamming the door behind her.

Adrastea dusted her hands. She pulled up a chair next to Mor-Lath. She rested an elbow on the table and cupped her chin in her hand. "I see you've been busy."

"What do you want?"

"As I recall, you asked that yesterday and I didn't have an answer for you. I do now. Do you want to know what I want?"

The look he gave her told her he was in no mood for games.

She sat up straight. "Very well, then. I want to divorce you."

A moment. "No."

Adrastea didn't flinch. "Am I that important to you? I don't think I am. If I was, then you would have taken better care of me."

"Bitch."

"Bastard."

His hand shot out and grabbed her by the hair. She stifled a cry but didn't fight him, though tears welled in her eyes. "I will never let you up as long as you continue to behave like this." She gritted her teeth against the pain.

He didn't let her go.

"I don't need you, Mor-Lath." Tears ran along the edge of her face and dripped onto the table. You have given me nothing I've wanted."

He gave her head a shake. "I gave you immortality, ungrateful wretch."

"I never asked for it. I would have been happy as a mortal as an immortal." She felt her scalp lifting under his tightly clenched fist. Would he succeed in tearing her skin from her skull?

As suddenly as he caught her, he released her, shoving her head away from him.

Adrastea leaned over his face, knowing she risked more pain. "Do you regret marrying me? Do you want your precious gift of immortality back?" She gripped the front of her gown. "Shall I give back everything you've given me? Shall we call it quits? I would be more than happy to go far away and never see you again."

"You could do that now."

Adrastea gave a bitter laugh. "Oh, no. No, no, no. Not without a divorce."

"No."

"Give me a divorce."

"No."

"If you want to be married to me so much, at least tell me why."

"You know why."

"What? Full godhood? Really?"

He glared at her. "Don't mock me."

"Well, guess what? You're not a full god. How can that be?"

He didn't answer her, though she left him plenty of time in which to do so.

"Could it be that vows spoken before a priest isn't enough? What more could possibly be required? Do you even know?"

He didn't answer.

"It wasn't a rhetorical question."

He looked away from her.

She kept her gloating to herself. "You really don't know, do you? And you've got too much pride to ask Lucea and Phyl."

"They told me I had everything I needed."

"Yes," she conceded. "But you never thought to ask what it was you were supposed to do with it."

He didn't answer her. His expression changed ever so slightly. So, she had given him food for thought.

"So, let's see. You married me but that didn't do it. You gave me immortality. That didn't do it either. What's left? Consummation? No. We tried that." Her voice grew cold. "And look at what a disaster that was."

"You tricked me." He kept his face neutral, but his pain rolled through the lines on her face.

"You betrayed me. I guess we're even." She put her finger to her chin in a mockery of thought. "Oh, wait. One more thing. There's this little issue about my sterilization. I guess we're not quite even yet."

Adrastea drew upon the Deeper Power, letting it fill her body. She stepped closer to the lower half of Mor-Lath's body and lifted her hand. For a moment, she enjoyed the sweetness of Creation as it coursed through her.

"Adrastea?" There was a tinge of panic in his voice. "Please, no!" He drew his knees up.

She let him squirm. As much fun as it would be to see him panic, she gave her attention over to some serious thought. She couldn't kill him but that didn't mean he couldn't kill her. It would even things if she sterilized him as he had done her. He, in turn, would then wreak vengeance upon her. Not necessarily by killing her but by doing something equally nasty. Maybe dismember her and scatter her body across Creation. Perhaps she could pull herself together, or perhaps not. Then, she would do something as nasty to him. The cycle would continue. Maybe he'd kill her then, destroying his one chance of his greatest dream.

Her hand came to rest on his knee. She put some further thought into the tangled web they were caught in. She didn't let go of the Deeper Power.

He would never grant her a divorcement. She knew that as well as he did. She was his only key to his greatest dream. Without her, his defeat in the final battle was all but guaranteed.

That was what she wanted, wasn't it?

Instead of carrying through with her threat, she asked him a question. "What will you do to me after I sear the manhood from between your legs?"

"I would kill you." He still held as much of the Deeper Power as he could. His hands were poised to grab hers, should they wander too close to the family jewels.

"And divest yourself of one wife? Divorce would be easier, and you get to keep that which you hold so dear."

She didn't say anything more. He watched her warily, in case she tried to use surprise.

She lifted her hand and he jumped. The Deeper Power he held slammed against hers. But instead of fighting back, she let it flow past. She gave into it. As a result, it passed by her harmlessly.

"What the—" Mor-Lath stuttered.

Adrastea gathered the Deeper Power to her once more and held it. Thoughts tumbled through her head. Why did she bother with him? Why didn't she just get her vengeance, then let him get his? They could descend into destruction together. Or why didn't she just walk away and leave him pinned here for the rest of his life? Let the Light destroy him when the time came.

Adrastea turned from him so she could let the tears slide without him seeing. She didn't dare breathe in case her breaths turned into sobs. Why did Phyl put her in this position?

She simply stood there. It would be so easy to walk away and leave him. She could go have a life of her own. Nobody would know who she was, nor would they care. She had a useful craft, augmented by her talent in the Deeper Power. She would not lack for a living. She could help people. She could find her own brand of happiness and live thusly for the rest of her days. Perhaps she could find love. Tears ran down her face at the thought of impossible dreams.

"You're crying, aren't you?" he sneered.

She looked over her shoulder. "Yes. But why should you care?" She turned completely to him. "Mor-Lath, there are things I want, things I need. You are perfectly capable of giving me everything I desire but you won't. Therefore, I have no need of you, as a god, as a husband, and certainly not as a friend.

"Because of that, I shall not harm you further. I don't see how it will benefit me. But I am going to leave you there. I will not remove the knife. You will spend the rest of your days pinned to the table. Oh, I may return now and then, for reasons I can't avoid. But you have given me no reasons to free you and every reason to let you be.

"Goodbye, Mor-Lath." Adrastea turned in a swish of grey skirts and walked to the door. She wiped the tears from her face.

"You will be back," Mor-Lath told her.

"I don't care." She stepped through the door and closed it gently behind her.

⚜

Adrastea stood in the corridor of the palace, properly dressed. After having left Mor-Lath, she returned to the bedroom. With the aid of the Deeper Power, refigured her current gown into something more like what the young woman had worn. The skirt she shortened not quite to the knee but mid-calf. It would do. The leftover train provided more than enough fabric to put together some sort of pantaloons.

When she felt adequately dressed, she returned to the Duchess' antechamber. Dassie was gone, as she said she would be. A stern-looking matron with steel hair pulled back into a bun had taken her place. The short skirt and baggy pantaloons did her no favors. If her fashion victimization wasn't frightening enough, the wicked knife at her waist would discourage all comers.

Was the weaponry a fashion statement or necessity?

The matron stood by the desk, sorting through paperwork. Her piggy little eyes lifted up at the sight of Adrastea. They lowered as they took in her apparel. She sniffed but offered no further comment on what she may have seen. "You're that grey woman young Pennexter spoke to earlier?"

Adrastea had the sudden impulse to slap the woman for her curtness. But that would not do. She had already had a fight with a god; a fight with a mortal just wasn't worth it. If Saraym chose to surround herself with women like this, that was her business. "I am."

The woman sat at the desk and shuffled through a black folio. "Did you make an appointment?"

Adrastea sent her senses back through the door. Her Grace still slept. Although the Duchess felt like she could have used three years' worth of sleep, Adrastea had no desire to wait. She sent an impulse along the lines that connected her and Saraym. *Wake.*

Saraym awoke. Her wits gathered from the nebulous regions of slumber and resolved into consciousness.

There.

"That's why I'm here."

The matron sniffed again. "I don't have an appointment."

"Make one."

The matron gave her a look of thinly-veiled intolerance. "Can't make you one if there isn't one to be made."

"Does Her Grace have a busy morning, then?"

"That is not your business."

Adrastea smiled. While her recent argument made her want to just wipe this woman out of her path, she had to be civil. After all, it had been more than a dozen years since she'd seen the Duchess. Abusing her staff was not the best way to rekindle the relationship.

"Everything is my business." Must not slap ugly secretary. "I am merely being polite. I am not sure if Her Grace would wish to see me this early in the morning, but I do know she will wish to see me sometime." She hoped. What was she going to say to her? Offer an apology? An explanation? Or did she hope that Saraym would offer her more information?

The door behind the secretary opened. One groggy and grumpy Duchess stomped out. Her hair was more silver than dark. She still wore black, even after all this time. "What is all this noise?"

She opened her eyes, took one look at Adrastea and stumbled against the secretary. "I thought you were dead. High Priestess Desideria said you were."

"Desideria? How do you know her?"

Saraym didn't answer her question. "Why did you desert us?"

Adrastea wasn't sure how to answer that. Not that Saraym gave her a chance to answer.

She took Adrastea's hands and dragged her backwards into the sitting room. She slammed the door, leaving one bemused secretary behind.

Chapter 21

The sitting room decor had not changed much. Pillows and blankets stuffed the window seat. Did she still sleep here after all this time? The simple chairs remained. A big table, scattered with maps and reports and other paraphernalia, dominated the center of the room. Above her hung a little round globe that glowed, similar to the ones in the Temple. Only this light was rather stark and not at all muted. The pale colors contrasted sharply with Saraym's black clothing. The Duchess wore a simple blouse, uncorseted, and black pantaloons, no skirt. The fashion did her figure no favors.

Once in private, Saraym shook Adrastea. "Where have you been?"

"I've been busy." Uncomfortable with explaining her story, she changed the subject. "How do you know Desideria?"

"She was the Tredan ambassador when we signed the Tredan treaty."

"The Tredan tribes and Feown? Allies?"

"Against the Cithrans for over a decade." She went over to the table and selected a map. "We'd pulled an army of women together, but it was only good for a few skirmishes. Put a bit of fear into the Cithrans. Then a year later, Desideria comes. Your husband sent her. We negotiated a treaty; our combined forces have quadrupled. They also sent women for their army, as well as men."

Radelisa once told her about warrior women. She thought they were glamorous.

"For a while, we did rather well. Towns and villages fell readily enough. Cities, we couldn't touch. They were too big.

"Then the Cithrans recovered their army. Boys grew old enough to lift a rifle. Women and girls, likewise, were recruited to fight. Cithra's greater population meant they were able to recover their army faster."

Saraym bent over the table as if the weight of the world on her shoulders increased. "We're outnumbered again and have been for quite some time. We've adapted our tactics. Guerrilla warfare, booby traps, poisoned food and water. Despite that, we are nothing more than an annoyance to the Cithrans."

Adrastea felt something stick in Saraym's head. "And there's something else?"

She nodded. "My coffers are dry. Feown is bankrupt. I've even spent my own personal fortune. At least I have no heirs, so there is no one to inherit nothing. Despite what the council thinks, I believe it's best this way."

"What will you do?"

She gave a sad laugh. "I don't know. I've tried keeping the state of affairs from the council. I can't fool them forever. They know how to read a ledger."

"Is the whole council against you?"

She shook her head. "No. There's a few I trust, like Jonathan Pennexter. He's a funny one, that priest. He comes up with the most brilliant ideas but refuses to claim the credit. Says it's inspiration from the Light."

"Perhaps it is."

Saraym shrugged.

"And what does he advise next?"

The Duchess drew a deep breath. "He wants one strong push into Cithra. Disrupt their food supplies just before winter." She shook her head. "I don't think I can afford it. So, if you have any magic at all up your sleeves, anything that can replenish coffers very much to let, I'd greatly appreciate it.

"I'll see what I can do." Even if Adrastea had to dig the gold out of the earth itself. Say, there was an idea. "Assuming you have the money you need, what would your plan be?"

Saraym consulted the maps on the table. "If I could, I would push in and strike at the Cithran capital. I'd sneak in the subtle forces and destroy their High Council. Disrupt their leadership from the top."

"That wouldn't stop them."

"No but it would throw them into chaos." Saraym pulled one map closer. "Most wars are conducted over land. Who's holding what hill, who's holed up in what trench. But we've been sneaking in and mingling with them. For us Feowans, it hasn't been too difficult. Dye our hair blonde, wear their clothing. Tredans aren't so lucky in their colorings, so they've been providing front-lines troops. Keep them distracted on the war lines, while we sneak in and wage guerilla warfare. Blowing up supply lines, random buildings, spreading terror and unrest. Believe me, nothing is scarier than thinking any two random women may be sporting explosives under their skirts. Also makes them suspicious of each other."

Adrastea felt chills roll up her spine. "You've been busy."

"Yes, but it does cost more in lives." Saraym deflated, all her drive gone. "I wish there was an easier way, but this is it. So yes. If I could destroy the top, then the rest of their nation would splinter. We could pick off counties individually. But we need more training and troops, and that means more money."

"Your council has no solutions?"

Saraym shook her head. "We've tried them all. If something doesn't happen soon, the Cithrans will win through our financial attrition." She gave Adrastea a pointed look. "So, if you've got a pile of gold hidden away somewhere, I could put it to good use."

Adrastea wished she did.

Mor-Lath had much to think about after his wife left. She had declared she would leave him alone but how long would that last? It had been a close call when she threatened to emasculate him. For a moment, he wondered if she was going to present him with the choice between that and divorcement.

He did not want to make that kind of a choice. He did not relish the thought of having to convince her to marry him again.

As he lay there, staring at the knife that had held him to the table for the past day, he considered the disaster he called a marriage. Nothing had turned out as he planned.

What really stung was that she was right. He was not a full god, nor was he—they—likely to become a full god any time soon. Is this what the Light planned? They always seemed to be one step ahead of him. He should have suspected something from the beginning when They agreed to his request of a wife.

"You lied to me," he told Them.

You know We didn't, came Their reply. *You're on your own, dark lad.* As They withdrew their subtle touch, the absence of Their Light and influence left an empty pit in his stomach. Only then did he truly feel alone.

He closed his eyes and sought his wife. She was nearby in the temple. She blatantly ignored him, even though he knew she felt his questing in the lines he implanted in her skin. She drew upon the Deeper Power. Did she plan on using it against him?

No, she simply left, going far away to Feown.

So be it. He didn't need her. There had to be another way to remove this knife from his chest. He'd tried removing it by hand, by sheer force of the Deeper Power and even having someone else try to pull it out. It wouldn't move. He'd even tried sliding his body against the edge, hoping to widen the cut. However, she did it, she'd bonded the knife well.

His heart ached. It protested with every beat the foreign object imbedded within it. The flesh objected but the blood didn't mind as much. It flowed around the knife and continued on its merry way. The wound hurt whenever he prodded it with his finger. He could almost ignore it if he didn't touch it.

He tried translocating himself elsewhere. Even tried dissolving the wooden table beneath.

Nothing worked. Creation defied his every attempt to remove the knife. That Creation would obey her and not him grated on his nerves.

"My goodness, you have gotten yourself into a pickle." Tanat appeared at the end of the table. She pushed back her hood and shook out her hair. "I say it's about time your bad luck caught up with you."

He lifted his head. "What do you want?" he growled.

"I came to judge some souls."

"I'm not dead yet." Mor-Lath let his head fall back.

"Pity. We could use a new God of the Dark, one who would do his job."

Bile rose in his throat. "Not this again."

"Did you ever stop to think the reason for the final confrontation is because you haven't been doing your job? Creation craves balance. You've thrown everything out of equilibrium. Just shrive the souls and we'll all be happier for it." Tanat roamed the library, running her hands along the walls. As she moved, the souls of the dead drifted out and followed her about.

Tanat shook her head in disapproval. "You've taught Adrastea bad habits. Here she's brought all these souls out of Dom-al-gol and hasn't had you purge them. I shall have to speak to her about that."

Mor-Lath didn't respond.

"Anyhow," Tanat continued, "I'm looking for some specific souls. She took them before their time." Tanat frowned. "No wonder her luck has been so bad lately. But then, she's had bad luck since the day she was born, hasn't she? I don't blame her for hating you, but her actions will do the world good."

Tanat found one soul and scooped it into her hand. She approached Mor-Lath on the table. "And yet I have to admire her. Who else in Creation can bring down the mighty God of the Dark simply by doing nothing? Even the Light has to work hard when it comes to you.

"But Adrastea?" Tanat laughed. "It's too elegant. I can't help but watch. Creation won't tolerate you much longer, and then…" She snapped her fingers. "No more Mor-Lath, no more Dark God. Then the evil and the bad luck you cause through your selfishness shall depart and plague mortality no more." She sighed with an ecstatic shudder of delight. "Balance, once again."

His knot of fear expanded until it threatened to overwhelm his common sense. "And what if I win?" he declared.

Tanat gave him a smile that sent shudders down his back. "My dear Mor-Lath, I guarantee as long as you are pinned to that table, you have no hope of winning."

"You don't know that."

"I am Judgement," she stated. "I know imbalance when I see it. And you, my dear?" She shook her head in pity. "I am shocked. You were given every single thing you needed to succeed and what do you do? Not only do you shoot yourself in the foot, but you keep pulling the trigger.

"I've been watching you, with your little quest. I have no idea what or whom you're looking for. The Cithrans have no god. They don't even have a poser of a god. The One True is nothing more than an idea of their High Council."

This got Mor-Lath's attention. "If so, then why are they seeking Adrastea? Their One True has commanded it. They certainly don't believe in me, so why should they believe in her?"

Tanat shrugged. She caught another soul, reeling it in along the Line of Deeper Power that connected it to Creation. "I don't know. I don't think it matters. You've dropped the pebble you held in your hand to catch the shadow of a cloud. The pebble that has skittered away was a diamond of the first water. She's not coming back." Tanat came to sit on the table. "So now I get to watch you squirm until your destruction, which is sooner than you think."

"I don't believe you."

Tanat shrugged again. "You never do, yet I am always right. Will you never learn?"

Mor-Lath muttered something under his breath. Even if she had the power to release him, Tanat would never do it. So, he wouldn't bother asking. He had his pride.

Tanat ignored him, her focus on the two souls in her possession. The first she had tucked into her belt for safekeeping. The other, she weighed carefully in her hand. "I know you, Lanne Farmer's wife. I see the sins on your soul.

Lanne squirmed on Tanat's palm, trying to fold in upon herself in shame. "I'm so sorry for what I've done," she groaned. "Truly I am."

"I believe you. Loneliness is an easy path to sin. No wonder you're burdened down by lust, selfishness and envy, though not as much as you could have been. That at least is in your credit."

Mor-Lath closed his eyes. He did not want to watch her suffer. He'd tried to prevent her death, though why eluded him for the moment. Everything had been fine up to the point she got married. Even then, he didn't care. Nothing Tanat said or did would make him care.

"If I had known what I was getting into," Lanne explained, "I would have been stronger and resisted."

Tanat nodded as she listened. "That is the way of sin. It disguises itself and entices us, luring us into captivity. And while your soul may still have a glorious future, you cannot progress while you remain unshriven."

She held the soul out towards Mor-Lath. "Should I bother asking or you just going to squirrel them away to Dom-al-gol, to feed off their misery and anguish?"

Mor-Lath refused to justify that with an answer.

Tanat withdrew the soul. "Just as well. Your wife has bound this one to her. She would take great umbrage at you mistreating this soul, as you mistreat your mantle of authority and as you've mistreated her."

"Shut up."

Tanat released a thoroughly-judged Lanne. "Back to your box." Lanne fled.

She drew the soul out of her belt. She held this one to her face and sighed in pity. "Oh, my dear, your soul is dark, no doubt because he promised you many things, especially concerning the afterlife but now you know different."

"I am not ready to be shriven," Desideria replied. "I still feel anger."

Tanat nodded. "I would too, if he had mistreated me as he did you." A sullen feeling turned the essence of Desideria's soul opaque. Tanat sighed and let the judged soul go. The priestess had damned herself to spend more time away from the glory of the Light.

Mor-Lath did his best to feel indifferent about that.

Tanat insisted on capturing all the escaped souls and making sure they were where they belonged—or were supposed to belong.

"You've let far too many souls out of Dom-al-gol and haven't shriven even one of them. You know what this is going to do to the mortal realm?"

"I don't care." He knew he should but right now he wanted to hurt someone. This was the closest he could get.

Tanat looked around. "There were supposed to be six. Where is the last?"

Mor-Lath gave her a pointed look. Like he was supposed to know?

Tanat turned to the judged souls. "Do you know?"

Udevrien knew. Mor-Lath could see it in her. "That would be Desmone," Udevrien said. "She would be with Adrastea. Her Holiness has singled her out for her own reasons."

The immortal of Judgement beckoned Udevrien forwards. Udevrien had no choice but to obey. "And why is that?" she asked the dead soul.

If Udevrien had cheeks she would blush. She turned her gaze to the Dark God before dissolving into great despair.

Even Mor-Lath felt it. He took offense at that. How dare she blame him? Why is it everyone thought everything was his fault?

Only most everything was his fault.

Tanat did not pursue further information. "I shall have to retrieve that soul from her."

"Good luck," Mor-Lath scoffed.

Tanat nabbed Udevrien and lobbed her towards Mor-Lath. "Why don't you do your job and shrive this poor soul? You got her into this mess; you get her out."

Mor-Lath flicked her back to Tanat. Udevrien let out a soft wail of disappointment and betrayal. Her sorrow twisted, bringing her more pain. He would not do it, not with all these other souls watching, expectantly. "Her sins aren't that bad. Make the Light do it."

Tanat gathered the soul to her. "Alas, her sin, thanks to you, is a shade on the heavy side. It is not the Light's duty but yours."

Again, she shrugged. "I know what you're doing. It's not going to work. It won't give you what you need. Doing the right thing will."

He wanted to bang the back of his head against the table several times. "Giving up power does not make one stronger."

"Hm." That was all she said.

"Nice knowing you," she tossed at him before her presence departed.

Yet Mor-Lath was not left alone. Before Death had left, damned souls had been oozing out of the woodwork, to gather around the table and stare at him. They appeared corporeal, so they had clenched hands, tight expressions and accusing eyes.

His heart struggled against the knife as a bad feeling came over him.

Only Udevrien expressed any feeling, as she sobbed away in a corner. Must she wail and moan like that? What did she want him to do? Didn't she realize there were more important things than her delicate sensibilities? Terribly selfish of her, he forced himself to think. Better than to dwell upon his own guilt. That terrified him.

Two other souls comforted her. Several more gathered around. He recognized the two as Desideria and the anchoress who'd forgotten her own name. The others in the loose circle were all the souls Adrastea had freed from Dom-al-gol.

His sense of uneasiness increased.

As more souls poured from the walls they pressed forward around the table, gathering closer and closer. Still more came.

They couldn't hurt him, he told himself. They were separated from their bodies. He was an immortal. He had power over them, not the other way around.

Mor-Lath held out a hand and by sheer force of will, commanded the nearest few to him.

To his consternation, they resisted his pull but eventually they came. But before he could open the gates of Dom-al-gol to thrust them in, some of the other souls spoke.

"So, God of the Dark," one began. "The rumors are true."

Another approached. "We have issue with you."

As they closed in, Mor-Lath had a dread within that whispered to his knot of fear that he might not be as safe from these souls as he thought.

⌘

Adrastea's heart weighed heavily after her conversation with Saraym. Wars needed money. Adrastea had not given any thought to money in a very, very long time. Even before her marriage, she never gave it much thought, as Sacred Spring worked more on a barter system. Money was little more than ticks in Rop Storekeeper's books.

How to help Saraym?

When she returned to her bedroom at the Temple, her mind had not come up with any viable options.

Desideria's soul had been waiting for her. "Someone new has visited your husband," she reported. "Now she is looking for you."

Adrastea forgot about Saraym. "Oh? Who?"

"She called herself Judgement."

Tanat. Adrastea's heart beat harder. "What did she want?"

Desideria settled on Adrastea's shoulder. "She is looking for you."

"So you said. Did she say why?"

Unvoiced thoughts swirled in Desideria, ones that took Adrastea aback. "She's unhappy with me? Why? What have I done?"

If Desideria had a throat she would have swallowed. "She says you're guilty of murder."

Adrastea's heart tightened up into a cold, hard lump. "Ah." Yes, she was very guilty of murder. Already, her guilt weighed heavily inside her. She should have never killed all those women. Oh, why did she let her temper get the best of her? She'd failed as a daughter of the Light.

Adrastea should have known better. Because she had the power to destroy those lives, she should also have practiced the wisdom not to take those lives. Tanat would judge her harshly.

Adrastea sank to her bed. She'd done a terrible thing. Phyl had said nothing of her sins, only spoke of her relationship with Mor-Lath. Had he left this for her to atone for? He couldn't absolve her of everything she did wrong.

"Let her come. I am ready to be Judged." She cradled Desideria in her hands. "You were far more patient with me. I treated you terribly in the beginning and you forgave me every time."

Desideria patted Adrastea's thumb. "I knew you were inexperienced and bewildered. You were trying to make sense of your new world. As I got to know you, you showed your thoughtful side. Had we met under better circumstances, we would have gotten along splendidly." She sighed. "There was something about Mor-Lath that brought out the worst in you. And you in him, come to think of it. I hope you get your way and you can be free of him. I think you both would fare much better apart."

Adrastea watched Desideria's unvoiced feelings swirl around. Desideria missed the old Mor-Lath. Anger at the new one darkened her to near-opacity. Bitterness, disappointment and sorrow. Her heart ached at Desideria's misery. "I wish I could shrive you."

Desideria shook her head. "I do not think your Glasskisser god will have me."

"They would have everyone, if They could."

Desideria did not believe her. "Though I would take some pleasure in all dead souls going to Them, and none for Mor-Lath."

Adrastea held the dead priestess close. Someday, Desideria would be willing to forgive, to let go of her anger and disappointment. Some day she would truly be free.

She closed her eyes and thought of Tanat, who preferred balance in Creation. *I am ready to be Judged.* Adrastea gave herself over. However, Tanat weighed her, she would accept.

She felt the immortal arrive. It was as if Creation bowed to Tanat's presence, to await her order. Adrastea kept her eyes closed.

"You cannot be Judged," Tanat replied. "You are not dead."

Adrastea's eyes flew open. "But I'm guilty of terrible acts."

"And you will have to do what you need to do to set it straight." Tanat stood before her, her fingers inspecting the carving on a bedpost. "Though I don't know how you will ever fix death. Not only did you take life, but you deprived the influence of that person on those around them."

Her words pressed on Adrastea's heart. "I know. I don't know what to do."

Tanat held out her hands. There reposed five souls. "I have Judged these, but you have bound them to you. As you claim responsibility for them, I insist you make Mor-Lath shrive them of their sins."

Adrastea recognized the souls in Tanat's hands. Lanne sniffled and pressed her head into her hands. Udevrien looked pensive. The anchoress and others simply waited. She took delivery of these souls, cradling them, as she had Desideria. "What, none of them are raised to the Light?"

Tanat touched a finger to their heads: "Dishonesty," she said of the merchant's daughter. "Wrath and pride," she said of the rancher. "Pride in ignorance," she said of the anchoress. Her hand hovered over Udevrien. "Neglect."

Her hand rested on Lanne. "Loneliness."

That surprised Adrastea. "Loneliness is a sin?"

"Reveling in loneliness, wearing it like a hair shirt, is sinful. It locks you away from others and leaves you vulnerable to all sort of other sin."

Adrastea lifted up the scrap of Lanne. "No wonder you were so vulnerable to him."

Tanat held out her hand. "There is one more soul I must Judge."

Adrastea offered her Desideria.

"No, I want the one in your pocket." Tanat plucked out Desmone.

Adrastea snatched at her rival. "Not her. Not yet."

Tanat waved away her protests. Her focus was on the soul in her hands.

"Ah," she said, as she examined the soul in her hand. "You have been a very sinful woman."

Adrastea looked at Desmone, to see if she could see what Tanat's not-eyes observed. Fear, that was quite obvious. It whirled and swirled through her like sticky yellow smoke. Guilt, those were the blue streaks. What else had Tanat seen?

"Woe be unto you," Tanat replied. "Your soul was heavy before Mor-Lath found you. Betrayal, oath breaking, pride, selfishness, self-centeredness. It makes me wonder; why did you ever choose a religious life? Ah," Tanat uttered. "Lust for power, as well as for flesh." She held the soul up close to her lips and whispered in her incorporeal ears.

Whatever she had said caused swirls of misery in Desmone.

When she was finished, she dumped her back to Adrastea. "She is tied to you, as they all are. Now, take them to the Dark God and make him shrive them. Make him shrive them all."

Before she left, she pointed a finger to Adrastea. "Mind how you comport yourself, daughter of the Light. Only you can redeem your soul while you live."

The immortal disappeared.

Adrastea looked at the souls in her hands. They were as confused as she was.

"What happens now?" Udevrien asked. "This is not how I envisioned the afterlife."

Desideria floated away, uninterested in their possible fate.

Adrastea didn't know what to tell them. "What should happen?" she asked, "or what will happen?"

The anchoress spoke. "The scriptures claim when we die, we are sent to His Holiness, where we can join him forever in the underworld."

Lanne, who had wrapped her incorporeal arms about herself added, "In our faith, if we are not good, we are damned to hell, to suffer torment."

From her corner across the room, Desideria snapped, "Sounds much one and the same."

Udevrien insisted, "Mayhaps. But what happens now?" She looked about the room.

"So... what?" spat Desmone. "We're supposed to live in your skirts until... what?"

Adrastea snagged Desmone out of the group and held her up by the scruff of the neck. "You, I think I shall pin to a tree. Every morning after breakfast, I'll use you for target practice with a rifle. I am accorded a good shot."

That shut her up for the nonce.

Lanne spoke. "I don't want to be here. I'm not happy. I feel like I won't be happy ever again."

Udevrien replied, "That's the sin doing that. Haven't you noticed? It weighs us down and drags us away from up there."

Up where? Adrastea wanted to know.

"I'm not sure how to describe it," said Udevrien. "Ever since I died, I've had this desire to go somewhere. I know where it is." She pointed off in a direction. It wasn't so much up, as it was eastward. "But I can't seem to get there."

The others nodded. Likewise, they pointed in the same direction. "It doesn't matter where we are. Even if we try to go there, it keeps moving farther away."

Adrastea focused on Udevrien. "Think about where it is you are supposed to be," she ordered.

Udevrien considered where the "up" was. As she dwelt upon it, Adrastea could sense the faintest of Lines between Udevrien and somewhere else. She laid her hands on the Lines and quested along.

The Lines went a very long way, farther than Adrastea could see. "That's a far place you want to go to. I'm not sure where it is."

"Perhaps it is your god," Desideria suggested. "I imagine they would be as far away from Mor-Lath as possible."

This could be it. "If so," Adrastea replied, "the easiest path there is to be shriven."

"Can you shrive us?" Lanne asked, hopeful.

Adrastea shook her head. "Only he can."

"Oh." Lanne's disappointment echoed with the other souls.

Disappointment swirled through most of them.

Only Desideria was unfazed. "I think you should make him do it right now."

"What? Now?" Adrastea blinked at the priestess. "I'm willing but I don't know how to make him do anything he doesn't want to do."

For the first time in a long time, Desideria laughed. "Oh, you ignorant girl. From the very beginning, you could have received anything you asked, so besotted with you he was."

Was he?

Of course, he had been! Adrastea felt like thirty-six kinds of stupid. Had she realized from the beginning he'd stop at nothing to win her troth, she could have used that drive to get whatever she wanted.

Instead she had dug in her heels and stuck to the moral high ground. "Well, I certainly can't now. He's not going to forgive me for pinning him."

Udevrien snorted. "Oh, don't be so sure." She shook her head in disappointment. "Didn't anyone teach you how to lead a man around?"

Adrastea refused to answer that.

Desideria said, "She's right. I believe most of your troubles have been that you've been trying to get your own way without thinking of him. You always clashed. When I wanted him to do something, I convinced him it was his idea."

If Udevrien had had a forehead, she would have smacked it with her palm. "Even now, you have something he wants."

"What?"

"Freedom."

"I'm not letting him up." Adrastea folded her arms and set her ways. That bargaining chip was off the table.

Desideria stroked Adrastea's hair. "You don't have to let him up. You only have to give him the promise that you might let him up."

"He's not going to fall for that."

Desideria shrugged. "Then leave him there forever."

Udevrien leaned closer to whisper in Adrastea's ear. "As long as you have any power, you can use it against him." To herself, she muttered,

"Country girls."

"I have to think about it."

Desideria shrugged. "Take as long as you want."

"No," replied Udevrein. "I'm quite ready to be shriven now."

With that, the two priestesses descended into argument. Adrastea fled the bedroom, leaving them to duke it out.

Even so, it took them three weeks to convince her.

Adrastea stood outside the door of the library. A quick check of the Lines told her Mor-Lath was alone. He would be spending much time alone from now on.

Behind her, thousands of souls waited. They had heard, one way or another, that the God of the Dark would be shriving souls today. It had been their multitudinous voices, as well as the pleadings of five murdered women that had won her over.

Desideria had stayed out of the conversation. Recently, she'd pulled Desmone aside. Adrastea was not sure of what they spoke, but the younger priestess looked worse and worse, the more a stern Desideria spoke to her. The only thought Adrastea picked out was, "You have no other hope."

All the rest, by sheer force of numbers, had propelled Adrastea to this point. "You will tell him to shrive us."

Udevrien said, "He exists for no other reason." She'd been slipping in and out of the Library, coursing through the books as if they were smoke, acquiring knowledge. She leaned close to Adrastea. "He knows this."

Adrastea nodded. She'd had enough of his shirking of duty—to her, to the world, to the undead. Gathering her courage and the Deeper Power, she opened the door to the library.

Of course, he expected her. She did not feel any surprise through the Lines but a resignation.

However, once he saw her companionship, his resignation turned to wariness.

She sat on the table next to him. "You will shrive these souls for me."

He turned his face away from her. "I will not."

"How about I put it this way: If you do not do this one thing Creation requires of you, I have absolutely no reason at all to let you up. If you do not shrive souls and send them to the Light, then you are useless to everyone. I will leave you where you are until the end. I will lock this room and no one, living or dead, shall come here again."

Mor-Lath turned back, a look of horror on his face. "You wouldn't do that."

Adrastea held forth the soul of Lanne. "Prove your worth or I leave you here forever."

Lanne squirmed and tried to climb back into the safety of Adrastea's pocket. Adrastea wouldn't let her. "I'm sorry," she said to the soul. "You don't belong there. You belong somewhere much nicer. It's my fault you're here. I can't restore you to life, but I may be able to send you on to a better place."

Murky panic swirled in Lanne's interior. "I don't know if I want to go."

"Of course, you do," Adrastea replied. She held Lanne close. "I am sorry I killed you. I acted hastily and unjustly. You did not deserve my wrath. Please let me do this one thing for you."

Adrastea presented Lanne Saponer to Mor-Lath. "Shrive her."

Mor-Lath looked at Adrastea and all the souls behind her. Disquiet stirred in them, hinting at potential violence. He'd tried tossing several of them back into Dom-al-gol a few weeks ago but their connection to Adrastea brought them out again. That Line he could not cut.

Adrastea knew this. She pushed Lanne closer to him.

With a sigh of resignation, he accepted the soul. As he held her, she grew so opaque she looked substantial.

Then all the darkness within her fled, leaving only a bright being.

"AH!" she cried in joy. She floated upwards, spiraling towards the heavens, before disappearing from sight.

Lanne had been redeemed.

Udevrien pushed her way forward, jumping into his hand. The whole of the spirit host moved forward but Adrastea held them back.

The priestess said, "It could have been so beautiful."

Mor-Lath shook his head. "You would have been jealous, had you learned about my wife any other way." He cleared her soul. She flew off as Lanne had.

Next were the other three. They were quickly released and disappeared.

Desideria brought Desmone over to Adrastea. "Before you shrive this one, she has something to say to you."

Adrastea frowned. She did not know if she wanted to listen to Desmone.

But the words that came out of the young priestess' mouth rattled her core. "I'm sorry," she said, Desideria looming behind her. Contrition swirled in her soul. "I am sorry I took your place. I am sorry I let my actions be thoughtless and selfish."

Adrastea put a hand over her mouth. Tears welled up and spilled out her eyes so much she nearly choked.

Desmone was not finished. She shot one nervous glance at Desideria. "I am sorry I did not know my place and I continued to antagonize you. I acknowledge my role in not preventing the deaths of others." She shuddered. "Please forgive me. I want to be shriven."

Adrastea turned away. What could she say to that?

She wrestled with her anger, until it gave way to the forgiveness that had to come. If she didn't allow it to, she would be as trapped in her fate as Mor-Lath.

Wiping her face, she picked up Desmone. "I am sorry I killed you. I am sorry I let my anger get the best of me." She dropped her in front of Mor-Lath.

To her god, Desmone asked, "Before you shrive me, I must know. Why did you choose me?"

His brow furrowed. "You do not want the truth."

But Desmone shook her head. "There is nothing but truth now."

"You were convenient. Nothing more." His words filled her soul with anguish.

As she collapsed into a mound of sorrow, he scooped her up and shrived her of her sins. It took some time for him to unravel the regret. It came undone in the end.

The resultant soul, barely visible, wisped upwards and faded away.

Adrastea pulled forth the next soul. "Desideria."

When the priestess looked at her god, sorrow swirled in her heart. "No. I am not yet ready." Without a by-your-leave, she fled, taking her unshriven self as far as she could go.

Mor-Lath stretched out a hand towards the fleeing soul. "Dessie?" But she was gone. He did not call her back. His hand curled up and he pressed his fist to his mouth. Regret emanated from him.

Adrastea turned away, her heart heavy. Waving her hand, she gave permission for the rest of the souls to come forth.

Mor-Lath shrove every single one of them.

As he worked, she wondered: Phyl had said he had two tasks— redeeming the dead and... what?

Chapter 22

Adrastea watched as the sin fell away from the final soul. The soul shined with unburdened relief. As Mor-Lath released it, the soul soared up to glory and to the Light.

"That is the last." He watched it go. "There are no more ready to be shriven."

Adrastea nodded.

"I do not like your bargains much, Bride of the Dark," he said.

She leaned from where she sat on the table to lay down next to him. "You were in favor of it at the time."

He turned his face away from her. "I shall not be making another any time soon."

She reached out and caressed the handle of the knife. "Shame. I was thinking of offering you another." Her hand lingered on the knife as she waited his response.

His breath caught. She watched him carefully. He considered it, even before he had heard it. He did not look at her but stared at the ceiling of the library. She could almost hear the thoughts tumbling through his head.

"No," he said with a weariness. "I will not free you from our marriage."

"I know," she replied. "I've come to accept that." She didn't elaborate further but let him wonder what it was she wanted.

He put his hands behind his head. He put thought into the silence between them. She let him think, for what was a few minutes more? He had prior so many lonely hours and days and weeks in which to turn things over in his mind.

"You want me to heal you, don't you?" he stated.

"Yes." She rested her head on the table. "Wholly and completely."

He sighed and thought some more. "You are asking a great deal."

"So are you."

His eyes turned to her. "But is it a balanced bargain?"

She lifted herself up so she could look at him better. "Of course, it is. The reason you're pinned to the table is because you sterilized me."

"No, the reason I'm pinned to the table is because I damned you to Dom-al-gol for fifteen years."

"I know why you did it. Did you know why I did what I did to have you damn me?"

"We're getting away from the original question. Not that it matters, because you haven't posed your bargain yet."

But Adrastea wouldn't be distracted. "You know why I killed those women?"

He sighed and gave in. "Was it because you were bitter or because you were jealous?"

"Envious. Jealous means fearing losing something one had. Envy is about what one doesn't have."

He sucked in a strong breath. "Oh, you got what you wanted, didn't you?"

"You made me pay a heavy price, far heavier than any of the others."

He pulled his hands out from behind his head. "You didn't think I would tryst with you if you were hale, did you?"

"You could have told me first." Her answer was low and dangerous. "I might have accepted it." Or not. She'd always assumed that her path in life would include marriage, and children would follow naturally.

Perhaps he sensed he would lose his bargain before she offered it. "But that is in the past. We can't change the past."

She put her hand back on the knife. "We can correct the mistakes of the past."

He wearied of their fruitless banter. "Just make your offer."

"Restore my womb. In return I shall visit you every day, where you can try to convince me to free you."

His lip curled. "That's not much of a bargain. In fact, I don't see any advantage at all."

"What? An opportunity to be free?"

"Empty promises." He looked away from her.

"Not exactly," she countered, her hands stroking the knife handle.

"Before, our bargain was that I would not desert you forever. But I didn't say how often I would return. You know, I could only pop back once or twice before the end and my part of the bargain would be fulfilled. This bargain determines how often I visit you."

He rolled this one over in his head. He countered. "How about this. I heal you, you free me."

"No. My patience is wearing thin, Mor-Lath."

He considered this. "You realize I shall not touch you if you are fertile."

"Can't miss what I've never had." Her heart faltered for one mournful moment. She pushed away the sorrow of the untaken path. Curse him for awakening her passions in the beginning.

He rolled his eyes away in a mockery of thinking. "As I recall, that's not quite true."

Her hand stroked the knife hilt, then dropped to his belly. "It wasn't impressive enough for me to want to repeat the experience."

That got his attention. "What?" Then he thought she was joking. "Oh, ha."

She wasn't laughing. He returned a frown that told her he took umbrage at that. "You wanted it bad enough to seduce me."

"I'm sadder but wiser, now. Like you said, we can't change the past, no matter how desperately we want to undo it. Anyhow, you never really wanted me that way. I don't see how things have changed. It will be no great sacrifice for you to restore me to completeness. I give you the opportunity to convince me to free you. After that, we can go our separate ways, rarely seeing each other except when necessary."

More thought on Mor-Lath's part. "And how often would that be?"

She shrugged. "Except for the one little moment when I watch you die, absolutely not at all."

His frown tweaked into a moment of worry before he smoothed it away under a mask of cynicism. "You're my wife, whether you like it or not. I could still win the final battle."

She cupped her chin in her hands. "Well, if you win, then that means one thing: you're a god after all—we're a god." She gave him the same mocked look of thought he gave her earlier. "But guess what? That won't happen before the end, will it? Because you need my good will for that."

Her face hardened as she realized something. What was she doing? Sure, she wanted to be healed, so she could get on with her life. He had no compunction tumbling other women; he probably wouldn't care if she sought to warm her bed with other men. It changed nothing as far as their marriage was concerned. She may not have had a husband except in name only but that didn't mean she couldn't have children of her own, fathered by someone else.

It was a silly dream but the only one she had left.

She felt little jabs of pain as this last dream died. He wasn't going to heal her. She was a fool to think she could bargain it out of him. If she walked away now, she could still find some scrap of happiness somewhere, far away from him.

Adrastea pushed herself up to sitting. She knew when to walk away. "Never mind. I withdraw my offer."

She scooted to the edge of the table and leapt off. Not another word she would speak to him. He could have his life, such as it was. She would have hers. The souls were freed, he was doomed. Perhaps she could find a few last days of temporary happiness before their mutual destruction.

Adrastea was certain that when he died, she'd die too. She wouldn't put it past the Light to have set that condition on their marriage. After all, if marriage was supposed to unite them as one god, wouldn't it unite them in their failure to become a god?

Not that Adrastea minded the thought of death. She'd grown up with the idea that someday she, like everyone else she knew, would die.

"Adrastea, wait." His desperation touched the lines on her face. Until that moment, he'd kept his thoughts close.

She was at the door when the Lines of the Deeper Power wrapped around her, preventing her from leaving. She didn't struggle, she didn't turn around. She didn't even ask him what he wanted. She waited patiently until he either released her or the day of their death came.

"Please don't go."

She said nothing but waited for him to release her. Instead, he pulled her towards him. This she resisted. She closed her eyes and asked the Deeper Power to flow around her and return to its master.

Her eyes flew open. To her consternation, it didn't release her, because it came from within her. She glared at him over her shoulder. How did he do that?

He made his own offer. "Release me and I will heal you." It sounded like a plea.

"No."

He sounded confused. "But isn't that what you just asked of me?"

"I changed my mind."

She half-expected him to make some comment about the fickleness of women. Instead he asked an honest question. "But why?"

It took her aback. "Why should you care?"

He didn't answer. Still, the Lines of Deeper Power pushed her toward him. His will overpowering hers did not improve her disposition. She reached out and caught the edge of the table, halting her progression.

Finally, he said, "Because you are my wife."

"Like that means anything to you beyond my bondage. Otherwise, I have no other meaning to you."

In too-measured tones, he replied, "Perhaps that should change."

Her eyes narrowed. "You want me to let you off that table. I'm not falling for your tricks."

His hands clenched then released. "No, you will let me off the table so I can heal you."

"Then what?" She had no reason to trust him. Not one.

A moment. "Can hatred kill your dreams so quickly?"

She ran her tongue over a tooth. "Indifference can." She wanted to leave but the Deeper Power held her there. "Let me go. You've got everything you're going to get out of me."

"But you haven't got everything I want to give you."

Her patience wore thin. "I gave up on petty revenge."

"Then why am I still stuck to this table?"

Her answer was simple. "Justice."

They stared at each other. Adrastea tried to keep her frustration out of her countenance and that seed of anger, which she thought was dormant, under control. He studied her with slight narrowing of his brow, as if trying to read her thoughts. She pushed them away—anger, desire, yearning, frustration.

"Let me up, I will heal you and we shall go our separate ways. Deal?"

She considered. She closed her fingers in a fist. There had to be some trick in there somewhere. He would do anything, say anything to be free of her imprisonment.

The pain she felt the last time she walked out on him came welling back. It, too, had not died. "No." Tears stung her eyes. She shut them tightly and let the sorrow of her life overwhelm her. "Because I want you to hurt as bad as I do." Her pain made her weak. Why couldn't she walk away?

Mor-Lath drew her closer until he could reach her hand. He closed gentle fingers about her clenched fist. "I am not ready to die. Are you?"

She nodded. "I am."

He drew in a sharp breath. His hand tightened about her fist.

"I am ready to die and be Judged."

"Is being married to me really that bad?" He couldn't hide the pain in his voice.

She swallowed against the tightness in her throat. "Yes. I wish I never married you. Even if it meant the destruction of the world." She collapsed to her knees and laid her head upon the table. He still held her hand, her arm outstretched.

She surrendered to misery and cried in great big wails of grief. It loosened from its restraints and flowed through her body like sloshed water. It wanted to get out but there was no egress. Back and forth it rolled, unable to escape.

Mor-Lath held her hand, even though she tried to pull it away or slam it to the table a few times. He held on tightly as if afraid she'd flee, ere he let go. He let her cry until the exhaustion of it quieted her keening to shuddery sobs.

"I'm so sorry," he said after a very long while. It sounded like he meant it.

Her head lay against the polished grain of the wood. Her tears pooled and made the surface slick. Her face was hot as was the wood beneath and she ignored the prickles on her skin.

"Adrastea. Come here. I will heal you."

She shook her head.

"No tricks, no bargains. Just..." he hesitated. "Let me try."

She didn't respond.

The Deeper Power made it easy for him to lift her body from the floor and settle it on the table next to him. She curled up fetally, her back to him. This made it hard for him to reach her belly, to apply his hand and perhaps restore her. He couldn't roll to the side to embrace her properly—she heard him hiss as he moved against the knife—so he laid his hand against the small of her back.

Adrastea did not resist the flow of the Deeper Power he commanded as it entered her body and swirled within her, seeking, searching.

But she felt no changes. She let out a small sound of confirmed doubt.

"Wait," he said. "It's hard from this angle."

She turned around and sat up. "It shouldn't matter." She wiped at her hot, damp face.

He held a hand out in supplication. "Let me try. Please. Either I will succeed, or nothing will change."

"Either you will succeed, or I will learn just how powerless you really are."

"No." An edge entered his voice. "I can do it. Really."

Adrastea dried her face on the edge of her shortened skirt. "Can you?" She straddled his legs and sat down hard. If he felt it, he didn't wince. "So, do it."

Mor-Lath drew a deep breath. He called upon the Deeper Power. As he did, she did too, matching him in intensity. She didn't trust him. But deception didn't seem to be what was on his mind. Focus is what she felt from the lines. Deep, serious focus, and a determination to succeed.

He placed both his hands on her belly and tried not to think about how she was positioned on him. If it wasn't for the knife and if she wasn't his wife, this would have stirred his blood. Perhaps it did, though it did not manifest itself in any physical sign, much to his relief. It had been far too long.

Adrastea shook her head. Had she sensed his thoughts for a moment? "Don't get distracted," she warned.

He looked up at her. "Who said I was getting distracted?" he said a little too quickly. Flash of guilt.

The way she laid her hand upon the hilt of the knife conveyed that she meant business. His heartbeat pulsed through the knife. Did it pound as strongly as hers? The tempos matched.

His hands on her belly twitched as if they wanted to slide to her hips but he made sure they stayed put. She watched as he closed his eyes and requested Creation obey his will. An aura surrounded his form, growing stronger the more he pulled on the Deeper Power.

His hands felt warm, then hot against her belly, filling it with the sweetness of the Power. It continued in this manner for several heartbeats, then several more.

Nothing happened.

He concentrated. The table beneath began to groan and crack. Adrastea clenched her legs in case it collapsed. She did not want to fall.

Still, nothing happened.

Her hand clenched around the hilt of the knife. "It's not working," she growled, slow and deliberate.

His eyes opened, and he looked up at her, desperate. "Just a little longer," he pleaded, glancing at her grip on the knife before closing his eyes to concentrate.

She, too, closed her eyes and turned her focus within. She'd tried, fruitlessly, in the past to heal herself. She could not work with what was no longer there. Had he left even a scrap, even a cinder, she could have restored her womb from that. But he had left nothing.

She touched the Power he sent through her. It entered her and left, doing nothing.

Nothing?

Cold suspicion rolled through her. "Why aren't you doing anything?"

The sense of concentration she felt from him froze. Panic rolled over him; he'd been caught.

With a cry of anguish turning into a shriek of rage, she gripped the knife and ripped it out of his chest.

He gasped in surprise. "Adrastea, what—"

Her anger boosted the one thought in her head. *If I can't be whole, neither can you.*

⌒◎⌒

*I*f I can't be whole, neither can you. When she had ripped the knife from his chest, stars of pain danced across Mor-Lath's eyes. The focus of Adrastea's rage and betrayal slammed into his psyche.

As she lifted the knife to plunge it in him again, he sat up to catch her wrists. That knife was aimed much lower than was comfortable.

"Let me go!" she growled as she pushed against his hands.

The Power burned in her, focused and dangerous. Her anger scared him. He fought her wavering knife. Her focus gave Adrastea more strength than he anticipated. The knife swooped close to his stomach. He deflected her aim so the knife sank into the table and not into his flesh. His physical strength was his only advantage, and a slight one at that. Her fury was hers. And what a glorious fury! Her eyes burned, and her skin radiated. The sheer energy that rolled through her body flowed over him. His traitorous body responded. As she wanted to bury that knife in him, he wanted to bury himself in her, to get lost in all that temper and passion.

Adrastea grabbed his shirt as she pulled the knife out of the wood. "I will end you!" she cried as she jabbed the knife at his face. He blocked her arm but not fast enough. The sharp edge of the knife slid against his cheek, slicing it open. The sting brought back his focus.

Adrastea had put more power into her thrust than she needed. The strike overbalanced her as Mor-Lath deflected her arm past him.

She fell against him. The knife flew from her hand. In a quick thought, he sent the knife away, it disappearing before it hit the floor. Feown was far enough.

An angry, focused Adrastea was the most dangerous being in Creation. If he did not defuse or distract her, there was a very good chance she'd do him some serious damage, knife or no knife. His sticky, burning cheek was only the beginning if he did not do something.

How could he distract her? What caused her to lose focus? He'd pulled her close after her unbalance, so she could not strike him again. They struggled together as Mor-Lath failed to gain purchase. With her on top and his chest aching every time he flexed a muscle, he could not gain the upper hand. If only he could flip her over, pin her down and talk some sense into her.

Her disarmament distracted Adrastea enough for Mor-Lath to fill himself completely with the Deeper Power. A moment later she matched his capacity to counter him.

Of course. She could never resist the siren song of the Deeper Power. She gave in to its sweetness every time.

Mor-Lath's hand slid up to the back of her head. He pressed his cheek to hers and fed her tendrils of Power through her skin. Very specific tendrils.

She struggled against him. "Stop that..." With his arm about her waist and her knees to either side of his legs, she couldn't get enough purchase to push away.

"Shh, my darklet." He was such a fool. He'd used her sensuality to woo her during their courtship. Why didn't he use it to keep her on side after their marriage? Had his fear of a mashiah overwhelmed his common sense so much that now he faced dismemberment, or worse, desertion at the hands of his wife?

His skin buzzed against hers. He gave himself over to the seductive call of the Deeper Power. Let its awakening sound stir her soul as it stirred his.

How it stirred him! For thousands of years it had sung to him and soothed him. It ignited his senses and filled him with delight. While he had learned mastery over the sensations, the intensity had never decreased. All mortals had varying capacities for the Deeper Power, but nothing could beat an immortal filled with the full glory of Creation. Only Adrastea's capacity matched his.

As he shared the Power with her, her hands trembled. One hand was tangled between them, the other gripping the back of his shirt. She drew a ragged breath as she fought the sensation. "I..." she gasped. "...will not..." How breathless she sounded, "...give in."

Oh, she had a firm grip on her anger. She used it to battle against his determination. Could he turn that anger around? Could he redirect that fury into something sweeter?

He bent his head and ran his lips along her neck. A soft cry of ecstasy escaped her lips and her whole body shuddered. As she arched back against the sensations, he released her head enough to deliver to her a lingering kiss. All the while he fed the Deeper Power back to her, wisps at first, then rivulets, then a flood.

As her fist tightened on the back of his shirt he heard the cloth tear. Her anger had turned to frustration. Good. He nudged it with yearning. Half her frustration came from her physical unfulfillment.

Of course, she was unfulfilled. She had always been a woman of great potential, whose soul had always sought to fulfill that potential. She'd stimulated her mind, she'd kept her hands busy, but her heart had been locked away and starved.

He offered it the feast it craved.

Adrastea attacked his lips with a fury all her own, drawing more Power from Mor-Lath. She released his torn shirt and pulled his head closer to hers.

His free hand slid down her back, past her waist, to pull her closer to him. Let her feel how aroused he was. He would not hold back.

As she kissed him until he couldn't breathe, he kept his focus all on her. His fear he shoved away lest it distract him from his task or redirect her focus. Her self-control was in tatters. He aimed to keep it that way.

Adrastea lifted up on her knees, forcing him down to the table. Pain shot through his bare back as the knife wound hit the wood. His focus wavered. If he was to be violently ravished, a wooden table was not the preferred surface for ravishment.

Her anger still burned but had interwoven itself with hunger. Her need rolled over him and sunk into his flesh.

Mor-Lath had unleashed a monster, one he could not, dared not, stop. If she came to her senses now, her anger was fresh enough it might return. He dreaded what would happen then.

When she came up for air, her fists tangled in the remains of his shirt. As she pulled at it in her frustration, he willed it to part, lest she take an arm off with it. After she had torn it off, she threw it to the floor. Her eyes burned dark with need for him as her fingernails raked across his chest. Would she remove his skin as well? Thankfully, she missed the knife wound that bled on his chest.

Risking the distraction, he ran his hands up her thighs, pushing up her skirts. The skin of her legs felt so soft. He had often daydreamed of stroking her here, stopping himself short before he got into trouble.

Couldn't be in more peril than he was now. He gripped her legs and closed his eyes.

Shift. His back settled onto the bed he never thought he'd occupy, certainly not like this.

Startled, Adrastea's hold on the Deeper Power weakened. Her gaze darted about. In response to her confusion over the darkness the globes of light illuminated.

Uh oh. Mor-Lath sent a flood of Power through her skin. As it rippled over her, she closed her eyes and threw her head back. Crisis averted. A soft cry escaped her lips as her hands sought his, still planted on her thighs. As she guided them higher, he couldn't help but tremble.

A frission of the old fear ran through his heart. He fought it off. She was safe, she was safe, he chanted to himself. She could not carry a child, she was safe.

Her eyes flew open and she looked at him. Confusion flitted through them.

Mor-Lath's breath quickened painfully in his damaged chest. He pushed himself up and reached out for her face. He stroked the lines on her cheeks with the back of his hand, making them sing. "Adrastea," he murmured. "I need you."

Her hands tangled in his hair and drew him close for a kiss, reigniting her passion. She bore him back down to the mattress.

Mor-Lath gave in. Let her do what she wanted. If it kept him alive and intact, he would let her devour him.

Her motions were desperate and artless. Her fingers scrabbled uselessly at her bodice until he assisted in freeing her skin. Likewise, he assisted her to remove the rest of his clothing, lest she tear that off as well and do him an injury. He could not move fast enough. She hissed in annoyance as her own skirt tangled about her limbs. Fueled by the Deeper Power, she pulled it to pieces.

This frustration she turned back on him. He gasped as she bit his shoulder. "Easy," he said, as he stopped her from taking another bite.

Adrastea paused, panting. Her hands stroked down his chest, over his belly and lower. He reached for her hands, lest she take out her frustration on his poor member by squeezing too hard.

Her grip made him gasp. "Gently!"

Gentle was the last thing she was. He grasped her wrist to still her hand and loosen its grip. The maiden had no idea what to do with a phallus.

Or perhaps she did. She lifted up on her knees and with her hand to guide her, she sank onto him until she enveloped him completely.

Her tightness made him shudder with pleasure. He threw his head back and let her have her way with him. He kept some vestiges of control, for it would not do to spend himself before she'd reached her own climax.

Her arrival came sooner than he expected—too soon. The wave of heat washed from her over him and threatened to ebb. Oh no it mustn't! He laid his hands on her hips to still her motion.

In frustration she pulled his hands away. How dare he stop her!

If her hands had his, then he had her arms. He spread out his arms and drew her downward. He captured her mouth with his, running his tongue over her lips. Yep, that distracted her. The rhythm of her hips slowed as she gave herself over to a kiss.

And thus, he distracted her throughout the night, and occupied her, and aroused her, and brought her to completion several times until exhaustion overcame them both.

As she collapsed into the bed next to him, chest heaving with her final ecstasy, he dropped one arm over her waist and nuzzled her damp neck. *Sleep*, he suggested to her, waiting until she'd dropped completely into unconsciousness before submitting to sleep himself.

What had he done?

n the morning Mor-Lath stood by the bed and watched his sleeping bride—or rather, wife. She was his wife now, not just by vow but also by deed. Now that was a proper consummation—more violent than he preferred but his ends had been met. He had been freed.

He leaned against the bedpost, his arm raised above his head. Something very important had woken him but there would be time enough to deal with that later. Right now, he had to cope with his wife. Neither modesty nor cold bothered him.

His thoughts did. If he hadn't realized in time just how close he came to destroying himself, he would still be pinned to that table without a wife or a hope.

Her earlier words haunted him: "I wish I never married you," she had said. "Even if it means the destruction of the world." That moment had turned the blood in his veins to ice.

It irked him to realize he'd spent their whole marriage acting like an immature, selfish little boy, so concerned with being right, so put out at not getting his way. No wonder she hated him.

He'd treated her as if she had been nothing more than a means to an end. He paid for it now. He had been so worried about the Cithran's goals, especially those of the One True. Mor-Lath was certain One True was a real person, even if Tanat and the Light did not believe so. He'd focused so much on that vague threat that he neglected the one with the real power to destroy him: Adrastea.

She very nearly did. It would have been entirely his fault.

He'd woken this morning, a sleeping Adrastea cradled in his arms. He couldn't remember a time when he'd slept—actually slumbered—with someone. Not that he needed much sleep, being immortal. But to have someone curled up next to your skin, simply resting, was a pleasure he'd completely forgotten.

As he looked at her sleeping face, he saw the fresh young naïf he'd originally courted. Her brow was uncreased and relaxed. He'd grown so used to seeing it furrowed with anger.

When he said he was sorry, he meant it. Not so much for causing her pain but for putting them both in a position where her only option would have been walk away or dwindle into destruction. He ached at the thought that she would rather have died than remain with him.

Or she could have gone off into the world and live the quiet life she wanted. She might have figured out how to remove those lines from her face, thus removing the last traces of him from her. He would still have known where she was, vaguely but she would have to concentrate to sense where he was, not that she would have needed to. He would have remained forever stuck to the table in the library, forgotten.

Thank Creation he averted that disaster. Had he not come to his senses, he would well and truly have deserved his fate.

His wife was a force to be reckoned with and not one to be avoided or ignored. She did not know even half of what she could do until after she'd done it. That made her all the more dangerous.

Oh, she was all kinds of danger.

He wanted to believe last night was more seduction than rape. Once he'd set her loose, he couldn't have said no, even if he'd wanted to. In his final attempt at self-preservation he'd unleashed a most fierce creature who had treated him rough. Whether or not she saw it in the same light depended on her mood when she woke.

She laid fast asleep, her dark curly hair pooling around her bronze face on the pillow. A hand rested next to her cheek, slightly curled yet so relaxed. Her heart beat in a steady slow rhythm. No dreams danced on the stage of her mind. If she regretted her actions of last night, it didn't show.

He would have to proceed carefully. It was like having to court her all over again—no, worse, because before, he only had to fight his reputation. Now, he had to counter every single bad deed he'd committed.

His senses warned him before the door opened.

Berengaria and Radelisa burst through the doorway. "Mistress!" they shrieked as they dashed in.

Both skidded to a halt in a flutter of draped veils when they saw who stood by the bed. They cried out in startlement and Radelisa turned back to the door.

With a wave of his hand, the door slammed shut. "Shh," he said to the two startled priestesses. "You'll wake her."

Too late. Adrastea's eyes opened. She remained where she was, unmoving for a moment, then bolted upright. She looked around until her gaze fell on her husband. Then her heart filled with emotion. It was not benevolent. "You and I have unfinished business."

"We do. I will be more than happy to discuss everything with you later. But first," he gestured to the two still priestesses. "We have guests, my dear."

Berengaria stared at him, or rather, past him, for he was rather naked. He sensed her embarrassment, some hurt, and a few other emotions she was not pleased to entertain, all mingled in with a very solid fear. That one did not dare turn her back to her god. Radelisa remained turned towards the door. That one did not dare face him. She gripped Berengaria's arm as if to pull her sister priestess away from danger.

That was how they perceived him—dangerous. They broadcasted their fear and wariness of him so strongly that he had no doubt. It was not only Adrastea he had done wrong by.

But his priestesses could wait. First, he had to deal with his own concern and not take his eyes off his wife.

Adrastea leaned over to see past him. "Oh!" she gasped, then pulled the bedclothes to her nakedness. A flush suffused her face. She pulled up as much of the sheet as she could and wrapped it around her body before sliding off the other side of the bed. "Why did you let them in here?" Blood streaked her body; it was not hers. She dashed for the closet.

Mor-Lath didn't move, nor did he attempt to cover himself. He looked down at the wound on his chest. It had closed over but had not yet healed. He hadn't felt too much pain during their trysting last night. Blood smeared his skin as well. He dabbed at it and rubbed his fingers together to check it. Mostly, it was old, but some still wept from the wound if he prodded it too much. "They have come to bring us news." Also, his shoulder ached. She had not been gentle. Could he convince Adrastea to heal him now?

Adrastea emerged, clad in a simple robe. She pulled the belt of it tightly around her waist. "What news?"

Berengaria and Radelisa did not move. They remained clutched to each other. Radelisa couldn't meet Adrastea's eyes. She looked anywhere but him and her mistress. "Originally, we came to tell you he was free." She jerked her head at the god standing by the bed. "But I guess you knew that." There was some bitterness, possibly pain of betrayal, in her voice.

"Oh, yes. I shall have to do something about that." Her eyes narrowed.

Mor-Lath kept his expression blank; she was still dangerous. This would bode some caution. His eyes remained on Adrastea, but he spoke to the priestesses. "And what were you going to tell me before you made your unfortunate discovery?" At least they'd thought to approach him first with the news.

Berengaria's looked darted between Adrastea's scowl and Mor-Lath's bare back. Her gaze settled on Adrastea. "We've just received news through the telegraph. Feown had been attacked."

Chapter 23

He knew. It was what had awakened him that morning.

Adrastea stared at Berengaria. "What?" The low-simmering anger in her heart fled as dread took its place. The conversion from hot to cold rolled over him. Still, Mor-Lath kept his eye on her.

The priestess repeated her news. Adrastea's knees collapsed. She crumpled to sit on the ground. "When? How?"

Berengaria clutched at Radelisa. Radelisa refused to turn around. "Not more than an hour ago, if the telegram was sent immediately."

Adrastea wrapped her arms around her stomach and rocked back and forth. "How bad?"

Radelisa looked to Berengaria. "Pretty bad. The message was listed as urgent."

Berengaria said, "Other than that, we don't know anything."

Adrastea lifted her face to her husband. "And you knew about this?" Her voice held the same hurt he heard last night.

"I've known for a little while." His sources moved faster than any telegraph ever could.

She climbed to her feet while menace crept into her voice. "And you did nothing?" She advanced around the bed. "Did you cause this?"

Only then did Mor-Lath move. He stepped back from the bed, hands up. "No. I would never condone the destruction of Feown."

By now, Adrastea was close enough she could give him a shove. "But you could have stopped it. Why didn't you?" She drew on the Deeper Power.

He backed up even more, nearly to the head of the bed. "I had my mind on more important things."

"Oh yeah? Like what?"

"You."

That gave her pause. He took advantage of her momentary confusion to distract her. He took her face in his hands and drew her close for a passionate kiss. "I'm afraid we'll have to postpone our discussion for later." He motioned the two priestesses forward. "Dress appropriately, Bride of the Dark. We go to Feown."

When they appeared on the top of the Maiden's Tower, Adrastea's eyes welled up when she cast her gaze about Feown.

Smoke from countless fires blanketed the city, turning the morning sun ruddy. Buildings lay toppled, more so the ones near the borders of the city, rather than in the middle. The palace had sustained some damage. Towards the port side of the city, nearly every warehouse burned. Even up here on the tallest tower in Feown, the cries of the anguished people reached her ears.

Adrastea gave in to a sob. She closed her eyes and buried her face on Mor-Lath's chest. After a moment, he wrapped his arms around her.

"How did this happen?" she wailed.

Mor-Lath drew in a deep breath as he surveyed the city. "This was planned well in advance. The outer damage came from cannons, angled to fire cannonballs far over the walls. The inner damage, however, was due to planted powder kegs. Someone, several, no, many someones entered into Feown and planted them. At the appointed time, they lit the fuses and ran like cockroaches." Someone in Feown had betrayed that city. "I'm sorry. There was no way Feown could have defended against an attack like this. Her ancient defenses couldn't keep up with modern times. Now she suffers."

She pressed her face into the softness of his shirt and cried harder. He let her vent her sorrow and rage. It was best that way.

"Come, let us seek out Saraym."

Her Grace was out in Feown, surveying the damage and the battered people of her city.

The destruction was worse at street-level. Stones and other rubble lay scattered across the roads. The smell of burning buildings and goods stung their eyes. Occasionally they heard the distant explosion of gas. Many people cried as they worked to free others from collapsed houses. Some people simply wandered the streets, their minds shocked into stillness, neither seeing nor hearing the chaos about them.

Likewise, unclaimed souls flitted about, disoriented. Their deaths had come as a surprise. A few angels could be seen, resting near the dying, to give them comfort in their last moments. Mor-Lath had a few demons about, their only purpose to scout. Today was horrific enough; no mortal needed additional grief.

He and Adrastea found the Duchess dressed in the same serviceable wartime fashion the others wore. Her body, unfettered by a corset, looked like lumps of cold pudding under her bodice. Her hair hadn't been brushed and her skin wore a fine coating of dirt. She slouched wearily on a toppled statue of herself and watched with a grim eye as another search and rescue group uncovered another dead body. She did not move but raised her monoscopic gaze when the Dark God approached. "We never saw it coming."

Mor-Lath offered no comment.

"I don't think we could have stopped it even if we did. How could we be so vulnerable?" She rose to her feet. "You could have stopped it."

"And what becomes of mankind if I go around making all their decisions for them?" Creation didn't work that way. Every rhythm had its nadir as well as its zenith.

Saraym wouldn't accept that. She flung her hand towards a fallen building. "You couldn't prevent this?" It looked to have been a shop with a residence above it. An exploding cannonball had struck the corner of it. While the initial explosion didn't do that much damage, the weakened structure had later collapsed under its own weight.

Mor-Lath's expression darkened as he folded his arms. "I had something extremely important to deal with, far more important than one little shop."

"More important than an entire city?"

He threw his hands in the air. "Why does everyone keep asking me that?" He looked at Adrastea.

She returned his gaze, that brow that had been so soft at dawn was back to its usual furrow. "I am the last person to ask."

More buildings than not were damaged by the initial onslaught. Fire threatened the rest. Saraym's council had ordered the military divisions to pull down entire streets of houses as firebreaks. At least the water supply to the city functioned, mostly. The pump engines sprayed white sheets of water over the flames.

Saraym pointed her finger at him. "You failed," she accused. "You promised to spare Feown." She spread her arms. "And look what happened. I'd hate to think of the state of my poor city should it not have been under your protection."

Mor-Lath didn't reply but Adrastea spoke. "It's not your day, is it, God of the Dark?"

He shot her a serious look. No man needed two women's scorn.

Someone shouted a warning. A building was collapsing. The would-be rescuers dropped what they were doing and fled a creaking structure. It fell slowly, a few bricks and shingles at first then folded in upon itself in a groan. Plaster dust billowed as it came to rest.

Saraym sprang from her seat and pushed her way forward. "Anyone injured?" she shouted.

Shouts in the negative answered back. They were safe. The panic that drove her drained away. She returned to her fallen statue. She sank her weary chin in her palm and closed her eye.

Adrastea approached her with a hand out-stretched. "You're tired."

Saraym cracked open her eye. "Don't bother with me, Grey Lady. No doubt there are others in this city who require your talents more than I."

But Adrastea did not leave. "I'm so sorry. I would have done something, had I known."

Saraym shrugged. "So, the gods are good at picking up the pieces. I am tired of the gods failing to catch the glass before it falls."

Mor-Lath snorted at her. "Would you have us remove a mortal's agency for your convenience? The Light gives you far more power than you know."

Saraym waved a finger around her. "So, what do you call this?"

Adrastea looked about at the dust and smoke and disorder of what was a great city. "I would say that someone exercised the power born in them."

Mor-Lath pointed over to the fallen shop. "I believe you are right." He strode over and picked up something from the rubble. He observed it, or rather, he listened to it. What did it say to him?

Plenty.

He closed his hand and returned to Adrastea's side. He held his closed fist up for closer scrutiny. Then he raised a finger to illustrate his point. "Someone has been disobedient."

Saraym's brow wrinkled. A glance at Adrastea who shrugged

revealed no more answers. "Who?"

Mor-Lath pressed his closed fist against his lips for a moment as if forbidding the wrong words from escaping.

"You know who did this?" Adrastea asked. She climbed over the rubble and held out her hand.

Mor-Lath gave in to her demand, placing the piece of shrapnel in her palm. "What does this say to you?"

Adrastea closed her fist about the piece. As she concentrated, the Lines thickened between her and the shrapnel.

It remembered exploding after being launched from a cannon. It remembered the language of the loaders, the supply-sergeants, the manufacturers.

Her surprise flowed between their connection. "Avelian?" she whispered. "But I thought we were at war with Cithra."

Mor-Lath did not confirm nor deny. He lifted his head and sensed the Deeper Power. Adrastea did the same. They felt the vibrations through the Lines from the memories of things. Mor-Lath felt Tanat, working on the far side of the city near the docks. She would have many souls to collect today. He even felt the presence of a few mashiahs, their influence on Creation pulling on it like a dimple in a girl's cheek. Then he felt more of what he was looking for.

Still distracted by what he felt, Mor-Lath waved a commanding hand at his wife. "I need to check a few things. Stay here. I shall return shortly."

As if Adrastea had any intention of listening to Mor-Lath.

First and foremost, she was a Healer. Too many people needed her help here and now, starting with the Duchess.

Saraym had slumped back to her fallen statue, her head in her hands. "I don't need war on two fronts," she muttered. "I can't afford it."

Wars cost money. While the Feowans enjoyed ongoing victory, the Cithran war nonetheless continued to drain not only the ducal coffers but the coffers of everyone else. Now the damaged city would demand its share of funds.

Saraym groaned. "I think I'm getting a headache."

Adrastea placed her hands over the Duchess' and focused. "Smoke and tension." She relieved her suffering. "I'm afraid it will return."

"They always do."

While the workers escaped harm from the collapsing building, others were not so lucky. Adrastea roamed the streets of Feown, restoring crushed limbs, sprained ankles, lacerated arms.

Once she came across a courtyard full of injured children. The building missing a wall must have been a school. Ari had told her about the schools of Feown, where parents sent their children for education. She said it was different from the little dame school Mira had attempted from time to time. Adrastea's heart ached. How the parents must be worrying.

Some adults were among the children, their sorting and comforting efforts inadequate. The dust from destruction floated about the air, to mingle with smoke. A white film of dust settled over everything, making everyone look like ghosts.

Adrastea felt the children's pain as it rolled along the Lines. She gathered the Lines together as an idea sprang into her mind. As she had killed the Cithrans so many years ago, could she likewise heal everyone at once? When she had as many Lines as she could hold, she closed her eyes and concentrated. She formed the word *Heal* in her mind but couldn't direct it properly.

This Line wanted mending, that Line needed fixing, the other Line craved repair. It was not enough to simply command them to *Heal*. They wanted specific directions. How do they heal? Not everything was a simple request to reconnect. With the injuries came missing parts—skin torn away, blood seeping out, and more. How does one recreate missing parts?

How vexatious! Adrastea wanted to shout at Creation for being so complex. Still, when she went from person to person, the Lines spoke clearer to her. Bones were the easiest to mend. For something that was simply cracked, a command of the Deeper Power knitted them back together. Lacerations cooperated almost as well. More complex injuries took time.

And then there were those she could not save. For some, they were dead the moment the building collapsed on them. Someone had taken their time to lay them out and drape their poor little broken bodies with a sheet. Adrastea knelt down beside one child. She laid a hand on the unmoving chest. Yes, the souls freed from mortality would not go back if they had a choice. But what about the anguish of those left behind?

Why couldn't she heal death?

The Lines that sang of life were missing. Even if she wanted to bring back every lost soul, she couldn't because the Lines were no longer there. The bodies had returned to the ownership of the earth, the souls to the ether.

Before her, two angels appeared. Adrastea rose to her feet before them. "I know you, don't I?"

One smiled and tilted her head. The other beckoned to her. "Come, child of the Light," he said. You are needed."

She followed.

The angels did not take her far but led her to a stable of what was once a butcher shop. They pointed to the farthest stall.

A young woman cried out in pain, horrible gripping pain that did not release her even when Adrastea entered the stall. Only then did her body let her go, to give her a few minutes respite.

Adrastea stared at a very young woman, no more than a girl. Her belly was swollen with child. She had fine blond hair that plastered itself in damp wisps on her forehead. She whimpered and lay on her side. The too-short skirt of the current fashion did nothing to hide the nakedness of her lower body as she lay on the blanket-covered straw. More angels surrounded her, including two very fierce ones who had taken the stance of guards. Did all births come with such an honor guard and she never noticed, or was this baby special?

Adrastea knelt beside the young woman. "I am a healer. What is your name?"

The young woman licked her sticky lips. "Aril." She held up an empty mug. "Please, may I have a drink?"

Adrastea found a water trough outside and returned with cool, if not clean, water. Aril drained the cup. "More please?"

Adrastea wiped Aril's brow. "In a moment." Aril had a familiar country accent. "Where are you from?"

"A town called Crossroads."

Adrastea's heart lifted. Crossroads was almost home. "I'm from Sacred Spring. What are you doing here?"

If the revelation had any meaning for Aril, she did not show it. "Marcus was called up for war. We couldn't bear to be separated, so I followed him here."

Adrastea had been studying Aril's face to see if she recognized her bloodlines. What she saw instead disturbed her. She was far too young to be on her own, much less having a baby. "You ran away from home?"

Aril frowned. "It's not running away if you leave together." She licked her dry lips and looked at the empty cup. "But we got separated. Then the army surrounded Feown." She swallowed dryly. "I haven't seen him since. I can't go back, not now." She put her hands on her belly. "Back home, they won't let me keep the baby."

"I can see why." Adrastea put her hands on her hips. "How old are you? You can't be much older than sixteen."

Aril swallowed and looked away. "Um, aye. I'm sixteen?" Her voice rose in the end, discrediting her statement.

Adrastea closed her eyes in disbelief. Had Aril been sixteen, she would have claimed an older age. Since sixteen was a lie... No. Adrastea shook her head. Fifteen, at most, possibly younger. Too young, way too young.

"Uh oh." Aril breathed hard. "I'm gonna have another pain."

A contraction took over her body. Aril gripped her hand until the pain subsided. She fell back to the straw beneath her with a whimper. "How much longer will this go on?"

Adrastea put her hands on Aril's knee. "If I may?"

"May what?" Aril sat up in alarm.

"I can check to see how far along you are in labor."

"How do you do that?"

Adrastea explained how one checked the cervix. Aril's mouth shot open in disgust. "You can't do that."

"Can't or shouldn't? I think you mean shouldn't, because I've recently learned there's not much I can't do."

Aril squirmed. "But, but... do you have to?"

Adrastea sighed. "When a woman is about to give birth, her birth canal widens. As soon as it is as big as a fist, the baby's head pushes against it. I can feel that and know it's time."

A shudder ran through Aril. "But does it have to be done that way?"

Adrastea ran her hands through her hair. "Can you think of a better way?"

Since Aril couldn't, she put up with the indignity of Adrastea checking her ripeness.

"Wait, wait, wait," Aril called before Adrastea had a chance for a good feel. "I feel another one coming on!"

Adrastea helped Aril sit up for the contraction. "You're close to ready, if I counted that right," Adrastea said as the contraction faded. "Let me check you."

Aril only nodded. Tears dampened her face.

Adrastea checked. The baby's head pushed well against a fully-dilated cervix. As soon as her fingertips brushed the scalp, the head pushed forward.

"Very soon." Adrastea withdrew her hand. "If you sit up for the contractions, it'll come even sooner."

Aril nodded before giving in to sobs. Adrastea held her hand until the next contraction came. She lifted Aril up to a squatting position through the ordeal. As she did so, the two angels who guarded her well, assisted her.

"That felt... different," Aril said when the contraction finished. She swallowed dryly. "I need a drink."

Adrastea fetched more water.

After Aril had a good, long drink, she said, "I want to name the baby Tomias if it's a boy and Harianne if it's a girl. Tomias was an uncle who helped raised me because my ma died when I was a baby."

"And Harianne?"

"It's kind of after me and I was named after an aunt I've only met once. But I thought it was pretty— Ooh!"

Another contraction came, robbing Aril of her powers of speech. Adrastea held her upright while she strained through the pain.

The sweat renewed itself on Aril's forehead. "I don't think I can take much more of this," she confessed.

"Then we're close. Try pushing with the next contraction."

Aril did. "Oooh," she grunted at the end of it. "That really hurts. That really, really hurts."

Adrastea gave an unprotesting Aril a quick check. "You're ready. Push again at the next contraction."

She did but stopped as soon as the baby started to crown. "Ah, ah, ah," she gasped. "It stings!"

Adrastea groaned as the head of the baby pulled back up. "You've got to push despite the pain. The baby's got to come out sometime."

"But I can't," wailed Aril. "It hurts too much!"

"You can do one more. You can push through the pain. One more and that'll be it."

But Aril shook her head. "I can't."

Her body didn't give her a choice. Adrastea lifted her up as the penultimate contraction struck. "Bear down." Adrastea hollered while she supported Aril from behind. "Push! Push!"

Aril wailed as she pushed the baby's head through. Then she collapsed in a torrent of tears. "I can't do that again."

Adrastea patted her on the back. "The head's out. Do you want to feel it?"

"Ew, no!"

Adrastea sat back and wiped her own sweat off her forehead. "One more easy push and you'll be done."

Aril nodded, still bawling like the child she was.

The contraction came. Adrastea lifted Aril up and over onto her hands and knees. "You push, and I'll catch."

But Aril was already pushing. In a gush of fluid, the baby slid out. Adrastea laid the new infant on the harsh blanket while she helped Aril lean back. Adrastea lifted the baby and placed her—for it was a girl—on Aril's chest. "Welcome to the world," Adrastea murmured.

Aril wrapped her arms about the squirming child. "Oh, she's bigger than I thought."

Adrastea had to admit this was the biggest baby she'd ever seen. "Give her something to eat. It'll help with the afterbirth."

Aril looked up at her with worried eyes. "I don't know how."

Adrastea showed her how to attach the baby properly. Immediately little Harianne began to suck.

She stood back and let the mother nurse the child. She laid a hand to her own barren belly. Unless she could figure out a way to be healed, she would never have a child of her own. All this knowledge but only for the benefit of others.

Aril began to shiver. "I'm cold," she complained.

Adrastea's hands went automatically to her own shoulders. But she hadn't worn a cloak. "Hold on a moment." She closed her eyes and thought of a cloak hanging in her wardrobe back at the Temple. A request of the Deeper Power and the cloak fell into her hands. She spread it across Arianne. "There. That should help."

She picked up the cup and went outside to fetch more water. When she returned, Aril lay back, still and quiet, her eyes closed. Arianne continued to nurse. "Here, I've brought you some…"

How pale Aril was. Water forgotten, Adrastea fell to her knees and shook Aril. "Don't go to sleep yet. Wake up."

Aril's head flopped.

Adrastea sat back to think and put her hand in something warm and damp.

A pool of blood spread under the straw. Adrastea jerked back the cloak to see it pour out of Aril. "NO!" She wadded the cloak and jammed it against Aril.

The afterbirth had detached itself from Aril's womb but not completely. "I am fifteen kinds of idiot," Adrastea cursed as she tried, with the Deeper Power, to push the placenta back. But it didn't want to go. Of course not. Placentas were meant to come out. The bleeding continued, and Adrastea sensed the faltering heartbeat. Then she tried to pull the placenta the rest of the way, but it tore. Then she squeezed her eyes shut while she searched for the bleeding vessels. Perhaps she could pinch them off until they stopped. So many little ones. She sealed off this one and that one and...

A feather touch stroked her face. "It's all right," said Aril.

Adrastea opened her eyes and looked behind her. Aril hovered there, pale and transparent, with the two angels who had brought Adrastea here and the two who supported her in birth. "I'm okay now." Behind her a multitude of angels appeared, familiar and comforting.

Adrastea turned back to the body, pale and still and peaceful. "But you were so young." Her heart ached.

Aril's soul smiled. "But I knew love." She turned to one of the angels next to her. "Great is the life that knows love."

"Take care of my baby," said Aril. The angels faded away, leaving Adrastea alone, taking Aril's soul with them.

"I will," Adrastea whispered. She looked down on the baby who was unaware of the passing of her mother. She still sucked at the nipple, more from instinct than hunger.

Adrastea used her pinkie to disengage the small mouth. Then lifting the surprisingly heavy child, she wrapped her in the remains of her mother's dress.

Arianne smacked her lips a few times, nuzzled about, then settled to figure out her new world.

Adrastea felt someone behind her.

"There you are," Mor-Lath said. Then he saw the dead girl. "Uh. What did you do?"

Adrastea turned to him with scorn in her eyes.

Then he saw the baby. "Put that down and come on. We've got work to do."

"No," said Adrastea.

Mor-Lath frowned but his expression changed. Instead of

demanding she comply, he asked, "Why?"

Adrastea clutched the baby tight. An old familiar hurt welled up inside. "No, I will not put this baby down."

"Well, you can't bring it with us."

She took a deep breath to gather her patience. Nevertheless, the moment she opened her mouth, it fled. "Mor-Lath," she said in a dangerous voice. "I will keep this baby." she drew herself up. "And there is nothing you can do about it!" Mor-Lath took a step back.

He looked at his wife, then the baby, then back to her. He took another step back. "Do you really want a baby so much? Do you know how much work they are?"

"I know exactly how much work they are. Before you came along, I assumed I'd marry someday and with marriage comes children. I was ready.

"You will never give me children. I know that now. But that doesn't mean I can't have one, even if it's not of my body." Her arms tightened around the newborn.

There was something about that baby that unsettled him. But when he saw how fiercely she defended the infant, he capitulated. Perhaps this was just the thing to soothe and distract her. "You want some little plaything? Fine. Have your little doll. But you keep it away from me. I will have nothing to do with it."

Adrastea studied him longer. "You promise?"

"If it pleases you, keep the child. All I ask is that you do not set the importance of this child over the importance of us.

"Now is not the time but we have much to discuss regarding the sorry state of our marriage, and I... I wish to make things better."

Her eyes narrowed when he made this admission. Of course, she did not believe him; he did not blame her. He would have much work to convince her he was not the beast she'd always believed him to be. "I'm sorry." He took a step closer to her. Her arms tightened around the baby and she shrank away from him. "Let us try again—rather, start again. We— I, didn't do things right the first time." He spread his arms. "I've never been married before. It's just as new to me as it is to you.

"Please," he begged. "Let us make this right."

She'd listened to him, her expression tight and closed. "I don't know if I believe you," she finally uttered, after having weighed his words. "I certainly can't trust you. You really want to make this right? Prove it."

He nodded. "I will do everything I can to make this right. All I ask is that you stop being angry with me. Give me that chance."

Again, she didn't reply right away. She exhaled through her nose and shook her head to herself. She held the baby close and replied, "Actions speak louder than words."

He nodded again. No way was she going to accept his word. He would have to prove his new sincerity to her. "So be it."

An explosion from several streets over rumbled through the air. The tension between them faded away as they turned their attention to this new destruction. "I have some business to take care of," he said to her. "I beg your leave while I go deal with some rather disobedient children." And with that, he disappeared, leaving Adrastea alone in the stable.

Once alone, Adrastea looked at the infant, silent but alert, in her arms. "Harianne, your mother named you. I wonder if you have family back in Crossroads?" The thought of returning the child to her family made Adrastea's heart ache. Surely no one would mind if she kept her. From what Aril had said, it sounded like her family wouldn't be too happy with a sudden, unknown, possibly unwanted child.

She belongs to Sacred Spring, came a thought to Adrastea's heart. Adrastea looked up, expecting Lucea to appear but the goddess remained away.

"So, I can keep her?"

Affirmation, warm and comforting, filled her heart.

Harianne was hers. The Light Themselves approved.

Adrastea ran her hand over the little head. "Hello, little baby." She pulled her even closer and buried her face in the infant's softness. "Mine."

End of Book Two

###

A Note from the Author

Thank you so much for reading Bride of the Dark. I hope you enjoyed it. If you did, please leave an honest review on the site where you purchased this book. Alternatively, leave a review on a reputable review site of your choice. Reviews are not only the highest compliment you can pay to an author, they also help other readers discover great books. Share the love by telling others. Thank you!

Other Books by Heidi Wessman Kneale

Available where all good ebooks are sold.

<u>Of The Dark series</u>
God of the Dark
Bride of the Dark
House of the Dark

<u>Romance Novels</u>
A Lady of Many Charms and Other Stories
Her Endearing Young Charms
The White Feather
For Richer, For Poorer
Marry Me – A Candy Hearts Romance
As Good as Gold

Acknowledgements

It's amazing how many people are involved when one is writing a book. From mentors and fellow authors to critters, beta-readers and general fans, many eyes, hands and hearts help bring this project to light.

First, I mention Dr. Anne Wingate and Kathryn VanRoosendaal who both read the earliest first chapters of Bride of the Dark and who suggested that Of The Dark should be a trilogy, not a single novel. How right they both were.

Many critters of the Online Writing Workshop who also gave valuable feedback on those first chapters, and the Vicious Circle and Stromatolights who helped me refine my craft.

Beta-readers: Hannah Whitehead, Jen Kilshaw, Gary Herdsman, and Melody LeBaron, all who cried over the deaths of people, of dreams and of ideals in this rather dire book, and who all expressed a desire that somehow, some way, things will get better in the third book (or at least, some comeuppance).

Various members of the Romance Writers of Australia had advice of much usefulness when it came to the final draft, which helped immensely.

Also glad for the support of my fellow NaNoWriMo participants. Let us always encourage each other to become the authors we want to be.

Finally, I acknowledge the Whadjuk tribe of the Nyoongar people, past and present, who are the traditional owners of the land on which I live and write.

About the Author

Heidi Wessman Kneale is an Australian author of moderate repute. She is best known for her escapist fiction. Like most humans, she's got a family and a cat. When not writing novels, she can be found composing music and staring at the stars.

Socialize!

Hang out with me online:
Twitter: @heidikneale
Blog: Romance Spinners
Web: Heidi Kneale, Author

Want a free story?

Of course you do!

Get Heidi Kneale's short story "Within Her" when you sign up for her quarterly newsletter at http://tinyurl.com/heidikneale/ plus get news of upcoming releases, special deals and more.

⚜

House of the Dark
Book 3, Of The Dark series

Read on for a sneak peek into "House of the Dark"

Chapter 1

Adrastea laid the sleeping baby on her bed in the Temple of Mor-Lath. She stood back and studied the new life. A new baby, fresh and pure, helpless. What was she going to do? She'd never been a parent—had never given it much thought, really. She always figured if she did get married and had a family, she'd have Ari and her own mother to help her. She never thought she'd parent alone.

The infant didn't stir—the pinkness of her cheeks and the slow movement of her chest the only signs that she was a living thing. How soft the skin felt when Adrastea stroked it. Could she be a mother?

Aril trusted her in life. She gave her approval in death for Adrastea to take care of her child.

Adrastea knelt beside the bed and stroked the baby's downy head. So much to consider. The past two days since releasing Mor-lath felt like riding on the cart behind a runaway horse. And here came the bottom of the hill.

The baby's eyes pinched up. The little shoulders squirmed before settling back into sleep.

What should she do next? Surely the baby couldn't stay here in the Temple. The Light had said Harianne belonged at Sacred Spring. There, at least, she could be safe.

What about herself? Should she stay here, or should she leave? She had promised Berengaria and Radelisa she'd stay and make things right.

What to do?

And then, there was Mor-Lath. He'd changed his tune quickly when faced with utter destruction.

She was still married to him. Probably always would be. Pity.

He said he wanted to make everything better—make a new start.

Did he really?

He'd tricked her into releasing him from the table. That was her fault. She should have known he'd never have healed her. And she should not have let him goad her into such rage as to snatch the closest weapon, despite the fact it was already buried in his chest. And then she—

Not that it mattered now. Adrastea pushed her finger into the fist of the baby. Look at the tiny fingernails. She ran her thumb tip over them. Someone had to take care of this baby. Adrastea had promised Aril and stood up to Mor-Lath. He'd relented, calling the child a 'plaything'.

She sighed and looked about the luxurious bedroom. This was no place for an infant. She could not stay here, not permanently. Even if it meant deserting the priestesses for the time being.

She would have to return to Sacred Spring.

Mor-Lath appeared at the foot of the bed, startling her.

He wore a brown robe, hood thrown back, looking very much like a Light priest. He leaned on the wooden bedpost. "There you are. Come on, we've got things to do—"

Her rage flared up; she had thought it dead. Her mind reached out to find the nearest weapon she could use.

Her thoughts settled on one of the fashionably long and wickedly sharp hat pins that were scattered on the dressing table. It had to be as long as a butcher knife and as thick as a leather needle. She'd emptied them out of their wooden box so she'd have somewhere to dump Desmone's and the others' souls. It would do.

In one fluid movement, a hat pin flew to her hand. She drove it through his hand and into the wood.

"Aaah! Damn!" He hissed in pain. "What was that for?" He grabbed the pin and pulled.

It wouldn't come out. A small well of shimmery blood dripped from where the pin emerged from his hand.

Adrastea simply folded her arms. "You tricked me into releasing you from that table. You said you'd heal me. You failed. So back you go."

"What?" His temples pulsed with his quickened heartbeat.

"Adrastea?"

She went to the wardrobe. She'd need clothing. The fine dresses would do until she could get sensible things again. One of the fine shawls would make an adequate sling for the baby. And this time, Adrastea planned on taking every single jewel on which she could lay her hands. It's not like he'd wear them. If there was another woman in his life (best not to think upon't), Adrastea did not want her to be decked in these. These were hers. Really, they were.

Would any of the priestesses go with her? She'd grown used to their company, especially Radelisa and Berengaria.

Mor-Lath attempted to free himself. "You can't leave me here forever," he pleaded.

She didn't even glance back. "The hell I can." She returned with an armful of clothes chosen not so much for their cut, but for their fabric. She dumped her load on the other side of the bed from the baby, who, despite the noise, slept on. Did he even realize the child was there?

He snarled at his failed attempts. "You expect me to stand here for the rest of my existence?"

Adrastea shrugged as she folded the gowns. "According to you and the Light, that's not such a long time. Anyhow, I'm going back to Sacred Spring."

When I've had too much of reality, I open a book.